*Nomi Eve*

❧

# The Family Orchard

Nomi Eve lives in Brookline, Massachusetts. She has an MFA in fiction writing from Brown University and has worked as a freelance book reviewer for *The Village Voice* and New York *Newsday*. Her stories have appeared in *Glimmer Train Stories, Voice Literary Supplement,* and *The International Quarterly. The Family Orchard* is her first novel.

INTERNATIONAL

# The Family Orchard

# The Family Orchard

A NOVEL BY

❧

## Nomi Eve

*Vintage International*

VINTAGE BOOKS

A DIVISION OF RANDOM HOUSE, INC.

NEW YORK

FIRST VINTAGE INTERNATIONAL EDITION, SEPTEMBER 2001

*Copyright © 2000 by Nomi Eve*

All rights reserved under International and Pan-American Copyright
Conventions. Published in the United States of America by
Vintage Books, a division of Random House, Inc., New York, and
simultaneously in Canada by Random House of Canada Limited,
Toronto. Originally published in hardcover in the United States by
Alfred A. Knopf, Inc., a division of Random House, Inc.,
New York, in 2000.

Vintage is a registered trademark and Vintage International
and colophon are trademarks of Random House, Inc.

Some of the chapters in this novel were originally published as follows:
"Esther and Yochanan" in *Glimmer Train Stories* (June 1996);
"The Water Dance" as "Al Jud" in *The International Quarterly*
(Winter 1997); "The Double Tree" in *The Village Voice Literary
Supplement* (*VLS*) (March 1994); "To Conjure the Twin"
in *Glimmer Train Stories* (August 1997).

The Library of Congress has cataloged the Knopf edition as follows:
Eve, Nomi, 1968–
The family orchard / Nomi Eve.—1st ed.
p.   cm.
ISBN 0-375-41076-7—ISBN 0-375-72457-5 (pbk.)
1. Jewish families—Fiction.   2. Jews—Israel—Fiction.
3. Israel—Fiction.   I. Title.
PS3555.V32 F36   2000
813'.6—dc21   00-040566

*Author photograph © Marion Ettlinger*
*Book design by Rebecca Aidlin*
*Family tree designed by Karen Schloss*

www.vintagebooks.com

Printed in the United States of America
10  9  8  7  6  5  4  3  2  1

To my mother, Rita, who gave me the space
in which to create art

To my father, Yehoshua, who gave me the material
with which to fill it

To my grandmother, Rivka, who gave me her stories
and her blessings

To my cousins, Burt and Joan, beloved friends,
first readers

And to my husband, Aleister Jeremy, prince of all
my pages, with whom I love to dance

# CONTENTS

## Part Four

## Part Five

## Part Six

# The Family Orchard

*T*he word *legend* comes from the Latin "*legere*," which means "to read." The word *fiction* comes from the Latin "*fingere*," which means "to form." From *fingere* we also get the word *fingers*. We form things with our fingers. The word *history* comes from the Greek "*istor*," which means "to learn" or "to know." I believe in original etymology. I believe that fiction is formed truth. I believe that history is a way of knowing all of this. I believe that legend is how we read between the lines.

JEWISH FAMILY ON MOUNT ZION

# PROLOGUE

I TELL:

*J*eremy, if I had to choose a beginning, I would tell you that
there is no beginning and then I would tell you that there are
many ends. But you would not be satisfied with this. So I
would go back to work, and then I would return to you and
tell you that the beginning is in the trees. All of them. In the double
tree, half blood orange, half mandarin dancy. In Al Jud, charted only
on the map of myth, anchored in the corpse of the Jewish spy. In the
tool tree, mostly wood, but a good bit metal. Citrus graft, corpse root,
abandoned tools that rust through to the rings. Yes, if I had to choose
a beginning, I would tell you that these trees are where the story
starts. At least that is where it starts for me.

But then maybe you would look at me with doubt. You, who
know the parameters of this story. Maybe you would put your arms
around me and say, softly, "Is that all, my love?" And then I would
look up at you and say, "No, that is not all, my love." And later that
night I would tell you that the beginning is in my father's trees—his
family forest, our own old and ongoing groves. Brother branches,
citrus graft, corpse root, abandoned tools that rust through to the
rings. Yes, that is all. If I had to choose a beginning, I would tell
you about all of these trees.

# Part One

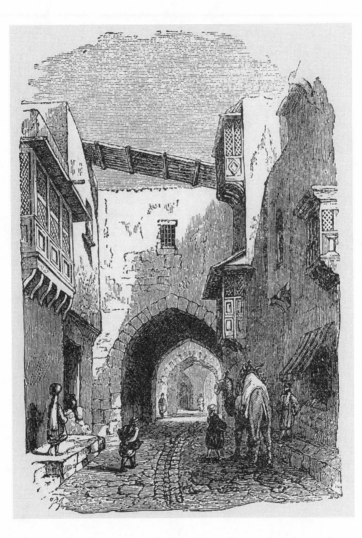

Esther Sophie
Goldner Herschell
1820–1854

Yochanan
Schüne
1815–1875

## Chapter 1

## ESTHER AND YOCHANAN

*My* father writes:

Rabbi Yochanan Schine, a student of the famous Chatam Sofer, was engaged to Esther Sophie Goldner Herschell, the grand-daughter of the chief rabbi of the British Empire. Esther and Yochanan were my great-great-grandparents. They immigrated to Palestine and married in 1837 in Jerusalem.

I write:

Esther was pious but in a peripheral way. She knew the *mitzvot*, she knew to make the Sabbath holy, but she felt that there was no real harm in putting her own creative interpretation on the old rules because certainly creativity was an essential and blessed quality of Man and it would be a sin not to use it.

At first she did not like Jerusalem; she was from a long line of people who lacked sense of direction. The stony city, with all of its obscurant walls, twists and turns seemed to her a nasty place without any recognizable plan.

Three months and two days after the young couple arrived, she ventured out alone for the first time. Quickly lost, but not frightened, Esther decided she would just wander. She knew that if she wanted to she could ask someone to show her the way back to their house, which was a half-grand, half-decrepit habitation on Rav Pinchas Street. It was located across from the Peace of Israel Synagogue in the center of town.

And then Esther smelled the bread. She turned a corner, walked a few more steps. Soon she was standing outside an arched open door watching a bare-armed baker slide a tray of dough into a furnace. Esther stood and stared. The steam and sweat and dough and bare baker skin created in the room an atmosphere magnetic, carnally alluring. The baker was a young man, no more than twenty. Esther, married less than four months, was nineteen.

Although she was not ordinarily a believer in astrology, and had absolutely no idea how sailors used the night sky to tell them where to go, she felt certain that crucial stars had descended into that tiny bakery room to make for her a perfect navigational tool. In short, she was inspired, and knew for once in her life exactly in which direction she was supposed to go.

The baker stood before her—a destination slim and brown. He was lithe and beautiful in a coltish, boyish way. Small. Only a bit taller than she. Esther immediately took in his huge almondy eyes, and his hair—thick dark brown hair—gathered in a low braid at the back. He seemed to her like something carved out of precious wood; miniature, masculine, and muscular all at once.

The bakery was only two rooms. One with a low, wooden baking table rutted and eternally floury from years of use, and the other with a brick furnace that had been hewn, by the baker's grandfather, out of the limestone wall. It was behind what would later be the public pavilion but was then a rubbly clump of lower-class homes bordering the more prosperous center of town. When the baker saw the young woman with the full skirt, cinched at the waist, when he saw the big brown eyes of the woman, when he saw her white skin, full lips, and attractive face, he invited her in. He gave her a fresh roll and asked her, in nervous, clumsy Yiddish (which, like a mule, kicked and brayed itself off of his tongue; he was embarrassed at his language's lack of manners) if she would like some sweet mint tea. This was the start of her nine-year love affair with the baker and her lifelong passionate entanglement with Jerusalem, the city whose twists, turns, bakers, and twin arcane whispers of piety and perversity ultimately spoke straight to her heart.

Esther would make love with her husband at night "through her front door" and then, in the daytime, she carried out an affair with the baker, a third-generation Palestinian Jew. Their sexual game was ruled by the fact that the baker would only enter into her "rear door." Both euphemism (which in the entire nine years they never breached) and position (which in the entire nine years they never varied except slightly in angle) suited them. Titillating not only the tenderest parts of their anatomies, but also the deeply humorous sense of sex that they found they shared.

She came once a week, on Tuesdays, in the late afternoon when her husband would be busy participating in his civic meetings and the rest of the town, in classic Mediterranean style, would be indoors either scheming, studying, or sleeping. The baker, whose hands Esther always thought were strangely thin-fingered and uncallused for a baker, would lock the door to the back of the shop. And as he walked over to her, she would be laying a clean cloth down on the baking table. She loved lifting a finger to his lips, putting her fingers in his mouth and then tracing the graceful outline of his face, from mouth to nose, eyes and into ears.

Always, when they were both ready, she would turn away from him and lean her body over the table. He pulled up her skirts, pulled down her undergarments and his own pants. Then he licked the fingers on his right hand and slowly, passionately, opened her up. Soon he slid right into her. She loved the feel of his body angling its way upward. She loved the feel of her heavy breasts hard pressing into the wooden table. He gripped her hips and thrust himself deep.

They kissed and panted and hungered at and for each other's skin—more, not less, fervently as the years went by. Theirs, they agreed, was an ancient elemental passion that must have existed, like sand, earth, and sky, long before either of them had been born. And despite the intense physicality of their togethering, both

Esther and the baker always felt insubstantial, flimsy, oh so light in the presence of this passion. But this was not a bad feeling. When they made love, it was as if they were wrapping their bodies not only around each other but also, and more essentially, around something else that had before been naked. It was, they agreed, as if the passion were the real creature, and they, though temporarily deprived of the normal trappings of personhood, were lucky to have been chosen as its favorite clothes. They dressed the passion in carnal finery, and the passion wore them with secret frequency.

My great-great-great-grandmother, Esther Sophie Goldner Schine, granddaughter of the chief rabbi of the British Empire, thought her husband's coming in through her front door and her lover's coming in through her back door was the perfect arrangement for a Jewish woman. The notion of separate facilities fit nicely into the ready framework of *kashrut*. Milk here, meat there, and as long as there was proper distance between things, everything stayed quietly kosher.

*M*Y FATHER WRITES:

Yochanan came from a part of East Prussia called Sheinlanka, which means "pretty terraces." Today it is part of Poland, not far from the town of Posnan. He came to Palestine under the following circumstances:

In 1836, the chief rabbi of the British Empire, Rabbi Shlomo Berliner Herschell, sent out a messenger to search for a *shidach* for his granddaughter, Esther. A *shidach* is the Yiddish word for a marriage match. The marriage was to be bound by the condition that the young couple marry and reside in Jerusalem. This was before the existence of Zionism. Most Jews still believed that Israel should not and could not be established until the Messiah came to Zion. Rabbi Herschell disagreed with prevailing thought. He was among a group of radical European Orthodox Jews who believed that moving to Palestine was not in opposition to the messianic ideal.

The messenger traveled for almost an entire year. Finally, he arrived at the city of Pressburg, at the house of study of the famous Prussian rabbi, the Chatam Sofer. Yochanan had long been a student there. Like the chief rabbi, the Chatam Sofer also disagreed with prevailing thought—that is, he believed in Israel as a realistic homeland, not just a spiritual one. In response to the rabbi's messenger, the Chatam Sofer promptly sent his prized student, Yochanan. Yochanan and Esther met in London and became engaged almost immediately.

I WRITE:

On the third Tuesday of Chesh-van, four months after they arrived in Jerusalem, Yocha-nan finished early with his civic meeting and decided to make for home. He was just about to walk past the Glory of Israel Synagogue when he saw Esther step out of the front door of their house and turn to walk the other way. It was late fall, and chilly. She was wearing her long maroon coat and the wide-brimmed black hat that tipped down over

JERUSALEM STREET

her right eye and made her vision, she always explained, "a bit drunk feeling, you know, only half there and wobbly, but not too bad, I find my way after all." Yochanan loved his wife's way of speaking. Her sentences were curvy and full of original character.

Yochanan called out to Esther but he was too far for her to hear and so he walked on and meant to call again, but then he found himself walking quietly, stealthily after his wife around a corner, and again, another corner, and then down the street and into an alley. He stopped at the mouth of the alley and watched his wife walk through the bakery's back door. Her maroon coat wafted behind her for several seconds and then too, disappeared into the warm realm of dough and yeast.

Pulling back and into a doorway on which was graffitied the word *sky* in sloppy Aramaic, he looked up at the real sky, which was darkening with the foredream of a storm. He watched as the baker poked his head out and then shut the front door of his shop. Hidden, but only ten feet away, Yochanan didn't say a word. Then he walked to the closed bakery door and put his ear to the old wood of it. Soon he could hear his wife groaning. He stepped away from the door and looked up and down the street. No one was in the alley, nor walking toward it. He walked back and listened some more.

He became aroused almost immediately, and soon was picturing the baker holding Esther's naked breasts, petting them gently and then lifting up the nipples to his mouth. First one and then the other. And the baker's hand, Yochanan imagined the baker's left hand reaching in between Esther's legs, which she pressed together tightly. Soon, in his mind, they were pressing their naked bodies together and moving, back and forth, toward and away, with the tempestuous ease of a storm just brewing. The storm outside began to blow. Yochanan huddled into his coat, raised his collar, and ducked deeper into the doorway. Shutting his eyes, he leaned into the images as if they were the real door, open and welcoming, while the wooden one, closed and cold against his body, kept him out of all this. Now he heard the baker groaning. Esther let out a small passionate yelp. And as the two lovers inside reached satiety, the one outside reached down and touched himself, pressed there, pressed and pulled himself to solitary, intense pleasure. Only then did he leave.

Yochanan put his hands over his hat and ran through the rain.

His feet swish-swished into puddles already forming in the narrow, stony streets. As he ran, he heard himself reciting an angry litany like an opposite prayer.

*The baker has a face of moldy clay.*
*The baker has hands of heavy stinking wood.*
*The baker is a deformed gentile in disguise.*
*The baker is an eater of clams.*
*A descendant of Amalek.*
*The devil of devils.*
*The baker is . . . the baker is . . . the baker is shtupping*
    *my wife!*

The rain hit him harder now, pelting from every angle and also straight up from the ground. He felt slowed by it, slowed and assaulted, as if each raindrop were a separate obstacle. Reaching home, he went inside, took off his great coat and hat, and set them upon the fine wooden rack that they had brought with them from London. Shaking out his beard and hair, he ran his fingers through them. Then he held his hands up to his mouth and breathed into his open palms. The warm air hovered there, but only for a second, and soon his skin was cold again. He breathed again, felt warm for several seconds and then cold again, warm and then cold. Cold. He dropped his hands down to his sides, thrust them into his pockets, and sighed deeply. But then everything changed. His mood rocked and swayed, and Yochanan felt a smile flutter to his lips.

Laughing out loud, he turned and looked at his image in the gilt hall mirror. My, how shaggy! Wet! How disheveled! But happy! Happy! He found himself possessed of an excited and yet cautious confusion.

He had taken great pleasure outside the baker's door and yet there were so many sins and so much shame growing on the fields where this kind of pleasure bloomed. Where was his anger? He could not feel it now. Where was his litany, his sour prayer?

Yochanan loved his wife and trusted her too. Strangely, he still trusted her. The image of Esther in the baker's arms was an excruciatingly beautiful flower. Vicarious, criminal, devastating, and yet thrillful. He ached with every petal, leaf, and fresh-cut stem of it.

Once again, he imagined the baker's dark hands thrusting upward into Esther's body, her mouth half open, lips wet. Yochanan imagined and imagined, and grew once again aroused while standing alone in the antechamber still dripping from the rain. But he didn't touch himself this time. He was in his own house and the walls were lined with holy books. Yochanan could not bring such odd illicit flowers home with him. Rubbing his hands together, he put them once more through his beard. As if he could comb out the confusion. A servant walked into the antechamber.

"Oh, sir, I didn't hear you . . . come in, sit by the fire, take off your wet clothes and eat some fresh rolls just come from the baker. Esther, the lady, your wife, she has just brought them in through the kitchen courtyard door."

*M*Y FATHER WRITES:

> In 1837 there was a horrible earthquake in the northern city of
> Sefat, home to devotees of the mystical branch of Judaism called
> Kabbalah. More than five thousand people were killed and those
> that escaped left the city and wandered throughout Palestine.
> Many half-mad old kabbalists made their way to Jerusalem.
> The streets were full of their ragged and deranged numbers.
> Yochanan and Esther, working with the British Consul, set up a
> charitable foundation to aid their cause. Amongst other projects,
> they raised money for an orphanage. Once the money was
> raised, Esther became its de facto director.

I WRITE:

hile her husband had come in wet, Esther had arrived home soaking. She had gotten caught in the brunt of the squall. And although both her color and her spirits were still lifted from her doughy tryst, everything else about her dragged. Her hair had come loose under her hat and lay in sopping tendrils all about her face. And her long maroon cloak, drenched at the bottom, hung heavily around her feet.

In the kitchen she threw off her floppy hat and stepped out of the cloak, gratefully peeling its wetness off of her body. The only dry thing about her were the rolls, which were curled into a cloth that she had stuffed under her cloak and which she had held tight into her chest as she made her way home. Suddenly laughing, she thrust the rolls away from her body and into the hands of the servant who laughed along with her for no reason at all. They continued laughing, Esther and the servant girl, as Esther unconsciously ran her hands up and down her bodice. Her nipples were cold and hard. And they stung a bit too. Esther dropped her hands and walked upstairs to change into dry clothes for dinner.

When she saw Yochanan standing in the front vestibule she stopped, gave him a smile. His look was neither vacant of affection nor full of any familiar warmth. She didn't know how to respond. Again, she tried to smile. And this time was successful. But the smile brought another shiver. As if there were a bit of cold contained in the subtle upturn of her own lips, which, with her smile, spilled out of her whole body. She hugged her arms about her. And she needed to speak. It was odd to stand there not speaking.

"One of the Sefat men begged to be—let into our house, out of . . . ," she began.

". . . And so you let him, it's raining, of course you let him."

"I led him to our door but at the last second he . . ."

"Ran away. Yes, they always run away."

"My husband. You look tired."

"My wife. You are very wet. Go dry yourself. And then we will eat. I smell the bread. It smells good."

Esther walked toward her husband and continued to speak. "But just as I opened the door, the man ran from me." She stopped in front of her husband and held out her hand to touch his. Yochanan felt how cold she was. Esther spoke again.

"The baker put in an extra roll. He is a good baker."

"My wife. Esther. You are very wet. Go upstairs, dry your—"

"My husband, I am going."

Yochanan watched after her as she climbed the stairs and rounded the landing. And as Esther disappeared from his view he felt that he could hear his own heart and smell his own blood and even feel his skin encasing his face and fingers, his legs and feet, his toes too. He felt taut and uncomfortable inside of himself. As if he were more a creaky machine than man, more a sum of mismatched parts than any sort of ethereal spirit. Whereas usually he felt the opposite. So comfortable with the feel of his own soul. And so familiar with it.

But now was not a time for soul. Actually, he couldn't feel his soul at all. Only his bones, and his body and all the blood running through it. Looking up the stairs again, he saw only emptiness. Then the green spot at the top of the hall snared his eyes; it was the picture, a landscape that his father had sent them, a present from Sheinlanka. Sent with the messenger whose eyes rolled this way and that, and in whom Esther had recognized a distant cousin's husband's younger brother or at least the form of someone remote and inconsequential whom she had once known.

"Well, maybe not you," she had said when the messenger protested, "but definitely someone like you or, at least, like your face." Then all three, Yochanan, Esther, and the messenger had laughed at her rather silly if not poetic persistence.

"At least, like your face." Now Yochanan mouthed his wife's words to himself, "At least, like your face." The words didn't mean anything, but he felt an odd and pressing need to repeat them. As if this one fragment of nonsense could save him. Yochanan knew that he would not mention what he had seen to his wife but that she knew that he knew and that this was to be their secret. And he also knew that the secret would become over time a mistress to both of them, a silence that they would share and take into their bed and ultimately believe in. For what is a secret, he mused painfully, but a kind of religion that leads the silent to constantly pray.

*M*Y FATHER WRITES:

Yochanan's father, the chief assistant of the Chatam Sofer, was the blind rabbi Mordechai Schine. A legend has been passed down that his students never knew he was blind. According to the legend, Rabbi Mordechai Schine tricked his students into thinking that he could see by listening for the turning of pages as they studied the Talmud and following the text in his head. He must have known the entire Talmud by heart.

I WRITE:

sther changed quickly out of her wet clothes and came down for dinner. They ate in relative silence, whereas usually both chatted comfortably about their days. Then right after they had finished eating, the couple went up to their room and got into bed. It was much earlier than usual, but neither knew what else to do.

Esther was pious in her own way. She knew how to keep the Sabbath holy but in private she often broke the rules. Yochanan was pious but in a serious way. He knew the *mitzvot* and he always kept the Sabbath holy. To him, creativity could come only as a consequence of prayer and piety, not as a shaper of it. Esther and Yochanan lay in their beds, side by side, barely any space between them. As it was not her time of the month, the beds were pushed together. On the days when she was bleeding they would be pulled far apart. Esther fidgeted and couldn't lie still. She sat halfway up and flipped her pillow over, fluffed it up and then lay down again, resting her face in the cool linen. She watched Yochanan's back. He was turned away from her, facing the window that looked out over the Mary Church. As he gazed at the church, his thoughts traveled in the opposite direction to the garden the Christians call Gethsemane after the olive trees that grow there crooked and squat.

Esther sat up again and turned the pillow another time. But the linen on the underside wasn't cool yet and this made her fidget some more. She did not know what or how or how much he knew, but she knew that Yochanan knew something. And Esther wondered how this something fit into his prayers. He was a most prayerful man, her husband, from a long line of rabbis reaching all the way back to Rashi, the great eleventh-century commentator.

Shutting her eyes, Esther tried to sleep but she could not. She kept seeing images and having odd thoughts and memories. She felt filled with them. Her whole body dreaming, remembering, thinking. One image would not leave her alone. It was of Yochanan's father. She could not stop visualizing and thinking of Yochanan's father, a man whom she had never met but whose story fascinated her. Esther had a picture in her head of an old man sitting at a table in the House of Study. He was surrounded by many students and many books.

The image dissipated, leaving her alone with Yochanan in the almost-dark. Esther closed her eyes and listened to her husband breathing. Heavy and deep were his inhalations, and every couple of breaths a restless comma of a cough inserted itself into his repose. Sighing, Esther feared that he had caught cold in the rain. She rubbed her eyes and took a finger up to her right nipple, which was still tender. The baker had taken her nipples into his mouth and sucked them until she felt like screaming in pleasure but she hadn't screamed; instead she turned the yell inward as she had taught herself to do, inviting it into an inner cavern where voices were always echoing and the trick was never to try to contain them but just to let them joyously be. She moved her hand away from her breast and traveled it down in between her legs, but only for a second. Not for pleasure, but for the feeling of comfort and warmth. And then she curled over on her side and shut her eyes.

THE GARDEN OF GETHSEMANE

She pretended that every time Yochanan inhaled was the turning of a page and every time he exhaled was the ending of a chapter. In this way, she read the Talmud of their togetherness. It was a big book. A book that contained all that had already passed between them as well as all that would ever pass between them. Past and present and future all were written there. She read for a long time, so many shared stories, some intimate, some silly, others dark and uncomfortable, some so beloved that she almost cried from them.

The night passed heavily. No, thought Esther, Jerusalem is not a place for regular sleep. Only for a kind of restless burrowing inward that leaves a soul dreamily awake all day long. Yochanan slept deeply; his breath was a parchment of air that she read from for a long time. And then, as the sky lightened, Esther moved toward her husband and roused him gently. Yochanan wrapped his arms around her and nuzzled his lips into her forehead. She pressed her body into his, and together they slept, adding another page there.

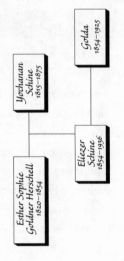

Esther Sophie
Goldner Herschell
1820–1854

Yochanan
Schine
1815–1875

Eliezer
Schine
1854–1936

Golda
1854–1925

## Chapter 2

## GOLDA AND ELIEZER

MY FATHER WRITES:

The 1850s were very hard times for our family in Jerusalem. In 1851, Esther's father, who had immigrated to Jerusalem after she did, was murdered. I will discuss this mysterious tragedy in detail in a later chapter of this family history. In 1854 Esther died in childbirth when she was thirty-four years old. The child, my great-grandfather Eliezer (after whom I am named), lived. He was their only offspring.

Many years after Esther's death, Yochanan remarried a widow named Ruchama who had a daughter Eliezer's age. Ruchama and her daughter were immigrants from Prague. The daughter's name was Golda. When Yochanan married Ruchama, Eliezer and Golda were both fifteen years old.

Yochanan and Ruchama had three children, and one of their great-grandchildren was the Ramat Kal, the commanding general of the Israeli Army.

I WRITE:

The year they both turned seventeen, Golda came to Eliezer's bed for the first time. For most of that first night, Eliezer lay wide awake in bed, stunned by her closeness, paralyzed by his desire for her, terrified of who they really were and what he really wanted them to be. He kept going over it in his head. How the night was unusually cold. How her fire had gone out, how she had come to his door, knocked gently, explained how she was freezing and then how she had asked him if she could climb into his bed. He noticed that her night voice was softer and higher than her day voice. Her blond hair was loose, she wore a blue wool nightgown buttoned up to her neck. Eliezer had put his arm around his sister, and tried to warm her up. She was so cold. Her teeth chattered. But when she fell quickly asleep he moved away from her, and inched as close as he could to the opposite side of the bed. Golda slept on her belly, her right leg bent, her behind slightly up in the air.

Eliezer stared at the ceiling but then he felt as if the ceiling were staring at him, at both of them. He inched even closer to the edge, hanging a whole leg over—which was very uncomfortable so he pulled it back up and tried to make himself into a skinny little line. He looked over at his sister. He did not know if they were sinning by sleeping together in the same bed, but it felt as if they were. And yet, he told himself, one had a moral as well as religious obligation to relieve the suffering of others, and wasn't cold a kind of suffering? And didn't cold lead to illness? And didn't illness lead to death? And aren't all Jews commanded to break almost all of the commandments if it is in the service of saving a life? Again, he looked over at his sister, and tried to convince himself that her lips were blue, even though he knew they weren't and tried to tell himself that she looked feverish even though she didn't and then he stopped trying to tell himself anything and concentrated instead on the startling evidence of life in his own pajama pants. Eliezer spent the next agonizing hour trying to figure out how to relieve his own suffering without breaking any more commandments or God Forbid waking his sister with an unseemly creaking of the bed.

But he did not wake her up, and somehow Eliezer did manage to fall asleep, and in the morning when he woke up, she was gone. At breakfast, Golda did not mention anything, she didn't say anything in front of their parents—Yochanan with his long beard and tired eyes, Ruchama clearing away the dishes. Only later, when they were both walking out of the house together to go to school did Golda look at Eliezer and smile and say "Thank you" in her day voice, which, he noticed, was much deeper than her voice of the night.

All that day as he bent over his books and pretended to study, Eliezer felt himself trying to shrink, trying to make himself very small, but instead of becoming a little line on the edge of a bed (or on the edge of a creamy yellow page of Talmud) he felt his life force expanding, and even though she was not there with him, he could feel Golda's life force expanding too, so that by the time the day was over and they met to walk home from school through the windy streets and alleys of the Jewish Quarter, no bed or book or room or alley was big enough to contain either of them, and the world itself was filled with their blushing forms.

❧

Soon after, she began coming every night, after their parents were asleep. Night after night they slept all curled up, his big arms around her little ones, her face on his chest. Eliezer thought that it was as if their nights together existed in a parallel universe, a place just above or below their parents' house. When he was younger, long before Golda and her mother came to them, he would run up and down the stairs and into all of the musty rooms where he would knock on walls trying to find a secret passage. As a little boy, he had been sure that one of the walls in the house on Rav Pinchas Street was hollow and that if he could only find it, and knock in exactly the right spot, the wall would swing open and the house that he had been born in would be revealed to him as a hollow shell with secret hallways leading into magical rooms filled with golden treasure. Sometimes he even imagined that his poor dead mother whom he had never known was the treasure, that she was alive with pink cheeks and sparkling eyes, just waiting for him to find her.

Now, lying next to Golda night after night, Eliezer often thought of himself as a little boy knocking on so many walls: how he used to rap with his knuckles and then press his ear to the cold stone, and then move a bit and rap again, and again, all the way through the house. Golda made a smooth umming sound as she turned over. Eliezer watched her hair fall over her eyes. He wondered if time perhaps had folded over on itself because he felt as if a wall had indeed swung away, and he was staring at himself on the other side of all the dark and rubble. He saw himself lying in the middle of a room full of riches, his arms wrapped around Golda, her arms wrapped around him. And as he finally fell asleep, Eliezer saw the two of them walking down the secret passageway that he had always known existed. They walked behind and above and below the walls of their parents' house. They held hands as they walked. They did not know where they were going. Golda held a candle to light the way.

❧

The first time he touched her he felt as if he were crossing an ocean. They had been lying awake for hours. Usually she fell asleep quickly, but on this night she didn't, and instead whispered to him in her high night voice, charming his earlobe with her cool breath, her fragrant syllables. She told him stories of where she and her mother had lived before coming to Jerusalem. She said, "It was a city of one thousand golden spires." She said, "When the sunlight hit the spires I believed that we were living in the realm of enchanted castles." She said, "The fairy tales my mother told me seemed real there. Princesses, dragons, magic spells." His hands were on her cheek, and then down on her shoulders, and then his hands were exploring distant territory on the other side of the ocean where there was more oxygen, and the ground was more fertile, and as his hands pressed into her bare skin, he knew he was home even though it was the first time he had ever been there. She kissed him back, she put her tongue in his ear and swirled it around, she nuzzled into his chest. And he breathed deeply and put his hands on her breasts, which were small and firm and beautiful. With his fingers, he played with her nipples, making them rise, and then he leaned over her and took one in his mouth, tickling the tip with his tongue and then biting just hard enough and licking, suckling again. And even though they were both silent, he heard her high voice in his head saying, "Princesses, dragons, magic spells." He knew that there was a never-going-backness to what they were doing. They would never again be able to pretend that they were just sister and brother. Every one of those first kisses, his tongue in her mouth, on her teeth, her fingers on his chest, her lips on his neck, and then lower, made every previous second of their lives different. And the future was in the quickness of their breath, and the future was in the brightness of their eyes as they stared stunned and enraptured at each other, and the future was in their sighs as they pulled each other close.

My FATHER WRITES:

Yochanan Schine was a very forward-thinking man. Though he himself lived in the house on Rav Pinchas Street all of his life, in 1870 he built another house outside the city walls. This property, in the neighborhood of what is today called Nachlat Shiva, or "the settlement of the seven," was in the tiny heart of the nascent Jewish community outside the walls. It was the first two-story building outside the Old City walls, and the eighth house ever to be built by Jews outside of the Old City. Yochanan maintained the house as a rental property.

I WRITE:

The house in the New City was a grand affair. It had six rooms—four on the first floor, two on the second. Yochanan only rented out five of them, leaving the smallest of the second-floor rooms for his own occasional use. This room was decorated sparsely but elegantly with a bed and a desk, a comfortable cushioned chair and an imported Egyptian rug woven with bright colors in an intricate geometric pattern that made everyone who ever looked at it a trifle dizzy. The rest of the house was rented to an Austrian musician of some renown. The musician was a kind man with a graying mustache and a prominent forehead that shaded his eyes and made it seem as if he were seeking shelter from the sun even when it was cloudy. The musician always greeted Yochanan warmly, but the two were of different temperaments and never really made much conversation. There was no separate entrance to the little room, and so Yochanan had to walk through the musician's house, as it were, in order to reach his own space. But the musician never seemed to mind and respected Yochanan's privacy whenever he was there.

Yochanan was a man of regular habits and could be counted upon to visit his house at three-thirty on Tuesday afternoons at the beginning of each month when his civic meeting convened in the New City to broach subjects pertaining to modern municipal business. On these days, in addition to his civic meeting, Yochanan would check on his business interests or visit a friend who had recently moved, or just peruse the growth of the new neighborhoods of which he was at once proud and suspicious. After he finished his business or his visiting, he would stop by the house for a short rest before starting back to the Old City and his house on Rav Pinchas Street.

During these "reposes," as he liked to call them, he would sometimes drift off to sleep in his comfortable cushioned chair, or if he was very tired he would lie in the bed. As he slept he would dream that he actually lived in the New City and that he had always lived here and because of this, his entire life was several shades different. In these dreams he always saw his first wife, Esther, down in the parlor of this house. They would both of them be young in the dreams, younger than when Esther had died. Yochanan would approach her from behind and, as he reached the chair in which she was sitting, she would turn around and smile at him with her head half-tilted. He would put his hands on her shoulders and plant a kiss on her head. They would stay like this for a moment before Esther began telling him something mundane in an astonishing way or something astonishing mundanely. In the part of his sleeping soul that was conscious, Yochanan would note happily that Esther's gift of creative speech had survived the journey to the Next World, and in the part of his sleeping soul that was truly sleeping Yochanan would delight in his first love's lopsided diction, loving to hear her sidewinded stories again and again and again.

Yochanan never dreamed of Esther while he was lying in his bed in the house on Rav Pinchas Street. He only dreamed of her here, in this house she had never even seen. Of course, he thought it very strange that she should appear to him outside the geographic realm they had shared. But he never thought about this too long, and instead, as the years passed, and the dreams kept coming to him, he grew more and more grateful to this new house in the New City, grateful for the new dreams of his old life that it so kindly afforded him.

⚜

The first time Eliezer and Golda knocked on the musician's door and asked to "rest" in their father's room, the musician happily obliged. It was quite a long walk from the Old City and it made perfect sense that they should want to sit down for a while before starting back. But after they began to "rest" regularly in their father's abode, it became clear to the musician exactly what kind of "repose" the "siblings" were up to. He was aware of the history of the family, and knew that the two were not blood-related. He would watch them ascend the steps to the little room. Golda always went up first. She was so light on her feet, it almost seemed to him that she flew to the high branches of the house while Eliezer followed after, his heavier steps more earthborn and mysterious.

At first the musician was not quite sure that he approved of the young couple using his house as the site of their illicit liaisons. He was the sort of musician who could hear whole symphonies in his head. He understood the intricate workings of the many different instruments and could hear notes speaking to each other from in between octaves and movements. He often heard his own life as a symphony—the different instrumental people he knew casually overlapping or reaching intense crescendos that filled his inner landscape with a constant music. His fingers were ever re-creating this music on the strings of his own violin. And he had a talent for hearing other people's life symphonies. A talent for hearing their secret songs. When they first started to use the little bedroom for their trysts, the musician could only hear Eliezer and Golda's seventeen-year-old drums—taut, eager instruments beating with nubile passion that shook the stones of the house and made him somewhat uncomfortable. But as time passed and they kept coming to the house, he began to hear more deeply the true music of their connection. As they smiled hello to him, and then shyly made their way upstairs (Golda flying, Eliezer stepping hard on each step), he could hear the airy flutes, lutes, lyres, and harps of their love and he soon decided that their lust was natural and their attraction was as spiritual as it was sexual.

As they lay together on the little bed, Eliezer's arms around Golda's slight shoulders, the musician would serenade them from down below. And because he was a man who appreciated intrigue and had had his own grand and secret passion in his youth, the musician found that he played better, stronger, and with greater purpose when the young lovers were in his house. The pair grew used to embracing to the melody of the often quite naughty notes floating up the staircase and through the floor. They appreciated the beautiful music, and were also grateful that the sounds of their lovemaking were naturally muffled by the normal goings-on of the house that Yochanan had built in the New City. They would lie on the bed and Golda would lift her arms and open them up to embrace as much space as she could while saying, "This is our enchanted castle," and Eliezer would believe her. She would take in the whole room with a hungry, happy gaze and say, "We are the keepers of this magic chamber," and then she would bend over him and make him raise his neck and as he shut his eyes she would kiss him on the sensitive skin of his throat, saying, "Here are the keys we need to lock the door. Here are the spells we need to become invisible." But this last thought would make both of them somewhat sad, because their love was so visible to them that it hurt to have to hide it from their parents and from the rest of the world. And yet they also craved invisibility, needed to be not seen, needed to hide, needed no one to really know who they were, who they had become together. Eliezer would say, "Tell me more about the castle." And she would point to the walls of the little room and say, "The walls of the castle are as thick as a full-grown man is tall. And the castle is surrounded by a moat in which there are alligators and sharks always swimming." He would say, "Alligators?" And she would say, "Yes, but we are safe inside the castle. We are invisible here, safe behind these walls."

⚜

No, Yochanan did not come too often to the Beit Hachadash, the New House, as he called it. No more than once a month. And whenever he returned to his *real* house, he always felt somewhat guilty as he kissed his second wife, and he always avoided her for most of that evening—for he greatly feared that she, this new wife, who was dear to him too, could somehow tell that he had been keeping company with a beloved ghost who lived inexplicably outside the walls of their neighborhood. He did not want to hurt Ruchama, and yet he could not resist his New City naps, his unearthly Esther dreams.

CASTLE

In the dream he sometimes reached out and touched Esther on her breasts, rubbing his palms against her hardening nipples, and she would look at him with delight and desire, but most of all with surprise—for in her lifetime he had never been so casual with their lovemaking, they had certainly never made love in the parlor, only in the bedroom with the lights out, the curtains drawn. He would rub her nipples and then take hold of her full breasts, squeezing them over and over again as she would pull him to her, her mouth wide open in a smile of such perfect pleasure, and he would fall over her, and then lift her up and place her gently on the Egyptian rug whose wild, puzzling pattern made them both dizzy, and in their dizziness they would consummate the dream with a passion of such tenderness and intensity that when Yochanan finally woke up alone in his little chamber he would often be sweaty, light-headed, blessedly shaken.

Sometimes, as he made his way back home from the New City, Yochanan would muse at how strange it was that as an old man—

he was now almost sixty—he would find himself involved in per-petrating a betrayal against his own, very-much-living wife, Ruchama. He, Yochanan! He, who knew what it felt like to be on the other side of desire's door, leaning heavily against a love that had locked him out and yet also queerly had included him. Yochanan was a deeply spiritual man, and even though Esther only came to him ethereally, he still felt as if he were cheating when he lay his hands on her dear shoulders, or bent down with passionately aching lips to kiss her on the top of her sweet curly head. He would walk more slowly when he had these thoughts. Or if he were in his carriage, he would sometimes forget to cluck and the horse would slow down to an almost-stop. Then Yochanan would suddenly come out of his thoughts and cluck the horse or begin walking again. And as he made his way home, passing through the Old City walls, crossing the Street of Death's Angels, life would seem a very strange thing to him. Sometimes, in the house on Rav Pinchas Street he dreamed that the tiny New City was hovering just over the sprawling Old City and all the inhabitants of both domains were climbing onto their roofs and singing psalms in a language he could not recognize. Yes, it was all very odd, but over the years he had learned not to fear the strangeness at all.

They surreptitiously visited the musician's house for many months. During this time Eliezer and Golda loved to pretend that the entire house was theirs and that they were a proper couple, husband and wife, living in it. After spending time alone in the little room they would venture outside and take long walks around the new neighborhood, commenting on the local style of architecture, their favorite subject being the subtle variations of color in the stones used in each dwelling. They made a game of trying to name the palette of a particular mountain from whence the stones had come. The house closest to theirs they called Ruby Rose of Sharon, the next one was Golden Gift, then Rainbow Glow, Angel's Blush, and Laughing Sunrise for the stones of the house of the British adventuress with smoky blue eyes. But Yochanan's new house they did not name. And when they were back in their little room and they shut their eyes and saw the stone in their heads they were both embarrassed and stunned by the beauty and intimacy of the color. The stones of the house that Yochanan built and that now surrounded them seemed like flesh to them.

Of course all the stones in the city were more similar than different, all of them golden and blushing in the Jerusalem sun. In the evening, Golda and Eliezer would walk toward a little well at the bottom of the small settlement where rose bushes grew wild. There they would smell the roses, rest for a bit, and then walk a little farther before leaving the New City and heading back for the house on Rav Pinchas Street where their parents were expecting them for dinner.

As they walked home, Eliezer would glance over at Golda and think. He knew that Golda was no regular sister. He knew that he was no proper brother, but they were bound together by these pale integument words while the other words—lover, beloved, husband, wife—floated out of reach. He knew and feared the prohibitions all too well, knew that as the daughter of his father's wife, she was technically forbidden to him, that their union was considered incest. And yet, the part of him that prayed, prayed for her, and the part of him that blessed, blessed her, and the part of him that danced on Shabbat, danced for her and the part of him that believed in God, believed in a God of different dictionaries, a God of great wizardly books whose words leapt off the pages and dressed your life in the right syllables and stories, no matter who or what or how you were.

❧

Later Eliezer went over it in his mind. How the door had opened quickly, without a sound. How Golda had been sitting up in the bed, naked. How she had first tried to cover her breasts, but then hesitated, and instead covered her face in her hands. How he had reached for her, and tried to cover her with his own body, and how they had been pulled apart, and how the faces of their father (his) and their mother (hers) had been so angry, but also at the same time full of love and sorrow and forgiveness. Ruchama had thrown a blanket around Golda and then hustled her out of the room. Yochanan had ordered his son to dress and then he had led him out of the house, nodding austerely at the musician who was standing just inside the front door, cradling his violin like a baby. The musician had not given them away. Yochanan himself had found his children out. He had grown suspicious one night after getting up for a drink of water and finding Golda's door open, her bed empty. Soon after, he and Ruchama had followed them to the new house one afternoon. When they had appeared at the door the musician, who was really a good man and did not mean to betray anyone or anything, had confessed the truth. The musician confessed because the refrain of reality was already in Yochanan's sad and wavering voice, and he could not bear to go against the score of such delicate and dangerous music.

Eliezer walked behind his father with his head down. They walked out of the little neighborhood and then got into an old carriage that was waiting for them by the rose bushes, by the well. Eliezer could not look at his father. Nor did Yochanan look at his son as he heaved himself up into the carriage. Eliezer focused on the horse's rear, and watched its muscular undulations as it pulled them away from the house where he had so often lain with Golda. He had no idea what his father would do, and for a few minutes he feared that Yochanan would hit him, that he would just turn around in the seat and begin to pummel him with his fists that were speckled with age, the knuckles beginning to grow knobby. Eliezer clenched his gut in anticipation of defending himself—he would cover his head with his hands, he would crawl up in a little ball, he would become invisible. But Yochanan did no such thing, and instead he just drove them both through the various skeletal new neighborhoods without saying anything. When they finally entered the Old City walls and began making their way back to their own house, Yochanan turned to Eliezer and asked him, very simply, if his intentions toward Golda were honorable. Eliezer heard himself answer and saw his father nod, and then saw Yochanan nod again pensively, and then pull at his long beard before continuing once more toward home. They rode under the split half arch, down the Street of Death's Angels, and then around to Rav Pinchas Street.

Inside, the house was quiet. But Eliezer could see from the coats in the hallway that his stepmother and Golda were there. He looked at the hallway, the coatrack, the fading painting from Sheinlanka hanging above the stairs, and then he looked at the floors, the ceiling, the walls, and that was when Eliezer realized that the walls of their house had always been hollow but that he had it all backward—the secret rooms were the ones they inhabited every day. And the other rooms, the hidden ones, were hidden not because they contained treasure but because they didn't.

※

Nobody noticed that evening when Golda slipped out of the house, but soon they realized she was missing. Eliezer found her. He found her sitting on the ground in front of the city wall to the left of the Tower of David, just beside the Jaffa Gate. The Gate, having closed over an hour before, was quiet but for a trio of Turkish gendarmes playing some game with colored stones and a big red stick.

When Eliezer came to her she lifted her arms and they held each other tightly in a way that was most improper for married couples out of the privacy of one's bedroom, let alone for unmarried couples out on the streets. Eliezer nuzzled Golda's head. She pressed her face into his chest. He held her so tightly, her spine, her hips, the small of her back. Her hands were just above his buttocks, holding him tightly in the small of his back. And as they stood there together, embracing, Eliezer had the strangest feeling. He felt that when he and Golda hugged like this someone else was there too. Putting its arms around their shoulders. Hugging them, and by hugging them, recognizing them, like they had recognized each other in their first conversation. Eliezer wondered if every couple had one of these—a secret spouse, cosmic and gentle, who fell in love with them at the same time they fell in love with each other. "This creature," he mused, "is partner to our privacy. It comes when the soul wants witness." Golda was breathing deeply. He could feel that she was shaking. After several minutes, Golda took herself out of his arms and walked away from him. Her eyes were dry, but very tired-looking. Her face was pale, her hair tousled. When she reached the wall she stopped. She lifted a hand and brushed its cool dusty surface. Then she leaned forward and pressed her forehead against the huge old white-gray wall stone, her fingers spread wide out on either side of her face. She stood there like that without speaking. And even though Eliezer was several feet away, he could feel the cool of the stone on her forehead, and he could feel the weight of the stone on her forehead, and he could feel all the world's walls rising up, called by her evening voice, which was both lower and higher, sadder and happier than her voices of the day or night, to do the hard work of protection.

※

That night, Yochanan, sitting on the side of his bed with his head in his hands, swore to himself that he would never visit the little

TOWER OF DAVID

room again. Ruchama, already in bed, was crying. Yochanan pulled at his beard, tugging the strands from his cheeks, his chin. He wondered if the room in the new house was haunted by the carnal spirit of his first wife. He wondered if his dear late Esther's incomparable lust for life and love were somehow responsible for the mess these children were now in. He wondered if by going there, and by dreaming his dreams, he himself was somehow responsible. He thought, "Maybe my illicit thoughts have infected the paint on the walls, the linen of the sheets, the tiles of the floors, and by inhabiting that same space they could not help but be influenced." But then he thought of the look on his son's face when Eliezer had sworn that he loved Golda and would care for her for the rest of his life, even if their love were unsanctioned. Yochanan remembered how they had entered the house just an hour earlier, after Golda had run away. How Eliezer had his arm around her shoulder, how they had climbed up the front stairs, moving, step by step, together forward. And even though part of Yochanan knew that it was the wrong thing to do, he found himself shutting his eyes and asking his dear departed Esther a question. He was not a man who often consulted spirits or believed in spooks. But this time was different. He conjured her image before his eyes and said, "My wife, did you haunt these children?" And the Esther in his soul looked straight at him with her lopsided loving gaze and said absolutely nothing that he could comprehend.

Before he fell asleep, Yochanan swore to himself once again that he would never again visit the little room in the house in the New City. He kept his pledge for several months before finding himself there again. Downstairs, the musician played a sweet serenade while upstairs, Yochanan spent a precious hour dreaming of an Esther whose gazes had always been cryptic and whose influence over his life he would always love but would never understand.

*M*Y FATHER WRITES:

**Would you believe that when they were old enough, Eliezer actually married Golda? Imagine, a father and a son married to a mother and a daughter! They married very young, and according to family stories were always very much in love.**

I WRITE:

*T*he night of the day they were married, Eliezer's eyes stayed open for a very long time. He held Golda close and watched over her. She slept curled up on her side, her back curved into his body like a little spoon. He encircled her, a big spoon. The room was dusty with a gray-white Jerusalem glow. Eliezer watched the shadows on Golda's face, there in her eyebrows, the curve of her nostril, the indent above her lips. It is said that every child spends the nine months in their mother's womb learning Torah. They learn everything that there is to learn. And then, at the moment just before birth an angel enters the mother's womb and presses his finger above the baby's lip, thus making the almost-born child forget everything.

The little indent remains—the physical mark of all forgetting. Once born, the child must spend a lifetime struggling to relearn all that it once already knew.

Eliezer reached over and lightly touched Golda's forgetting spot. It was so soft. Under her nose. Above her lips. She didn't seem to notice his touch. He took his hand away quickly though, wondering if the phenomenon continued, if there was some spot on the souls of the dead, angel-marked or otherwise mystical, where all of Life's Torah leaked out. This dusty light on the walls, the warmth of Golda's slim body, the sound of the Austrian musician's violin. The little room in the New City. Surely these memories would leave him one day. Would leave her too. What then? Eliezer breathed deeply, and then he shut his eyes and hugged her tight.

That night, as always, they shared their sleep, not just in form but also in function, and when they awoke the sun shone brightly through the window. They were blessedly mingled in the morning light, his arms wrapped around her shoulders, her head on his chest. And even though the violinist was far away, they lay in bed for hours embracing to the shadow sounds of a naughty serenade whose melody wafted over their bodies, casting away forever the need for castles with thick walls, houses with secret rooms, and spells that make love invisible.

MY FATHER WRITES:

Golda and Eliezer had two daughters, my grandmother, Avra, and her sister, Zahava. Yochanan died in 1875 after a short illness. Upon his death, the house he had built in the New City was supposed to be inherited by my great-grandfather, Eliezer. But Eliezer did not keep the house. He never really explained to anyone why he didn't want it, but it was well known in the family that he felt a solemn duty to live in the Old City, where he was born. Eliezer sold his share of his inheritance to his younger half-siblings—the children of Yochanan and Ruchama.

Today, the house that Yochanan built sits in the center of downtown Jerusalem. The property is beautiful, built in the old arching dome style. The descendants of Eliezer's half-siblings all own shares of this house. There are many of them—sons and daughters and cousins and nieces and nephews and grandchildren and great-grandchildren. I recently visited the house with my daughter, Nomi. We found it quite easily. It was amazing to walk around inside and think, "Here is where Yochanan stood so many years ago. . . ."

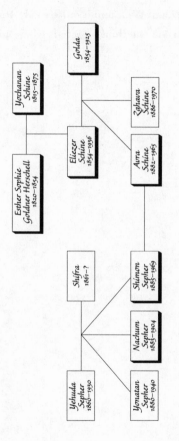

## Chapter 3

# AVRA THE THIEF AND SHIMON'S LOVE
# AND GRIEF

**I WRITE:**

Avra was a born thief. As the great-granddaughter of a murdered man and the great-great-granddaughter of the chief rabbi of the British Empire she was born with a mixture of pageantry and poison in her blood that manifested itself in a compulsive desire to take other people's nice things. In her heyday, in between the ages of seven and seventeen, the Old City of Jerusalem—all of its quarters—entertained a constant parade of lost objects. Her audience cursed. Police hunted. But she was never caught. Avra was a pro.

**MY FATHER WRITES:**

Yochanan and his second wife had a daughter named Avra—she was known in the family as Avra the Big. Eliezer and Golda also had a daughter whom they named Avra—she was my grandmother. I have no idea why they used the same name. In order to confuse us, I guess. My grandmother was called Avra Hayafa— Avra the Pretty. The great Israeli lexicographer, Eliezar ben Yehuda, wrote in his memoirs about his daughter playing with Avra Hayafa. That's right, he was writing about my grandmother when she was a little girl! Avra was born in the Old City of

Jerusalem in 1892. Her younger sister, Zahava, was born two years later.

As you can imagine, the relationships in the family were all very confusing. In fact, my mother once told me that somebody was his own uncle. And when you look at the relationship, this is actually possible! You cannot easily make a family tree because the roots are intertwined all over the place.

I WRITE:

When she first started, she stole only small domestic objects: her cousin's blue left shoe, her mother's bronze thimbles, her father's Sardinian eyeglass case. Someone in the house was always missing something. But who would suspect a child, let alone their own child, of committing a crime? And so her petty thievery continued. Avra was fair-skinned and dark-haired like her grandmother Esther. But unlike Esther, she was skinny. Esther had been curvy and soft even when she was small. Avra had no curves. She was a tiny little wisp of a girl with a flat little stomach and wrists the size of a grown man's thumbs. Daintily small like her mother. And very pretty. Who could suspect such a fairy child of anything illegal? She seemed to have a body too small for secrets—where could she hide them? And a smile too big for breaking rules.

But things kept disappearing, and by the time Avra turned eight her parents had begun to suspect something. By then, the thimbles and the shoes and the eyeglass cases had been joined by an entire congregation of books and socks and buttons and pieces of imported Armenian lace. But Avra wasn't one to get caught. Before her parents' suspicions could ripen into disciplinary surety Avra had moved on. Her habit roamed and raged out of the house. When she was nine, she stole a precious purple geode from out of an Argentinean stone merchant's satchel in the middle of the main street of the Arab bazaar. Also an intricate rendering of Jesus' face from a local tattooist's work table. Her habit had no religious qualms; it sat down at all of the city's three monotheistic tables, and even occasionally sampled the pagan fare. At nine-and-a-half, she stole two pairs of men's shoes from the front porch of the Omar mosque. And when she was ten, she stole the heirloom silver spoon from out of the third drawer in the breakfront in the living room of the French rabbi's walnut bureau while all the other guests, including her parents, were listening to a viola recital in another room. At ten-and-a-half she stole seven mosaic stones from the face of a second-century B.C.E. Roman goddess that had just been unearthed behind the Temple wall by an American archaeologist with a lisp who had called Avra "Thweetie" when he found her sitting primly on a low stone wall at the edge of the dig one winter afternoon. Smiling, Avra had hopped off the wall and skipped childishly, charmingly, by and away. She returned that evening after dinner when the archaeologist and all of his diggers had gone and the night watchmen had left their posts to drink some hot Syrian ale. Avra climbed down into the pit of the dig and slipped the goddesses' eyes, nose, and lips into her pockets—not because she really wanted them, but because after her great-grandfather's murder, the line between legality and life had been, in their family, organically broken. At least in her genes. And anyway, her fingers just itched.

She never kept what she stole but scattered it all around, taking particular pride in occasionally giving something back. So, for example, she might replace the Jesus tattoo with the goddess's lips or the silver spoon with the Jesus tattoo, and though no one ever caught her trail, if they had, they would have seen that her intent was not so much to take as to confuse, and that at heart she was not so much a criminal as a clown with a misguided sense of self-expression.

ℳY FATHER WRITES:

Avra married Shimon Sepher, an emigrant from Russia. At the
beginning of the nineteenth century, the Russian czar permitted
some Jews to move from Lithuania to the south. In the Black Sea
region, they were allowed to be farmers, to own and work the
land. This was very unusual as the Jews in Europe were typically
not allowed to own land or to be farmers. Among the families that
moved to south Russia was our family—the Sephers.

The Sepher family generations known to us lived in the city of
Tokmach in Tavria County, north of the Crimean peninsula. The
family was well educated and received a good, solid Jewish education. Some of them were very religious and spoke Hebrew fluently.

My father's grandfather, Yehuda Sepher, married a woman
named Shifra. Together they had four children, three sons and a
daughter. I have not been able to find out the daughter's name,
or to trace any of her descendants. Their three sons were
Yonatan Sepher, born 1880, Nachum Sepher, born 1883, and
Shimon Sepher, born 1885. Shimon was my grandfather.

Yehuda's uncle, Zeev Sepher, had immigrated to Petach
Tikvah in Palestine from Russia in 1842. According to Turkish
law, if a Jew died with no relatives in Palestine, his property
would be confiscated by the Turks. This caused great distress in
many families. In order to prevent the confiscation of his property, Zeev willed his property to his family back in Russia and
entreated the family to send a child to inherit his farm in Petach
Tikvah. The letter was found, along with other family documents, in an old suitcase under my grandfather Shimon's bed
when he moved into a nursing home in 1968. The following is a
copy of this letter:

To my relative Yehuda,
I send you greetings and much love. And I ask you
from my heart, dear nephew, please send a child to us.
We are very old and God forbid our property may be

taken by strangers. You must send one of your sons. And when the boy comes, tell him not to bring prayer books, we have enough. Also tell him not to worry from the sail on the boat. The same God that rules the land also rules the sea and everything will be fine. . . . Thank God I have bread on the table but I do not have a barn for the cattle to be in in the winter. It will cost 50 rubles to build it and I have only 20 rubles now. When your son comes to me he can work in my fields or for Baron Rothschild in the vineyards. If he comes, all will be well. Send a child so that the property will not be lost!

Happy New Year,

Zeev Sepher

Nachum, Yehuda's middle son, decided that he would go to Palestine to inherit his uncle's property. This was probably because Nachum was the most religious of the brothers. But before he could go, war broke out in Russia. In 1904, the Russian-Japanese war erupted, and the czar's draft increased its scope. All three Sepher brothers—Yonatan, Nachum, and Shimon—were in danger of being drafted.

Of the many hardships faced by Jews in Russia, being drafted into the czar's army was one of the worst. Many young Jewish men fled Russia in order to avoid being drafted into the czar's army. Others pretended to be lame when they were called in front of the draft board. Some even maimed themselves rather than serve. A popular technique was to bend and tie a finger until it lost its use permanently.

The reason they attempted to avoid the draft was that they were abused in the army, and were not allowed to practice their religion while serving. The period of service could be as long as twenty-five years! It was, for most, a death sentence. Also, many of the young Jews in the czar's army were forced to convert to Christianity. If there was only one boy in the family he was spared military service. Sometimes, if a Jewish family had more than one son, they would give one of the boys to close friends or relatives who had no children to raise as their own. In this way, both boys would be spared from service. This happened in our family—not on the Sepher side, but in another branch, the Leibs. Rabbi Menachem Hakohen Leib, my great-great-great-great-uncle, had two sons. The second was adopted and raised by the Plotnick family. I have recently contacted the descendants of this cousin. They live today in San Francisco.

In the winter of 1904, the eldest Sepher brother, Yonatan, had a hearing with the Russian draft committee, which was called, in Russian, the Prizawe. Yonatan wasn't drafted because he managed to convince the committee members that he had a problem with one of his legs. He did this by pretending to limp. Years later, Yonatan would show his children and grandchildren how he was an expert at perfectly imitating a limp.

Soon after Yonatan successfully evaded the draft, the middle son, Nachum, was called into the Prizawe.

I WRITE:

Ever since he was a little boy, Nachum had believed in spiritual geography. He knew that he had been born with a map in his brain and that the map had a course on it, a course in bright red ink, flowing through all of the moments of his life, and charted straight for Jerusalem. He was smaller than his brothers, which made him very short. He was more religious than his brothers, which sometimes made him the butt of their jokes. He would leave them in the morning and walk to the House of Study as they went to thresh the hay.

"Ahh Nachum," they said, "tell me when you find Mount Sinai on those pages, I'll climb it with you, could use the exercise." Nachum, carrying his books to the House of Study, wondered if God was a mountaineer, or if he lived in valleys. He wondered if

God was hay or if God was grass. Or if God was both hay and grass.

Nachum was called to the draft board on a Sunday morning at the end of May. It was the late spring of 1904. The czar's army had just been defeated by the Japanese at the Yalu River. Nachum planned to travel to Palestine the next fall, leaving Russia right after the Jewish New Year. The night before he went to the draft board he had practiced his limp with his brothers. Yonatan was the best at it. He had shown Shimon and Nachum how to pretend that they were squeezing a pin in between their two biggest toes. "The trick," Yonatan had said, "is to try to walk without dropping the pin or letting it poke into you." That was the trick. An imaginary pin. They had all tried it several times, limping the length of the cottage and then outside, all the way to the barn. Yonatan had done it with his left leg, Shimon with his right. Nachum, too, chose his right one. Then, when they got tired of limping, Shimon had yelled, "Take these pins and race me all the way to the river!" And they had all crouched down to the ground, their fingers pressing into the dirt like the legs of spiders, and then suddenly they were running, running, their feet hitting the ground with hard thumping echoes.

In the morning, on the way over to the draft board, Nachum had practiced his limp again—stumbling clumsily down the dirt roads, stumbling as he walked by the Moscow schoolteacher's house, stumbling, clenching the invisible pin in place. It really worked, limping, limping as he made his way down to the other village where the draft board sat. He had limped by the old egg woman. She had waved and said, "Nachum, son, what is wrong?" But he hadn't answered her. He was concentrating on not letting the invisible pin fall out from in between his toes, and when she saw in which direction he was going she had thought, "Oh, dear God in Heaven, please put a universe of clumsiness in that boy's foot. For just one morning."

Nachum limped all the way to the draft board. And he limped into the hall where the tall Russian men were sitting at a table with their legs stretched out on the floor in front of them, their feet crossed at the ankles. The one in the middle who was calling out names had a zigzagging scar on the side of his neck and a crisp, cold voice that made Nachum think of old snow. Nachum wondered if the czar also had a voice like old snow, but then he thought, No, the czar's voice probably sounds like a glacier.

He took his place at the back of the room with all of the other draftees, some of whom he recognized, but most of whom were strangers. He waited all morning and half of the afternoon, his limp keeping him company, sitting next to him like a good friend. Then finally, the officer in the middle with the zigzag scar and snow voice called Nachum's name and Nachum got up from his seat. His limp got up with him and walked with him past all of the other young men, the invisible pin perfectly clenched in between Nachum's biggest toe and the one next to it. But just as he was about to cross the room and take his place in front of all of those uniformed Russian men the pin fell out, and he was abandoned. His heels hit the ground with equal force. And even though he tried to conjure the pin back, even though he tried to will himself to stumble, he could not fall, he felt his feet lifted, lifted up, walking the walk of a healthy man. And as the Russian officers inspected his body with their eyes, his right leg spoke to him. It said, "I can run one million paces. And yes, I can even climb Mount Sinai if you want me to." Nachum stood in front of the uniformed men, his hands behind his back. His wool hat in his hands. A prayer cap on his head. His long hair flapping into his eyes like a decorative fringe. And as the officer with the snow voice and zigzag scar called his name a second time and asked him his parents' names and asked him if he was in good health, and he answered their questions, Nachum wondered if God lived in Russia, and if he did, he wondered if God ever had supper with the czar.

*M*Y FATHER WRITES:

Nachum was drafted. He was killed on the Russian-Japanese front later that year. When Nachum was killed, my grandfather Shimon decided that he would travel to Palestine in Nachum's place. That is how our family (on the Sepher side) ended up in Israel. Had Nachum not been killed, my grandfather would probably have stayed in Russia.

I WRITE:

When Shimon heard of his brother's death he had been out chopping wood. He sat down on the woodpile and remained there for a very long time; even when it got cold he did not leave the woodpile. After it got dark he built a fire. Some of the wood was dry, but most of it was wet, and so the fire did not take immediately. Shimon added small twigs to the two logs, and then he put more twigs under the tent of wood and kept feeding it until the logs caught and the fire began to travel from the edge of one piece to the edge of another, until finally all of the wood was bathed in flames. Shimon stared and stared at the fire, the way you can only stare at fire or at running water. He watched the fire spark in yellow and orange and red flame. He had never had his own Grief before. He felt as if he did not exist. And that this Grief, this dead Nachum Grief, had dreamed him up. He rubbed his hands over the fire, and breathed in and out quickly, blowing air through his lips in short staccato. No, he did not exist, he was only a dream and he would fade and in his place the Nachum Grief would walk the world, a more permanent creature.

They did not bury Nachum. His body was lost somewhere on the southern Russian border. But the family sat *shiva* for the traditional period of seven days, sitting on low stools with their clothes and their hearts rent. Several days after they finished sitting *shiva*, Shimon walked to the next village and to the House of Study of Nachum's rabbi. He knocked gently on the door, and asked to be let in. It was a smoky room. A stove in the back left corner puffed and leaked gray scarves of smoke into the air. But no one seemed to notice. Shimon surveyed the crowded room, the dirt floor, the wheezing stove, the students and their books. He noticed a crumpled-up dark-green handkerchief on the floor under one of the tables and wondered where it had come from. Whose pocket? He walked further in. Nachum's study partner had big hands and huge feet and a mouth that was little more than a line. Shimon let the study partner put his arm around his back and walked into the crowded room with him, but he would not sit in Nachum's empty seat and instead just leaned against the wall. The old rabbi nodded at Shimon from across the room.

On the second day, Shimon stood against the wall again.

On the third day he took a seat under the window, and on the fourth he sat there too. Shimon continued to come for two weeks. He would chop his wood way into the night, and work at the dye factory from midnight to dawn so that he could go to the House of Study during the day and just sit. He wasn't sure if he slept during this period. "Maybe my eyes are closed on the inside," he thought, "and all of this waking is really a queer way of rest." He didn't really feel the need to sleep. He did not know what he wanted to do there, in the House of Study, but he knew that he needed to go in. And in return, the pious young men read Shimon's presence with kind glances and cantillations of silent acceptance. Their rabbi had taught them that although the Holy Ark is home to God's greatest revelation, there are other Torahs, one written on human pages, the kind you can't roll up and return to the ark. Nobody asked him to join in their Talmudic conversations, nobody pressured him to learn. They just let him sit.

On the eighth day of his vigil, Shimon found himself sweating even though it was not very hot. The ends of his fingertips felt numb. And there was an uncomfortable throbbing from out of the crook of his right elbow. Shimon felt his body was mixed up and that maybe his face would soon migrate down to his feet and vice versa and he would have to walk home upside down.

On the ninth day of the vigil, Shimon got up from his seat, walked across the room, and approached the rabbi. For several seconds he stood and just watched the rabbi read. The rabbi looked up from his book with a two-mouthed gaze that said simultaneously, "I am glad to see you my son," and "I have already seen you, my son," but Shimon was not put off by this contradiction. He crossed his arms across his chest and asked the rabbi the following two questions:

"Rabbi, how far is it from here to Palestine? And, please sir, tell me what is the nature of its terrain?"

The rabbi got up from his table and walked over to a bookshelf leaning against the left wall of the room. He walked with a forward-leaning shuffle. Reaching the bookcase, he bent nimbly down and pulled a slim green volume with frayed cloth and a battered spine from the second shelf up from the floor. He gave the book to Shimon and said, "You go west and then south, my son. The entire journey should take you no more than several months if you are lucky. In the middle of the ocean trip you will reach a depth equaling the height of the Tower of Babel, and I would highly recommend that at this point you watch day and night for schools of elegant intrinsic puffer fish. They are rare, you know, most rare, and live only at that latitude, and swim on the surface of the water only several days a year. Watch for them, my son— each year they choose a different time to rise up and show their fins, which are yellow with magnificent red spots."

Shimon laughed out loud, he couldn't help it. The rabbi, who had a very big red nose and a beard that split into two pieces— each reaching all the way down to his belly button—smiled widely and twirled the left piece of his beard. Shimon kept laughing. He had the strangest feeling. He thought that he could feel his Nachum Grief laughing too. The rabbi handed him the book and their fingers touched together across the spine. Shimon thought, How strange that a Grief can have a sense of humor. But it does. Several of the students looked up from their books.

Shimon thanked the rabbi for his gifts, and he walked home with a book full of the names of Palestine's birds, minerals, and flowers, its absolute elevations, distances, and depths. Shimon read the book voraciously. And he began to recite litanies. The trees are this, he would say, the soil is that, the birds are such, the clouds are those. There seemed to be something very important about knowing all of this. Shimon stopped going to the House of Study, returning only once, two years later, the day before he left Tokmach. He had gone to return the rabbi's book, but the rabbi had refused it, and had pressed it back into Shimon's hands.

※

Shimon left Russia with his pockets almost empty but for a few precious rubles stuffed there by his older brother, Yonatan, and a fancy carton of Russian soap. Yonatan earned more than anyone else in the family by selling fancy soaps to wealthy vacationing Russians in the Ural Mountains. The soap was made out of minerals that came from a secret cave underneath the river Volga. It was packed in blond wooden cartons of various sizes, and the cartons were stamped with an intricately rendered image of the czar's face.

On the day that Shimon was set to leave the village on his long journey to Palestine, Yonatan had taken pity on his penniless sibling. "Take these rubles and run," he had said to Shimon, and then he had reached a hand over and tussled his baby brother's hair in the way that only older brothers are allowed to do.

THE RIVER JORDAN

Shimon smiled. He put the rubles in his pocket and then crouched down on the dirt floor of their parents' house in a sprinter's classic starting pose.

They had grown up racing each other.

The trick was you had to come up with a silly sentence to launch you off. "Take some sticks and sprint to the stream!" "Take a ticket and I'll beat you to Babel!" And then you could run, race, fly around the village like crazy Cossacks, your brothers at your shoulder, the three of you reaching the end of the race simultaneously and then each of you swearing that you got there first. Gifted with gazelle speed, always flying around the shtetl with the swiftness of sweaty angels. Yonatan ran with his palms open, his fingers held straight together like soldiers. Shimon ran with his chin first and his fingers clenched into fists. Nachum had run with his tongue between his teeth and he kicked up high and funny with his feet so that from the side it looked like he was dancing.

Shimon looked at Yonatan. "You say when, brother, I'll run you all the way to the Jordan River and then loop back around the world to your beloved Volga. You just say when."

Yonatan had laughed and then, with a sneaky sideways motion, he kicked Shimon on his backside in a strategic place with a strategic amount of pressure so that the physics of the playful kick made Shimon fall flat on his face. Shimon landed with a growling thump. Shimon, who was really the swifter one but was also the less steady on his feet. They were so fast, the fastest boys in southern Russia they would boast, even though they had never raced a Christian. Because Jews ran against Jews. And Jews ran *away* from Christians. This was the way it worked.

Shimon stood up. He leaned into his brother with his left shoulder—a hard, I-will-push-you-down sort of lean. But Yonatan stood his ground, and the lean led to a rare hug. Shimon suddenly, awkwardly, wrapped his arms around his surviving brother's muscular middle. And then with equal awkwardness, Yonatan wrapped *his* arms around Shimon's broad, barrel-shouldered frame. Yonatan was the taller of the two. Resting his head on Yonatan's shoulder, Shimon breathed in the sweaty musk of his brother's neck. And they stood there like this for several seconds, caught in the horrible crush of what each knew would probably be a lifelong goodbye.

"Goodbye."

"Goodbye."

"Oh, and take that carton of soap," Yonatan softly offered. They were still hugging and so his words were spoken into the side of Shimon's head. "Take it, I left it outside the door. Fancy Russian soap. Take it with you, brother, trade it for some domestic goods. It's worth a good amount of money."

"Take these rubles and run." Shimon respoke his brother's last challenge. And though they were both standing still, as they continued to hug, each brother felt possessed by the power and spiritual flow of a good hard sprint.

"Thank you, my brother," Shimon said. "Thank you." And they parted.

❧

Shimon thought often of his brothers during the trip. Many nights, before he went down into the hold, he looked up into the starry sky and thought of the prayer that his brother Nachum had liked best: "Blessed be God who arranges the stars in the Heavens." Nachum had told Shimon that he liked this prayer because it helped him think of God in the process of actually setting the world up.

"Physically fitting things together. You know, like a sculptor or a painter or even an engineer." Nachum had had a very physical way of speaking. When he spoke he waved his hands wildly as if he had extra vowels in his fingers and verbs in his fists. He was also always nodding his head down at the end of sentences, so that his hair, worn long and rather messy, flapped into his eyes. Shimon, standing on deck, stared at the stars and wondered if God would be so kind as to arrange his dead brother up there alongside the other twinkles, bursts, and heavenly glows.

But Shimon's thoughts were not only about the heavens. After walking under the stars he would go down into the hold and try to sleep. He suffered from strange dreams in which Yonatan was diving into the Volga and frolicking naked with the czar. He tried not to dream this dream but it kept coming back. Shimon tried to force the dream away, or to keep himself awake so that he wouldn't dream anything, but nothing worked. He kept falling asleep and the czar and Yonatan continued to flip and somersault and dive backward into the water.

Halfway through the trip Shimon looked for the rabbi's yellow fish but could not find them. He leaned over the rail of the deck and said softly, under his breath, "The intrinsic puffer fish have yellow fins. They come to the surface of the water only once a year." But no fish came to the surface of the dark and grinning waters. Shimon leaned farther into the wooden side of the ship.

For the past few days he had been seeing faces in the waves, and waves in the faces of his fellow passengers. He felt lonely and all mixed up.

By the time he docked in Jaffa he was a shadow of the Shimon who had left Russia. A skinny shadow with only those few rubles in his pocket and that fancy carton of soap with the czar's face stamped on it. He had only one other piece of baggage—a battered gray suitcase packed with two sets of clothes and one pair of winter shoes and Nachum's small black Bible with his uncle's letter pressed in between the pages.

⚜

They met in the Turkish police station inside the Old City walls, just to the right of the Jaffa Gate. Shimon was behind bars. Avra was not. She was in the hallway, waiting for him to be released. For although it *is true* that she *had filched* a miniature olive-wood carving of the Last Supper from a Christian knickknack stall that very morning, Avra wasn't in jail because she had been caught stealing (she hadn't been) but because she had witnessed the crime that had put an innocent and angry Shimon behind bars.

It happened in the early afternoon. Avra had been wandering through the bazaar looking for something to steal. Her eyes rested on a miniature oval olive-wood carving of the Last Supper, no bigger than the middle of her palm. And she decided to take it. She reached out and put it in her dress pocket. (That was how she usually did it, authoritatively nonchalant—as if she were *supposed to be* taking whatever it was she was taking.) Then she walked next door to the shop that sold spice, soap, and fancy perfume. What she wanted to do was to leave the Last Supper in the middle of the cloves and cardamom and cinnamon and pepper and salt. She liked the idea of Jesus eating his last meal on top of the warm-smelling packets of spice. But just as she was about to take the Supper out of her pocket, she saw the pickpocket with no front teeth reach his right hand into the jacket pocket of the handsome young man who turned out to be Shimon. Both the thief and Shimon were in the middle of the shop. The pickpocket reached in and tried to take the small satchel of money out. Shimon felt the invader's hand reach in and smashed his own hand down on it, breaking the man's fingers. The pickpocket immediately withdrew his wounded limb and started screaming. His hurt hand was flopping around like a dead fish in the air. A crowd gathered. The shopkeeper backed up against the wall of his wares, not knowing what to do. Soon a Turkish gendarme came running to see what the fuss was all about.

Now Shimon was a stranger in Jerusalem. He had never before traveled to the Old City. He was living on his uncle's property in Petach Tikvah, two days away from the Holy City if you took the fast donkey, three if you took the slow. The fast donkey was busy carrying Shimon's new friend, Alexander Tsarfati, to Jaffa where Alexander was meeting some relatives at the port, so Shimon had taken the slow donkey and had stopped many times along the way in order to sightsee and rest. He had come to see Jerusalem and while he was here he wanted to try to sell his brother's fancy soap so that he could buy some lumber to build his own small house and barn.

So, Shimon was a stranger, come to sell his single crate of wares. In contrast, the beggar was a natural-born filter-feeder in the holy ocean, the sort who skimmed Jerusalem's silty bottom. Born and bred on the Via Doloroso, he had a reputation for having stolen the splinters from the original cross. When the pickpocket wasn't wandering off with other people's possessions, he could always be relied on to sell you a genuine John the Baptist eyelash or a prime piece of Saint Peter's scalp. A merchant of the lowest order, but a merchant nonetheless. The Turkish gendarmes treated him with a certain measure of respect because he always gave them a decent cut.

The gendarme did not doubt Shimon's story of self-defense and probably would have let him go immediately, therefore punishing neither man. But Shimon couldn't control his temper, so the situation got out of hand. After breaking the pickpocket's fingers, Shimon had stood in the middle of the shop with a look on his still-too-skinny face that made the shopkeeper and the bystanders, and then the gendarme, more than a bit afraid. The gendarme, closing his hands into fists, wondered if his would be the next fingers broken. Shimon was not generally an angry man, but when he did get angry, his temper was loud and violent. He closed his mouth very tightly when he was mad. Instead of answering the gendarme's standard questions, he got more sullen and more angry and his lips just kept squeezing tighter together. So the gendarme, along with his reinforcements, hauled the angry, kicking, now yelling young Jew down to the station.

But Avra had been watching the whole thing. And the young Jew with the strong fists and serious temper had caught her fancy. She liked the way he looked. His strong skinny body. His light coloring. The way his chin squared off at the bottom and his forehead rounded off at the top. She thought that he was very handsome. So she went to her father, who, like his own father before him, was in close relationship with the British Consul. Eliezer managed to pull some Turkish strings. And Shimon was let out of jail in just a few hours.

❧

Avra led Shimon through the Old City to her family's house on Rav Pinchas Street. The police station was in the Armenian Quarter, and they had to pass through the Arab bazaar on the way home to the Jewish Quarter. Shimon walked behind Avra. Or rather, he trotted. She did not seem to be running, but she moved so fast that even though his legs were substantially longer than hers, he had to jog to keep up. And he was afraid of losing her. The spice merchant's shop where he had gotten arrested was right at the entrance to the bazaar. This was the farthest he had ever wandered into the Old City. From the little he knew of it, the Old City of Jerusalem seemed whirlpoolish and scary. More like the entrails of some petrified prehistoric creature than a proper place to live. And they were going deeper and deeper. Down small steps. Right now. Now swerving left. Down a narrow side street. Across a street half blocked by a big green carriage and two languid donkeys in bright red halters swishing their tails. As he jogged past the carriage, the donkey on the left lifted up his tail and swatted Shimon on the arm. Now back to a main street. There were so many people. It seemed like hundreds of people. They passed a bakery with trays piled high with pieces of pistachio baklava, the bright green nuts in the center. Shimon was amazed that Avra moved in a straight line. She was so little that she fit through cracks in between bodies like an arrow. But he had to swerve constantly. Even though he was skinny he was also muscular, still somewhat bulky, and felt out of place, as if his frame belonged to a different scheme of space entirely. Shimon felt panicky and afraid, and wanted to yell, Please slow down! But instead he kept swerving and jogging, and then they were there. Avra put one foot up on the second step of the house and bent down to tie her boot. As she tied she said, "This is where I live," and she motioned toward the arched door. Shimon looked up. The house on Rav Pinchas Street, seventy years after Avra's grandparents had moved into it, had suffered some rearrangement in its fractions. It was no longer half-grand and half-decrepit, but was one-fourth grand and three-fourths decrepit, the front steps falling apart, the facade chipping and cracked in one hundred places. Even the door that Avra was pointing to was gashed in several places, as if someone had once tried to break in.

Avra looked at Shimon looking at the house and decided for certain that she would marry this man. Maybe it was because she liked the thought of meeting her husband at the scene of a crime. Maybe she just wanted to get married. Maybe she just really liked the way Shimon looked. For whatever reason, Avra knew that she needed him, and something in Shimon's gaze told her that he needed her too. Shimon scratched his nose and half smiled. He leaned on the stone wall in front of the house. The sun was high now over the Mary Church. Avra squinted so that she could see Shimon better. She smiled back at him, and they both let out a little laugh.

Shimon joined the family for lunch. Before the meal was over Avra reached her hand into her pocket and touched the smooth little olive-wood Last Supper that was still there. It must be noted that that Last Supper was one of the only things that Avra ever stole that she actually thought of keeping for herself. Not as a religious totem of course, but because it had become an ambassador from the country of her and Shimon's first meeting. But she didn't. As she had with all of the other objects she stole, Avra eventually found herself secretly giving it back. Not to the original owner, but to someone else who owned something else she had once taken.

The next day, Shimon and Avra took a walk through the Jewish Quarter. This time, Shimon did not have to jog to keep up with Avra. They walked together, in close companionable strides.

Shimon joined the family again for lunch. And then for Shabbat. He had planned on returning to Petach Tikvah right after he had sold the soap. But he didn't go anywhere. Instead, he stayed in the Jewish Quarter with the family of Avra's mother's brother, a ritual slaughterer with a strange absence of eyebrows and a patchy grizzled beard. Avra's uncle traded Shimon board for help in his shop. Shimon courted Avra in the evenings. The rest of his time he spent learning how to carve, weigh, muck out, and stuff the intestines of what seemed to him an entire herd of cows. At night he thought he heard them mooing. The work did not suit him at all. He knew that his fingers were meant for the soil and not for all this blood.

Five weeks after their first meeting, the young couple brought together by that carton of still unsold aromatic river Volga Russian soap were married. The night before the wedding, Avra stole a long beautiful feather from the tail of a priceless golden parakeet kept in a fancy cage by one of the Russian Orthodox priestly brothers. Then she took the feather to the face of the goddess whose eyes and nose and lips she had stolen so many years before. And for no good reason, she left the feather there, outside in the dark, resting on the ruin of an archaeological wonder. There, where the lips should have been.

This is how my great-grandmother, Avra Schine, a born thief, came to marry Shimon, a man from southern Russia with strong fists and very fast feet. She moved with him to Petach Tikvah, far from the Old City. But the dirt roads and wide, open pastures of Petach Tikvah were airy and empty, walled only by the wandering eyes of the neighbors who watched closely and carefully protected their things. So Avra stopped stealing (for a while) and turned her art inward, so that, like her grandmother Esther, she became a woman of fiercely original speech.

*M*Y FATHER WRITES:

Shimon and Avra were married in 1909. That year, Shimon, with the generous help of his uncle, purchased building materials from two merchants in Jaffa—the supply store of Mr. Briteman and the hardware store of Mr. Rokach (the father of the first mayor of Tel Aviv). Among the documents that were found under Shimon's bed in 1968 were the detailed bills of these purchases. On one of the bills there is a unique handwritten comment, "Ship by 20 camels." With the materials, Shimon built a tiny house on his uncle's lot. Shimon and Avra were very poor. They lived in this house for more than forty years.

I WRITE:

our months after they married and moved into their own house in Petach Tikvah, Avra woke Shimon up in the middle of the night and confessed to him that she was a compulsive thief. She did not confess because she wanted to be honest with her new husband, but because in the absence of the ability to continue doing what she was born to do, she needed some other release. That night, Avra told Shimon the life history of her sticky hands, from thimble to silver spoon to shoes and precious stones. She told him the stories of everything she had ever stolen and everything she had ever put back. With her first confession, Shimon moved several inches closer to his side of the bed, and then drew his legs up to his middle and wrapped his arms around them, so as not to be touched by her words. He would not look at Avra, and instead nervously stared at the door. Would the Turks be coming to arrest her? He thought that he could hear the heavy tramping of boots coming toward their house, though there was no such noise, only the insistent, high-pitched chatter of his wife's revelation. No Turkish police in sight, only crickets and Avra's confession and the late-night rustling of leaves and branches.

As her stories grew in number, Shimon felt his stomach clench up and his lips tighten. He felt his anger coming toward him from across the darkened room, like the hand of an outstretched stranger. Pulling the covers up to his ears, he tried to hide from his wife's words, but she kept talking and talking. He didn't respond. Soon his lips were locked painfully tight over the anger that was inside of him now, making his head horribly heavy.

Avra kept speaking. And though Shimon tried not to listen, what happened was that in a couple of hours he found himself letting the covers drop away from his face and looking at Avra as she spoke. Eventually Shimon sat up and began to ask questions. By the time the sun came up, he found himself completely engaged in what she was saying. Eventually the stories actually began to amuse him. The anger left his head and joined the invisible crowd of spare emotions congregating on the far side of the darkened room. Shimon scratched his left ear and licked his lips. He felt curious and warm. From the moment they first met, Shimon thought that Avra's lips were the most beautiful and reddest lips he had ever seen, and they seemed even redder now, made up with the tantalizing pigment of petty crime and confession.

Soon he wanted to know the specific details of each lift. He began asking: "The French rabbi who lost his heirloom silver—what city in France did he come from?" . . . "What was the viola recital like? Who was playing? Were they any good?" . . . "And how far was it from the Omar Mosque to the Soap and Spice stall? Exactly?" . . . "The Jesus tattoo was being drawn for a member of what Christian sect? And for what part of their body? Back? Shoulder? Or maybe hips?"

Shimon asked Avra some things that she obviously knew and others that she obviously didn't. But no matter what the question, she gave answers. She would say, "Hip. The tattoo was for the hip of a Dutch pilgrim who wore an eye-patch and whistled as he walked down the Via Dolorosa." Avra spoke with a delightful authority in her voice, and like Nachum, she was verbally physical. Her hands built the word houses of her mouth and soon the husband and wife were lying not in bed but in a very sudden and very stolen village that had landed between their sheets.

Shimon asked on: "What pagan goddess was it who was missing her eyes, nose, and lips? Athena? Artemis? Mistress of Love? Wisdom? Of the Hunt?"

Avra told him everything. And as she spoke, Jerusalem, the city of gold, made a guest appearance in Petach Tikvah, city of gentle fields, palm trees, and too much summer dust.

Finally, at dawn, Avra finished. She was leaning on her side now; her small face was flushed and her eyes were sparkling. She licked her lips and then said, "There was a bird. I do feel somewhat bad about borrowing its feather." And then she told Shimon about the tail feather she had stolen from the Christian brother's rare bird the night before their marriage. As Avra spoke, the feather landed a second time on the goddess's face (with equal softness and yellow grace). And as it landed, Shimon had an image of a giant yellow bird flying over their wedding canopy just as he was stomping on the glass. He smiled in the waning darkness. He felt as if someone had just read him the best chapter in a good book. "Or perhaps," he mused, "this was all a play; perhaps my wife just gave a star performance?" He had not thought of Avra as an actress before. But there was definitely good drama in her criminal indiscretions. Reaching out a hand, Shimon tenderly touched his bride's cheek. She kissed his fingers. He felt the heat of their connection. Soon they moved toward each other and embraced, and then they both fell asleep.

When Shimon awoke, he was newly horrified. Avra was still sleeping. She was curled on her side, facing him, her hands open, fingers spread out wide. He felt once again crushed and crowded. And he cursed himself for not having gotten angry. He had the awful feeling that all of the things Avra had ever stolen were there in the room with them. There in bed with them both. Stacked in the curve in between Avra's flat belly and open hands. Surely the police would track her down and throw her in jail! And maybe him too, for harboring a criminal!

He got out of bed and left the house without waking her. All that day he was tired, angry, and tense. He felt as if some awful trick had been played on him. As if someone had actually copied Avra and misplaced his real wife. Or maybe Avra had done it to herself. Taking herself elsewhere, leaving him with a talking shadow. He didn't know what to think. He didn't know what to do. But he did know that the woman in bed last night had been some other Avra, a woman he neither recognized nor wanted in his home.

Shimon came home from the orchard that night in a miserable mood. He did not know what he would do, but he knew that he needed to do something. Avra smiled at him, and asked him how he was. He just nodded and grunted and sat at the table in a nervous lump. She served him dinner, and then sat down to eat her own platter. But before she even cut her meat, she told him, without a bit of nervousness, shame, or fear in her voice, that their neighbor had a string of turquoise beads mined from somewhere in Australia that she was just longing to lift. Shimon was astonished. She looked at him with a smile and added, "But of course, I won't do it." And he did not respond. That night they barely spoke. The next day when he came home from the orchard she told him that the local rabbi had a miniature copy of the Book of Psalms bound in purple leather that she desperately wanted. And again, she smiled and said, "But of course, I won't do it."

More days passed and more objects were coveted—this little hoe with a red handle, that baby's blue knit cap, a letter from Baron Rothschild, written to the settlement's most prestigious citizen and on display in the local museum explaining the importance to the Jews of developing local industry, specifically, an industry for the domestic fermenting of wine. Avra wanted to steal many things. Each time she ended with the same words, "But of course, I won't do it."

Aside from her confessions they barely spoke. Shimon was miserable. He was ashamed that he had actually listened to her entire litany that first night without offering a single rebuke. And he was mortified that he had asked all those questions. And now, why wasn't he reacting? Why wasn't he telling her to be quiet? What was happening to him? How could he condone her criminal lust, let alone goad her on?

Soon Shimon decided that he needed to take action. To do something either to prevent or repent for his wife's crimes. So he began making rounds. First, he went next door on the pretense of borrowing a hammer and in this way made sure that the turquoise beads were still decorating his neighbor's neck. Next, he went to the rabbi and asked him a basic question that he knew the answer to about *shmita* year and the proper religious way to grow wheat—and in this way made sure that the miniature Book of Psalms had remained on the right-hand corner of the rabbi's desk. Later he checked on the Rothschild letter. He also visited the young Polish couple with the new baby and admired the child's knit blue cap.

When he saw that the things his wife coveted actually remained in their proper places, he started to think that in speaking to him about stealing, his wife was finding a harmless way to sate her bad habit. Shimon went home and walked inside quietly, without letting the door bang. Avra was out back in the garden. He could hear her singing to herself as she planted seeds.

That night, just as he had that first night, he asked questions. In response, Avra talked them all over the world. She talked them to Poland where they visited with the grandmother who had knitted the baby's blue cap. They sat with her for several minutes and admired her handiwork. Both of them felt the longing and family love that she used to connect each stitch. Then they took their leave of the old Polish grandmother and Avra talked them to England where they visited Baron Rothschild himself, and advised him on the drafting of his letter, telling him that "Yes, the Jews need work. Yes, the land needs planting." Next, they traveled back in time. Going to the ancient realm of the Psalms where they picnicked on a hilltop with the author of the rabbi's miniature book, dreaming toward Zion, loving God in each blade of grass growing there.

Avra's stories filled the evening and made their house warm. Whereas in Jerusalem she had stolen objects and put them in different places, now the objects Avra coveted remained in place and instead, Shimon, her new husband, felt himself the one transported. He wondered how far it was from their bedroom in Petach Tikvah to the places Avra told. But he knew that there was no accurate or easy way to measure. Resting his chin on his palm, he watched his wife talk. Wisps of dark hair were coming loose from her bun and falling into her eyes. She didn't brush them away, but spoke from behind the tendrils. Shimon breathed in deeply and thought, "If my Nachum Grief could have a sense of humor, perhaps my Avra Love can have a sense of crime." Smiling, he reached out and took his wife's hand. There seemed no harm in this.

# Part Two

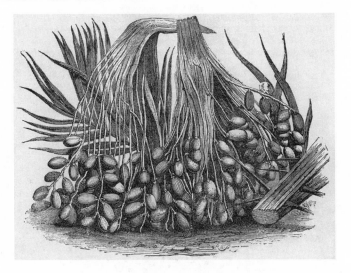

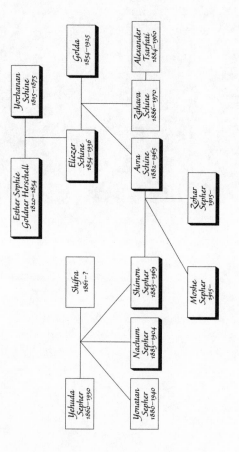

## Chapter 4

# THE WATER DANCE

*M*Y FATHER WRITES:

In 1914, Avra, a small woman, began working as a charwoman in a Turkish army base. Shimon, who was short, dark, and very muscular, worked in the citrus groves of Petach Tikvah. In 1915, they lived next door to Avra's sister, Zahava, who had married a man named Alexander Tsarfati. Shimon and Alexander Tsarfati worked together as *pardesanim*, that is, as orchard men.

About my great-uncle Alexander Tsarfati, there is an interesting story. My father once told me that Tsarfati had been deeply involved with the NILI spies. The NILI spies were a group of young Jews spying against the Turks, for the British. They believed that only under the benign protectorate of a European power, like the British, could the Jews ever establish their own country. The spies were led by a beautiful young woman named Sarah Aaronson. Sarah Aaronson was an incredible figure in Israeli history. Supposedly, she had many lovers. It was even rumored that she had an affair with Lawrence of Arabia. Several of the other spies were always known to be in love with her. NILI is an acronym for a biblical phrase from Samuel XV: *Netzach Israel Lo Ishaker*, "The Eternity of Israel will not Lie." The name was chosen randomly. The spies took a dead compatriot's Bible, let it fall open to any page, and took these words from it.

| MY FATHER WRITES: | I WRITE: |
|---|---|
| Conditions in Palestine were terrible then. There was mass hunger, malaria, crop failure, and the Turks were expelling Jews from their homes. Refugees were wandering the country. | Alexander Tsarfati showed Shimon how to do the water dance of the orchard. And in Shimon's mind, it was the water dance that afterward (years afterward) most reminded him of Sarah Aaronson. Not the bullets, not the many deaths, not the story of the spy in the desert—none of these things |

led Shimon's mind to Sarah Aaronson quite so quickly as the water dance did.

The point of the water dance was to irrigate the orchard trees. It was the only form of irrigation used in Palestine at that time because it required no pipes, only legs. This is how it was done. The orchard men dug trenches in between the rows of fruit trees. The trenches were all connected, and each tree had its own trench that allowed the water to flow directly to its roots. Shimon stood in the middle of the row of trees. Alexander Tsarfati was at the end of the row. Alexander yelled, "Yalla, now! Jump in! Here it comes!" along with an expletive that was not directed at Shimon but at a mosquito landing on Tsarfati's knuckles as he struggled with the pump to let the water flow. Alexander Tsarfati slapped the mosquito but did not kill it in time to stop it from drinking his blood. A red welt rose up there. Shimon, in the middle of the orchard, stood with his feet spread wide out, left foot in one trench, right one in the other, so that when the water reached him it flowed not into the two trenches he blocked off but into the two that he had left clear. The water flowed to the two mandarins. The lemons to his right remained dry. Alexander Tsarfati sucked on his knuckles. He yelled, "How is it going?" And Shimon yelled back, "Very muddy!" He was deep in mud by now because one of the trenches had given way and was caving in. Now Shimon jumped out of the first group of trenches and into the second. He felt as if his body had become machinery and wondered if perhaps next it would become the trees.

I WRITE:

On the twelfth day of April, in the year of 1915, Avra found herself in a very unlikely and awful situation. Avra was in the pasha's inner office in the Turkish army camp outside of Petach Tikvah. Six months pregnant with twins, her first babies, she was crouching behind the inner office door, so that the people outside the office, in the entrance way, could not see her. In the entrance way sat an officer with a pug nose and bad allergies. He was horribly mean and had once yelled at Avra for upsetting a bucket, reacting as if she had not just spilled water but had committed a vicious crime. The officer snorted and sneezed at least once every fifty seconds, so that she, Avra, crouching inside the office, could hear him there. Avra was alone in the room. Her skirt was hiked up almost to her hips, and her knees were splayed and her right hand was thrust under her underwear, her fingers reaching high up into her vagina. High. Higher. One by one she put four bullets inside of herself. Just underneath her heavy womb. The officer snorted. She knew that if he came in and found her now, she would be hanged as a thief or a spy. Avra pressed the bullets higher up. This made her cramp up, but she kept pressing higher. She was so afraid that when she stood up they would fall out. The bullets were cold and hard and she felt a grim and nauseous fever swell through her as she stood up and straightened her skirt. The bullets stayed in place. Avra bent down again. This time she dipped her hand into the bucket of soapy water that she had been using to mop the pasha's floor. Swirling her hand around in the bubbles, she washed her own smell off.

Then she mopped the floor, making sure to get the corners extra clean because the pasha checked. And then she dusted the tables and the vases and chairs. Then she dusted the wooden box sitting on the right-hand corner of the pasha's desk. The box had contained the four bullets and still contained many more. The officer outside was blowing his nose. She lifted up the heavy bucket and left the inner chamber.

As she passed by the officer, she noticed for the first time that he had a red birthmark behind his left ear. The bucket banged against her knees. The metal handle dug into her palm. She threw the water into the parched brown-gray soil behind the barracks. Avra watched it trickle into the earth in random squiggles and lines. She could not move from this spot. And as she stood, riveted and revolted, she clenched the muscles in her vagina around the hard metal. She could feel each bullet lodged there. And although she knew it was impossible, she thought that she could feel them stacked as high as her lungs. "Dear God," she said out loud. "Dear God." Though she was not the least bit religious, Avra knew the proverb: the mother who, while pregnant, takes a fright, gives birth to a child wearing the face of the mother's fear. For several seconds Avra felt as if she were some kind of mystical mirror and all of the world was reflected on her skin. "Dear God," she said again, this time in a whisper, "what will my babies look like?" Leaning over the earth, she retched. The twins in her belly began to kick as the last of the soapy water disappeared into the earth, leaving a splotch of darkness on top of the droughted soil. Avra stood up and wiped her mouth on the back of her hand and then she put her hands on her lower back, pressing there with her palms in an effort to ease the pain of carrying such a burden.

*M*Y FATHER WRITES:

In 1916, a NILI carrier pigeon was caught by the Turks. The message the pigeon carried tipped off the Turks as to the existence of the spy ring. Soon they came for Sarah. They took her and her elderly father, and they tortured them both for several days. Sarah's torture was severe. Her fingernails were ripped out, her palms burned, the hair was pulled out of her head; her body was beaten repeatedly. But she did not give up any information.

Sarah Aaronson begged to be allowed to return home one last time before she was to die. Her captors acceded. She was walked home in chains. When she arrived home she went to the bathroom. There, she wrote a letter to the other spies telling them to be brave and assuring them that she had not given away any secrets. Then she took a pistol out of a hidden cabinet and shot herself in the mouth. She did not die immediately. Paralyzed, floating in and out of consciousness, she died four days later.

According to my father, my great-uncle Alexander Tsarfati was actually the man who acquired the gun Sarah Aaronson used to kill herself. Supposedly, when things began to look very dangerous for the spies, Sarah asked her companions to procure her a weapon, "for self-defense." And Tsarfati was given this assignment.

I do not know if this story is true. My great-uncle would never speak on the subject of the spies, and my grandparents, Shimon and Avra, who were very close to Tsarfati, always remained silent on the subject too. My father heard the story when he was a child. He heard it from an older cousin, who, along with my grandparents and great-uncle, died many years before I began writing this history.

I WRITE:

Avra sewed the bullets into the stuffing of a dark purple saddle pillow. The cloth was very thick, and afterward her fingers stung from pushing the needle through it. Shimon took the saddle pillow, tacked his horse with it, and then rode up north with Alexander Tsarfati. Shimon tore open the pillow and gave the bullets to Sarah Aaronson. He put them in her hand. Alexander Tsarfati gave her a gun. Sarah held these things for several minutes, not saying anything. She curled her fingers around them and then she thanked the men pro-fusely. Later that night, Shimon and Alexander went with Sarah down to the beach to wait for the messenger ship from Cairo. It was a cold night, the water was choppy in a dark silvery way. Sarah spotted the swimmer first, but before the man could make it to shore, they all heard the horse-thud and jangle of a Turkish patrol. Everyone scattered. Shimon ran after Sarah. She was very fast. She led them into a cave where they waited together in silent darkness until someone came to tell them that it was safe to go back outside again.

The next morning, Alexander and Shimon traveled home. On the way, Alexander told Shimon stories that he hadn't wanted to hear before. Stories about Sarah Aaronson whose legendary beauty was no longer legendary to Shimon but as real as his own heart beating. Shimon agreed with his friend that she was the most beautiful, the most alluring woman he had ever met. They traveled on. Alexander was quiet for a very long time, and then he suddenly said, "We spies are now spying on each other." Shimon did not ask him what he meant but he was stricken by the image of Sarah running ahead of him in the dark, and he wondered if the sand knew who ran across it, and if the darkness knew her name, and if the seawater too were in love with Sarah, or if it just seemed as if it should be, like all the rest. When they finally arrived back to Petach Tikvah, Shimon was very weary. Avra held out her arms to her husband.

*M*Y FATHER WRITES:

Avra went to her father's house in Jerusalem, which was very near to "Dr. Wallach's hospital," in order to deliver the twins. She went two months before the birth. This institution later became Shaare Tzedek, one of Jerusalem's best hospitals. The birth was difficult, but the twins were born healthy on July 7,

1915. Avra and the babies stayed in Jerusalem for a month, then Shimon came to bring them home. The boys were absolutely identical. Avra tied different colored strings around their tiny wrists in order to tell them apart.

I WRITE:

*L*ater, she would think about what she had done. Avra would remember how it had felt to crouch down behind the inner office door. She would remember how, as she had pushed the bullets into her body, the words *unlikely* and *awful* had come into her head. They had come into her head and had hung there, as if describing not only this one moment but also the entire universe for several seconds.

Time passed. Avra would go about her housework and would think about how she had stolen the bullets, how she had swirled her hand around in the water, how she had walked past the officer with the pug nose and she would tell herself that it had been wrong to think *unlikely* and *awful*. Because what she had had to do on that day had been so antithetical to life that such words— unlikely, awful—spoken in the language of the living, could in no way describe her deep grief toward the task she had volunteered to do. Could in no way describe the residue of this grief, left behind forever in the wake of the bullets, left behind in the cave of her own body. But as she did not know the language of the dead, and as it had not really been a death moment either (no, not a death with the twins suspended overhead, shading the bullets with their yet unlived lives), Avra could find no right words to tell herself the story of what she had done that day in the pasha's office.

She would think about these things over and over again after Sarah Aaronson died. Sometimes Avra would catch herself dreaming about Sarah Aaronson, and she would reach out and try to touch the other woman's beauty in her sleep, but then Avra would wake up in the darkness and feel jealous of her dear husband sleeping by her side. Shimon had had a chance to see Sarah Aaronson when she was still alive. All Avra had ever seen was a photograph. And still the words bothered her. Unlikely, awful. Awful, unlikely. They kept her awake, came to her at odd times and made her nervous.

And then one day, Avra was mopping her kitchen floor while the twins took their afternoon nap. She stopped and leaned against the mop. Her bare feet were covered with cool water. She looked down at her hands and then up at the ceiling and then down again at the mop, at the bucket, at the water. She told herself to hush. She told herself that in order to speak the truth about the day in her life when she stole the bullets for Sarah Aaronson's gun, she would need a grammar of skeletons and a vocabulary of fruits and flowers. "For this," she said, almost out loud, "for this I would need other mouths." And then she mopped her kitchen floor until it sparkled.

❦

The water dance always reminded Shimon of Sarah Aaronson, more than the feel of bullets in his hand, more than the memory of all the deaths and the secret conversations. And when the years passed and technology changed and pipes came to Palestine, huge and heavy lead pipes that they had to carry into the orchards on their backs, Shimon did not really believe in their existence. After he had laid the heavy pipes into the earth, and checked their connections and then turned a spigot and listened as the water coursed through their metal bodies, he would sometimes walk to the middle of a row of trees, and when no one was looking he would do the water dance anyway, even though there were no trenches for his feet and no water to divert, and even though the trees now got their nourishment from other sources. Shimon would stand in the middle of the rows of trees and jump from one imaginary trench to the other, thinking, We are each an orchard. And this life is a water dance. And God is the one who jumps between our trees.

Shimon would always remember running with Sarah on the beach in the dark. And he would always remember how Sarah had leaned back in the cave pressing her body into the cold stone. Sometimes as the years passed by, Shimon would think about his dead brother Nachum. In his head Shimon would see him walking to the House of Study. Or sometimes he would see Nachum, as if out of the corner of his eye, running next to him, always a stride ahead or a stride behind. And then Shimon would think about Sarah again. And he would wonder if on the day she shot herself, God had been dancing in Sarah's orchard with particular skill and gymnastic fervor, or if the opposite were true and that on the day that she shot herself, God had chosen not to dance the steps of Sarah's dance at all. Causing some of her roots to parch and others to flood. Causing her orchard to wither.

My FATHER WRITES:

Sarah Aaronson did not lead the spies alone. She was joined in the leadership of the operation by her older brother Aaron Aaronson. Aaron was an agronomist and was famous throughout the world for discovering the biblical "Mother Wheat" growing wild in the hills of Palestine.

There is a fascinating story about one of the NILI spies who died in the Sinai desert. The spy's name was Avshalom Feinberg. Long before Sarah Aaronson was killed, Avshalom Feinberg and his partner tried to cross the Sinai Desert in order to reach the British in Cairo and give them information about Turkish troop movements. At that time, a trip through the desert was very dangerous. One risked losing the way and dying from thirst or hunger; also, travelers were often attacked and killed by bandits.

Avshalom Feinberg was rumored to be Sarah's lover. According to legend, his companion spy was also in love with her. The two men entered the desert together. Sarah remained behind in

CLUSTER OF DATES

Palestine, waiting to hear if they made it across.

Feinberg never made it to Cairo. His partner arrived alone. He said that they had been attacked by Bedouins who killed Feinberg and dragged away his body. The body was never found, but many years later, a group of Israeli soldiers were in the Sinai Desert when Bedouins led them to a date palm tree that they called Al Jud. In Arabic, *Al Jud* means "on the Jew." Although there was no proof, the soldiers surmised that the tree called Al Jud marked the grave of the NILI spy. Supposedly, Avshalom Feinberg had had dates in his pockets, and after he died the tree grew out of his body from the seeds of the dates. There is one version of the story in which the soldiers gathered around the tree and picked its fruit while saying the prayer for the dead. And there is another version of the story in which nothing of the sort ever happened.

For many years, the spy who made it out of the desert was blamed for the other's death. People

DATE PALM TREE

believed that he killed his comrade in order to eliminate Feinberg as a rival for Sarah Aaronson's affections. People believed that the spy who lived killed his companion, buried his body, and then made up the story of being attacked by the Bedouins. Only after many years was his name cleared of suspicion.

**I TELL:**

*T*he word legend *comes from the Latin* "legere," *which means* "to read." *The word* fiction *comes from the Latin* "fingere," *which means* "to form." *From* fingere *we also get the word* fingers. *We form things with our fingers. The word* history *comes from the Greek* "istor," *which means* "to learn" *or* "to know." *I believe in original etymology. I believe that fiction is formed truth. I believe that history is a way of knowing all of this. I believe that legend is how we read between the lines.*

*Proof? There was no proof Al Jud really marked the grave of the NILI spy. But I think that this does not matter. Certain kinds of stories don't need legs of proof to walk on, don't need water facts to drink. Unlike the spy, the story of Al Jud made its way out of the desert, and it lives among us still. No, there was no proof. Shimon danced the water dance, and Avra was a thief. And we lean against the date tree, because the absent body offers so little to hold us up.*

## Chapter 5

## ZOHAR

**MY FATHER WRITES:**

My father Zohar, and his twin brother, Moshe, grew up in
Petach Tikvah. Petach Tikvah was the center of the citrus-
growing industry in Palestine. When they were very young,
Shimon began taking the twins (my father and uncle) out to the
orchard with him. The family would joke that the boys knew how
to graft before they knew how to walk. Of course this is absurd,
but it shows just how immersed their lives were in the orchard.
Unfortunately, it also shows how poor the family was. The twins
had to leave school and begin to earn money at a very young age.

**I WRITE:**

Zohar was seven years old and nobody's fool. He knew that
Piki Kleinman was the biggest boy in school—almost
seventeen, or some other astronomical number. And he
knew that when Piki Kleinman asked you to do something you did it, even if it meant peeing on your neighbor's dog,
or giving some pretty older girl flowers. For Piki, of course. Piki
Kleinman, who was the biggest boy in school, was also the most
handsome boy. He was always courting the prettiest girls in
Petach Tikvah, and one of his favorite mating rituals was getting
the little boys to bring his dates little gifts from him. Flowers or

candy lifted from the British soldiers' store on the corner of
Pardess and Amnon streets.

Zohar had already peed on a neighbor's dog, a brown puppy
terrier, at the behest of Piki Kleinman. Piki Kleinman wasn't
watching. He wasn't anywhere nearby, even. But he had told
Zohar that if he peed on the puppy he would take him with him
into the orchard, which was quite an honor considering that
everyone knew that Piki Kleinman always tended the groves
alone. Zohar hadn't asked any questions.

*M*Y FATHER WRITES:

Petach Tikvah was not a quiet place to grow up. Even when my
father was a little boy, he saw his share of violence and fighting.
In 1917, the battle between the invading British and the retreat-
ing Turks passed through Petach Tikvah. My father and his twin
were only two years old, but he remembered hearing the story of
how the family had run all the way to Jaffa, to an aunt's house,
to escape the war.

Later that same year, the British passed the Balfour Declaration. It included the following crucial statement: "His Majesty's
Government view with favor the establishment of a national
home for the Jewish people and will use their best endeavors to
facilitate the achievement of this object." The Jews in Palestine
were of course overjoyed at this proclamation, but the Arabs felt
that they had been double-crossed. They had previously been led
to believe (by Lawrence of Arabia and other British officers
sympathetic to the cause of Arab nationalism) that Great Britain
would "view with favor the establishment of a national home"
not for the Jews, but for the Arab people in Palestine.

In 1920–1921, in response to rising Jewish immigration, the
Arabs reacted with a series of sporadic attacks across the country in which many people, both Arab and Jew, were killed. The
worst of these "riots" began in Jaffa on May 4, 1921. On that day,
a group of Jewish Communists marched through the center of

ORANGE GARDENS NEAR JAFFA, WITH THE PLAIN OF SHARON AND
THE MOUNTAINS OF EPHRAIM

town immediately after a Zionist labor parade. The Arab nation-
alists saw the strong show of Jewish political presence as a
challenge to their claims. They erupted in fierce riots, which, for
the first few days, were contained within the Jaffa area.

I WRITE:

Now Zohar held the flowers carefully, by the middle of
the stems with both hands. He held them straight in
front of him, not even bending his elbows one bit.
Pink petals and white petals. And thorns. Zohar
thought that they were roses but he wasn't sure.

He delivered the flowers to the girl with the red hair and seventeen and twenty-one freckles on the backs of her hands. Zohar
knew how many freckles she had because one day Zohar and
Moshe had counted them. It had started with the Purim parade.
The redheaded girl was dressed up as Queen Esther. The twins
were dressed like court jesters and were roly-polying this way and
that, making everyone in the entire school laugh, jumping up and

down, doing somersaults and their favorite trick, looking at each other and making silly faces, and funny synchronized movements with their hands and feet, as if the other were a live mirror out of control. But then their teacher clapped her hands and the twins had to "attend the queen." Each had taken one of her pale, speckled hands and led her in his best courtly manner in a procession around the school yard. Afterward, the twins had become obsessed with the question, How many freckles are on the hands of the redheaded queen? Moshe, the more practical twin, said at least forty-five. Zohar's estimations went much higher. Fifty, sixty, eighty, even. Finally, the problem was solved when Zohar and Moshe spied on the redheaded queen in her own backyard. They hid under a bush to the left of a bench that she sat on to do her family's darning. As her hands went up and down with the needle, they counted one freckle for the in, and one for the out, until the entire hem had been completed.

❧

After Zohar gave the redheaded queen the flowers, Piki Kleinman appeared in the yard. He came right out of the orchard wearing a dark-blue work shirt and dirty dark-blue pants. His forehead—just above his right eyebrow—was bloody from a straight scratch parallel to the brow that Zohar knew was from the kiss of branches. And the backs of Piki Kleinman's hands were also bloody from the bottom root thorns that everyone called pigs. The pigs were hearty wild-citrus stock and grew at odd angles and sapped the strength of the rest of the tree so you had to cut them. But when you went to chop them off, the thorns always cut you back if you weren't wearing gloves, which no one ever did.

The big boy winked at Zohar, motioned away with his head while saying *"Yalla Kofiko,"* which meant "Let's go now, little monkey" in a blend of Hebrew and Arabic slang. Zohar understood that his services were appreciated. But he didn't really want to leave now. So, instead, he left through the front yard of the house, and then doubled back around and hid in the bush by the bench where the couple was standing, and where the redheaded queen usually did her darning, and where the twins had so earnestly counted the freckles on the backs of her deft hands.

*M*Y FATHER WRITES:

But then the violence spread. My father told me that the fighting in Petach Tikvah erupted suddenly, "in the middle of a very normal day." He said that it lasted for only several days, but that it seemed like "forever." The experience was, for my father, as well as for all the other children and men and women of Petach Tikvah, one of extreme horror. The first afternoon of the fighting my father remembers having to stand in the middle of the main street of the town in a group with all the women and children. There were over two hundred armed Arabs on horseback, gathered at each end of the main street of the settlement. The village men, as well as some armed women, gathered around the rest of the women and children and stood there in a ring of protection until the Arabs went away. On the first day of the "Petach Tikvah riots" there were not many serious casualties.

But then the worst thing happened. The next morning, May 9, 1921, the corpses of four "big, popular boys" were found at the edge of Petach Tikvah. They were found by the night watchman, and brought back to the school yard and laid out there. My father said that every Jew in Petach Tikvah—children, women, and men—came to see the corpses. "We all filed by, one by one. I don't really know why they took us children, I guess to show us the horrible extent of the fighting. It was truly horrible. There was much crying and screaming. Some praying." My father said that the boys' bodies had been "dishonored" in an awful way. Their bellies were slashed open from chest to groin. Inside of their gaping chests, on top of their innards, rested each boy's pair of shoes.

It was later ascertained that the four young men had gone into the neighboring Arab village with torches in the middle of the night. They were on horseback and were armed. People speculated that the boys were trying to scare the Arab villagers into leaving the town alone in the morning. Some said that they were just being dumb, others called them too brave, or not brave enough; some called them troublemakers, others called them heroes. There is a memorial in Petach Tikvah in honor of the four young men.

That day, the riots spread, full scale, throughout the region. More people were killed. My father and his brother hid with their mother and other women and children in a half-dug-out shelter for more than twenty-seven hours. The British arrived to put an end to the violence. But before it was all over, forty-seven Jews and forty-eight Arabs had been killed.

I WRITE:

Zohar walked with the rest of the family and neighbors and friends to the school yard. His mother held his hand. His father was holding his brother's hand. As they walked close, then filed by the corpses, Zohar saw the belly and he saw the shoes and he saw the blood and he saw the surprised expression on the older boy's face. Piki Kleinman was surprised, yes, but it was the surprise of the dead, not of the living. A lopsided look that said that this big boy had discovered something grand and odd and horrible, not about life, but about the ever-after.

The redheaded queen was in the school yard, too. She was kneeling down by the bodies. Her mouth was wide open but she wasn't screaming. She had the boys' blood on her knees. Her freckled fingers were spread out wide and she was patting the air back and forth with her palms in one weird continuous motion.

Zohar did not sleep that night. He was, after all, a little boy, and such big thoughts left no room in his head for rest and sweet dreams. He lay awake for hours and hours. He saw the belly and he saw the shoes. And all Zohar could think was that the shoes were untied, and that Piki Kleinman would surely trip if someone kind didn't quickly reach in there and tie them.

# Chapter 6

## ZOHAR AND MOSHE
## OR CHASIA / MARY

*My* FATHER WRITES:

Once a year, Avra would take the boys back to Jerusalem to visit her parents. Shimon did not go with them. He couldn't afford to leave his work as an orchard manager in Petach Tikva. Avra would travel with the twins in the back of whatever vehicle was available. Over the years, they went by donkey-cart, horse-drawn carriage, truck, car, and eventually bus.

Golda died in 1925. Eliezer did not remarry. When the twins were fourteen, they didn't go to Jerusalem to visit Saba Eliezer. They didn't go because that year, 1929, the Arabs rioted again throughout Palestine. Many people were killed, and more were wounded. Jerusalem, especially, was the scene of much discord. This is because the catalyst for the riots was a dispute over the rights of Jews to pray at the Western Wall. The Wall was officially owned by the Muslims of Jerusalem, but Jews were allowed to pray there. But when the Jews put up a screen to create separate prayer areas for men and women, the Arabs accused the Jews of violating the "status quo" and of threatening to take over the Al-Aqsa Mosque, which lay just beyond the Western Wall. Violence quickly erupted and spread.

During this dangerous time, Avra and Shimon begged Saba

JEWS' PLACE OF WAILING, JERUSALEM

Eliezer to leave the house on Rav Pinchas Street and come live with them in Petach Tikvah. But he refused to leave Jerusalem, saying, "I am one of the guardians of the Walls." He kept close to home and thank God didn't get into any trouble.

In 1930 the violence died down, and the family decided to return to Jerusalem for a holiday. This year Shimon joined them. The four—Shimon, Avra, Zohar and Moshe—had not been to Jerusalem together since the babies were born. It was, in my father's memory, a very special vacation.

I WRITE:

### SUNDAY, THE DAY OF TRAVEL

MY FATHER WRITES:
On the first picture of the twins, Avra wrote their names by punching holes through the paper with a pin. Otherwise, she could not tell who was who.

Avra was the first one into the carriage. She hoisted herself up into the back of the carriage and perched on the edge, her legs happily swinging. She was glad to be going to Jerusalem. She liked

her new life in the open plains of Petach Tivkah, but the whole
first month of the boys' lives, while they were still in Jerusalem,
she had whispered to them to breathe in extra deeply. She hoped
that the city would be kind enough to coat them in the color of
the early evening light, "so that you will be pink and gold and silver, so that you will glow, my sons." She kissed their tiny cheeks
and noses, whispering, "That's right, breathe deep." The babies,
as if spurred on by their mother's coaching, had breathed most
joyously, most gratefully, that first month. They had lapped up
their first pools of air as if aware of the high quality of the
source. Avra had held her twins close to her breasts and quietly
thanked the city for helping her nurse them.

Now, of course, they were long past nursing. Avra winked at
her boys as they scrambled up into the back of the carriage. They
didn't wink back; rather, they scrambled over her, racing each
other for the best seat on the pile of blankets all the way in the
back. Shimon, last to enter the carriage, neither winked nor smiled
nor scrambled. He climbed slowly in and settled down next to his
wife with a sigh. Avra took his hand and tried wordlessly to reas-
sure him. As the carriage began to move, she closed her eyes and
envisioned the house on Rav Pinchas Street, and her father,
waiting for them there. "Home is reunion," she said to herself,
"and family a dwelling, too." This thought made her smile as they
rolled along.

Shimon took his hand from Avra's and wiped his sweaty forehead. Then he shifted on the bench and breathed deeply. He was
both nervous and excited. Excited in anticipation of the vacation,
nervous in dread that his wife, this sweet wife who was sitting by
his side humming a very pretty tune, would once again fall prey
to the spell of the city she considered personally responsible for
her thieving habits (though, Shimon noted, she always blamed
Jerusalem with a smile). The carriage jangled out of Petach
Tikvah.

*M*Y FATHER WRITES:

Now, in order to describe the character of my great-grandfather
Eliezer (after whom I am named), I must digress. When I was
thirteen years old, I asked my father what his grandfather was
like. He told me that Eliezer had been a "very kind, very enthu-
siastic man." And then my father had laughed out loud before
telling me that when he was around my age, his grandfather had
been obsessed with the story of a murder that happened in our
family. This was the first time I had heard of any murder. As you
can imagine, I was fascinated. With a smile on his face, my
father told me that every time he and Moshe would visit their
grandfather in the Old City, they would spend days with him
"trying to solve the ancient crime." That day, when I was thirteen
years old, my father told me the following story. And this is how I
learned about the murder of my great-great-great-grandfather
Rabbi David Berliner Herschell.

🌿

Rabbi David Berliner Herschell was my great-great-grandmother
Esther's father. In 1845, seven years after Esther and Yochanan
married and moved to Jerusalem, Rabbi Herschell, a widower,
emigrated from London to Jerusalem with his youngest daughter, Sophie, and her husband, Jacob Silverman. Silverman, an
Austrian citizen, was a businessman. Soon after he arrived in
Jerusalem he became the part-owner of a factory that produced
phosphorous wicks. Rabbi Herschell and the Silvermans lived
with Esther and Yochanan in their house on Rav Pinchas Street
in the Jewish Quarter of the Old City.

Herschell had a very impressive lineage. Not only was he the
son of the chief rabbi of the British Empire but he was also a
direct descendant, through the intertwining bloodlines of three
daughters, of the famous spiritual teacher, the Ari of Sefat. The
Ari lived in Sefat in the fifteenth century. And it was there that

the Ari taught the Zohar, or "The Book of Splendor," which is the core text of Kabbalah. Rabbi Herschell considered himself to be a spiritual descendant of the Ari. He devoted his later years to the study and practice of mysticism. According to family tradition, during the last years of his life, Rabbi Herschell wrote a mystical treatise "in the tradition of the Ari." But no record of such a work exists today.

Soon after his arrival, Herschell became a very prominent member of the Anglo-Jewish Jerusalem community. Consequently, his deathbed was attended by the British Consul to Jerusalem, James Finn. James Finn was an avid diarist—he kept daily journals of consular affairs for the years he spent in Jerusalem. These diaries still exist today—they have been published under the title A View from Jerusalem, and are considered important historical documents. Much of what modern historians know about daily life in nineteenth-century Jerusalem comes from this source. I have supplemented what I remember from my father's telling of the tale with Finn's firsthand account of the tragedy.

The story of the murder is as follows. Six years after they moved to Jerusalem, on November 10, 1851, Herschell had completed his morning studies and was in the parlor of the family house eating his lunch. After just a few bites, he took seriously ill. Doctors were called immediately, as was British Consul James Finn. It was quickly ascertained that the rabbi's lunch had been poisoned.

Immediately, Jacob Silverman and his son, seventeen-year-old Anshel, were suspected of the crime. This was for two reasons, both having to do with the fact that Herschell was a very wealthy man. First, there was the matter of Jacob Silverman's bad investments. Silverman had wanted Herschell to invest money in his factory for the production of phosphorous wicks. At the time, phosphorous wicks were used to kindle fire. They were considered a technological revolution. A dry wick would be laid on a flint and then struck with a stone hammer. The impact produced sparks that set the wick on fire. Rabbi Herschell, conservative in matters of money, refused to contribute to the venture. Silverman invested in the wicks and lost a large amount of money— not because the technology was deficient, but because his investment partners absconded to Syria with the bulk of the business's cash. But perhaps more important was the matter of Herschell's recent marriage.

Herschell had recently married a young woman named Chasia. Chasia was at least forty years younger than Herschell! According to family lore, she was very beautiful. Together they had a son who was still a baby when Herschell was murdered. It was widely suspected that the Silvermans murdered Herschell in order to prevent him from making a new will in favor of Chasia and her child. But the murderers were too late—on his deathbed, Herschell dictated a new will to British Consul Finn. In the new will he left a fortune to Chasia and her son.

After a lengthy trial, the defendants were acquitted for lack of "irrefutable evidence." However, they were always popularly considered guilty. So much so, that even today, more than 140 years after the crime was committed, at large family gatherings, if any descendants of the Silvermans are present, someone from our branch of the family will inevitably point to them and humorously whisper, "Murderers!"

Chasia Herschell inherited her husband's fortune. The only part of the inheritance that remained in our family was a pair of silver candlesticks willed by Herschell directly to his eldest daughter, Esther, my great-great-grandmother. Today, the candlesticks are in possession of my distant cousins who live in Jerusalem.

Not long after her husband's death, Chasia left Jerusalem with her young son. They moved to Sefat where she remarried. There is a legend in our family that in addition to the inheritance,

thought, "flowers." Eliezer reached for a towel and patted his face with it. Then he began to say his morning prayers.

After it had plagued him on and off for almost a year, a very, very tired Eliezer Schine began to think that he needed a new strategy. He realized that he could not dislodge the image, that it was stuck fast in him. But that he could do what he came to call "his duty toward it." This duty consisted of a combination of investigation and aggressive imagination. He would seek the events that led up to Chasia's departure. In time, the image and its attendant story saw that their host really was trying his best to accommodate them, and so they gave Eliezer back his sleep.

MY FATHER WRITES:

My father told me that in addition to Eliezer's "preoccupation" with the murder story, what he remembered most about those yearly visits was that he and his brother, Moshe, loved to run on the walls around the Old City. They would run for hours, exploring, playing, or just horsing around. I once asked my father if he had been scared to run around Jerusalem after the riots. But he said that life quickly went back to normal, and that the city streets were filled once again with both Arabs and Jews.

My father and Moshe would run on the walls almost every afternoon of their visit. The walls, which were built in the sixteenth century by the Ottoman sultan, Süleyman the Magnificent, have six gates. Eliezer once told the twins a story about the Lions' Gate. He said that the lions carved in the gate symbolized a pair who played an important role in the city's history. Süleyman's father, the first Ottoman sultan, had threatened to raze Jerusalem. But a pair of hungry lions had appeared to the sultan and scared him off. The lions remained in the city as stone sentinels against future such threats. My father remembered being terrified of lions because of this story. He would always walk a wide circle around a lion's cage in a zoo.

**MY FATHER WRITES:**

In school, Zohar was good in history and literature, and Moshe was good in math and science. Zohar and Moshe used to take each other's tests in their best subjects; as a result both always had good grades.

At the age of five, Moshe was ill and knew that his mother was about to come and give him castor oil, which he obviously hated. So, in the last second, he switched beds with Zohar. When their mother came, not only did she force Zohar to take the medicine, but she also hit him for telling her that he was Zohar and not Moshe.

**I WRITE:**

An optimist and a lover in his youth, Eliezer Schine had aged into a not-quite-so-optimistic old man, but he prided himself on the fact that he was still every inch the lover he was born to be. His dear wife was now dead. But when she died he had set himself seriously to the task of loving other things. He loved his daughters and his sons-in-law, he loved his city, he loved his old friend Bartok's spicy cooking, he loved his house. As he got older Eliezer became known in the neighborhood as a good fellow, a man neither too earnest in his prayers nor too lax in his worship, a wise friend, a perfect neighbor, the sort of safe, genial putterer with whom young mothers often left their children while they ran to the store. When his own grandchildren were born, Eliezer felt his love for them well up. What always astonished him about finding new loves was that they never took the place of old ones. They simply added more to the world's store of affection. When the twins were babies he rocked them to sleep, one in this arm, one in that arm, while marveling at their tiny bodies.

On the day that the family was due to arrive Eliezer woke up smiling. Stretching his arms, he cracked his knuckles and climbed out of bed quickly. He did not put on his regular clothes. Instead, he put on a special pair of pants reserved for exercise and a loose-fitting lightweight shirt that he had bought himself many years before in the *shouk* in Jaffa. When he was done dressing, he patted down the pockets on his baggy trousers and said "humph!" The pockets were too puffy for his liking, and he wished he had another pair. Still patting, he said his prayers briefly. Then he walked down the stairs and out into the tiny courtyard behind the kitchen.

There, in the company of a stray chicken, Eliezer jumped up and down twenty times while flapping his arms this way and that. Next, he put his hands on his hips, and twisted his old torso that way and this. Then he touched his toes ten times, and reached for the sky ten times. Finally, he executed a grand finish with eight astonishingly deep knee bends. When he was done, he smiled and patted himself heartily on his old chest. He was breathing heavily, but at the same time, he could feel his blood sparkle with vigor. "Indeed," he said to himself (and to the chicken), "I'll run those walls, no problem."

When they were babies, Eliezer had carried them. When they were toddlers, he had held their hands and watched as they stumblingly navigated the chinks and twists in the elevated path. Now they all three raced along the top of the wall together, Zohar and Moshe running ahead, the grandfather who was quite fit for his age following after, his pace jaunty and purposeful.

They followed the wall as it encircled the different quarters of the city. Each day they ran a slightly different path. They never went the whole way around, because the wall was so very long— but they always doubled back again over favorite parts, so people got used to seeing them. And by the time the boys were in their teens, the threesome had become rather famous. A kind of aerobic emblem, a lively, moving addition to Süleyman the Magnificent's magnificent wall. Tolerated by Christians, Armenians, Arabs, and of course by their fellow Jews, they ran wherever they wanted.

First came the boys. Brown hair flopping, blue eyes glinting. They were so beautiful, so identical, so charming. When Moshe and Zohar ran by, people from all four quarters forgot that they lived in a place whose soul was so divided. And then twenty yards behind came the old man. Fists clenched, arms pumping, lower lip thrust out as if in a pout, a supremely entertaining old man in his baggy big-pocketed pants. The Arab bookseller who spotted them running behind the Lions' Gate wanted to know, "What makes an old man run like that?" Theories abounded. This one said the old Jew ran for the future. That one said, "No, can't you see, he runs for the past." That one said it was boredom, of course. Another that he ran to cure heartburn, numb limbs, sour breath, sore teeth. In certain neighborhoods, betting pools began. But the real reason Eliezer Schine "ran like that" was never discovered.

### SUNDAY, LATE AFTERNOON

The boys sprung happily out of the carriage and into their grand-father's arms. Avra and Shimon hung back, shaking the distance of the journey out of their stiff backs and legs. But soon they, too, were enveloped. The old man wrapped his arms around his dainty daughter and her muscular husband. But then he stopped himself mid-hug, pointed to his outfit, and told the boys that they had exactly forty-three minutes until the setting of the sun. Within seconds the boys and their grandfather could just be seen disappearing under the split half arch, Moshe in the lead. Avra and Shimon, standing on the steps of the house of Rav Pinchas Street, watched them go, laughing.

As they ran, all three waved at this neighbor and at that shop-keeper. People were glad to see that the boys were back in Jerusalem and that Eliezer was back to his grandfatherly tricks. Moshe was still in the lead. Zohar was several paces behind him. Eliezer smiled with pride. He was aware that his identical grand-sons were extremely handsome. He was also aware that their double image on the golden wall, against the orange-and-red-

MOUNT OF OLIVES, FROM THE WALL

and-pink setting Jerusalem sun inspired awe in the different communities. He too felt awe.

## SUNDAY EVENING

Eliezer eyed both boys with a wide glance before he began speaking in a soft voice. "My grandfather was murdered, you know." Zohar and Moshe looked back at their grandfather, their glances not quite as wide as his, but their attention truly all given. They nodded. Eliezer pointed to the indentations left on the rug by the long-sold peacock chair. "It was here," he explained, "that my grandfather ingested the poison." Eliezer pursed his big lips and nodded his head back and forth.

It was always the same. Every year on the first evening of their visit, after they had run the walls and returned home and eaten supper, they would gather in the parlor and Eliezer would retell the story. He told the boys that Chasia and Herschell had lived "here in this house" and that Chasia and Herschell had had one child, "a baby boy." According to Eliezer, Rabbi Herschell had been not only a brilliant scholar but also a very wealthy man. And Chasia was "rich in her face, yes, a stupendous beauty." At this point he would hold his own face and say with lilting pathos, *"Oy Gut in nu! Oy veys mir!"* Oh our God! Oh woe is me! "My beloved mother's sister's evil husband," he seethed, "a cursed man named Silverman and his cursed son named Anshel killed Grandfather Herschell by poisoning his lunch! And why did they do it?" Herschell would look at one boy and then at the other. Then he always paused and breathed deeply. When he spoke again Zohar and Moshe always joined in, "The Silvermans murdered Grandfather Herschell," they all three would say, "so that Herschell wouldn't make a new will in honor of the beauty and her babe."

There were clippings and old photographs. Court transcripts and several pieces of yellowed paper that Eliezer insisted were original pages from the diary of James Finn. Pages on which Finn presented the "clearest evidence" that the Silvermans were indeed the killers, their hands stained with kin blood. The twins surveyed the evidence. They read the clippings, and spent the days of their vacation walking behind their grandfather in the approximate footsteps of the murderous grandson, Anshel Silverman. They stood by the side of the sufferer's "actual deathbed" with their eyes averted, their hands clasped behind their backs. They sorted through the dusty remnants of what had once been the old man's robust collection of books. As they did these things, they knew that they were witnessing something simultaneously inappropriate and grand. And that this something had taken up residence, making their grandfather only a tenant to the landlord prose, the living story. It seemed to both boys that while this creature was certainly interesting, it wasn't at all mindful of the house. The house was dusty and dark. Half-grand, half-decrepit no more, its decrepitude was creeping up and its grandeur was drawing to a close. But still there was a softness, a sweet mellowness to the air there that was not at all uncomfortable.

❧

Every year after the original tale had been told with identical drama and identical detail, Eliezer would serve his identical grandsons a small helping of tantalizingly different information. His soft hands pointing to Herschell lying on his deathbed, "wearing a blue cap and a nightshirt with antique buttons." Pointing to Anshel Silverman, "who in his youth had a fondness for pet rabbits and a talent for math." Each year the clippings grew more and more faded. Each year the details grew more elaborate. At first Chasia was simply "slim and sweet." The next year she had "a beautiful voice." The next, she "often went about the house singing operas of the old Italian master, Verdi." Eliezer would hum a few bars with his eyes closed. The boys never contradicted their grandfather, they never pointed out his blatant anachronisms or little inconsistencies.

One year, Grandfather Eliezer told the boys that he had learned that the poison, the "instrument of murder," was "a noxious powder used in the production of phosphorous wicks." This revelation was followed by a full-scale expedition to the local factory on the corner of Choulda the Prophetess and Amnon Streets where such wicks were still produced. At the factory they had a very serious conversation on the "nature of the toxic product itself" with the foreman, a small Bohemian immigrant who was sure that this curious old man and his blue-eyed grandsons were up to no good.

Another year, Eliezer told the boys that Chasia had been the stepsister of a certain baker, "a Yemenite whose reputation for rolls and challah was unrivaled in the Jewish Quarter." Supposedly, Eliezer confided in the boys, the baker had been friendly with "my own dear mama and papa" and it was through this "warm family connection" that old Herschell and young Chasia actually met. "I imagine," Eliezer confided, "that Chasia was working in her stepbrother's bake shop when Grandfather Herschell came with my mama one morning to pick an order up."

The next day, Eliezer and the twins spent the afternoon wandering around the Jewish quarter trying to locate the certain Yemenite bakery "whose family history," Eliezer noted poignantly, "is with a mixture of mourning and love so intimately connected to our own." They visited all of the bakeries. They searched, they sampled, they nibbled, they asked. But none of the bakers admitted to having a step-Chasia in his family tree. Eliezer was convinced that one of them was lying. But the boys just smiled at their grandfather. Eventually, each took one of his hands and gently directed him toward home. Zohar and Moshe were content with so many answers of sweets and cakes and rolls and bread.

## MONDAY

While the boys were out with their grandfather, investigating a report that an "aged and sallow-looking" Anshel Silverman had been sighted in the section of the Jewish Quarter closest to the Roman wells, Avra and Shimon also went out for a walk. They walked down Rav Pinchas Street, through the split half arch. Slowly, they wound their way into the *shouk*.

Avra breathed in deeply. Shimon noticed that his wife looked very beautiful. Her big brown eyes, dark hair, and white skin were browner, darker, and whiter than they seemed in Petach Tikvah. She looked like a precious etching. He reached out a hand for her. They walked deeper into the market past the carpet sellers, shoe merchants, bakers, and peddlers of spices; past stalls selling children's toys, candies, camel halters, metal tools, undergarments, guidebooks, gentleman's hats, and assorted tourist trinkets. They hadn't been back to Jerusalem together for a substantial visit in a very long time. They walked on. Sometimes with their fingers touching, sometimes with their bodies several feet apart. Sometimes they had to separate to let a boy with a wheelbarrow pass or

A STREET IN JERUSALEM

a woman with a huge basket on her head hurry through the center of the street yelling *"yalla yalla yalla"* in a high, loud voice.

Soon they turned down the "meat street," the lane of kosher butchers where Shimon had worked while courting Avra. "It was here," one part of Shimon told another part of Shimon, "that I learned the ritual intricacies of cutting up a cow." His hands, whose memories of the feel of flesh had been long ago erased by the warm soil of Petach Tikvah, whispered to the rest of him that they did not believe this new information. Meat was hanging everywhere, innards and outerds, fleshy necks and ribs and spongy lungs and hearts slick and shiny and stomachs and coiling piles of blue and red kishka along with the occasional sheep head, cow brain, headless chicken, and live bleating baby lamb. Blood was on the stones, and the air was laced with it. Shimon shuddered and tried to walk quickly, but his wife was moving slowly. Shimon tried not to breathe through his nose. He had never taken to the sour smell, never reconciled himself to the weird intimacy that develops between a meat-man and his wares. "After all," he used to think with the cleaver in his hand, "if I cut out my own *poopik* and told customers that it was the button from some kosher creature's belly, wouldn't they make a soup from it?"

Avra, it seemed, had no such thoughts. She was looking at everything with interest and admiration. Several strands of her hair had come loose from their knot and were wisping down on her neck and forehead. Reaching a hand up, she quickly moved them out of her eyes. So beautiful, Shimon mused, as she bent forward toward a butcher's tray. So beautiful, he mused, as she stood back up. Stood back up?! Shimon was horrified. Had she really? Could she really have? "My God! Dear God of meats and markets," he prayed. "Dear God, avert your eyes from this *treif*, this unkosher moment!" It was only after the organ had been secured on her person, he knew not where, he could not imagine where, for she had neither bag nor pockets, only after the organ was definitely gone from the tray, that Shimon acknowledged to himself that Avra had really come home.

Put simply, she had stolen a cow's tongue. A huge pink-white tongue that had been lying on that butcher's tray next to ten or twelve others. Shimon said, "My wife," and she winked at him and gave him a very sweet "my husband" and then "come, my dear, let's walk on." Fifteen minutes later she had modestly transferred the tongue to the Seventh Station Beauty Bazaar. A place she thought perfectly appropriate. It fit in nicely, even Shimon had to agree, on a purple-cloth-draped low wooden table spread with "imported and domestic lotions, potions and balms for the brain and body."

And while it would be an exaggeration to say that in that one afternoon Shimon had been converted to his wife's frisky material religion, it is true that when he reflected upon the experience, he had to admit that he had enjoyed tagging along. Perhaps in the future, he thought, he would not be averse to praying to

Avra's gods of goods and chance should his fingers begin to itch like hers, and the city continue to conspire with the criminal he didn't know he had in him. That night, when they climbed into bed, Shimon smiled as Avra nuzzled up close to him. She fell asleep with her arms around his chest, her head resting in the slight indentation between his belly and heart. Shimon did not fall asleep so quickly. A glowing moonlight infiltrated their bedroom from a crack in the shutters. His head was filled with the thin streak of strong light. It illuminated things he had learned here a long time ago but thought he had forgotten: a rule concerning sacrifice. When a Jew brought an animal to the Temple for ritual slaughter, he was required to lean into the creature as he cut its jugular. God had decreed that for the sacrifice to be holy, the man must actually feel the animal's life flowing out of it. Shimon fell asleep imagining that he was walking through the market, Avra by his side, her laughing hands holding his own.

❀

The story of the murder affected the brothers differently. It was for Zohar a kind of maze. When he shut his eyes at night after his grandfather's telling, he would walk its twisty walls, following a path straight toward Herschell, right into Chasia, sideways toward the motive, slantways toward the murder weapon and then, with a crash, he would bang right up against the fact that a grandson could kill his own grandfather, just like that. The maze was a monster. But it was also a mystery and a bastion of old magic because it held him in its spell year-round. He wanted to know what Chasia looked like. He wanted to know where she came from. He wanted to know what she smelled like. He wanted to know if she was a hummer or a whistler. He wanted to know if she was pious like his great-great-grandfather, or if she, like himself, had grave questions concerning soul and piety and the nature of God. Zohar would work the rows. Climbing under boughs, binding new grafts, checking on old ones. And by the time they would all break for lunch, the maze would have let Zohar into its secret chambers in which he would have seen at least seventeen different Chasias. This one humming and that one whistling, this one pious, that one proud, this one nimble, that one with a voice like an angel's, this one with an adventurous spirit who longed to travel the world.

Moshe was also amazed by the story. But he was less lost in it than his brother. Not that he was less captivated, just that he wasn't particularly horrified by its monstrosity or interested in its minutiae. Zohar could spend hours wondering what Anshel Silverman was wearing on the day of the murder. And he wanted to know the exact words that Anshel's father had used to goad the boy on. But most of all, Zohar was forever contemplating what he called "the holes in that boy's soul" and saying things like "surely only a soul in tatters could do that." Moshe did not really care for such details or spiritual searching. He was mostly interested in one thing, or rather, one person. Like Zohar, he dreamed of Chasia. And like Zohar, he wanted to know what she looked like, smelled like. But if Zohar was the poet of this family story, then Moshe was the peeper. He wanted to know what Chasia looked like without her clothes on, and what she smelled like in her private places. In his daydreams, as he worked the groves, Moshe was forever lifting the curtains in the room of his mind that she inhabited.

And while he was definitely more prurient than Zohar, Moshe was also more personal. Zohar saw Chasia in the trees, but Moshe saw her in the real live girls of Petach Tikvah. She was in their house and on the street. She was next door, she was in the school yard. She even occasionally held Moshe's hand and kissed him on the lips if he was lucky. Simcha Rabinowitch, a lanky beauty with skinny legs, was a lanky, serious Chasia who loved to talk about the poetry of Bialik and the plays of Chekhov and the evils of socialism, fascism, and war. Madeline Feldman, the petite blonde with big gorgeous breasts whose father was a Paris-trained shoemaker, was a shapely Chasia whose frisky incipient sensuality and gorgeously shod feet made Moshe half mad for a woman whose story he had only just begun to explore.

*M*Y FATHER WRITES:

On their visits, Grandfather Eliezer would tell my father and his brother all sorts of stories—stories about the murder of Rabbi Herschell, stories about the Old City, family stories from Europe, stories about his own life. One of their favorites had to do with the Dormition Abbey. According to Christian tradition, Mary never died, but fell asleep and was taken sleeping up to heaven. The Dormition Abbey was built on the supposed site of her ascension, which was on Mount Zion. Strangely, this site is just outside the walls of the Old City.

⚜

Eliezer told the twins that the Dormition Abbey, which they called the Mary Church, was left out of the walls for a singular reason. When Süleyman the Magnificent built the walls, his purpose had been to enclose and protect all of the holy places in the Old City. But his two chief architects, in order to save money, had demanded that the monks of Mount Zion pay for their portion of the wall. In addition to the site of the Dormition, Mount Zion is also home to the room in which the Last Supper supposedly took place as well as the supposed burial place of King David. The monks refused to pay. And so the architects left Mount Zion out of the wall. When Süleyman found that his architects had betrayed his purpose, he was so enraged that he had them murdered and then buried side by side just inside of the Jaffa Gate. The graves are still there today, but they are unmarked, and although the story is commonly believed, there is no real proof that the architects once lay within them.

I WRITE:

## TUESDAY EVENING

liezer again gathered the boys to tell them what more he had uncovered, "this year, in the archaeology of our recent ancestors." Grandfather Eliezer pursed his lips and paused for a second while he thought about what he was going to say. As he paused, the image of Chasia sitting in the carriage suddenly came back to him. There she was again. Chasia in the carriage. Then the woman in his head turned *her* head, and smiled at him before her carriage began to slowly move away.

Eliezer began to speak quickly. He told the boys that he personally believed a rumor that the great Italian sculptor Giovanni Giovanni, who had been commissioned to create an effigy for the new Dormition Abbey, had modeled his sleeping Mary after Chasia, otherwise known in polite circles as "the widow Herschell." "Supposedly," old Eliezer said, looking directly into the very blue eyes of first one twin and then the other, "several decades after the abominable murder was committed, Giovanni Giovanni was on a sojourn in Jerusalem when he heard the story of the young widow and was captivated both by reports of her beauty and by the pathos of her tale. According to local lore, the sculptor interviewed old-timers as to what Chasia really looked like. And that is how," Eliezer added with emphasis and a wagging finger, "the face of your grandpoppa's poor murdered grandpoppa's true love was fashioned into the face of the mournful Madonna who fell asleep but never died."

Eliezer took a deep breath. The twins wanted him to continue. He could see this. So he explained to them how he himself, a pious Jew, could of course never set foot in a church, even if it weren't illegal, which it was. Consequently, he had never even considered seeing the sleeping woman. "But I hold a deep conviction," he added, "that it is our Chasia lying there in the belly of that Church." He nodded in its direction. "And contrary to what you may think, my boys, I view her presence there as an advantage and not a sacrilege. You see, she may be sleeping but she is also a sort of spy, and in times of trouble, it is not such a bad thing to have a member of the family in perfect position to watch and think and listen."

The twins were not exactly sure what Eliezer wanted Chasia / Mary to be listening or watching for. Zohar, peering out of the window toward the Mary Church later that night, envisioned its great circular hall filled with renegade priests doing all sorts of secret calisthenics. Moshe lay in bed with his eyes closed. He had inherited his great-grandmother Esther's sexual sense of humor and was imagining that the Chasia / Mary statue busied itself peeking under the robes of the faithful as they knelt by her side to pray. "Isn't a statue made of stone?" Zohar whispered to Moshe. But Moshe didn't answer. He was already dreaming of a beautiful woman lying so close to their house, with a body not made of stone, but of skin and breasts and lips and breath.

The next afternoon, Zohar and Moshe ran the walls alone. They ran longer than usual. It was a hot day and both boys grew instantly sweaty. Their hearts were beating hard. But they kept running, arms pumping, lips pursed. Only when they came to the edge of Mount Zion did they stop. They leaned over the wall and stared at the Dormition Abbey for several minutes. Moshe had hoisted himself up and was sitting on the edge of the wall. Zohar was leaning against him. Though they hadn't exchanged a word, both knew what the other was thinking.

"Served the architects right," said Moshe.

"Yep," said Zohar, and both boys stood there for several minutes, silently thanking Süleyman for what they saw as just retribution.

## WEDNESDAY EVENING

The boys wanted to hear more about Chasia / Mary, but Eliezer refused to be swayed. Instead, he sat the boys down and talked to them at great length about Herschell's will, a document that both boys had read several times and which held for them little fascination. Eliezer spent an hour explaining how "if a certain key sentence of the will had been punctuated differently, then the entire document would have had different meaning. This," he explained, "would have meant dramatically different monetary consequences for Chasia, and of course for our family." The boys couldn't help shifting uncomfortably in their chairs. Moshe coughed a lot though he didn't have a cold. Zohar pulled at a thread on the already threadbare chair on which he was sitting. Finally, Eliezer sat back. He took a sip of water, cracked his knuckles. He was quiet for several seconds before smiling slyly and saying, as if in the middle of a different conversation, "According to my good friend Bartok (who has big ears and hears all sorts of things), directly above our Chasia/Mary's sleeping statue-body is an inscription from *Shir Hashirim* that says, 'Arise my love, my dove, my beautiful one and come.' " He winked at the boys, "Perhaps our Chasia, she is only sleeping too! Eh?"

Zohar turned away from his grandfather, blushing. He felt his face weirdly from the inside out, as if his skin had disappeared and his soul had been left suddenly unprotected. He reached up a hand and patted his cheeks, pressing down on his sinuses, his lips, his eyebrows, his eyes. Sometimes, in his dreams, Chasia *was* sleeping. She was lying in his bed. He was watching her. Watching her breasts rise and fall with a breath that rosed her cheeks and made her eyelids flutter. Whenever he had this dream Zohar would wake up in the morning with a deep sense of grateful pleasure and would then find himself flirting throughout the day with the earth, the air, even the sunshine. And when he would lie in bed again at night, he would float off to sleep pleasantly aware that somehow he had grown attracted to a natural phenomenon. Moshe glanced at his queasy-looking brother and gave him a knowing, reassuring smile. He was also taken aback. But not to the extent that Zohar was. "Arise my love," he mouthed the words and then bit his lips. "Arise my dove." He was somewhat scared. He was completely enraptured. And he was sweating even though it wasn't very hot in the room. Quickly, the twins kissed their grandfather goodnight. Then they crossed the parlor and kissed their parents too. Avra and Shimon retired soon after their sons. Eliezer was left alone in the parlor.

## WEDNESDAY NIGHT (THURSDAY MORNING), VERY LATE

Zohar sneezed and Moshe shushed him. But the shush was louder than the sneeze and when combined with the creaking of the old stairs, their exit was so loud anyway that Zohar's small sneeze was really of no consequence. In truth, the twins were not worried about the leaving part of this expedition. They thought that their parents, who were vigorous sleepers, and their grandfather, an old man, were not likely to wake up, despite the sneeze and the shush and the creak of the old stairs.

It was after midnight. Moshe smiled at the half-moon. Zohar also smiled and then quickly they both ran down Rav Pinchas Street, under the split half arch and into an alley that led out of the Jewish Quarter.

They ran silently. Past the fringes of the closed bazaar. Across the sleeping camel camp. Around the corner of the Sacred Well. Silently. Zohar led. Moshe followed but only in spirit. He had planned this expedition. He had bribed the monk. He had convinced Zohar that they "absolutely must go in there." He was the twin with the sense of crime, his mother's son truly. But Zohar was faster and had a better sense of direction. They ran on, down the Street of the Beatitudes across the Street of the Cross. When they reached the church that they referred to in code as "the big bed" the twins were panting but neither let out a peep. They looked at each other and proceeded to walk into the Dormition Abbey.

Though never having set foot inside a church before, the twins were single-minded in their mission and not distracted by the moonlit glint of the gold mosaics on the dome above their heads. They had no business in the dome. And they moved quickly to the stairway to the right of the door. This led to the catacombs. The crooked monk had supplied this information, and for good measure he had left the oil lamps burning.

The stairway was narrow and circular. The twins were down it quickly. Zohar was still ahead. He saw her first. But he did not go toward her immediately. He stood by the base of the stairs for several seconds feeling sweat drip down his forehead. He reached up to wipe it off. As he did so, a little pulse began to beat in the right of his neck. He was so excited and so scared, he could not tell which emotion was more the marrow and which more the bone of him. One filled him, but the other was holding him up. He looked back at his twin. Moshe, too, was sweating. And Moshe, too, looked scared and excited. But there was no mistaking that fear made up the bones of his soul at this particular moment. Moshe shoved his hands into his pockets and shifted his feet. He hung back while Zohar, feeling for the first time inexplicably bolder than his brother, moved closer to the sleeping creature in the center of the room. Sure enough, it was Chasia/Mary, her hands clasped over her substantial bosom, her beautiful features reflecting permanent repose. The twins recognized her immediately. Zohar was so close, he wanted to touch her. Reaching out one hand, he patted the woman's robes while his other hand climbed up onto her perfectly smooth, perfectly draped belly. Soon he let both hands climb farther up until they were on top of her own hands, on top of her breasts. Zohar thought he could feel a heart beating beneath his fingers.

Moshe approached the other side of the effigy. But still, he did not touch Chasia/Mary. He was surprised. And as the two boys stood breathing deep enough to fill not only their own lungs but that of the statue, they noted with twin frustration that since her eyes were closed, they could not tell their color. Zohar and Moshe stayed there for several minutes, but then Chasia/Mary's beating heart stilled itself beneath Zohar's fingers and instead the church seemed to come alive with creaks and whispers. They ascended the stairway and ran out of the abbey. Neither said a word. Soon they were climbing up onto the wall. And they began running. The city was loud with their running, but also soft with it. They ran through the sighs of ten thousand sufferers on ten thousand deathbeds. And they ran through the sighs of ten thousand tears falling from the eyes of ten thousand lovers. The city was cold in the moonlight. The effigy was cold in the catacomb. There were murderous children everywhere. And so many women sleeping, sleeping never to wake. Zohar and Moshe ran on, racing the rim of the night. It was almost morning when they climbed back into bed.

## THURSDAY MORNING

*M*Y FATHER WRITES:

Zohar and Moshe would often think alike. Their thoughts would overlap and one would finish the other's sentence. But much stranger than this was what happened when they slept. They were "opposite dreamers." If Moshe would have a particularly vivid dream, then Zohar wouldn't dream at all that same night. And vice versa—if Zohar dreamt well, then Moshe's sleeping mind would be blank.

I WRITE:

Moshe woke up long before he stopped being tired. He yawned and looked at his brother still asleep in the bed next to him. Zohar was sprawled on his belly, his arms flung out, his left leg straight, his right leg bent in a triangle against the other. Moshe pushed his brother's arm away from his own elbow and groaned. He was so tired, so groggy. It was eleven o'clock. Much earlier, at around eight o'clock, their mother had been to their room, their father had been to their room, their grandfather had been to their room, and all three had drawn the same conclusion, that the boys, for some inexplicable reason, had not gotten their proper sleep, and so they left them alone. After all, it was vacation. Moshe willed himself back to a half-sleep, eyes closed, mind half open. In this state, he dreamed about the orchard. No, this is not quite true. The orchard was second. First, it was Chasia. He saw her lying in the catacomb and he reached a hand out in his mind to touch her smooth belly, her rising bosom. Her body was soft and her eyes opened the second he lay his hands on her face. Her eyes were turquoise, bright bright turquoise, and Moshe sucked in his breath, unable to believe that such brilliant color could produce anything but brilliant sight, and he was greatly disappointed when Chasia/Mary did not recognize him. She looked scared. He did not want to frighten her. So he took his hand away and slowly backed out of the catacomb. Still dreaming, he ran up the windy stairs, and then out of the abbey door. The abbey was surrounded by a small grove of olive trees. Moshe took shelter in their squat shade where he told himself that it wasn't that Chasia hadn't recognized him, it was just that she had her mind on other things. And from a warm corner of his memory, Madeline Feldman, the petite blonde with big gorgeous breasts, told Moshe a thing or two herself that Moshe had neither imagined nor expected.

That is when Moshe started dreaming about the orchard. Actually, had he had his choice, he would not have dreamed about the orchard at all. He would have continued to concentrate on Chasia/Mary, or on Madeline Feldman, or on another one of his female friends. But an orchard is the kind of thought you have when your soul is overflowing. Moshe's soul *was* overflowing. He leaned his forehead into the olive tree in his mind and felt its rough trunk against his skin. Rolling over onto his back, he pulled the covers over his head. In the muffled pinkish morning light he wandered back to Petach Tikvah. There he walked through his father's groves of orange trees. They were all grafted, some with head grafts, some with *temech* (support).

Shimon had taught his sons, "When we graft we create something unnatural." He spoke to them as he worked, asking the boys to hand him his tools, telling them, "But the unnatural thing becomes in its mature expression something that seems to have been given nature's approval. People are supposed to graft," Shimon told them. "As if it were asked of us. Part of our partnership in creation." When the twins had completed eight years of school, Shimon gave each boy a grafting knife, a tiny curved, almost sickle-like tool, and sent them to work in the orchards. He took them out of school, but he continued their education. He had shown them how to find the embryonic cells just below the branch nodes. He had taught them how to peel away the bark without killing the green-white flesh underneath, and how to cut the notch in the sapling and how to bind the wound of the union. But his best lesson, the one they would never forget and which would keep teaching them almost forever, was the lesson that the olive tree teaches the grafter.

Olives are the best example of natural grafting. They drop their own supports, their own *temech,* and in this way keep growing for countless human generations. When they were fourteen years old, Shimon sat the boys down, one twin on the right of an olive tree, another twin on the left of it. Then he left them there. They grew squirmy in ten minutes, annoyed in fifteen, but at twenty the tree started talking and the identical brothers sat for at least two hours listening to the mistress of all grafters discourse in woody whispers on her art. A branch entwining there, another one curling here, and the center trunk dissolves slowly in perfect sync with the pace of the furthermost branches dropping new roots into old soil. When Shimon came back, Zohar and Moshe were standing up. They were running their hands over the tree. Pressing their fingers and palms into its branches.

Soon after, the twins convinced their father to plant a row of

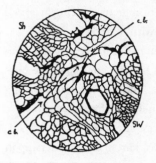

**Fig. 3.**

Bud union of Shamouli on Sweet Lime, 5 days after budding. Cross section showing callus bridges leading from the wood to the raised flaps. Sh = Shamouli. Sw = Sweet Lime. c. b. = callus bridges.

olives on the eastern periphery of his main orchard. The boys secretly hoped that the olives would tell their secrets to the oranges. Then their groves would be the first in the land to graft themselves, becoming bountiful for centuries—like the olives, only sweeter.

Moshe woke up at noon. As he got out of bed he had one last image in his head: Chasia / Mary had risen from the catacomb. She had risen, and had come back with them to Petach Tikvah. She was running in and out of the rows of the eastern olive trees, which had doubled in size since Moshe had last seen them. Moshe was there too. He wasn't exactly sure what they were doing there together, he and Chasia / Mary, but it looked to him as if they were playing some game, maybe hide-and-seek. The branches of the trees were obscuring them, one from the other.

Zohar slept a bit longer than his brother. When he woke up, he remembered the night only. Stealing out of the house, sneaking into the catacombs, standing by the effigy, and afterward the running. All of these things were clear to him. But unlike his brother, Zohar had had no dreams.

## THURSDAY NIGHT (FRIDAY MORNING), VERY LATE

Eliezer Schine peeked around the corner of the outer wall of what he had grown up calling the Mary Church, but was now properly referred to as the Dormition Abbey. He peeked and he stared into the darkness, squinting so that he could see better. But he saw nothing: the church was quiet, and the door the twins had disap-

OLIVE TREE

peared into remained closed. Soon he hid again, pressing his back against the wall, his fingertips into the cold chinks between the stones. It was the middle of the night, at least three o'clock, and Eliezer's teeth were chattering. Was this their first time? Questions pounded him. Or had they come before? Was it a dare? A joke? An obsession? Eliezer could not stop the questions. What would he do if they were caught? Were they actually praying to the statue? God forbid! Woe and shame! Were they touching her? Were they doing something lewd? A sin! A *shanda*! Swallowing hard, he turned toward the wall and rested his cheek against it until the questions had completely passed. When they had, he peeked around the corner again. But still he saw nothing. And he also heard nothing; the night was quiet, and there was, thank the Lord, thought Eliezer, no watchman, no guard, no British soldier in the vicinity making rounds. He let out a deep breath. And then he peeked again, this time with his eyes wide open. He was horrified, yes, but there was a curious center to his horror that winked out of him in a way that was only half horrible.

He had woken up and heard footsteps in the hall. Then, as he got out of bed, there were footsteps coming down the staircase. He put on his trousers as the front door opened, and he ran down the stairs just in time to peek out of the door and see in which direction his grandsons were heading. He began to run. If anyone had been watching Eliezer Schine at that moment they would have seen an old man in a white nightshirt and puffy-pocketed trousers running with his fists clenched, arms pumping, his lower lip thrust out in a pout. His pace was not quite jaunty but it was definitely strong. He followed the twins through alleys and around corners. Eliezer followed them to a gate in the wall and then he followed them through it. And as he watched from behind a lower wall they entered into the church. When they disappeared from his view he asked with a pious shrug of his shoulders for God to give his grandsons their object. "But, please, my Lord," he whispered, "please let their object be pure."

Soon he saw them come back out of the church. They paused and looked at each other and then started back through the gate in the wall that enclosed the Old City. Eliezer watched from not far away as Zohar and Moshe climbed up onto the wall and then took off running. Moshe was in the lead, Zohar close behind him. He tried to call their names, but no words came out. So he just stood there watching the emptiness where they had been. Then he began walking back toward Rav Pinchas Street. Eliezer was terrified that his boys would not return, that they would get lost or be caught or land in trouble.

Standing on the steps of his house, he held out his hands, palms up, and he watched as his old fingers with their yellowed nails and thick red knuckles curled slightly inward. For several seconds he thought that he could feel the boys running on the lines of his own palms. Their feet were as tiny as the heads of pins, and they pattered back and forth across his palms in a serpentine tickle. Quickly opening the door, Eliezer walked into the house, and up the stairs. He lay in bed for almost an hour, all the while holding his hands up on top of the covers, his fingers curled slightly inward. At four-thirty he heard the boys sneak into the house and climb into their own beds. Only then did Eliezer curl his fingers into fists and let himself fall into a deep sleep that was at once confused and warm.

## FRIDAY AND SATURDAY

Avra noticed right away that things were out of sorts with her family. Crossing her arms over her chest she pressed her fingers into the ribs under her breasts, a nervous habit. Then she let her arms flop down again as she walked straight into the parlor and looked around. Her father was standing by the window with his chin thrust out, frowning. Her sons, sitting in the far corner of the room quietly reading old books with tattered covers, seemed to have misplaced their habitual selves; they were quiet and in full control of their mouths and gangly limbs, not at all like the growing, going-this-way-and-that fifteen-year-old boys she knew her adolescent sons to be. She remembered for a second what it had been like to carry these boys. A little "humph" escaped from her mouth and unconsciously she put her hands on her stomach. They hadn't given her a second's rest. Avra liked to joke that her boys had played soccer in her womb. "The whole nine months kicking so many goals—by the time they came out I was a championship game!" But now they were quiet. Not anything like they had been as babies, and not like they usually were as boys. They looked very tired. At three o'clock, when they wanted to go out running, Avra barred the way, and sent them to their room for a nap.

Shimon was also strange. He was sitting in a corner with his fingers pressed together and he was looking intently all around the room. Avra was worried about her husband. Ever since their walk the other day he was different, and she wasn't so sure that for Shimon, different was good.

He *was* different. He had woken up that morning fascinated by all the little things in the house. The old brushes, shoes, sewing baskets, broken decorative *tchotchkes,* writing sets, mirrors. All of these things called to him. But he didn't know if they wanted him to take them and put them elsewhere, or to leave them be while adding to their numbers an array of interesting immigrants. Sitting in the parlor now, he surveyed the old objects in the room: a Turkish ashtray in the shape of a camel; a small decorative rug with frayed edges and faded colors; a blunt-edged knife; a children's book called *The Frequent Frog* lying on the bottom of a bookshelf no one ever browsed anymore. Shimon, who was not naturally a city dweller and actually was somewhat afraid of walking alone on the city streets, would have been just as happy to do this work without ever leaving the room in which he was sitting. But something told him that this wouldn't quite do. So he excused himself without giving a good reason, and quickly walked out of the house. Avra, who had no real sense of what her husband was up to but sensed rightly that he needed some time by himself, watched him walk down Rav Pinchas Street and disappear under the split half arch. Sighing, she closed the door.

Shimon returned within the hour. Among other things, he dropped a fancy bronze nutcracker in the middle of Old Herschell's dusty desk. A lambswool bootie he deposited to the left of the front door, and a lovely blue-and-gold needlepoint sampler with a bland psalm spoken into its mesh he let float down to the bottom shelf of the old bookcase, where it decorated *The Frequent Frog,* who, for so many years, hadn't known what a fine and pious dress it was missing.

Shimon tried to leave his offerings demurely. He wanted them to blend in. He wanted no one to notice. But Shimon was not naturally demure. Actually, he was somewhat clunky and, though muscular, possessed little of the sort of silent strength needed to keep secrets. Avra, who noticed everything instantly, was appalled. She spent all of Friday afternoon finding these out-of-place objects, and then quickly secreting them in the folds of her skirts. Then she ran around the *shouk* really trying very hard to find the stalls they had come from, putting them back, one by one—if not in the exact right place, then at least in a place that was less wrong than her father's parlor. When she was done, she returned to the house no less horrified. Not because her own sticky fingers had grown any less sticky, but because her husband was such a naturally honest man and she felt regret for the first time in her life for something she had taken.

The house was, that day, in remarkable disarray. Zohar and Moshe slept the afternoon away. Avra was distressed. Shimon was possessed of an unnatural euphoria. Eliezer was exhausted. And though he had a feeling that the Chasia-image wasn't lodged in his soul anymore, he puttered around the house refusing to sleep. That evening the family gathered around the Sabbath table quietly.

It was a strange Sabbath on Rav Pinchas Street. In the morning, Eliezer went to synagogue alone. When he returned, the family ate a hasty lunch. Then they said prayers. But the prayers felt big in their mouths, and the lunch not big enough, though all had several helpings. Had the family spoken, they would have agreed that regular things were taking on irregular dimensions. Especially the old house. The house, usually so spacious, suddenly didn't seem to have enough room. Eliezer kept bumping into Shimon. Shimon kept bumping into his wife. Avra kept bumping into her father. But none of the crossed paths led to genuine smiles or good conversation.

Upstairs, Zohar leaned out of the window and stared hard at the Dormition Abbey. He shut his eyes and imagined that Chasia was leading him around the orchard, alternately telling him the history of each tree and her own history. He wondered how she knew so much, but he didn't dare interrupt her. Moshe, lying in the bed in the same room, took a good nap. He dreamed that Chasia was walking hand-in-hand with all the beauties of Petach

Tikvah. They were coming toward him, lanky and dark and light and blond and well shod and well spoken, and curvy and skinny, and beatific, but in a sexy way. Meanwhile, downstairs, Grandfather Eliezer spent the afternoon unsuccessfully looking for his eyeglass case—a kindly, useful object that Shimon hadn't brought home but Avra had mistakenly taken back.

## SATURDAY NIGHT (SUNDAY MORNING), VERY LATE

Eliezer followed the boys again, but this time he did not stop outside the church. He went inside and stood under its glittery dome for several minutes before he descended to the catacombs where he knew the boys would be. Then he walked down the circular staircase and saw the boys standing together on one side of the sleeping Madonna. They heard him, and turned around in one synchronized sway. He could tell that they were surprised by his presence, but also that they could not really react to it. Somewhere in between bliss, religion, and puberty, this moment lay. The twins were far away. And he, only a grandfather, could not carry them any farther either toward or away from the woman sleeping so calmly in their midst. He walked up to them, and put a hand on each boy's shoulder. They stood there for a very long time linked by a private enthusiasm that gilded their insides much like the mosaics above gilded the dome. When he finally spoke, Eliezer whispered, "Well, if she is not our Chasia, then surely she is someone else's." Zohar nodded. Moshe didn't move. But both boys knew that their grandfather knew she was their own.

They left the church. And then all three began to run the walls together. The boys pulled ahead as usual. But not far ahead. They ran for a very long time. Past the Tomb of the One-Eyed Sheik, past the British Consul's residence, past the Wailing Wall. The sky turned from black to pale milk and then the sun began to rise, turning the city a fine shade of butter. Every so often the twins would look behind them. Their grandfather nodded, winked, urged them farther. As they neared home, early-rising friends, neighbors, storekeepers threw surprised waves in their direction. The word went out, "Old Eliezer and his boys are coming this way carrying the sun in on their shoulders." They ran on. Zohar and Moshe felt that they could run the walls forever, and Eliezer's jaunty pace took him farther that night than he had ever expected to go.

They returned to the house in the very early morning, entering without waking Shimon or Avra who were sleeping with their toes touching, Avra's mouth half open, Shimon's right hand on Avra's left thigh.

In the late afternoon of the day before, Shimon had seen Avra picking up one of the things he had taken. It was a little round jewelry box made of metal. She found it on the wooden shelf under the mirror in the front hall. He followed her out of the house and caught up with her in the middle of the Street of Death's Angels where, with a very red face, he tried to tell her something. Something about leaning and learning and taking precious things from God. He was stuttering. He couldn't complete his sentences. Avra felt sorry for her husband. Drawing the tiny box out of the folds of her skirt she said, "Sweetheart, just tell me where it goes. Then we'll go home. No tongues today, I promise." They put the jewelry box back where Shimon had gotten it—a fancy Armenian import store just behind the carpet-seller's street. Then they went home. And that night they spent hours taking and giving and giving back a marketful of love and pleasure.

Zohar, Moshe, and Eliezer had tiptoed up the stairs. The boys fell asleep immediately. They dreamed one dream, holding her from all sides. Lying down in his room, Eliezer nodded smilingly to the sun rising over the Dormition Abbey. Then he shut his eyes and enjoyed a sleep that was no longer flimsy gray, but was once again the deep velvet it used to be.

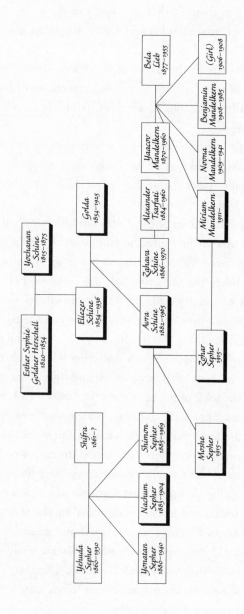

## Chapter 7

## MIRIAM

*My* FATHER WRITES:

My maternal grandfather's family lived in the southern Ukrainian village of Noviye Mlini, which means "New Mills." In 1900, my grandfather, Yaacov Mandelkern, married his first cousin, Rasia, in Noviye Mlini. In 1902, their son, Pinchas, was born. In 1903 Rasia died of tuberculosis, leaving Yaacov a young widower with an infant son. After the traditional period of mourning came to an end, Yaacov was advised by a matchmaker to visit a certain Rabbi Leib in the nearby village of Kodrovkah. The matchmaker told Yaacov that the rabbi had several eligible daughters of marriageable age. And since both families, the Mandelkerns and the Leibs, were Lubavitch, that is, they were both members of the same religious sect, it seemed very likely that the visit would result in a proper match.

Bela Leib was, relatively speaking, an old maid when Yaacov came courting. She was twenty-seven years old and had two older unmarried sisters. She had already turned down several marriage opportunities because of the age-old tradition of older sisters marrying first. Yaacov was a very attractive young man, he was highly educated and pretty well-off. Bela was the smartest and most attractive of her sisters. And Yaacov set his sights on her soon after he arrived in Kodrovkah. Bela eventually decided to marry him regardless of the tradition, and her parents did not object.

In Noviye Mlini, the couple lived with Yaacov's parents. The family had a large grocery store in which both Bela and Yaacov worked. In 1906, Bela gave birth to a daughter who died at the age of two. Their son, Benyamin, was born in 1908, their daughter Noona was born in 1909, and Miriam (my mother) was born in 1911.

I WRITE:

Of Miriam it could be said that she had a fashion sense from the moment she was born, and that when she emerged into the world, even her ordinary infant nakedness was not only beautiful but also somehow stylish. By the time she was six, she made her father, a religious man, think of queens (and smile), and her mother, a realistic woman, think of concubines (and frown) when she skipped by.

From an early age she had a talent for handiwork. She loved to knit and to embroider and to crochet. She learned first from her mother, who had learned from *her* mother, who had learned from an aunt of whom a story is told that she was really an uncle, though this rumor is only a matter of family lore. Miriam's mother, Bela, hailed from the village of Kodrovkah, a place renowned for its production of priceless tapestries that took at least six years and sixty pairs of hands to make. Bela, who was a slim sparrow of a woman with big, pretty eyes, taught her daughter everything she could remember. Miriam's quick white hands were like memory perches for the old images, bawdy gossip, and intricate stitches. Of Miriam it could be said that she held her art like doves. Her thread flew deep into the cloth.

MY FATHER WRITES:

Jews began to leave Noviye Mlini and other towns in the area prior to the outbreak of World War I. Some left in the late

nineteenth century and during the Russian-Japanese war of
1904–1905. At the outbreak of World War I (1914) and later,
during the Communist revolution (1917), living conditions for
the Jews worsened. Pogroms, murders, and rapes were daily
events. Many Jews left the small towns for large cities where
they were less noticeable. At least five of our family members
were murdered during this period by the gangs of Petlura, or by
the White Czarist Army of General Danikin.

Like many other Jews, my grandparents feared a pogrom. So,
in 1916 they moved with their four children to the city of Sartov
on the Volga River. In Sartov, Yaacov established a coffee factory.
They lived in a house that shared a large court with about forty-
five gentile families. When Yaacov was practicing his *torah* for
Shabbat, he had to keep his voice down so as not to anger the
gentiles.

They stayed in Sartov until 1918. When the Communists began
to take control of the area, the entrepreneurs knew that they were
in danger. Yaacov's strong desire to educate his children guided
him in their next move. They decided to move to Lithuania.
Yaacov knew that the Jewish communities of Lithuania had established a large and modern school system. The family planned to go
to the city of Riga but the first train to come was for Kovno. They
took that train and lived in Kovno from 1918 to 1923. In Kovno, the
children studied in the Hebrew Realick Gymnasia.

In Sartov, prior to their departure, Yaacov ordered from a
carpenter a small crate with hollow walls. In it he put his Russian rubles and the family jewelry. This was his daughters' (my
mother's and aunt's) dowries. By the time they arrived in Kovno,
the Communists had changed the Russian currency and the
rubles were worthless. In Kovno, Yaacov established a coffee and
cocoa factory.

The family's next move was to Palestine. Yaacov Mandelkern
was a Zionist. My aunt Noona told me that when the famous
Jewish poet, Chaim Nachman Bialik, received a permit to immi-

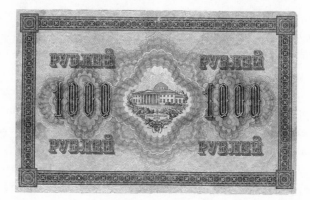

1OOO RUBLE NOTE SMUGGLED OUT OF RUSSIA
BY YAACOV MANDELKERN

grate to Palestine, she went with her father for a special farewell reception. The eldest son, Pinchas, was active in a Zionist youth movement. The family story is that Pinchas decided to make *aliyah,* that is, to move to Israel. But Bela said to Yaacov, "Pinchas will not go alone. He might get lost there." The result was that all six family members immigrated to Palestine in 1923. This is notable because Pinchas was Bela's stepson—this is just one example of what a wonderful and devoted mother she was.

On the way to Israel, the family visited their in-laws, Shai and Devorah Lieb, in the Polish city of Chopot. From Chopot they traveled to Berlin. This was right before the Nazi putsch in Munich (the beginning of Hitler's rise to power). They were in Berlin for exactly twelve hours. They took a night train to Trieste, Italy. While they were in Trieste, a vessel from Palestine came filled with Jews who had left the country. Most of these Jews were heading for Australia. They told Yaacov and Bela that the economic situation in Palestine was unbearable. My grandparents refused to be discouraged by this bad news and continued on their journey. From Trieste, they went on a boat to Port Said in Egypt. For this boat ride, they had to bring all of their

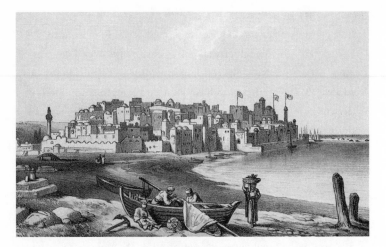

JAFFA

own food. From Port Said, they took a smaller boat to Jaffa,
Palestine. They arrived there on the sixth anniversary of the
Balfour Declaration, on November 1, 1923.

I WRITE:

By the time the family emigrated, Miriam had surpassed
her ancestors' expertise. She had learned how to sew
the scattering geography of Jews. Noviye Mlini, Sartov,
Kovno, Chopot, Berlin, Trieste, Port Said, Palestine. Each place
had its own stitch. And Miriam could tell the stitches, like a
story. Tracing the family journey of loss here in a black swirl, fear
there in a green half-moon, desperation in a gray star, hope in a
fancy purple cross stitch with little dots radiating eastward in
swervy flows. They traveled by train and cart, and foot, and boat
and foot and train again and boat again. By the time the family
reached the port of Jaffa, Miriam had embroidered so many
maps, and their ultimate unreadableness left her sick to her
stomach. "Too many legends," she murmured to herself while
ripping out a row of stitches. "Not enough firm ground."

*MY FATHER WRITES:*

Immediately after landing in the port of Jaffa, they went to
Petach Tikvah, a small city six miles east of Tel Aviv. They traveled by horse-driven covered wagon, called a *diligans* in Turkish.
In Petach Tikvah they purchased a lot on Herzl Street. First,
they built a barn in which they lived for about six months until
their house was completed in late 1924. It had three rooms and
an outhouse. There was no electricity in the town. According to
my mother, there were no locks on the doors to the house. They
usually ate on the porch where they had a table, chairs and a box
for dirty laundry. One morning they realized that the table cloth
had disappeared—it had been stolen. Bela, who was very generous and had a great sense of humor, said: "Somebody must have
been very cold and badly needed a blanket."

Soon after they first arrived, a family friend borrowed from
Yaacov five pounds (probably Egyptian pounds). This friend
planned to purchase a cow in Lebanon. Yaacov gave him ten
pounds for two cows—one for himself. Bela knew how to milk a
cow from their days in Noviye Mlini.

Petach Tikvah was the citrus-growing center of the Jewish
Settlement. Yaacov purchased a citrus grove. In addition to his
own groves, he was involved in planting groves for Lithuanian
Jews who planned to come to Israel.

Several years after they arrived, Yaacov signed a loan guaran-
tee for a friend. The friend went bankrupt, and Yaacov was
forced to sell his house and orchard.

*I WRITE:*

Once they were settled in Petach Tikvah, Bela sent her
daughter to spend afternoons at the knee of an expert
seamstress—an old widow whose name, Shalva, meant
"tranquil." Miriam walked slowly into the small house. Inside it
was surprisingly bright despite the absence of all but a single
window. The old woman reached a huge hand out and Miriam

stumbled forward. She raised her head and their faces almost touched. Shalva had huge breasts and a big soft middle. Shalva had a Yemenite sense of design, a Syrian sense of humor, the ancient eyes of an Indian, and the wide-open mouth of a loquacious Lebanese. She came from a kind of gracious everywhere, that country in the center of all maps called "nowhere in specific."

From Shalva, Miriam learned the patterns behind the patterns of lines and swirls. She learned the cloth behind the cloth, the stitch behind the stitch. Finally, she learned that there were fingers behind her own, and how to stop her own from getting in the way. And though Shalva never taught Miriam how to sew the old charms into her creations, over time the teacher realized that the student had learned anyway. And from the time Miriam was twelve they could be found sitting together—the big-breasted old mosaic of a woman and the lovely little girl, sewing entire oceans of incantations.

❧

When Miriam was seventeen, there moved into the settlement of Petach Tikvah a family of impossibly wealthy, impossibly rude Jews from the Island of Sardinia. This family bore the name of a kind of rare igneous rock that sounded like a cross between the Hebrew word for "mold" and the Yiddish word for "monster." The name—geological, grotesque, and inherently scorching to the tongue—was unpronounceable. And so, depending upon mood, and proximity to the principal players, people would refer to the matriarch and patriarch as either Mister Mold or Madame Monster. Or Madame Mold and Mister Monster. And the children—three young sons and a single daughter of marriageable age—were the Little Moldy Monsters.

They were imperious and proud, black-haired and big-shouldered and bony in the rear. They lorded over the city as if they owned its entirety, which they didn't, but almost did. They owned half of all the orange groves, a full quarter of the lemons, and all the best, most fertile land to the east.

Miriam was by now recognized as one of the best seamstresses in the entire settlement. She sewed stories into her cloth. Whoever wore these garments took on the mood and moment of the specific tale. She had first experimented with this technique on her parents, making for them a set of lovely pajamas into which she had embroidered a common fairy tale. But Miriam wasn't one for literary accuracy. So, during this queer period of time in the family history, Bela would bound about the house flexing her muscles while looking for a dragon to slay, while Yaacov would wake up feeling like a rescued princess and then be horrified when he realized that he had lost, or misplaced, or cut off his long golden hair.

❧

Seven months after the Moldy family invaded Petach Tikvah, Miriam was called to their compound. It was located on the far periphery of the city at a high and windy rise in the landscape. Miriam walked quickly; she carried nothing with her. Not even her measure. Not her samples of stitches or colors or cloth. Not because she was unprepared, but because the call had been accompanied by strict instructions for her to come empty-handed.

Miriam walked up to the gate of the compound and knocked on the door. It was opened by a hand that was neither monstrous nor moldy but seemed to her to have been fashioned out of precious silk. Skin so perfectly pale it seemed in danger of being stained even by the air. This was very disconcerting.

Miriam wondered if she had the wrong house. But of course, there was no other such house for miles. She walked in and stared at the silky young woman. Then she nodded and smiled.

The young woman nodded back but did not return Miriam's smile. At this point several other people entered the room. Miriam surmised that this was Madame Monster, who, like her daughter, nodded at Miriam but did not address her, and a young man whom she took to be the groom. He had a small round scar on his left cheek and eyes like cracked crystal. He strutted from wall to wall in a most clomping manner. When he was done walking, he said, "You are not accustomed to dressing figures of our caliber, but perhaps you can employ some opposite technique." And then he laughed, a laugh as cracked as his eyes and round as his belly. It hurt Miriam's ears.

The young woman didn't say a word to Miriam during the entire interview, even while they were alone, and Miriam was draping her figure with fine bolts of cloth. Miriam breathed deeply. She knew that her handiwork was magic and she saw no reason why magic couldn't mate with materialism. She nodded at the young woman. She would accept this commission.

Miriam walked home slowly. Her hands were heavily laden with silks from China, damask from the fashionable Parisian neighborhood of Neuilly, and linens from Morocco—white, purple, and black. When she reached home, Miriam put the cloth aside and joined her mother in the kitchen. She wouldn't start work until the next day. She needed time to choose a story.

That night, Miriam shut her eyes; she browsed through all the stories of their lives, and all the stories of their neighbors' lives, and all the stories of the lives of people she had never met, but only imagined. Finally, coming back close to home, she chose the perfect story for this wedding. In the morning, she took up her needle and began to embroider it into the cloth.

*My* FATHER WRITES:

My grandfather, Yaacov Mandelkern, was a man of high morals and good intentions. In 1918, before they immigrated to Palestine (and when they still had some money!), the family lived in the small Russian city of Kovno. They lived there until 1923. In Kovno, there was a very large, well-known *yeshiva,* or House of Study. Every day, Yaacov invited a *yeshiva* student home to share the family meal. Each day, a different student came. This was for two reasons. First, to give as many students as possible the opportunity to come, and the second was so as to make sure that they did not fall in love with his daughters—my mother and aunt, Miriam and Noona. Miriam had long brown hair. Noona was blond. Both girls were very beautiful.

I WRITE:

So Yaacov Mandelkern had made his rule. The young men came to lunch. One by one. And yes, each one came only a single time. Yaacov took great pride in discussing with the student a variety of topics: the latest Talmudic tract, the newest fashions in Minsk, the unfortunate way so many horses were losing their shoes in the deep, deep snow. The boys always answered with fumbling eloquence. They spoke in soft voices. They never looked at their host, but down at their hands.

Miriam and Noona refused to join in the conversation. They kicked each other under the table. And always, they tried to memorize the boys' faces so that afterward they could giggle about each one. The boys had scraggly beards and sad eyes. They had high cheekbones. They were fat. Or skinny, and had little mouths. Big mouths. Big noses. The boys had high, bushy eyebrows. Eyebrows that met in the center, over the bridges of their noses.

And so it went. A boy came to lunch. And always, the next day a different one replaced him. The system seemed to work. Yaacov Mandelkern felt his daughters' virtue safe and his sense of civic pride swell.

But then, just weeks after the inaugural invitations, the House of Study in the city of Kovno ceased to recognize itself. What happened was this. Every day a student came to lunch. And every day he answered Yaacov's questions. And every day he looked shyly down at his own hands, trying his best to avoid looking at the daughters. But every day the student was undone. Miriam and Noona's beauty wafted across the table toward him, colliding over the main meal—the chicken, the meat stew, the potatoes— with their father's attempt to prevent any alliance. The effects of this collision were severe and sensual, illicit, irresistible. Unexpected spice rained down over the food. The students ate of the food and were changed by it. By the end of the meal the young men's hands were shaking, and their shyness was turned to thoughts of seduction, love, and lust.

They left lunch possessed, returning to the House of Study with wide eyes and clammy skin and bulges below their bellies with which many of them were unfamiliar. And in this state, they began to read a new Torah. The young men, bent over their regular books, read the daughters of Yaacov and Bela Mandelkern. The matriarchs took on their mellow faces. The patriarchs and prophets (minor *and* major) began to touch themselves, touch each other, began to even reach out and touch the students in new ways.

The students kept attending the Mandelkern table. And they kept returning to the House of Study with new insight into their religion.

Kovno felt the effects. Students stumbled around its streets with odd loping gaits and funny twisted grins on their faces. And as time went on, the gaits got lopier and the grins grew more and more twisted. For the students were experiencing the indignity of Yaacov Mandelkern's injunction. Their portions of pleasure were true to their origins—they were unfulfillable, unrepeatable, and lasted only the length of a single meal. In just three months, the House of Study in the city of Kovno had metamorphosed into a container of pure carnal frustration. It was a school that had been known, prior to the onset of the invitations, as a place with an excellent reputation for close textual study.

All regular learning was abandoned. Many spent their days and nights flipping through the pages of the holy books, searching for the esoteric incantation that could save them, that could break the spell. Others searched in the opposite direction, looking for the miracle hidden in time that could bring satiety to Kovno. The young men searched through centuries mystical and epochs momentous. They searched the future, the past, the present. They searched the illicit epics of their own erections. They searched and they searched.

By the time three months had passed and more than forty boys had been to lunch, the House of Study in the city of Kovno was transformed completely. Its walls like sponges took the boys' sorrow into the paint. The floors and ceilings too, so that the building buzzed like a hive of bees aching in the eternal absence of all honey.

It was a strange time in Kovno. It was a frustrating time. A time of intensity, desire, and disarray. A time so transformative that the love and lust that those young students felt for the daughters of Yaacov and Bela Mandelkern became incorporated into their bodies, like extra hearts or special silken breaths. And when the family finally left Kovno it took many months for the matriarchs and patriarchs to disentangle their bodies and resume their ancient attitudes of sated grace. The students themselves were quite changed. All were left touched by the memory of a gentle madness that would serve them throughout their lives, especially in the most difficult moments when the seconds ticked away in shades of gray because time had lost its color.

Yaacov Mandelkern, my great-grandfather, a man of high morals and good intentions, never knew what trouble he had wrought. Noona and Miriam knew exactly what trouble *they* had wrought. They listened to the servants' gossip and then walked around Kovno with proud, jaunty steps, two girls commanding the gusts of local weather.

⚜

Miriam worked with fury. None of the young men from Kovno were recognizable on the white damask, the black linen. But Miriam translated their aching essences into geometrical shapes, into loops, and lines, and circles, and double circles, and squares, and rectangles, and flowers of feverish variety. She concentrated not so much on the lust and love as on the frustration. She worked with fantastical imagination. She used color combinations that had not been seen on earth since the days of the Temple when the high priest wore a garment embroidered with a magically hued design known only to select ancient initiates, and which had been revealed to her in a waking dream. She worked for ninety days, up until the day before the day before the wedding. And then, just before she was about to complete the task, she paused. She held the cloth up to her face, losing herself in it. And for several seconds she wondered if the Ten Commandments weren't a document like this, some queer history recorded as revenge. She wondered if there was no such thing as a prophet. "Maybe," she mused, "Moses was really a master tailor and revelation just a practical joke." She stitched the last border on the groom's waistcoat and then went to work on the veil.

⚜

On the night of the wedding, the bride and groom, under the carnal influence of the boys of Kovno, were possessed by a fierce sexual urge. And the urge was infectious. It seemed to waft through the wedding canopy, causing its cloth to billow upward even though it was a night with no wind, and causing all the men

143

who were standing under the canopy to press closer together and then bump violently backward when they realized what their pressing was all about. The bride and groom were, of course, the most affected. After the ceremony and feast, they retired to the marriage chamber and took each other to the verge of a pleasure never before experienced in Palestine. But just as they were both on the verge of satiety, a captivating flaccidity possessed the groom and they were undone. All sex jumped the ship of his body and he was left feeling like an embarrassed infant—deflated, tiny, shriveled, and with not a single tickle or tender touch left in his lips, hands, or hips. The mortification continued for days: in public his privates were stiff and ready—pressing up out of his pants in a way that made most members of the community avert their eyes against the indiscretion. But in private the groom's privates were flaccid, unfulfilled. He drooped and drooped and drooped. There was not even the tiniest possibility of a rising. Not at the sight of his bride's naked body, and especially not at the sight of her very frustrated face.

Miriam, down in the valley, heard all about it. She did not smile at her neighbor's misfortune, but knew that she had done the proper thing. One day, perhaps, she would send them a present: a small tapestry on which she would sew the story of her own parents' marriage. Yaacov and Bela had a love like an onion—with many interesting layers and a good strong flavor that stays long in the mouth. But not yet. No, not yet. Miriam liked to let things stew.

# Part Three

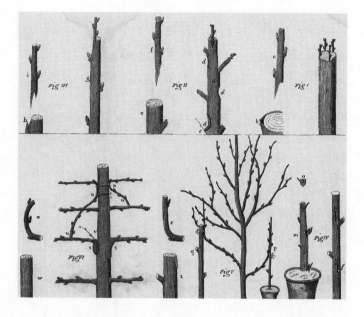

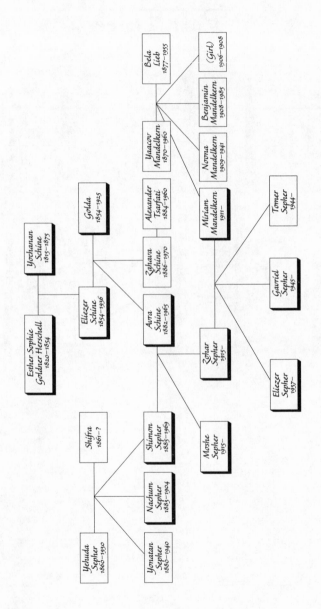

# Chapter 8

## ZOHAR AND MIRIAM

*M*Y FATHER WRITES:

Both my parents were excellent athletes. My mother was an accomplished gymnast and my father was a champion soccer player. When he played on the home field, the crowd used to shout: "Zohar-Koach! Zohar-Koach!" (Zohar-Strength!)

My parents met on the soccer field in 1933; she was twenty-two, he was eighteen. Zohar was warming up for a practice when he saw Miriam across the field. She was hanging upside down from parallel bars, doing gymnastics. He crossed the field, waited for her to come down, then asked her for a date. A fifty-nine-year romance ensued.

When my father was just sixteen years old, he bought a motor-cycle—a British Rudge license plate 536. The price was 100 liras. The motorcycle became a very important part of his life. He loved to drive and to travel up until his very last day. Back then, the borders were open, and he traveled all over the Middle East. One of my father's many motorcycle trips was to Syria. He went with three other young men on two motorcycles. They traveled all over Syria, and reached the Turkish border. They also spent several hours in jail, in Damascus, after fighting with "Arabs who attacked them." My father told me that the four of them had stood back-to-back with their fists up, warding off a whole

DAMASCUS

mob. Syrian and French officers came to the jail to see "Jews from Palestine who fight and do not run away." My father often rode to Beirut where he and his friends visited nightclubs; he traveled all over Lebanon.

The Rudge played an important role in my parents' lives. They often took rides together, when they were dating, and later, when they were married. They were really a wild couple. Perhaps with some exaggeration, my father once told me that it took them only six minutes to ride from Petach Tikvah to the Mugrabbi theater in Tel Aviv—a distance of six miles! And in those days there were only dirt roads. They rode everywhere on the Rudge: to Jerusalem, Netanya, up and down the Mediterranean coast. A popular place among the youngsters of Petach Tikvah was the ruins of the Fort of Antipater, on the Yarkon River near the town. My parents loved to ride the Rudge to the fort and then camp out there with a whole group of good friends, build a fire, cook some simple food.

My parents were married on the first of Iyar, 1936. After their wedding, they left Petach Tikvah on the Rudge. They went to spend their honeymoon in Jerusalem with Zohar's grandfather, my great-grandfather Eliezer, in the house on Rav Pinchas Street.

Grandfather Eliezer was eighty-two years old. He hadn't left Jerusalem since his seventy-fifth birthday—not because he was never invited but because, as he told people, he had "stopped believing that anything existed outside the walls." My father told me that in the latter years of his life Eliezer seemed puzzled by visitors, but also appreciative of their presence. Zohar and Moshe visited regularly and so he and the twins had remained very close. My father once told me that wedding ride up into the mountains of Jerusalem, with his "new bride hugging his back," was the most wonderful trip of his life.

I WRITE:

Zohar carried Miriam as far as the Rudge, which was leaning against the side of the house. Both climbed onto it, and they began their journey. She had taken off her veil, but for the whole ride she felt as if she still had it on, and it was flowing after them.

They reached Jerusalem just after dark. The family house on Rav Pinchas Street was now entirely decrepit and just the ghost of grand. Old Eliezer was quite excited by the prospect of hosting an active young Love in his house. He knew that the consummation of marriage was a special blessing, and he very much liked the idea of providing the proper place for this kind of prayer. Also, Eliezer suspected that the physical decline of his house had less to do with ordinary material aging than it had to do with the absence of inhabitants in love. He often walked around the empty rooms trying to conjure back kisses of generations past.

The grandfather welcomed the young couple in from the dark

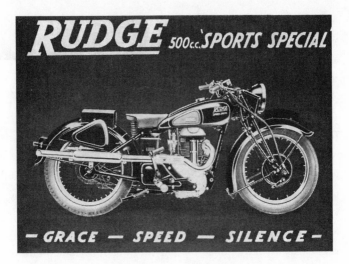

with strong cups of spiked tea and a hearty meal. But he barely let them finish it. Zohar and Miriam hadn't been in the house for half an hour before Eliezer was shooing them up to bed with an obvious utilitarian haste that made Miriam blush.

This was the bedroom where Zohar's great-grandparents Esther and Yochanan had slept and dreamed and prayed and curled close together and sometimes moved far apart. Their ghosts were not entirely present, but nor were they very far away. It was the sort of night when ancestors inhabit the middle distance of soul, a hazy curious place just left of memory and to the right of the current moment. Both bride and groom felt themselves possessed of a hushing, comfortable quiet. They shed their clothes and lay down in the bed whose linens were fresh but whose frame was a gossipy relic. They lay side by side, not speaking. Their silence seemed part of an old ritual that was joining them, kin to the wedding canopy, but also like the glass Zohar had broken with his foot—something simultaneously over their heads and under their feet.

Zohar stared at the ceiling and soon he found himself mur-

muring a silent self-prayer. Zohar said the prayer of first things in honor of his first night as a husband and Miriam's first night as a wife. *Shehechianoo vekiemanoo, veheegianoo, lazman hazeh.* The rhythmic cant of the words felt good in his mouth. He added a hearty inner Amen, and then he looked over at his wife.

Miriam was also immersed in quiet. But she was not praying. Rather, she was looking out of the window, at the Dormition Abbey in the distance, letting her thoughts slide up and down its dome and sharp apogee cross, because the Jerusalem in her soul was wakeful and warm and in its own twisty mystical way, unrelenting. Miriam wondered about the cross and the dome, and about the creak in the bed. She wondered about the darkness, she wondered about her new grandfather, she wondered about her new husband, she wondered about herself. And as she lay there, she felt her marriage well up inside of her, and begin to throb and pulse and protect her. She was surprised and amazed by this phenomenon. And she wondered why nobody had bothered to tell her that a marriage was an organ your soul grows. That it was every organ at once, and all of them together—that

CITY OF JERUSALEM FROM MOUNT OF OLIVES

marriage was skin and liver, and heart, and stomach and lungs. This seemed to her, at that moment, so obvious. Miriam lay in bed in the house on Rav Pinchas Street absolutely amazed. She began to think of the way she would embroider this new information. What color the cloth? What quality the thread?

It seemed to both of them as they held each other in bed that the other had become a kind of door. And that the door led to Love, a territory invisible, eternal, and accessible only like this. Miriam wondered if all people weren't created for this—as building tools in a secret city that otherwise had no entrance. Zohar also wondered. He told her, in between kisses, that he suspected that the rest of life was just a diversion, "to keep us humans occupied while we are busy doing the real work of life—being doors and windows, and other kinds of walls." They laughed out loud, and then pressed their naked bodies together and kissed some more.

Old Eliezer heard their laughter and the loud, tidal creaking of the bed and laughed too. He fluffed up his pillows and shut his eyes. In the dark of his own head he had a vision of so many shiny new Jerusalem stones flying through the alleys of the city, zooming right and left, under the half arch, down the Street of Death's Angels, toward Rav Pinchas Street, where they adhered, one by one, to the front of the house, on top of the stones that had molded practically to dust.

Meanwhile, the young "builders" were busy "constructing." Miriam reached around and squeezed Zohar's buttocks. She let a finger slide up and down the warm crack of his behind. He moaned, and then thrust his hips forward and then back again. Zohar shivered and then sat up and bent over his bride. He ran his tongue over the nipple of her left breast, nipping it with his lips until she moaned, and arched her back, and then he reached tender fingers down into the warm and most willing window between her legs.

## My father writes:

After my parents were married just a few months, they moved from the city of Petach Tikvah to Shachar-Chayel (Shachar), a small citrus-growing village in Emek Chefer near the resort city of Netanya. Emek Chefer is a large fertile valley in the central part of the country, just along the coastal plain. The valley has a biblical name. The Chefer daughters were the first women in the Bible to inherit their father's property. Their father, Chefer's son, owned our entire valley. After he died without leaving a male heir, his daughters went before Moses to fight for their rights to their father's property, and they were victorious. Our valley is named for the granddaughters of Chefer, who owned our land until they died and then passed it on to their sons.

I was born in Shachar on February 16, 1937. I was named Eliezer after my father's grandfather who had died three months before I was born. My brother, Tomer, was born on April 6, 1944, when I was seven years old.

Tomer was an incredibly active child, and a troublemaker from the time he was born. We have lots of family stories about him, because he was always up to something. He started walking at the age of nine months, and was talking at one and a half. As a baby in his playpen, he would hear my father coming on his motorcycle and would start going crazy, jumping up and down and rocking the pen. When my father came home, before he would even enter the house he had to take Tomer for a short ride (sitting in front of my father).

By the time he was two, Tomer was wandering by himself all over the village. I believe there were only two cars in the village—and my father had the only motorcycle—so there were no paved roads and really no cars to worry about. But of course his wandering off always drove my parents crazy and we were always running out looking for him.

We lived in a tiny one-room house. At first, my father supported the family by farming his *dunam*, his plot of land, but with the outbreak of World War II, citrus exports stopped entirely, so my father had to stop farming and work as a *gaffir* (officer) guarding a British oil tank farm. My mother also worked—sewing insignias for Australian army uniforms. She told me that this was incredibly hard work—the uniform cloth was so thick that her fingers would go numb from trying to push the needle through it.

In the mid to late 1940s, my parents were involved (like most of our village) with the Haganah, the secret Jewish defense force. Both my father and uncle joined when they were sixteen, and were sworn in, according to my father, "with one hand on the Bible in a secret ceremony in a dark room lit by candles." Once my father and his twin swam underneath the Yarkon River to put in place a bomb that booby-trapped an important British point of crossing. My mother was also active. She and the other women in the area often practiced throwing grenades, assembling machine guns, and other military skills. Often their work involved smuggling weapons. My mother told me that the British soldiers were easy to fool. The village women would rub up right against them and tell them that their husbands were away for the afternoon. In my own baby carriage, tucked underneath my blankets, would be a machine gun. In a neighbor woman's carriage would be enough ammunition to blow up the High Command itself. But, in my mother's own words, "those British were so strange." All the women knew that the way to stop them from searching was to flirt. The more the women flirted, the more scared the soldiers looked. Sometimes, for fun, the women would try to push their luck, rubbing up against the soldiers and making such eyes as could only be taken for an invitation. The soldiers always let the women pass when they acted like this. The women were proud of their war effort. They liked to brag that they smuggled half an arsenal in their baby carriages and under their skirts.

My parents, like many in our valley, were particularly active in Haganah attempts to help war refugees immigrate to Palestine. In the 1940s, tens of thousands of Jews, many of them right out of the concentration camps, were trying to escape from Europe. Many wanted to go to Palestine, but Great Britain had severely restricted Jewish immigration. So the Haganah, the Jewish Defense Force, organized an elaborate system of illegal immigration.

Shachar is less than a mile inland from the seaside city of Netanya. Boats carrying "illegals" sailed toward Netanya on moonless nights. The shore is very rocky and there is no port. Haganah members disguised as fishermen met the refugees far out in the water and guided their lifeboats past the huge rocks that jut up from the sea. Once close enough, they lifted the refugees out of the rafts and onto their backs, carrying them through the waves to safety. The refugees would then be led inland, through dunes and orchards, and ultimately taken to Shachar and other nearby settlements where they were dispersed among all the houses. If the British came searching for illegals (which they often did), the villagers would say, "This is my cousin Shlomo from Sefat," or "This is my sister Ruth from Jerusalem." Everyone in Shachar and in the surrounding villages always had relatives visiting anyway, since they were close to the beach and the air wasn't nearly as damp as in Tel Aviv.

I WRITE:

On nights they knew refugees were coming, all the young women and older girls would go to one of the restaurants in town where the British soldiers were congregating. Of course the Haganah girls were part of the plan. They would try to get them drunk. They would wear revealing clothes and dance with the soldiers, letting them press close and put their hands all over their bodies. And while the women were distracting the soldiers, the men would be on the beach. Zohar would wade out into the water, reach up into a rowboat, help a man off, throw him over his shoulders, and make his way with the refugee through the surf, and then back again, to deliver another.

Next to Shachar there is another village, called Neve Boker. Miriam had heard that the refugees who landed in Neve Boker received what you could call "a different kind of greeting." Evidently, there were a few ladies there who competed with each other to see who could extend the most "elaborate" welcome. According to rumors (which were very credible!) a woman named Sophie Gefen was the best at this. She was beautiful and very intelligent, with one blue eye and one brown eye, black curly hair, and delicate, almost Asian features even though she was Polish through and through. At the restaurants in town, the Haganah leader would make sure that Sophie went for the captains, or sergeants, or lieutenants if there were any around. Miriam and her friends always used to joke that if only Sophie Gefen could be wrapped up as a present and delivered to the British High Command they would have had their own country a whole lot sooner.

According to rumors, on nights that they had refugees sleeping on their back porch, Sophie used to get out of bed in the middle of the night. Her husband was a heavy sleeper. He never heard a thing. Sophie would walk out onto the porch without any clothes on and slip into bed with the refugees. All the girls from Shachar used to joke that Sophie probably woke them up with the words "Welcome to the Holy Land!" or "How about some native milk and honey?" Sophie Gefen was known to have "greeted" a pair of French Jews (cousins) from Paris, a wounded socialist from Cracow, two yeshiva boys from Kovna, and a Lithuanian rabbi who had lost his faith in the dungeons of Europe, but in Sophie's arms, rumor had it, instantly retrieved it. Everyone in the valley knew what she was up to. But no one ever told her husband, which, depending upon whom you asked, was either a great crime or an act of great compassion.

∗

Not long after Miriam and Zohar first moved to Shachar, one of the village leaders paid Miriam a visit. Zohar wasn't home that day, he was out working. The village leader, whose name was Horowitz, knew that Zohar and Miriam were members of the Haganah. Horowitz told Miriam that two pairs of British soldiers were searching through the village that very day, looking for weapons and illegal information. He asked her if she had any weapons hidden around the house. Well, they didn't have any guns, but they had a stack of papers describing how you take a Sten submachine gun apart and then put it back together. Miriam was an expert with the Sten, she always won contests for "breaking it down" the quickest. She told Horowitz that they had some papers, and he said that they had to get rid of them immediately. Of course, this was very complicated. Eytan Rimon, who lived at the other end of the village, had a *slick* in his chicken coop. A *slick* was an underground compartment where they used to hide weapons and other illegal things.

But for Rimon to come to Miriam and then to make it all the way to his house with the contraband material meant passing through the village and possibly running into the soldiers on the way. That's where Abraham Lincoln came into the picture. Abraham Lincoln was from Lithuania. His real name was Yoni Burg, but everyone called him Abraham Lincoln because his wife was American and they spoke English at home. Horowitz organized everything chick-chock. Abraham Lincoln's wife, Devorah, cooked a quick lunch while he ran through the village to find both couples of soldiers. When he found them, he engaged them in conversation and then invited them back to their house for lunch. The British loved Abraham Lincoln because of his good English. Later Miriam mused that maybe he even had that nickname as part of Haganah strategy to make the British interested in him. The soldiers all went back to Abraham Lincoln's house for lunch, Devorah made something delicious, and Rimon made it to Miriam and Zohar's house and then out again, all the way through the village to his *slick* under the chicken coop without getting caught!

*M*Y FATHER WRITES:

In the later days of the British Mandate there was a very strong British military presence all over Palestine. During this time of increased tension, our people continued to secretly train for war. Often, we were under curfew and movement was severely restricted. But even under curfew, people trained. The women in our valley often used their babies to camouflage their Haganah practice sessions. They would tell the British that they needed to go to the tool tree to give their babies some fresh air, and that they themselves were athletes and needed to practice for the All-Palestine games. The tool tree is an old ficus with tools embedded in its trunk. Nobody knows whose tools they were or when exactly they were abandoned, but it was probably sometime in the end of the last century. The tree grew on the spot, around the tools. Saw blades, a lathe, hammers, they stick half out of the wood. Twice a week they would meet by the old tool tree and practice throwing grenades. The British always thought that the mothers were just getting some exercise or, more ridiculously, "practicing throwing the discus for the All-Palestine Games," according to my mother.

Anyway, when my mother and the other mothers would bring us children to the tool tree, one of the mothers would take a turn watching the children while the others went a short distance away. They would stand in a line and throw stones at a target, which was a red splash of paint on a dead ficus trunk.

Sometimes the soldiers would come and watch the women. They would lean over the fence, a pair of them, and watch with what my mother describes as "gazes of lust and admiration." For show, the mothers would sometimes run races or do gymnastic routines when grenade/"discus" throwing was over.

The late 1940s were a very difficult time for our family, and indeed for the whole settlement. War was imminent. The Haganah was stepping up its campaigns against the British. The British were retaliating with curfews and by tacitly ignoring the campaign of violence being waged by the local Arabs against the Jews. As a result of all this, many people in the settlement did not have regular work, and consequently, did not have enough food to eat. Our family was no exception. My mother would go to the market with a girlfriend on Fridays to buy a single fish, which they would then split—half for each family. During those years we never went hungry but we miraculously made do with very, very little.

I WRITE:

She is on the front porch, leaning against one of the brick columns. *This is how I always see her.* Her back is against the column, and one of her legs is up against it too, forming a triangle. Her right arm is up by her head. She is wearing a light-blue checkered cotton dress and her left hand is on her belly, fingers spread out wide. She stays there for a few minutes. When she steps into the house, the screen door slams after her. It is very hot and very humid midsummer. Sweat drips down Miriam's forehead as she diapers the baby. Eliezer is out back digging little holes in the sandy earth at the edge of the orchard. When he hears the back door open and shut, he looks up, waves a shovel at his mother. Miriam sits down under the little porch roof, in the shade. Tomer squirms off her lap. She lets him crawl to his brother. Again she puts a hand on her belly. She knows that she is pregnant, but at the same time, she cannot believe that she is pregnant again. So soon. The two boys play in the sand. Miriam presses her fingers into her stomach. She presses hard, so that her hand indents her body.

She is a strong woman, a woman of courage and beauty. She has many friends, and when she tells a story, people always stop and listen. Miriam takes her hand off her belly and wipes sweat off her forehead. She looks into the orchard, first at her sons and then at the trees, which are green now, as it is summer, and unadorned with orange fruit. Then she looks up above the trees and into the sky, which is so blue, hot blue, blue with a vengeance.

※

She took the children. Tomer in his stroller, Eliezer holding her hand. She knew that she shouldn't be going at all, not in her condition, but she went anyway. To the tool tree where she left them in the shade, in the care of one of the other mothers. Then she stepped out onto the field where she raised her right arm and squinted so as to see better the target. The cool stone fit perfectly in her hand. Closing her fingers around it, she took a deep breath. With her left hand she pushed away the hair that kept falling into her eyes. Then she stepped back, letting her arm swing back, her hand drop down, and then bringing it up again with enough force so that the stone careened through the air, and crashed into the target with a loud bull's-eye that caught the other women's attention. Then she did it again. And again. Bending down to pick up another mock grenade from the pile of stones at her feet. And the other mothers stopped their own throwing to watch her, applauding when she threw the last one. Applauding at the way the stone left her hand like a bullet and at the strong grace of her body in the blue checkered dress. She shut her eyes and watched the stone on the inside traveling on a straight path but through a different war, a private darkness, traveling toward a target no one else could see.

Over the next few months her belly swelled. When the other women found out she was pregnant they wouldn't let her practice with them anymore. Everyone was always afraid for a new baby. A woman shouldn't exert herself in such a condition. And then there were those scornful women who looked at the squirming babe in Miriam's arms and then down at the one in her belly and said unabashedly, "How could you? In times like these when you don't even have enough food for the ones you already have?"

In the afternoons, when Eliezer was at a friend's and she was alone with Tomer in the house, Miriam would go out onto the back porch. First, she would shut her eyes and imagine the row of women, their dresses hitched up when they leaned into the throw, their arms reaching up. Then she would open her eyes, and raise her own arm high. Planting her feet strongly, she would step back with her right leg. Raising her arm, she would lean forward, and then shift back, her feet not moving, but her legs accepting the intimate exchange of energy from front thigh to back thigh, to calf to heel to toe, and then lift her left foot into the air as some invisible stone careened out of her palm. Out and over the orchard. Hitting a phantom mark. Stepping back, she would squint and then throw again and again, with perfect aim, at the ripening fruit on the trees.

❧

Zohar would always associate the birth of his third child with butterflies and ashes. The ashes because the year the baby was born, there was a premature frost accompanied by a severe hailstorm that ruined most of the crops on the trees. That spring, the village burned an entire season of ruined fruit. While the burning was in progress a thin film of citrus ash hovered over all the houses and seemed to coat everything in a gray but sweet, almost caramelized, carapace. The amber-colored ash settled on the porches and branches and windowsills like a death you could eat like candy. Then they buried what was left after the fire and even the most secular among the *pardesanim* was heard to murmur prayers as the earth was opened up and then closed again, full of the still-glowing orangy embers of an entire season's bounty.

The birth would always make him think of butterflies because when the infant was seen right away to be missing fingers and toes, the head doctor of the birthing unit had taken Zohar aside and told him that he must immediately visit "another child, an extraordinary child who was born with this very same deformity." So, the next day, with Miriam still in the hospital, Zohar had left Tomer with a neighbor, and had taken Eliezer to visit the other little boy, who, like their own new baby, had been born with blunted hands and feet.

The family lived in Zichron Yaacov. Their son, the parents told Zohar, had been inspired by the great local naturalist Aaron Aaronson, who was the brother of Sarah, and who himself had been one of the leaders of the NILI spies. Even as a baby, the poor child was enamored by "all things wild and natural." But while Aaronson had cultivated fruits and flowers, this child collected butterflies. The parents took Zohar through the house to a back room whose walls were lined with glass cases. In the cases were hundreds of mounted butterflies. "All in all," the little boy told Zohar and Eliezer proudly, "I have one hundred and forty-two varieties. Many from overseas." He then showed them a huge cage of fine wire mesh on a back porch. Inside the cage were five or so bright bright-blue butterflies. The boy explained that he kept them this way until they died, and then he preserved them, mounted them, and added them to his display. "Sometimes, though," he admitted, he "suffocated the creatures to prevent their wings from losing their color."

Zohar realized that the reason the doctor had wanted him to

come was to see that a child with deformed hands and feet could accomplish something. Could collect butterflies, and know many things about their spots and colors and the shapes of their wings. But later, when it became apparent that their own baby was not only physically deformed but also mentally afflicted, and catastrophically so, Zohar would think back to that visit. He would shut his eyes and see those butterflies, all one hundred and forty-two varieties of them—their brilliant, intricate wings in blues and magentas and yellows. He wondered if the doctor had known then that the baby's condition was much more severe than a deformity of the toes and fingers. And he wondered if it was not the boy he had sent them to see, but the butterflies. Because there certainly was a similarity between the baby that had been born to Miriam in the hospital, and those beautiful creatures pinned to the wall, or kept waiting for death in a cage.

❧

Zohar returned to the hospital. He looked at Miriam and she looked at him. Their gazes were made of grief. And though they were not a religious couple, the words on their lips turned to prayers. They named their son with a prayer, they called him a psalm, they asked every angel for an answer. They called him Gavriel. *Gavri El,* which means "God Will Help Him Overcome." They held their baby and they took his tiny blunted hands in their own. Zohar thought about the trees this boy would never graft. Miriam thought about the way people would stare at his deformity. And when he slept, they slept too, while their eldest child, Eliezer, hovered around their bed, aware of strange shadows falling on the faces of his parents.

On the morning of the baby's *brit,* Zohar walked into the orchard, the baby clutched to his chest, its face pressed into his shirt so as not to be scratched by leaves and branches. He walked deeper and deeper until he reached a clearing in between four

trees where he stopped and lifted the child above his head. Gabi
was so light. He didn't weigh anything. Zohar pressed Gabi
higher up, higher up still, and then he stood for several seconds.
Gabi floated in the citrus air like some sort of opposite anchor,
mooring them both in place by virtue of the absence of any heaviness at all. They stood there like this for what seemed ten thousand minutes but was really a single minute, stretched to full
capacity. Finally, Zohar brought the tiny baby back down to the
layer of leaves and trunks and branches. And then he brought
himself down to the layer of roots and stones and worms. It was
bitter here, and deathly dark, but at least in the dark he was comfortable. Zohar pressed the baby back into his chest, which was
heaving with sobs, and together they came out of the orchard.

⚜

One night, when Gabi was several weeks old, Miriam went over
everything in her mind. When the three children were finally all
in bed, she lay down and went over the possibilities. The first was
the most awful. The first possibility was that she herself had
caused the ruin of this child. She did not know when exactly she
had reached the decision or if she had ever really reached it at
all. It was in her second month, before she had even started
showing. She didn't even know if she had reached it alone, or if
Zohar had whispered, persuaded, persisted. She didn't know. She
couldn't tell. The memory seemed to her in retrospect a mess of
yesses and noes that her own mouth may or may not have
uttered. She remembered feeling, as she had taken the envelope
from the nurse's hand, as if she were stepping out of one version
of her life into another.

She had walked home slowly that day. Taking a circuitous
route, around Amnon Tered's orchard, past the bomb shelter,
through the old chicken coops and then around again, around
the back of the school where children were playing. And no mat-

ter how she had tried to make these moments last they resisted. She had reached home, and walked through the gate, and up the front walk, up the porch steps and into the house.

In the kitchen, she had paused for a moment. Then she had opened the envelope and examined the powder. It was white. Just white. Dipping a finger in, she had taken a tiny bit out and tasted it. But it didn't taste like anything at all. For a few seconds she paused and tried to tell herself why she was doing this thing. But when she spoke to herself of rationing and shortages, and of not having nearly enough food to feed the two children they had already, she began to panic and forced herself to stop thinking. She got herself a glass of water, poured some of the white powder in, and mixed it up. Then she had stared at it for a couple more seconds before drinking it.

But the pregnancy had continued. The nurse at the clinic told her it must have been fake, the powder, flour probably, nothing dangerous. They had been tricked. Miriam knew that it hadn't tasted like flour, and she tried to convince herself that the nothing she had tasted had been nothing indeed. Sometimes she believed it. Other times throughout the pregnancy, she felt a panicky fire flaming in her head, on the inside of her skull. And to be alone, to be quiet, was to feel that conflagration, the fear that she had indeed destroyed something.

Miriam was a smart woman. She did not blame herself completely for the darkness they now suffered. Intuitively, she knew that the nurse had not comforted her with empty words all those months ago and that there was indeed a strong possibility that the powder she had taken to abort the pregnancy had been harmless, a fake. The land was awash in pills and syrups and powders that were impotent. Miriam told herself over and over again that it was possible that Gabi was born the way he was born not through any fault of her own. The doctors had said that Gabi's condition could very well be the result of a congenital abnormality in the family that had been previously hidden. She had taken some solace in these pronouncements—especially in the latter, and found herself repeating those final words, "previously hidden," over and over again in her mind, like a totem to ward off the torture of self-blame and also to ward off the possibility that this "abnormality" could reappear again in a future generation.

And there were other possibilities, too. In her fourth month, Miriam had been stepping out of a bus from a visit to her parents in Petach Tikvah when the woman behind her had tripped, falling down the steps and straight into Miriam who had then fallen down to the ground. It was quite a fall. She had landed face down. Everyone had helped her up. She was okay, somewhat bruised, shaken up, but really okay. The small crowd that gathered didn't quite believe her. The women especially. They wore expressions of great concern on their faces, for they could see she was pregnant.

Now, Miriam rose from bed and walked over to the crib where the baby was sleeping. She watched him while trying to locate the disaster in time and space. Though she couldn't really remember what the woman who had fallen into her had looked like, now she imagined that she saw her face clearly. She gave her full lips and a big nose. Miriam shut her eyes and watched the woman falling over and over again down the bus steps and into her life with a bang and a crash that left no survivors.

I TELL:

*N*o, I do not write to hurt her. I write to build a word-museum. In my museum there is a hall of images. They are arranged in a series of subtly shifting life-sized pictures so that if you view them all, you are viewing one completed action, like a flip-book. One series of images shows my grandmother, a young woman, throwing a stone. Her feet are planted firmly apart, and her right arm is raised over her shoulder. She holds in her hand a heavy round stone. In the distance, to the right are the tree and the babies, you can just see them. In the next image the arm, bent at the elbow, is even farther forward, and *her whole body, taut, energized, wears the anticipation of the throw as if it were a garment. In the next image her fingers are open, the stone still in her hand. But by the next image she has let the stone fly. It explodes forward like a grenade and her body becomes the ricochet, reeling backward, but she doesn't lose her balance. Then there are several stills of the stone flying through the air. A single image of the stone hitting the target, which is a clump of thistles to the left of a crumbly stone wall. Then, there is the final image. She stands with her hands on her hips, her face satisfied, proud of hitting the mark. Grandmother, I museum you and you museum me, for what is a family but a living hall of a loved one's many faces?*

I WRITE:

When Gabi was several months old, it became apparent that not only were his hands and feet deformed but that there was something horribly wrong inside of his head. Miriam and Zohar had suspected this when he had first been born, but the doctors had assured them otherwise and had urged them to take him home and treat him like a "normal baby." But he wasn't a normal baby. He was not alert like his older brothers had been. Especially not like Tomer, his senior by only eleven months. Tomer was a wild, precocious spark. By the time Gabi was six months old, Tomer, a year and a half, was already talking.

Gabi at six months couldn't hold up his own head. He didn't try to roll over. His eyes were always unfocused. Zohar and Miriam went back to the doctors and they ran tests and they ran more tests and all the while Miriam held the baby to her breast. As he suckled, she imagined that his soul had not come out of her womb. That it was still inside of her and that perhaps it would come out with her milk, into his lips, and flow like the Jordan River into the banks of his tiny body, which, though misshapen, was still pink and sweet and warm.

THE RIVER JORDAN

She would hold Gabi for hours as Eliezer learned to amuse himself. Tomer toddled wildly around the village, and the housework was left undone. Miriam would hold Gabi and rock him to sleep in her arms and daydream. Miriam knew that she was crying. She cried all the time now. While he was still asleep, Miriam set Gabi down in a bassinet in the little porch to the side of the house—the little porch was closed in with a concrete lattice. Often she would leave him there as she tried to get some housework done. She began to clean some potatoes for dinner, but the baby woke up almost immediately and she had to go to him.

Years passed. And the child heavied Miriam's breasts and arms until she had no more breasts and no more arms and only the body of a spent woman who could not carry herself any longer in this way. Zohar, too, suffered. But his suffering was different. Miriam suffered from the heaviness of the child while Zohar suffered from his lightness. When they would walk with the baby through the village, he began to fear that Gabi would rise up. Rise up above the houses and the tops and the trees. He would take them with him. Not to heaven, but to a kind of floating hell. A hell of idiot angels whose eyes are empty and whose blessings are all for naught.

Nor did the earth seem much of a haven. Nor did the heavens seem to have much interest or influence in making good their lot. They lived in two tiny rooms in a concrete house. She cooked on a tiny primus stove and since there was never enough food to go around, she and her neighbor would share. Half a fish was a holiday. Two eggs for two families. If there was milk it was only for the children, of course. Bread, a piece now and then. A ration of coffee, sometimes some oil, some sugar. Meanwhile, the war was everywhere. It was in Miriam's own hands as she reached up and threw the stone, its awful arc exploding phantom or not, against the target. The war was in Gabi's eyes. When she took him from his crib in the morning she would try to get him to look at her. To focus on her face. But he just stared and stared, acknowledging neither her existence nor his own. And when she put him to bed at night she sometimes imagined that the war was being fought in his own little head. Even though it was clear to her that this was a battle long lost, she kissed his forehead anyway and tried with her mother's lips to stop this one private field from raging.

Miriam bent down to kiss her sleeping older boys. First she went to Eliezer. This boy, she thought, has the face and countenance of a deer—a serene and dreamy animal whose camouflaged coat blends so perfectly with the desert that sometimes you didn't even know he was there. She bent down and pressed her lips to the brow of her dreamy thoughtful older son. And then she turned to the other one, Tomer. His sleeping face was so different than his waking one. Asleep, he really was an angel. Miriam sat down by Tomer's bed, and then leaned to kiss his smooth, cool, relaxed forehead. *"Ma yeeye im Tomer?"* she whispered. What will be with Tomer? Nightly she prayed that this one would make it out of childhood safely, not because he was sickly like Gabi, but because he was the exact opposite—he had almost too much life in him. He was always getting into such trouble. Although neither of them would ever admit it, both Zohar and Miriam were proud of Tomer's wildness, proud of the life force fizzing and burning under his skin. Miriam shut her eyes and for a moment tried to feel her elder sons' souls adorning the darkness. She mused, "If Eliezer is a deer, then this one is a wild zebra, his improbable stripes demanding attention, the pounding of his hooves danger-ous, fast, and different." She pressed her lips to Tomer's brow and kept them there extra long, breathing him in.

## Chapter 9

# THE DOUBLE TREE

*M*Y FATHER WRITES:

In the years leading up to the War of Independence in 1948 there were several groups of Jews in Palestine actively resisting British rule. One, which I have already mentioned, was the Haganah. Some of the groups were more militant than others, a difference that led to occasional flare-ups of internecine friction. There was a group called Etzel, which was particularly militant and claimed responsibility for many of the bombings and booby-trappings of that era. In May 1947, the British hanged two militant Jews from the resistance cell Etzel. In retaliation, Etzel kidnapped and threatened to execute two British soldiers. They kidnapped the soldiers from outside a pub in Netanya, the city near our home.

The incident with the British sergeants occurred when I was ten years old and it had a strange and dramatic effect on our family. First, when the sergeants were kidnapped, the British put our entire valley under curfew and then they cordoned us off and wouldn't let us leave.

But what happened next was much more memorable. After a few weeks of holding the sergeants in a secret prison, Etzel hung them from a citrus tree in one of the local orchards. The night after the murders was my uncle Moshe's wedding. He was marrying Dina Yisraeli, a local girl.

I WRITE:

*I*n those days, all the guests came with food. The feast was prepared from rationed morsels by so many separate hands. The night of the wedding, Dina wore a lavender dress someone had brought her from England. She had lilies in her dark blond hair, and a pearl-inlay brooch above her left breast. Moshe stomped on the glass. Everybody yelled, *Mazel Tov!* and drank to the young couple's health. Then the dancing began. Zohar, like a Middle Eastern Astaire on the dirt-packed dance floor, waltzed with Miriam and tangoed with the bride. Then he folded his arms across his barrel chest, squatted low to the earth, and kicked up his legs like a Cossack to the tune of Russian music that for several minutes made most of the guests forget they had ever emigrated.

Then the groom joined in. Moshe also squatted down low to the ground; the twins danced together, kicking up their legs with equal energy, both yelling Ha! Ha! Ha! as the crowd clapped and cheered them on. Next they stood face-to-face and wrapped their arms around each other's shoulders. They began to spin and spin, their foreheads touching, their legs kicking back up in the air, spinning, spinning.

Then it happened. The dancing had ended. Moshe and Zohar were wiping the sweat off their foreheads. People were beginning to sit down. But before even one bite of the precious food was eaten, Amnon Avishai rushed into the party and stopped the festivities with a two-fingered whistle. His news was this: the British army was hunting through all the surrounding orchards for the corpses of the two British soldiers. Once the bodies were found, they would burn the closest village. The bodies were not in Shachar, but Amnon Avishai, who had a "contact" (though no one asked who) had heard that Etzel was going to try to move the bodies into an innocent orchard and in this way slough off the guilt and sure burden of retribution from their own people.

Not all weddings are consummated in the usual way, especially in times of war, when ordinary rituals unravel. What happened was that everybody, including the bride and groom, left the party immediately. The men stood all night long and deep into morning in a protective ring around Shachar's orchards. Throughout the night the women took the uneaten wedding feast and walked from man to man, feeding them. And so they warded off the sins of their own kind.

*M*y FATHER WRITES:

The kidnapping and execution of the British sergeants was an important event in the history of the emergence of the state. Etzel's fearsome success was accomplished against a background of the disintegration of British rule. The hanging preceded the British pullout by almost exactly a year. It was all over the newspapers for weeks, and all anyone spoke about for a very long time. In our family, though, mention of the "two poor sergeants" was always a reference to Moshe and Dina's strange but beautiful wedding.

I WRITE:

*M*any, many years after that night, Zohar found the book in a store owned by a South African man who had lived with the Bedouin for a year and made him a cup of sweet black mud coffee as he leaned against a bookshelf and read. When he opened the book he saw it immediately. The photograph was toward the middle of the book. Its caption read: MAY 1947: TWO BRITISH SOLDIERS HANGING IN AN ORCHARD NEAR NETANYA. Zohar saw a half-moon in the upper-right quadrant of the sky. Ashen light. There was no fruit on the trees. Closer. Little black lines webbed through silver-gray bark. Wet, waxen leaves like so many green tongues. Closer. The head of the soldier on the right slumped sideways, his toes pointed down, hands bound behind his back, hips thrust leftward in a pose that reminded Zohar of the Christian messiah. The other soldier

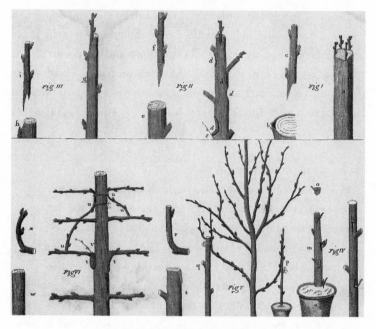

**GRAFTING AND INARCHING**

hung like a plumb line straight down from the tree. He had a mustache. His square chin was tucked into his neck, and his hands were tied primly in front of his crotch.

He turned to speak to the proprietor. But the man was busy with another customer, so Zohar looked down at the book. He wanted to say, "The hanging took place not in our village, but in one quite nearby." He wanted to say, "The night after the night of the hanging, Dina Yisraeli and my identical twin, Moshe, got married."

Now he remembered everything. How he and his brother had stood next to each other. Moshe by the double tree, Zohar just several trees over. They had spent the hours telling the stories of all the different times in their lives they were mistaken for each other. Moshe started, "When you and Miriam first moved to

Shachar and I came looking for you—when I got off the bus and asked for your house your neighbors thought"—Zohar interrupted—"that I had gone crazy, lost my mind. 'Imagine,' they said, 'the new neighbor is asking for his own address!' "

"Or the time I kissed Dvorah Ofek," said Moshe. Zohar smiled: "The time she kissed me back!" They kept this up for a while, before lapsing into silence broken only by the occasional kind words of the women coming toward them with smiles on their faces and heaping plates of wedding food.

Zohar had walked in circles around the grapefruit tree he was guarding. Then he had stopped and looked up at the sky. In the dark of the night the sergeants had seemed achingly anonymous to him but he had wanted to know: Which one was born on a dairy farm outside Oxford? Which one loved the taste of mangoes but hated how the roof of his mouth stung after he ate them? Which one had a mother who could speak four languages including Czech? Which one had a brother? Which one had a twin? Which one had a son? Which one, like Miriam and him, had borne an afflicted child? Fashioning his own details, Zohar had darned their blankness into something fiercely hard and personal.

Zohar knew all of his trees by heart. He had scratched the back of his neck and for the thousandth time that night, he surveyed the trees: the ones he could see, and the ones that were hidden. As he pictured each one, he had mouthed the names of the grafts, *rosh,* head, *temech,* support, *ayin,* eye. He saw which trees were the best bearers, which needed the most pampering, which shunned all but the slimmest attention, which were the oldest, the youngest, the sourest, the sweetest. And when he had finished the last tree, he found himself staring into the wounds of grafts he wished would not take. But the wish was in vain. The grafts too well executed. And as the sun began to rise over the valley, he knew that no matter where their bodies would eventually be found, the two British men had been grafted onto their trees forever.

**I TELL:**

*T*here are stories we tell ourselves over and over, all of our
lives. These stories, verbal vertebra, spine our minds—
help us stand, if not straight, then at least only a little bit
crooked. I know that war breeds mutant beasts. That night, a
frightened, two-headed dog had tried to bite itself in one of its own
necks. But it failed. Shachar wasn't burned. I also know that my
grandparents once stood in the sweetest of human walls. Sometimes, in my dreams I lean against this wall, brush my fingers into
its bodies, and read like braille the story of Dina Yisraeli and Moshe
Sepher standing in the uneven rooty earth by the double tree. Dina
wears her imported lavender dress and the lilies are still in her hair.
She stands in the uneaven rooty earth by the double tree and feeds
her new husband a cold potato knish. He eats the doughy pocket,
gently licks her fingers, and then reaches out and rubs her left nipple, just below the pearl brooch. She puts her right hand in
between his legs and squeezes lightly. For several seconds they stand
there, like this, the plate of knishes balanced in her open palm, far
below his right shoulder. For several minutes they think of leaving
the ring of their neighbors, of lying together, giving lust its first
night due. But soon Dina is moving on, feeding the next man in
line, asking him if he is cold, if she can bring him a sweater.

History tight-ropes toward family and I walk the strange soul
space in between. Jeremy, you ask me, "How far apart do people
have to stand to keep dead bodies out?" I say, "I don't know. Four or
five meters maybe, maybe more, maybe less."

## Chapter 10

## TO CONJURE THE TWIN

**MY FATHER WRITES:**

In 1948, on the seventeenth of Tamuz, during the Israeli War of
Independence, we lost Moshe. He died while fighting Iraqi
soldiers on a hill marked by the grave of a sheik. The hill was on
the outskirts of Petach Tikvah in a small place called Migdal
HaEmek, which means "Tower of the Valley." When he was
killed, Moshe had been married for less than a year. Dina, his
wife, his widow, was far away—in Haifa, visiting her sister, and
was informed only later. My father felt the bullet enter his twin's
back. I was just a little boy, but I remember that day too well.
My father had been out in the orchard when he came inside,
hunched over, with my mother, complaining of a terrible pain.
He knew that something had happened to his brother.

**I WRITE:**

Zohar could feel it. His skin was neither broken nor bleeding, but the wound was definitely there. Reaching his
right hand up over his left shoulder, he tried to press out
the hurt. As if maybe it were just a kink in the muscle
or a momentary misalignment of the bone. But the wound would
not go away; rather, as he pressed, it worsened, until it stabbed
and burned and blasted all through him. Falling to his knees,

Zohar let his hand come back around and slide onto the ground by his hip. Then he began to sob. Because the wound in his shoulder had neither logical source nor palpable manifestation.

After lying on the ground for several minutes, Zohar sat up, got to his feet and moved toward the house. He advanced in a lopsided shuffle, his right arm flung once more over his left shoulder, the palm of his hand pressing into the epicenter of the pain. "Moshe has been shot," he yelled to Miriam, as he emerged from the trees. Miriam, who was behind the house at the washstand, said nothing in response, but led her husband up the back porch stairs and into the little bedroom and then ran for the doctor. The doctor did not find anything wrong with the shoulder. He told Zohar, with calm voice and caring eyes, that no man can feel another's pain.

Miriam, sitting by the bed, stared at the floor. She did not see the doctor out. And when, just an hour later, Lazzie Friedman walked up the front path and into the house with the news of Moshe's death, she found herself listening not to the man in front of her, but to the messenger she could not see. That invisible invader who had been sent by some mad god or all-too-sane devil to hold horrible conversation with the muscular curve in the left side of her husband's back. Miriam reached out and held Zohar's head into her waist, her hands on his shoulders.

Lazzie told them that Moshe had died immediately. And that the bullet that killed him had entered just under the left clavicle. And that his body was safe in the bunker. And that he was a hero whom they all had loved. Lazzie cried as he spoke. Holding Zohar's sob-wracked body, Miriam wailed too.

When Lazzie Friedman left the house, Zohar got out of bed. He ran through the house, and out into the orchard where he retched onto a patch of knotty ground. His heaves were empty and painful. When the nausea passed, he looked up into the boughs and then back toward the house and thought, This is one death that will not be easily buried.

And Zohar was right. Moshe's funeral would be held the following day in the city of Petach Tikvah, the city whose name means the Opening of Hope. But the twin's death would not suffer earth to be laid upon it. A kind of phantom twinship remained adamantly above ground in Zohar's keeping for over fifty years. Moshe's death was like some queer fruit that neither ripened nor fell but remained pendant in stagnant unnatural grace on the tree.

❧

On the day that he was killed, Moshe had been planning to leave his unit for an hour and have lunch with his parents in Petach Tikvah. After he was informed of Moshe's death, Zohar immediately got out of bed and went to his parents' house to tell them the awful news. When Zohar arrived at Avra and Shimon's house, he walked up the front steps. Avra, who was waiting for Moshe to come to lunch, saw Zohar through the screen door. She thought that he was Moshe. When she called Moshe's name, Zohar fainted.

Avra opened the door and fell on top of her son who had fallen. When she landed, she found her face pressing into her son's chest and her knees twisted to the left of his hip. Her hands, which she had thrown out to break her fall, were firmly palming either side of his head. All in all it was not an awful fall. Just a strange one. The strangest thing about the fall, was, of course, that her son, whom she thought Moshe, had fallen in the first place.

"Moshe," she said nervously. "Moshe wake up." But he didn't wake up. Avra repeated, this time, yelling, "Moshe, wake up!" That was when she saw the subtle indentations on the side of Zohar's head. The indentations, tiny, almost unnoticeable, were really just flat spots no bigger than if a pinky finger had pressed there and left a mark. Zohar, the first twin born, had not emerged easily out of the womb. The doctor had pulled him out of her

with a pair of forceps. Avra, a new young mother, had first cursed
and cried over those marring spots, but then, rather quickly, she
grew to appreciate them, for the mechanical markings (which
were really so small that no one but a mother would notice them)
provided her with a sure tool of telling which boy was which. For
while her boys were always tricking the rest of the world, all she
ever had to do was look on the side of their heads. Moshe, the
second twin born, had slid easily out of her body after his
brother, and so his brow had stayed smooth.

Avra did not move. And Zohar's chest pounded up and down
underneath her. His was no faint of delicate repose, but seemed
a kind of eyes-closed struggle. It was a hot day and sweat covered
both of their bodies. The mother reached her hands to the side of
the son's head and touched lightly the spots that made him different from the one whom she had expected.

When Shimon came out of the orchard and round to the front
of the house and saw his wife lying almost astride their son, he
did not know what to think. He started to yell, "What are you
doing? What are you doing?" It was such an odd disturbing sight.
He started to run toward them, but was not in time to stop Avra
from pressing hard on the sides of Zohar's head. She was pressing not to cause her son pain, but to make those tiny forceps
spots disappear. No, of course this didn't make sense. One cannot just press and poke and refashion a skull. And if one could, to
press would only make the spots deeper. But Avra was not thinking of all this. Her logic consisted of the desperate panicked need
to conjure the twin named Moshe out of the twin named Zohar
between her palms. For she may have been a clumsy woman, but
she was also a very smart one. She had easily deciphered the
code: the forceps spots coupled with the faint, and with the fact
that Moshe was a commander in a war written like all wars, with
the blood-ink of so many beloved dead and wounded, equaled
the death of Moshe and the announcing presence of the uncon-
scious Zohar in his place.

Of course her pressing caused pain. And the son awoke with it, just as his father reached the front door, and bent down to push Avra's hands off Zohar's forehead.

All three huddled together on the front path, screaming and thrashing and sick with grief.

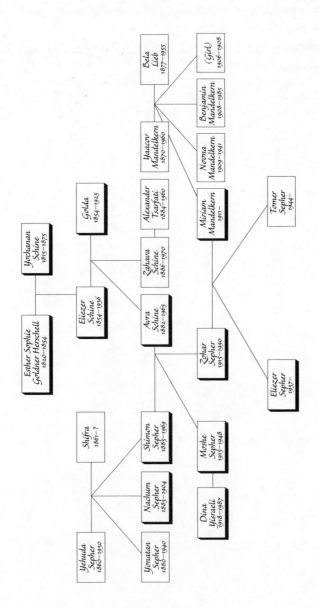

## Chapter 11

### UNDER BENT BOUGHS

I WRITE:

When Gavriel was five years old, they sent him to live among strangers. Doctors pointed to Tomer and then to Gabi and said, "What? You have one like this at home and one like that? Quickly, you must send the afflicted child away. Having Gabi at home will stunt the growth of your other children." Social workers said, "You must hold tight onto what is good in your lives. For the good of the older boys." Rabbis said, "*Lo Hametim Yehalelucha Ya.*" God, the dead cannot praise you. And even though they knew that Gabi was not dead but only trapped in a death-in-life, Miriam and Zohar listened to the doctors, and they listened to the social workers, and they listened to the rabbis. They sent Gabi far away. For the good of the other boys.

They tried to forget him. They pretended he did not exist. In time, he became buried. Buried like the roots of the trees, for, like roots, he pressed up into their lives unprovoked. And with their roots all tangled up, and under bent boughs, they sank into a theology of namelessness. They called their child nothing. They never again called on God. And they knew not what to call themselves anymore.

Zohar could not stop thinking about what they had done. Abandoning the child to the questionable care of strangers. Dozens of times he would climb on the Rudge and kick the engine into roaring, only to sit on the cycle and go nowhere because the road that led to Gabi was too winding, too treacherous, too far. "And anyway," he reasoned, "I am a stranger now too." Twinless and aching, he did not go to bring home his son. He just sat there on the roaring cycle, gripping the vibrating handlebars till his knuckles turned white. And he bit his own lips until almost drawing blood. Then he caught a glimpse in the chrome over the front wheel and panicked at the visage of his own distorted double. Dismounting the Rudge, Zohar was horrified for the millionth time since Moshe's death that a person could simply disappear. He felt queasy in his soul. And as he put the bike away, he cursed appearance and disappearance, he cursed strangers, and he cursed friends. And he did not go to rescue his son.

Miriam, too, was haunted by what they had done. She would turn her head and imagine, no, not imagine, but actually *see* her youngest son sitting in his hunched-over, rocking way on the floor of the bedroom. There was spittle on his fingers; he had a habit of licking his fingers and then shaking them in the air. He would do this over and over. Licking his fingers, shaking them. Sometimes he would hold a wet finger up to his eyes, not touching his eyes but getting the wet finger as close as he could, as if he could see something in the sticky little bead of water. Miriam would be ironing or darning, or putting something away in the drawers and would turn her head and see him thus, as she had seen him so many times before. She would wonder as she had wondered from the first time she had ever seen him do it, what it was that Gabi saw in the glob of his own spit. She would wonder if there was any meaning to the motion, or if it was just a spasm, a tick, a habit that meant nothing and was not a sign that her son was looking for something more. And she would go to him, her hands held out, but when she reached the spot where he had been sitting, there would be no Gabi on the floor and she would reel backward as if punched in the belly not only by his absence but by his persistent presence in her heart.

As the years went by they did what they could to help him disappear. First they took his photographs out of the family albums, hiding some of the pictures, tearing most of them up. Then they began to hide or throw out the documents that seemed to insist—despite the evidence—that such a person existed, had been born into their own house—the doctors' reports, the medical information, the copies of letters to this specialist and from that one. Then they began to mechanically take him out of their speech, inserting a pause where his name would have been. Over time, mechanics yielded to the fluency that comes with knowing something by heart. The pause disappeared and all that was left of Gabi was a shadow on their tongues.

And Miriam would continue to practice. She would stand on the back porch, plant her legs, and raise her arm. When she would throw, her aim would be slightly off, her strength not what it used to be. But she would keep throwing year after year, when no one was watching. She would throw placebos, mock grenades, soft rotten oranges, bright-green young lemons, hard as rocks. She would throw and throw, her arm coming up, fingers gripping something hard or mushy or invisible. Fingers gripping emissaries of recent aches and ancient grievances. And then letting them fly, one by one into the trees. Even though the British had long left. Even though the rest of the mothers had long since stopped gathering by the tool tree, and even though the babies they used for cover weren't babies anymore, but girls and boys who could grip their own stones and hold court over their own explosions. Miriam would throw, and occasionally hit her mark. Wiping her hands on her apron, she would walk inside the house to finish fixing dinner or washing the floors.

❧

As Eliezer and Tomer grew up they learned how to fill up the space where the other one once had been. They would stand up extra straight or puff out their chests to take up more room when they heard the emptiness in the house begin to roar. They became the best joke-tellers in the village, the best song-singers, storytellers, they were constantly trying to be amusing, to attract all attention so that attention would fall on nothing else. And so they grew up trying, with the clumsy grace of infant angels, to make the world smooth for the adults whom they loved, and for whom the roughness of everyday existence was obviously excruciating. When people asked, "How many sons have Zohar and Miriam?" it became easy, as the years passed, for people to look at the two boys or to think of them and answer with conviction "two." Easy, that is, except for sometimes when the sun shone over the valley at a certain unpredictable angle, and the outline of the third child suddenly appeared pale and queer-looking behind the body of his older brothers. But usually Gabi stayed hidden.

When enough time had passed, the phantom stopped appearing to Miriam, and Zohar no longer climbed on the Rudge and revved the engine, determined for brief seconds to rescue a boy who had once been his. Finally, the disappearance reached the shores of their souls where memory lives. Somehow, whether out of mercy or as a side effect of misery, or because this is what they had really intended all along, memory of this child almost completely eroded. They no longer held pictures in their heads of what life had been like in the years right after he was born. The pictures simply faded. Or rather, his image faded and everything else about that time, including the war, and Moshe's death, and the birth of the State, and the wars that followed, took on starker colors. And when years had turned to decades, and decades had turned into the kind of time that needs no counting, they knew with the finality that comes at graveside that he was no longer among them, even though there was no dead to bury and mourn.

❀

But there was a grave. A grave that floated around the house, through the bedrooms, the salon, landing in the kitchen on time for meals. While Eliezer and Tomer tried as hard as they could to pretend they didn't see it, Miriam and Zohar were wholly distracted by it. They saw themselves in the grave. Lying inside it, holding each other in a lovers' embrace. The grave drifted through the house like a tiny boat on a river of air. Sometimes the boys, while growing up, gangly, moving this way and that, would collide with the grave and suffer bruises. Other times they would just watch it pass over their heads and pretend that such a thing was actually normal. Pretend that every house in the village had a *kever*, a grave trapped within its walls.

The grave drifted through the house. And on the tombstone were inscribed the words neither Zohar nor Miriam ever said out loud, but yelled constantly, masking their words in other words, and those words in yet other words. No matter how they tried to disguise it, both knew the epitaph with which they were aching, "Here lie the Zohar and Miriam we might have been." Curled in a lovers' embrace. Suffering no affliction, no unspoken agony, no torment of conscience. "We might have been thus." No, they murmured no *kaddish* and they kindled no yearly flame, but each made a lifelong prayer out of the unspoken promise, "Never will we take him back."

When company came, everything was different. When company came, there was no grave in the house, there was no silence, no brothers or sons dead or otherwise disappeared. The presence of other people in the house provided the right shield. Miriam would put her hands on her hips and begin to tell a story. Zohar would smile widely and play the perfect host. They would be charming. Everybody loved them. They had so many friends. Nobody could tell a story like Miriam and no one was a better friend than Zohar. He would ask after your mother, your brother, he would call you by your old nickname, he took you seriously, he laughed at your jokes, and when he stood up and held out his hands to take yours in his own you would feel that the spirit of the land itself was giving you its warmest greeting. Zohar would smile at Miriam.

Food was more plentiful now. Miriam would serve coffee and apple cake. Noodle kugel and blintzes filled with potato or cheese puree. She served the confections, the coffee, the conversation. Zohar would smile at his wife, laugh lines radiating out from his eyes, then raise his head and look out over the orchard. In the distance he would spot the double tree, half blood orange, half mandarin dancy, and as he visualized its branches in his head, as he counted the small green fruit that were beginning to grow, he would feel for several seconds that he had tricked fate and found under the boughs of this blessed moment, sacred ground. But when the guests left the grave always floated in again.

I TELL:

*U*nder the boughs of the double tree all is quiet and the air is crisply fresh and cool. I press my head back against the trunk and stretch out my neck. I bend down and dig my fingers into the moist earth, tracing the roots of the tree swirling just under the surface of the ground. They are thick and curvy and I know that if I were to follow them, I would find not the center of the earth, but a spot close by where something crucial is in the making. I am very tired. I shut my eyes and think, We are not made of words: flesh and blood are not pages. We do not have a story, or tell a story even, but a story has us and tells us.

*The word* delete *comes from the Latin* "letum," *which means* "death" *and from which also comes the word* lethal. *The word* revise *comes from the Latin* "revidere" *which means* "to see again." *I would like to believe that somewhere in the past, in the realm of visionaries, scribes, and priests, there is some kind ancient who could scribble out passages with the power to hurt us, add those with the power to heal. I bend lower to the ground and with my fingers write a familiar name in the earth. It's not so much that I want to erase the past as that I want to create a present and a future different from all this. I want to delete our pain, revise our prose, until the story tells us all in a gentler manner.*

# Chapter 12

## THE STONES

MY FATHER WRITES:

Some of my favorite memories of life in Shachar are of my father and the *pardess*, the orchard. In the early days, we irrigated in open, small trenches. To see my father jumping from one row of trenches to another, diverting the water with his own legs in different directions, doing it in three rows at the same time— this was quite an experience. What a marvelous workhorse he was.

Soon after we moved to Shachar in the late 1930s, my father found mosaic stones under the soil of his newest grove. It was illegal not to report archaeological finds to the authorities. But my parents never reported the stones. They were afraid that if they knew about them, the archaeologists would come and dig up their orchard. So they kept the stones a secret.

I WRITE:

Zohar was watering the clementines. He stood in the trenches for several minutes, diverting the water with his legs. And then, just when he was going to jump to the mandarins, a single stone rose up from out of the soil. Bending down, he let it come to him. He let it rest on his palm and then he curled his fingers around it. Its cool cubic hardness told itself to his skin in a way that he knew was much older than the trees, much older than the water even. Shouting to the man at the end of the row to shut the *berez,* the spigot, Zohar put the stone in his pocket and told the man that they were done for the day. "The trees have had enough," he said, even though they really hadn't.

Later, that night, he came back out. He took the mosaic with him. The mosaic and a spade. He dug down to the roots of the tree. Soon he found it. A piece of ancient floor. The slender roots of the clementine tree were growing around the edges. He rubbed his fingers over the floor, counting the stones. Seventeen. He kept digging, careful not to cut any roots. On the other side of the tree, he found another piece. A little farther to the left he found a bit of a wall. And to the right, what seemed like a corner of a room. He stopped. The half-moon was high overhead. He wondered about the nature of permanent things. And he wondered if the fruit from the trees that grew atop the mosaics would take on the hard quality of stone—would their oranges be inedible? Or would they take on the secret sweetness of his find and prove more tasty than any regular harvest? Zohar reburied the stones except the single one that had led him to the others. This he put in his shirt pocket, and then went back into the house, to Miriam. That night they began what would be a lifelong game. A game they played at night in bed. Miriam would curl up close to her husband. She would wrap her arms around his middle, letting her breasts press into the hollow crook of his arm. She would start. She would hold the mosaic up in front of their faces and say, "Ancient Phoenicians lived here. A bustling community of homes and shops. Where our bed is, where we are lying, was maybe a bakery, or a spice stall."

Miriam would start again. She would say, "A Judean princess lived here. She had skin the color of golden wheat. This mosaic was part of the floor of her inner chamber. It was decorated with colorful images of beasts and birds with her beautiful face in the center, like a jewel. And the stones were scented with myrrh. Yes, myrrh, you can still smell it." She passed him the stone and Zohar sniffed. He would add his own sentences. He usually peopled his city with farmers and laborers. Canaanite farmers with bare feet and pouchy cheeks. Greek farmers in loose gray tunics and olive-leaf wreaths around their heads. Jewish farmers with familiar faces, no matter what century they hailed from.

They played the game. They told each other that their land had been lived on by the twelve tribes of Israel, and by some Eskimos even, who had lost their way. They told each other that Ezekiel had used the stones as a parking spot for his chariot once, when all the clouds were filled up. They played the game and they lived their lives. Zohar tended the trees, and Miriam tended the family. And the country around them was birthed, and the earth around them bled, and they, too, bled. Bled so badly that at times they played their lives while they lived the game, hungry all day for the hush of night, when stone became story and story became better plot than the one daylight offered.

❧

Zohar remembered those nights by the stories. And the seasons not by the changes in weather or politics or war, but by the words they exchanged. Words that defied curfew. Curfew: when the evenings were lonely and long, they got into bed early. Miriam held the stone; she was half sitting up, leaning against a light-blue pillow.

"Here lived a group of pioneers," she said. "They called their village Shachar, sunrise. This mosaic belonged to the floor of their bathhouse. They lived here for a long time. But besides this stone, they left no trace." Zohar reached out his hand and put it on Miriam's thigh. Squeezing softly, he nodded, and she continued. She said, "They called their village Shachar, which means dawn because the settling of the land was the dawn of their new day and they wanted to mark it. Shachar like a tide and like a today and like a tomorrow. They lived in a place named for a time of day and the longer they lived there, it seemed that time itself, whether out of gratitude or simple good nature, took on reciprocal qualities. Every second was a place they could plant in. And plant they did, until their original fifty *dunam* bore the fruit of double the distance. Their young trees took good root. And their oranges and lemons when they came tasted deliciously of some eras long gone and others yet to be, only imagined."

Miriam kept talking; as she spoke she looked out of the window, half smiling. She said, "They tried to explain this phenomenon. Some said that when the sun rose in Shachar its rays carried the special grace of continuous creation. Others subscribed to a more terrestrial magic, believing that the roots of their trees were watered from an underground spring whose source was yesterday's yesterday, and whose headwaters churned in a delta of a good tomorrow."

Zohar fell asleep wondering if it really could be like she said— as if by clearing away the rocks and draining the swampy malarial water one could actually find a way to alter time so that the history of the hills and valleys and the future, too, somehow expanded. Yes, they told their stories in bed at night. And during the day they planted their trees and their orchards bloomed. And when the oranges came in winter they climbed ladders and picked the fruit with care, always twisting the little stems, never pulling so as not to tear the skin. Then they would pack the harvest, cradling each orange like a baby, like bullion—the true bricks their country was being built on. Sometimes, though, the regular order of things seemed to reverse, and their country would begin crumbling back into the dust from which it was emerging, and their stories, the ones they only whispered, would begin telling them in loud voices.

Another night. It was Zohar's turn. He took the stone from the little table by the bed. As he closed his hands around it, he had the oddest feeling. All the things he and Miriam said to each other in bed, all the stories, he suddenly believed them. He opened his hands, and he looked at the stone. It was white and tan and mostly square, with tiny pits in one side and rough gray residue of mortar on the other. He began, "Here lived a wine-grower. This mosaic belonged to the decorative wall of his best press." He smiled, he was happy with that one. Then, he continued, "Here lived an encampment of itinerant Macedonian soldiers. And here"—he dramatically placed the cool stone on his wife's naked belly—"here lived a troupe of ancient Babylonian clowns." Miriam laughed and shimmied backward, away from his hands. The stone slid off her body. Zohar retrieved it from beside her right hip and then kissed her neck, her ears, her eyes. And the nights rose and the days set. And while they told and they touched, sometimes—out of grief, despair, and especially anger—with the stone as their witness and stories as their weapons, they tortured each other too.

Another night. Miriam began, "Here lived a child whose only story was a vacant stare. This mosaic was part of the room he was kept in." She looked over at Zohar and nodded, as if urging him to continue. But he refused. He turned on his side, away from her, as she went on. That night, Miriam talked for a very long time. She told her husband a story he already knew. He didn't know how he knew it, he just did. It was his as much as it was hers. Some stories are your flowers. Others are your meat and bread. This story was neither flowers nor meat nor bread. It was extra, and it was impossible. It was their shared cursed inheritance. As Miriam told on, Zohar wondered when the people she spoke of had lived there. Then, just before she finished speaking, he realized that they were living there now. Their existence was concurrent with Zohar and Miriam's own. A shadow family in a shadow grove with a shadow mosaic that floored all of their lives and forced them all together. Zohar looked at the stone in his wife's hand and wondered if the other people's trees, shadow or not, had had enough water.

❊

There were centuries in the soil and there were soldiers in their branches, and there were brothers missing and there were babies in all of their arms. Always Zohar was the brother, and sometimes Zohar and Miriam were both the warriors, and sometimes they were the parents, and sometimes they would look at each other and scream. Scream, loving the sunrise. Scream, hating the dawn. Once Zohar found himself by the clementine tree. He was trying to rebury the stones—not so that no one else would find the mosaics, but so that the stones would stop finding the two of them. The stones found them too often. Once Zohar dug down under the double tree, he dug down so deep. He did not know if he wanted to find stones, or if he wanted the earth there to be empty. The earth on which he had stood when his life became empty and the architecture of his every day was blasted to bits for good.

❊

Another night. Miriam passed the stone to Zohar, and he told her not about the people who lived on their plot before them, but about the trees living there now, with them. "This one is very serious," he said. "That one, the new grapefruit, has a sense of humor. This pummelo is proud. That shamouti, by the corner of the grove closest to the house, is very sweet and has a generous nature." When he finished Miriam looked at her husband and tried to giggle. But the laugh stuck in her throat, and as they lay there they heard each other tell another story. He heard her tell it. She heard him tell it. It went like this: "Here lived Zohar and Miriam, and their sons." That was all they said, all that could be said out loud.

They held the stone together, his hands over her hands, their hands over a bit of history so hard it defied the softness of their fingertips. They held the stone together in silence, thinking that in seventeen centuries someone digging into the earth of all this would find the remnants of their sorrows surely turned to stone, or if not stone then some other element just as hard and as perfectly resistant to the passage of time. And with these thoughts they climbed toward each other. Or maybe it was away. Far away.

The stone was in Zohar's dreams. In one dream the stone was in his hand, in between his thumb and fingers. He held it up in front of his eyes and looked into it. Its surface metamorphosed, swirled, became so shiny, so bright that it blinded him, giving him an excuse, at least temporarily, not to see. When he opened his eyes it had changed again, and was no longer shiny but was instead a radical shade of different. A different color, a different composition of matter that seemed less like stone and more like memory. He looked into it and saw its many faces. He saw the Judean princess reclining in her myrrh-scented chambers. He saw the Phoenicians and the farmers, the grape-growers, the clowns. He kept looking. Soon he saw the child of whom Miriam had spoken. Zohar saw the child's silence and suffering. He saw that the child was indeed in need of great strength, of great help, of great healing.

※

Sometimes when he couldn't sleep, Zohar would lie awake imagining that he was getting out of bed and walking out into the lower grove. He would crouch among the trees and begin digging a deep hole. In this hole he would lay his own stones, thus building their own century, their own seconds, endowing each tessera with a different tale and then burying them all. He would shut his eyes in the darkness and imagine that the stone he and Miriam traded back and forth in bed at night had originally been laid down like this. Not for shelter, no. But as the carrier of the histories of the people who had lived on their land before them.

In the morning when Zohar woke up, he would wonder if he had really gone out into the orchard. Or if the soil under his nails and on the knees of his work pants was just the residue of a real day's dreams.

Every so often they went out together, Miriam and Zohar, to the clementine tree in the lower grove where he had found the first stones. They didn't say much; they usually just sat there, on top of where they knew those original mosaics to still be. Early on, when he first found the stones, they had thought of looking for them elsewhere. Of looking under the grove of shamouti, under the pummelos, or under the old stand of lemons by the side of the house. But they never did. They didn't need to. In time they came to understand that the mosaics were not an isolated phenomenon. It became clear to them that underneath all of their groves, and yes, underneath the groves of their neighbors, and underneath the groves of their neighbors' neighbors was a secret city, a mapless ancient metropolis.

⚜

They played the game and they lived their lives. And in time, their lives became crowded with a crazy but endearing cast of characters. They had generations of farmers and merchants and clowns. They had Persians, Greeks, Babylonians, Macedonians, Gypsies, and Jews. They had children who taught them ancient games. They had hungry priests and thirsty prophets. Once they had a spy with a skin condition. They had the ghosts of foreign soldiers who sat slumped against the trunks of the trees telling them tales of mothers and lovers in languages they just barely knew. And all the while the scent of myrrh was everywhere, wafting up from the floor tiles, curling into their blankets.

"Yes, myrrh, you can still smell it." Miriam passed the stone to Zohar. She continued, "Here lived the Judean princess with wheat-golden skin." Soon she stopped talking, put her head to the pillow, and went to sleep. But Zohar couldn't sleep. He was awake and aware. He saw the faces of the princess and of the Phoenician farmers and of the grape-growers, the soldiers, the faces of children, and of parents and prophets. He closed his eyes and watched as the individual tesserae that made up their faces lost their distinctiveness. He watched as the birds and animals that swirled around the princess's head came to life, took flight, and began performing a delicate parade around the bedroom. Meanwhile the tiny lines on all of their faces faded until skin became smooth, eyes became bright, features no longer petrified assumed the air and expressions of the living.

Zohar lay for hours holding his sleeping wife in the darkness, listening to the night song of the birds, the purring of the beasts, while watching those other men, women, children who were simultaneously buried so deep underneath them and lying there right between them. He watched for a very long time. And then suddenly—perhaps he had looked away for a second—suddenly Zohar noticed that pieces were missing from all of their faces. There was a gap in the princess's right cheek; one of the foreign soldiers was missing half of his neck; a farmer had no left eye; a child, whom he recognized, had neither forehead nor fingers. These holes, these black, ugly marring holes disturbed the harmony of the whole. It destroyed them. Zohar watched sadly, as the lines of each individual tessera reemerged like some grotesque grid, first encaging their vitality and then destroying it.

He kept watching, but soon all were imperfect artifacts again. Unreal people with holes in their faces, lines in their skin, faded colors, and no real claim on life at all. The animals and birds also became stones again, falling with gravity out of the room. Miriam half-woke up. She looked at her husband with sleepy eyes and he whispered to her to go back to sleep. When Zohar finally fell asleep his dreams all revolved around the fact that something precious had been ruined, and that they, lying atop the wreckage, were either witnesses or accomplices to a crime buried so deep no one would take the time to excavate it, or investigate it, or even believe it had ever happened.

I TELL:

*J*eremy, when I was a little girl, my grandfather took me and *my brother out to the orchard. He showed us where to dig. We dug until we reached the mosaics. I will never forget taking those stones out of the cool soil, brushing them off, and then closing my palms around them. They were my first experience with buried treasure.*

*Whenever I go back to Shachar, I walk through the grove where the mosaics were once buried. After so many years of irrigation, the top layers of soil have been washed away, bringing the stones to the surface. They are almost everywhere now, decorating the soil with so many hard, white squares.*

# Part Four

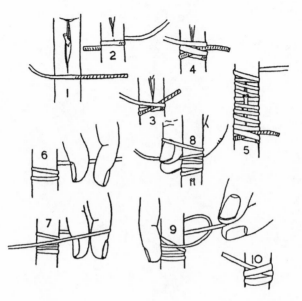

## Chapter 13

## ELIEZER, BY THE MANGO TREE

My FATHER WRITES:

The 1940s and early 1950s were excruciatingly difficult. At home in Palestine there were the constant terrors associated with the British and Arab conflicts. And although for a long time we did not really know what was going on in Europe, once the survivors began trickling in, there were constant revelations of unimaginable atrocities.

Despite all the troubles, we managed to get through these times. I think my mother is responsible for having helped our family through these times with her storytelling. Growing up I must have heard hundreds of her tales—she told stories about all sorts of things, but her best ones were about our own relatives.

I always loved the story she told concerning our ancestor the Chacham Tzvi HaAshkenazi. The Chacham Tzvi was my great-great-great-great-great-great-grandfather on my father's side. He was born in Vilna in 1660 and was a very important rabbi known throughout much of Europe. He suffered a horrible tragedy—his wife and daughter were killed by the Imperial army of Leopold I in Ofen. According to stories, the Chacham Tzvi never fully recovered from this loss.

Also, he was the center of a big controversy in his day. The controversy revolved around a *golem*. A golem is a supernatural

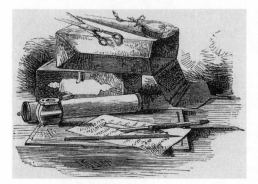

WRITING MATERIALS

creature conjured out of the earth by a rabbi in order to protect a Jewish community from danger. Supposedly, a golem has no soul. The Chacham Tzvi had a strong reason to believe in golems: according to folklore, his own grandfather, Elijah of Chelm, actually made a golem in his own day.

The Chacham Tzvi wrote a very famous opinion (responsa) concerning golems. He wrote that a golem would count in a *minyan*—that is, would count as an official member of a quorum of ten praying Jewish men. Many prominent rabbis were enraged! There was even talk of excommunicating the Chacham Tzvi for his heretical opinion. But this did not happen. He was also involved in a second rabbinic controversy. He was once asked if a chicken without a heart could be considered kosher. When he decided that yes, such a bird would be kosher, the decision made many people furious. A chicken without a heart? People wondered—how could such a creature be natural, let alone kosher? But despite the controversies, the Chacham Tzvi did have many followers and was considered a great teacher and scholar all of his life.

When my mother would tell me about the Chacham Tzvi, she would always add stories about golems. She knew many: "The Golem and the Bridegroom," "The Plot against the Golem," "The Golem of Prague," "The Golem and the Missing Maid." I don't know if she made them up, or if they were part of folklore, but she told them like adventure stories and I loved hearing them.

Sometimes I would go out to the neighbors' chicken coop and try to pick out the one without a heart and then imagine what it would taste like if I were to cook it and eat it. But I was even more interested in the golem story. I always wondered if the Chacham Tzvi himself had encountered a golem, and if he had, how he knew that the creature even wanted to pray?

THE CHACHAM TZVI'S OPINION:

> I shut my eyes and let the vision come to me. In the vision, a golem wandered into the synagogue just as a small community was gathering to pray. The golem was obviously not human—he moved in a stiff, unbalanced way, his face was pale as chalk, and his eyes were focused but empty. Yet there was no mistaking the creature's piety. He was wearing *tallis* and *tefillin*, a *kipah*, and as the community waited for ten men to make the *minyan*, he sat quietly in one of the pews, reading psalms. The community consisted of nine men. They were gathered on the other side of the room from the golem. They were standing with their arms folded, obviously refusing, in the company of the creature, to even begin to pray.

I WRITE:

Eliezer ran out of the back door, letting it slam. He ran down the porch steps and into the orchard. It was evening, nighttime almost, and he had just a little bit of time before he had to be in bed. He was in a hurry. He ran past the lemons, around to the right edge of the grove where there was a single mango tree that someone kind had once planted. The mangoes were ripe and the air around the tree was sweet and mangoey and Eliezer loved it. But he didn't come here to smell, not really, and not to eat of the fruit either. He looked around for the right stick, and when he found it, he cleared away some leaves from the ground and began to draw. A head, shoulders, two arms, two legs, feet, toes. He gave the figure eyes and a nose and mouth and ears. He even gave it a belly button and when he was sure no one was looking, he drew a penis, for good luck. Then he shut his eyes and began humming. He was a musical child and he was convinced, though he really had no reason to believe this, he was convinced that when God created the world there must have been some music playing. And now that he, too, was trying on a tiny scale to mimic the act of creation, he felt it was only appropriate that he hum. And hum, and hum some more. And so he hummed and hummed and stared at the figure and stood on one foot and then spit three times and then jumped on the other foot. But nothing worked; the figure on the ground remained a figure on the ground. He had chosen this spot for a purpose: since mangoes were his favorite food, Eliezer thought that it would be not only a kindness to the creature to conjure it from mango-scented ground, but also perhaps a temptation. He hoped that the golem would come to life, if not because he called it, then because the mangoes were calling out in a continuous fruity chorus of "come and get it." He knew that if he were a clump of earth and he had the opportunity to have a mouth and to eat a mango, he would listen to the humming of a little boy and beg all the molecules of his existence to turn from mud into man. And in his first moments on top of the ground, rather than in it, he would grab the fruit, take big bites, and then chew too quickly.

Eliezer apologized to the mango tree, and then he thanked the ground for trying its best, and then he left the orchard, walking very slowly back past the lemons, up the back porch steps, and into the kitchen where his mother berated him for having such dirty hands. That night, he decided that he had to do something regarding his technique. Obviously golems weren't for amateurs to conjure. He had heard that to make a golem one had to know the correct arrangement of the mysterious letters of one of God's more mysterious names. He wasn't in the habit of calling on God personally, let alone of contemplating the mysteries of the Divine Name. He had thought, with naïve enthusiasm, that his humming was some kind of approximation of God's name, or if not an approximation, then an endearment, or a nickname perhaps. But obviously he had been wrong. Eliezer had been trying for months now, and it never worked. For several minutes he wondered whether golems hated mangoes, and if maybe he should try the ground by another tree, a sweet orange perhaps, or maybe one of the lemons. Maybe golems liked sour fruit. But then he decided that if golems hated mangoes they weren't worth conjuring and so he would stick to his original plan.

And he would make it even better. In bed, he lay on his back with his hands behind his head and decided that he would study. Moonlight was dancing through the window decorating the ceiling in a lattice of excellent shadows. Eliezer asked the shadows to help him, to witness his solemn declaration. Sitting up in bed, he told himself and he told the shadows and he even told the moon—which he was sure was where all the golems lived when they were not living on the earth—he told them all that he would become a *Baal Shem*, a Master of the Name. He would learn the right combination of mysterious letters to conjure the creature from the ground.

THE CHACHAM TZVI'S OPINION:

But the vision did not stop there. The men continued to refuse to pray with the golem. They were making quite a fuss. Throwing their hands up, talking loudly, pointing angrily at the creature who every so often turned around and glanced meekly at the ruckus. Finally, the men walked out of the room and the creature, seeing that he was alone, stood up, and prayed all by himself. When the golem was finished, I followed him out of the door. I followed him out of air and into earth. I was filled with an awareness that I was visiting a muddy mystical realm. A realm of golem angels and archangels, golem prophets, golem priests. I saw underground seas part, fossilized bushes burst into flame, and roots become snakes and snakes become roots, and the earth open up to swallow more earth, and more earth rise up to build itself into a mountain so high that it threatened to reach not the sky but the ground that men walked on. And all around me were golems. Golems swathed in *tallitim,* golems praying, golems engaged in fierce theological arguments that they held by making signs with their hands. "I see," I said out loud. "Their prayers may be backward, but their God is backward too." And as I said this, I suddenly found myself back in my study, standing by the window, bound in my own *tefillin,* wrapped in my own *tallis,* saying my own prayers in a fervent forward whisper.

I WRITE:

He planned it all out. He would beg his parents to let him study with the rabbis in the nearby town. Of course they wouldn't be happy with his zeal, his newfound piety, but they would assent. After all, even though Zohar and Miriam themselves were not religious, there was religion in both their families, rabbis upon rabbis upon rabbis, reaching all the way back, they liked to joke, to King David himself. They would let Eliezer study as long as he agreed not to forgo his orchard work. He would agree. He would graft early in the morning and late at night. During the day he would study at the *yeshiva.* He would be an excellent student. The head of the *yeshiva* would even think Eliezer good enough to be a proper study companion for his own son. This would be a great honor. But Eliezer would not be looking for honors. He would want mostly to be left alone with the books that contained the mysteries he felt he needed. He would sneak back into the *yeshiva* at night, after he was done in the orchard, and open the books that were forbidden to one as young as he. The esoteric texts, the Kabbalah, the Book of Formation, would be his primary sources. He would pore over their pages, gleaning bits and pieces of the formulae he needed to make the golem, to conjure the mute creature from the ground. Eliezer took a deep breath. He heard a creaking noise from somewhere in the house, and a snoring, and then some more creaking, and meanwhile the wind outside had begun to blow. The shadows on the ceiling were waltzing about. Eliezer pulled the blankets closer around him.

He thanked the moon with its congregation of far-off golems for lighting up the night sky. And he told the shadows, which were slowly fading, that they were really excellent shadows, some of the best he had ever seen. And he finally fell asleep, dreaming not of golems but of mangoes, big red-green golden pulpy mangoes. He was biting into a mango; his hands and his face were becoming sticky and wet with its juice. And as he ate, in his head was a tune that sounded a lot like God to him. Yes, he thought, if I were in charge of things God would have song, not a name, and the names we call each other would also have notes. He thought about these things and fell asleep with a rather pious smile on his face, even though he wasn't the least bit religious.

THE CHACHAM TZVI'S OPINION:

**I opened my eyes and tried to block out the vision. I half roused myself from it, but soon it came back, with a vividness I recognized as a familiar harbinger of clarity. When I shut my eyes again, the golem was still there. The men were standing with their arms folded. It was clear that they were determined to prevent their prayers from mingling with the prayers of the conjured beast. The golem continued to sit in the front pew,**

**silently saying psalms. No sound came out of his
mouth, but his lips were moving.**

❧

**And then I began my work for the day. I left the golem
for last, choosing first to tackle easier issues. Sitting
down at my desk. Answering questions with questions,
questioning answers with answers. Of course, I would
have to say a scratch is the logical conclusion of an
itch, but an itch has its own esoteric ancestors in the
mysterious workings of the body and might therefore
be related, in some important but invisible way, to a
story the hand wants to tell to the skin. The logical
conclusion of this being my earlier opinion that the
story the hand wants to tell to the skin is mirrored,
obliquely, by the tale the skin wants to tell to the soul,
and by association, by the story the soul wants to tell
to the bones, specifically, the spine and the bones of
the head.**

I WRITE:

Eliezer was lying on the ground outside, by the mango
tree. Once again, it was evening; once again, he had
drawn the form of a human being in the earth, and now,
for the first time, he was trying something different. He thought
that maybe the earth needed some help, that maybe it wasn't
quite sure what he was asking of it and that maybe if it felt him
lying there, inside of the form, it would get the right idea. So he
put his fingers in the outline's fingers, his toes in the outline's
toes, and his head in the outline's head. He even tried to put his
own thoughts in the place where the golem's thoughts would be,
but he really had no idea what a golem's thoughts would be, so
he ended up thinking of rock candy, the sweet crystals stacked

like diamonds in his head. After all, he told himself, golems are probably mad about candy.

And so he lay like this for a very long time. In the distance he could hear branches breaking and he knew that his father was watering the lower orchard. He also knew that he was safe because this part of the grove wouldn't be watered again until the morning. Shutting his eyes, he tried to feel something. He thought that he would feel a rumbling underground. According to his own personal calculations, he had decided that there must be a golem waiting room in the center of the earth, somewhere in between the molten core and the deepest primordial layers. A waiting room where all the golems who have been mystically transported from their home on the moon were milling about, just waiting to be conjured. Yes, he whispered almost out loud, there must be a rumbling, a shifting, a tapping, maybe. So many golems in one place are probably rowdy, he thought, envisioning them knocking into each other playing golem games. But still Eliezer didn't feel anything. He pressed his elbows into the ground, he moved his head from side to side, put his ears to the earth and listened. But still, nothing. He shimmied like a puppy getting its belly scratched, trying through unorthodox but earnest movements to tell the ground and the golem within it that he was serious, that he really wanted it to come. But no mat-ter what he did there were no rumblings, no bumps, or pokes, or tapping on his back. The earth was quiet and unmystically smooth. So, on a final whim, Eliezer pulled down his pants and pressed his naked *tussik,* his bottom, into the ground thinking that maybe if he had some direct contact with the earth he would have a better chance of receiving some golem sign or crucial communication. The ground was cool on his backside, and a bit itchy too. But Eliezer persisted, and he even spread his fingers out wide in a four-fingered V for extra good luck like the priests did in their special high holiday blessing.

And still he inhabited the outline. When he shut his eyes he tried to feel it cleaving to him, tried to imagine the furrows he had drawn, rising up like little walls surrounding his skin. He wanted so much to feel it examining him, trying him on not quite for size, but for some other measurement not of human dimension. As he had kicked off his sandals, his bare toes were tickled by a gentle wind. And when he twitched his toes the furrows that had never really risen sunk back into the earth, and the earth sunk back into a cold slumber unadorned and undisturbed by either dreams or golems or the dreams of golems—"that is," Eliezer said to himself, "if golems have dreams at all." Eliezer exhaled loudly, and he continued to lie there for a long time with his naked behind pressed into the ground like an optimistic beacon or antenna. He lay there until his mother's voice began to call for him, until it was so dark that he couldn't make out the mangoes on the tree anymore, even though they were so close.

❧

Eliezer sat down and stared at the ground by the mango tree. He had drawn the figure and it was gazing up at him. The fruit was mostly gone now. He knew that he himself personally had eaten a million mangoes that season and he thanked the tree for its amazing bounty. Then he stared back at the ground and wondered if maybe he had been all wrong, and if maybe his *tussik* method had backfired. Maybe the golem was offended. Maybe the golem had actually heard him humming and had actually made the journey all the way from the moon to the waiting room and then up, up, up, from the molten core of the earth. And then, just as it was about to emerge, it had seen Eliezer's naked behind and had stopped in its tracks. Maybe the golem is bashful? he thought, sitting up straight, considering this new possible piece of information. Or maybe it thought I was being very impolite? But then Eliezer slumped back against the tree. He decided that a golem was probably not a modest creature because it came from the earth and the earth itself was completely naked—whoever heard of the ground wearing clothes? And also, any golem of his would have to understand that he wasn't being impolite; on the contrary, his bare backside was a form of greeting. He was trying his very best to say hello. So he tried the *tussik* method a few more times, until the weather began to change and when he decided that it was time for a different method, one more suitable for winter.

THE CHACHAM TZVI'S OPINION:

It is true. It is as they say. I am a deeply metaphorical man. I cannot but think that the rolled scrolls of parchment and ink are merely a way of making manifest the Torah of inner whispers. And I believe that metaphors occur commonly in nature. I tell my students, "Metaphors are wild creatures. They roam free, illustrating life with meaningful pictures." I tell them, "God is a poet, a painter, and the world speaks the language of image and art. We, like our forefather Yaacov, must learn to interpret the signs and wonders. And if we cannot interpret, then we must at least appreciate, holding out our open hands to catch raindrops we feel but don't see."

First a chicken. Now a golem. These questions were not intellectual exercises. They were more important than that. I felt, and still feel, that they were crucial. I sat back in my chair, pressed my fingers together at the tips. Crucial. Not because they dealt with matters of *kashrut* or synagogue propriety, but because of the way they entered my body. They way I suddenly needed them like sleep or like water. It was late afternoon. The men would be waiting. They would want an answer. I couldn't delay my opinion any longer.

But did they really want my answers? I believe many

unusual things. For example, I believe that when you marry, your soul grows a wife or a husband. A real and actual growth, like a bud or a branch. The logical extension of this belief is that when you have children, your soul grows a daughter, a son, and when you are born, your soul grows the sisters and brothers who make up your closest constellation. And so there is an inner family that corresponds to your outer family. I have argued this quite often. The two families reflect each other, like objects in a mirror. I rose from my chair. I wandered to the middle of the room, and I held up my hands to embrace my dead beloved. She was there, I swear she was, on my inside-out, my outside-in. In my garden of me. And this is why it hurts so much, I told myself. I tell myself over and over again. Because the mirrors don't match anymore and I am caught groping for yesterday's reflection.

A golem who prays. A chicken without a heart. I returned to my chair and sat still, feeling sure that these odd creatures and questions were obvious metaphors for my own mourning. And not only mine, I thought. No, of course, not only mine.

I sat and I sat. Finally, after hours of pondering, I took up the quill and wrote my responsa without flinching. I wrote thinking not of the chicken's absent heart nor of the golem's absent soul, but of the young wife and child in whose presence I still believe even though to others they are invisible.

Kosher? Of course!

To be counted? For sure!

I put forth my opinions and fought the opposition. I did not back down. And when they came asking for proof I was prepared. I stood up in front of them and with my right hand, I thumped the empty cavern of my chest where I knew my heart not to be, and with my left hand I tapped my skull, willfully conjuring the echo of all the emptiness inside.

I explained: "My friends, you ask if a chicken without a heart is kosher, and you ask if a golem, who everyone knows is a creature without a soul, can be counted in a *minyan*. In response, I tell you that I myself am a man with no heart, and that my soul too was taken from me long ago . . . long ago at Ofen. And yet, you pray with me, my friends. Eh, and yet you pray with me."

I wrote for a long time.

I wrote, "Somewhere buried in the earth is a golem Torah, but of course it is blank; the scrolls have no words."

I wrote, "Somewhere in heaven there is a kitchen where angels bake the sinews and souls of daughters and sisters and mothers and wives into the sinews and souls of sons and brothers and fathers and husbands— and in this way, the metaphysics of marriage and birth become manifest in the human body." When I was done writing, I said my prayers, and then undressed and climbed into bed. Soon I was saying the *Shema* in a fervent chant that testified with syllables of great sorrow not only as to the oneness of God but also as to the indivisibility of a family so violently rent. I lay awake for hours wondering, "Which was my heart— wife? Which was my soul—daughter? Or were they both, both?" When I finally fell asleep, both were both, and my arms were wrapped around my two beloveds.

# Chapter 14

## "A HEAT WAVE, LIVING FRUIT"

I WRITE:

The silence that was born with Gabi's disappearance did not come suddenly to their house as had the child's birth, or Moshe's death. Rather, it crept in on its belly, a slow-coming creature. No, the silence did not come to their house like the other tragedies had, with sudden shocks, violent collisions. It came slowly like a hot summer wind, a *sharav* from the desert singeing the words out of their mouths, a natural force that could not be reckoned with. Miriam answering a stranger's question, "Yes, two sons, sixteen and nine." And Eliezer marveling at how no one corrected her, but of course, neither did he or Tomer. The silence came blowing, airless and thick, blowing from out of their own lives, blowing between their eyes and bodies, blowing not to destroy but to protect. Protecting a mother, a father, two sons. And they prodded it along, doing what they could to facilitate its hot gusty journey.

This, Eliezer would always remember—standing in the doorway of the salon, watching his father taking the pictures out of the photo album. Eliezer knew which pictures Zohar was making disappear—he had no doubt that they were of Gabi. Looking back, Eliezer would always think it very strange that Zohar hadn't even tried to hide what he was doing. He hadn't taken the pictures out late one night when everyone was sleeping, or during the day when Eliezer was at school. He did it in the afternoon, and out in the open, in the middle of the house. Zohar looked up from his work and saw Eliezer staring at him. But Zohar didn't say anything to his son, he merely pushed out his lower lip and made a *tsk tsk* sound with his teeth. He stopped what he was doing, hands on the book, and stared at Eliezer. No words passed between them, but Eliezer understood completely. It was as if Zohar were saying, "We are colluding in all of this and that is part of the plan—to forget someone altogether, not by mistake, but on purpose." Zohar looked away, and then went back to work, inelegantly prying the pictures with their decorative wavy edges up from the black pages, and then not even bothering to rearrange the ones that were left to cover the spots where Gabi had been. All in all, it was a clumsy, rather quick operation.

Later on that night, when his parents were asleep, both of them snoring loudly, Eliezer crept into the salon and opened up the wooden cabinet where they kept the albums. He wasn't surprised at what he found. There was enough moonlight coming in through the windows to see that the albums were filled with empty spots that were darker than the rest of the pages. Darker because the photographs that had once been affixed there had protected the paper from the fading ravages of time or light. Eliezer put one palm over the emptiness and pressed down on it. On top of where the missing picture had been was a picture of himself, smiling with his mother. They were on a trip to the Dead Sea. He was eleven years old. His mother was smiling, too, and she was standing with her hands on her hips, looking out over the salty water. Eliezer pressed down on the emptiness with the heel of his hand. He pressed down hard, not at all concerned that his fingers were pressing into the photographs that had been left on the page, pressing down on his own skinny legs, pressing down his mother's face. He pressed down so hard that his wrist started to hurt. But he kept pressing; he was sure that he could

THE DEAD SEA NEAR MASADA

feel his hand pressing through to another dimension. There was no end to the dark space his hand was traveling. Finally, Eliezer stopped pressing down and the space snapped back up at him with a strange little thump.

He shut the album and when he went to put it away, he found the discarded pictures in an envelope at the back of the stack of books. Eliezer wasn't surprised that his father had left them there, for he had a feeling that he was supposed to find them. He flipped through them—there was the missing picture of Gabi and Tomer together on their mother's lap. And there was another one, Gabi wrapped in a baby blanket, and another, Gabi in his father's arms, another, Gabi in Eliezer's own lap, another, Zohar holding Gabi and Tomer with Eliezer draped over their father's shoulders. And when Eliezer closed the cabinet without returning these pictures, these tiny testaments to what had actually been, he knew that he was somehow both colluding with his parents and acting against them. He was stealing a piece of their silence—taking it without permission; but he was also adding to their silence, making it a darker shade of quiet, a more dangerous shade of missing, because now he, Eliezer, would be the only one who could see Gabi outside of his own soul. The only one who possessed visual evidence that such a son had actually existed. Eliezer slid the envelope into the waist of his pants and snuck into his room where he hid them in between the pages of a very big book that no one ever read but him.

Not long after this, Tomer, aged seven, developed a facial twitch. His right eye would jump open too widely, and then close too tightly over and over again. The psychologist whom Miriam took him to suggested that perhaps Tomer was afraid he would be sent away just like Gabi. Miriam and Zohar asked Eliezer to talk to Tomer about Gabi. "To see," they said, "if Tomer even remembers him." Eliezer decided to show Tomer the hidden pictures. At night, by the light of the moon streaming in their window, one by one they looked at the photographs together. Eliezer let Tomer hold the pictures while he pointed to Gabi's image and said, "Do you know who this is?" Tomer nodded, and held the pictures close to his face. When Tomer asked Eliezer what had happened to their little brother, Eliezer calmly said that Gabi was sick, and had to live in a hospital forever. "Forever?" Tomer asked. "Forever," Eliezer answered, covering his little brother's hands with his own. By the next morning, Tomer's facial tick had gone, never to return. And that was the one and only time Eliezer ever took the pictures out of his hiding place to show anyone else what Gabi had once looked like.

❧

The same year that Gabi was taken away, 1952, the year Eliezer was fifteen, President Chaim Weizmann died, and Prime Minister Ben-Gurion offered the Israeli presidency to Albert Einstein.

Einstein graciously declined, but the momentousness of this invitation was widely reported in the newspapers and was not lost on Eliezer. He knew that children from all over the world wrote letters to the great scientist. In school, his class had written letters asking Einstein about his childhood, and he had actually replied. Now Eliezer thought about writing to Einstein again. He wanted to write, "Dear Dr. Einstein, there must be a theorem, an absolute formula to explain what happened in our house." He wanted to write, "Dear Dr. Einstein, I know by now that ordinary math books won't contain it." He wanted to write, "Dear Dr. Einstein, is there something about your theory of relativity that can help us?" In the end he never sent the letter, he never even wrote the words down, perhaps because he was afraid the great scientist would have an answer, perhaps because he feared he would not. But in his head, Eliezer constructed many replies. Einstein would say, "My dear boy, your family is privileged to be part of a unique mathematical experiment." Or, "Relativity is yours, my son!" Or, "My child, I regret to tell you that math is not the field for you and you must instead devote yourself to philosophy and religion."

One night, as he was lying in bed, Eliezer told himself that there must be some way to explain what had happened to their family. He stared at the ceiling and tried to count himself to sleep but it didn't work. He was wide awake, even when he reached one thousand. He wondered about spiritual math, *gematria*, the kabbalistic system in which letters stand for numbers, and words have values, and through the matching of words with values disparate things get tied together. They were learning about it in school. He thought about when Gabi had been born. On the way home in the car with his uncle and father and cousin, night had been falling. Now, lying in the dark, Eliezer remembered that other darkness descending. And he counted up the night and counted up the stars and counted up the hospital. He counted up mother and he counted up father and he counted up uncle and brother, baby, new, our, all right. He almost said the word brother, *ach*, out loud. It did not surprise him at all that the *gematria* for "our brother," *achinoo*, equaled the *gematria* for "night," *lilah*. Eliezer had great faith in the goodness of numbers, but for the first time in his young life, he hoped that they were wrong.

The next day, in the tiny village library, Eliezer found a book of *gematria* that translated almost every word in the Bible into numbers, breaking the verses down into words that matched other words, not in meaning, but in value. He tried to add up all of their names and match the total sum with sentences in the Bible that were descriptions of disasters or harbingers of disasters to come. But in the end, this approach didn't work. Nothing matched; the sums were always radically different. Still Eliezer wanted to believe that there was an equation, and that if he were to solve it, he would have in his hands the right tools to use should the future dare to present him with a similar set of circumstances that threatened, on the same terrible scale, not to work out.

He tried another technique, once again translating their lives into numbers. But instead of leaving them as numbers, he then translated the numbers back into something else—another word or sentence with an equivalent value. Using this method, he would make the entire story disappear into a column of dry ones and twos and threes, fours, fives, sixes, and sevens that, when deciphered correctly, could stand for their story, but could just as easily stand for someone else's, or stand for nothing at all.

It's not that he wanted to do away with the numbers. He loved them intensely. He said them over and over again, staring at them, scratching their slim uncomplicated bodies with a stick into the earth. They never rebuked him. They never made fun of him. Then never stayed away, or looked at him strangely, or refused to look at him at all, averting their eyes, afraid to say the wrong thing. The numbers had nothing to say anyway except for the occasional gossiping about adding or subtracting or some other dry mathematical operation. The numbers couldn't hurt him. They couldn't yell, they couldn't shriek, and they couldn't fight. But when he tired of them, Eliezer could turn them into living words again. Not living words that rebuked. Living words that stood not for his family's tragedy but for random things in a random world of nonsensical juxtapositions. And yet, the juxtapositions all had the same value. And so the two lists were somehow equal. He wrote in four columns:

| | | | |
|---|---|---|---|
| "She had conceived" | *Harta* | 610 | They ran far away (*Ratzu rahok*) |
| "And there was born" | *Vayivaled* | 56 | He donated (*Nidev*) |
| "My brother" | *Achi* | 19 | Enemy (*Oyev*) |
| "But the hands" | *Aval hayadayim* | 102 | Deer (*Tzvi*) |
| "And the soul" | *Vehanefesh* | 441 | They joked around (*Hitlu*) |
| "Were afflicted" | *Hakuh* | 37 | The heart (*Halev*) |
| "And she nursed him" | *Vatenikehu* | 577 | Hard heel (*Akev kasheh*) |
| "Until five years old" | *Ad gil hamesh* | 465 | The support root (*Hatemech*) |
| "They quarreled" | *Hem ravoo* | 253 | Carpenter (*Nagar*) |
| "And the father's brother" | *Veach haav* | 23 | Pain (*Ke-ev*) |
| "Was killed" | *Neherag* | 258 | He snored (*Nahar*) |
| "Mourning" | *Evel* | 33 | A wave (*Gal*) |
| "The mother and the father" | *Haem Vehaav* | 60 | He will go (*Yelech*) |
| "Quarreled some more" | *Ravu od ktzat* | 878 | A salty rainbow (*Keshet melach*) |
| "Mourning and quarreling" | *Evel umerivot* | 697 | You will spread (*Tfasri*) |
| "Until they cast him off" | *Ad shehotziu oto mehabayit* | 1362 | In favor of drinking drugs (*Be-ad lishtot samim*) |
| "They fought some more." | *Vhem himshichu lariv* | 674 | He taught a lie (*Limed sheker*) |
| "And some more." | *Veod* | 86 | To us (*Lanu*) |
| "Now, there is a scar" | *Achshav, yesh tzaleket* | 1326 | Eli sat under the tree (*Eli yashav tachat haetz*) |
| "Through our generations." | *Bechol dorotaynu* | 734 | The fruit of the orchard is pretty (*Pri hapardes yafe*) |
| "A scar" | *Tzaleket* | 620 | Crown (*Keter*) |
| "In secret" | *Besod* | 72 | Dialect (*Niv*) |
| "I will hide it." | *Ani achbi et zeh* | 496 | Finished chapter (*Perek muchan*) |
| "But it says, 'Remember me.'" | *Aval hoo omer, 'zichruni'* | 585 | Sack of coffee (*Sak kafeh*) |

| | | | |
|---|---|---|---|
| "But I say, 'I lie.'" | *Aval ani omer sheani meshaker* | 1342 | And they walked slowly on the city walls (*Vehen halchu le-at al hahomot shel ha-ir*) |
| "He is forgotten." | *Hu nishkach* | 380 | A wooden shed (*Tzrif*) |
| "Of memory" | *Mehazikaron* | 338 | Weak (*Halash*) |
| "I was afraid." | *Pachadeti* | 502 | A heat wave (*Sharav*) |
| "And I am still afraid." | *Veani adayin poched* | 299 | Living fruit (*Pri chai*) |
| "He was afflicted." | *Hu hayah mukeh* | 103 | Was erased (*Nimchah*) |

He read the list of equivalencies over and over again. "Carpenter, Pain, He snored, A wave." He would run through the lanes of the orchard at night, saying the words over and over again—one word for each pounding stride: "Carpenter, Pain, He snored, A wave." It seemed to Eliezer that even the darkness took delight in their lack of meaning. They were a kind of poem. They were a secret communiqué about something distant and ridiculous. "Deer, They joked around, The heart, Hard heel." The words felt comfortable on his tongue, more comfortable than any words had ever felt on his tongue before. He thought that the way the words casually rubbed up against each other, without worrying about who was who or what was what was courageous. And he wanted to come from the planet where this alternate list was the real story. He stopped in the middle of a small clearing of lemons and twirled round and round with his hands held out, palms up, eyes open to the stars. "A wooden shed, weak, A heat wave, Living fruit!" It was an epic, it was a comedy, it was an epic comedy, and he wanted so much to come from the country where such things were spoken. He twirled around and around. "He will go, A salty rainbow!" He wanted to come from the poem's own planet. Then the other side of existence—the one that spoke the language that made his tongue heavy and life seem at times devoid of happiness or light, would be the nonsensical one; this life they were now living would simply be a list of random vocabulary that no one cared about because it made no sense.

❧

Eliezer did not give up trying to conjure the golem. Sometimes he got frustrated though, and with his foot, blotted out the figure he had so carefully drawn. He would kick the lines away, and then he would kick the ground some more until nothing was left but smears where a soul might have been, but then he reminded himself that golems weren't supposed to have souls. He decided that in his own sacred text, in his personal Book of Formation, golems would not only have souls but would also tell good jokes. His golem would tell jokes like a professional. He kept kicking at the outline until it was almost invisible. And then he stood back and surveyed his work. He was angry at himself, angry at the golem. Angry at the thought that the empty outline could ever be filled in.

And yet, he kept trying. After work in the evening, or late, in the middle of the night when everyone else was long asleep, he would slip out of the house and run into the orchard. When he got to the mango tree he cleared away the leaves on the ground, he kicked away shriveled-up rotten lemons whose peels were turning white with mold. Then he would find a good stick and crouch down. Holding the stick like a pencil he drew the figure of a man. He had not become religious, he had not studied in the *yeshiva*, he had not stayed up nights searching secretly in the Book of Formation for the proper arrangement of the letters of the Name. And no matter how good he was at math, the more he learned, the more he feared that there were no numbers—real or imaginary—that could give him the sum he needed. But he drew the figure anyway and tried anyway, shutting his eyes and whispering any one of a number of secret incantations that he imagined would do the trick. He walked the seven circles, though. This was easy enough. And as he walked he bid fire and water and earth and air to come forth and animate his creation. But this time, like all the other times, nothing happened. And Eliezer was disappointed that no golem rose up to keep him company, save the village, or do odd jobs.

And when the days were dark and nights were violently cold in the old stone house, Eliezer would wonder if perhaps he had it all wrong. Maybe the creature had conjured *them all* up. Maybe he and Tomer, his mother and his father, and his missing little brother were the golem's golem, if there was such a thing. But what wasn't entirely clear to Eliezer was why. For what purpose had the golem created them? For protection? From what? For revenge? From whom? The only thing he could come up with was that all the screaming and yelling that his parents did served to frighten someone away. The golem's enemies perhaps, evil spirits who wouldn't dare come near because—everyone knows— evil spirits are scared of loud noises. But then he would get very confused, because everyone knows that the golem is a mute creature, and if they were golems, too, then what were all these words doing coming out of their mouths? It didn't make sense. If we are the golem's golem, he thought, then are we really speaking when we think we are speaking? Are my parents really yelling when they think they are yelling? Or are we really all silent?

## Chapter 15

# THE CODE OF VILLAGE BOYHOOD

**I WRITE:**

*T*he seasons changed abruptly in Shachar. While in the rest of the valley it seemed that autumn gave way to winter reluctantly, in Shachar the cold just barged in. Even the city next door always seemed warmer, although there was no scientific evidence to support this fact. The villagers saw their breath in bed at night, little white puffs floating out of their mouths, and they curled closer to their husbands and wives; children slept with parents too, and whole families became used to dreaming similar dreams, a phenomenon no one could explain but all attributed to the very cold weather and the way it made them embrace each other somewhat more tightly than they normally would have.

Eliezer shifted his weight from foot to foot, and tried to keep warm by breathing on his own cupped hands. But he didn't really mind the cold. He had spent the night with his friends, and they, as a rule, were not so affected by the weather. For them, the coming of the cold meant the coming of the fruit, and for them, this was cause for celebration. But that was at the beginning of the evening, and now, at the end of it, Eliezer could not feel the celebration inside him. Instead, as he stood behind his house, watching his parents' dark sleeping window, he felt afraid.

Eliezer tried to be as quiet as he could as he contemplated

walking up the back porch stairs and opening the door and sneaking into his bedroom. But he knew that even his thoughts were too loud, and that his footsteps would be even louder, and that consequently he was doomed. His father would wake up. And so Eliezer didn't go into the house. He just stood there behind it. It was very, very late, probably close to three a.m. As he stood there, shifting his feet, watching his breath leave his mouth in little clouds, he thought back to the events of the night that had brought him here.

They were a group of boys, bored on an early winter's late night. It was already far past midnight when they had gathered. They had all stolen out of their houses and met at the bus station behind the bomb shelter. This is where they came when the village was sleeping. There was Eliezer and his friend Yoni who had freckles and could kick a ball incredibly far. Eliezer had known Yoni almost since they were babies. There was Moti Peleg whose family had moved in just three years ago. He was a skinny boy who didn't run very fast but usually won when they played cards. There was Micky Anderson whose parents were American, and there was Amos, who had huge blue eyes and dark skin and who was the most "mature" among them—Amos's voice was changing and he even had some facial hair.

They hadn't been at the bus stop for more than five minutes. Usually they weren't there for long. Because every twenty-five minutes or so the village watchman would come by and they would have to scatter. Or sometimes they would just stay in place, and the father of a friend or someone's own older brother would just nod at them and let them be.

But tonight they had no plans just to stay at the bus stop. Amos turned to Micky and said, "Happy times?" Micky ignored him for a minute and then shook his head and said, "Time to do what we do best." Eliezer nodded. Moti sighed and looked down at his feet. The bus stop had a metal frame, and Yoni was swinging by one of the bars that defined its roof. He was swooshing his body through the air like a gymnast. Yoni swung back and forth a couple of times and then dropped down to the sandy ground with a hollow, heavy thud. "What we do best," Yoni repeated. Then slowly, with a lackadaisical shrug and a look on his face that seemed like a cross between a question and a grimace, Micky held out pieces of straw to the small crowd. The ends were in his fist. One by one, all except for Eliezer chose the lots.

In the unwritten Code of the Orchard—which all of them, Eliezer, Moti, Micky, Amos, and Yoni—knew by heart, stealing fruit was an almost capital offense. Their fathers, the *pardesanim*, the orchard men, treated their groves like favored children, and each orange, each mango, each lemon, each grapefruit, was a precious prize that would lift not only their individual lives out of the sand, but also their whole country out of an epoch that should have been different than what it was. Stealing fruit was an almost capital offense. And yet, they were about to do it. Because in the unwritten Code of Village Boyhood, stealing fruit was a necessary delight. They couldn't resist. The codes clashed. All of the boys did it once they turned twelve or thirteen; it was a regular part of their adolescent play, their collective adventure. They even termed the night one of them first stole fruit as his "bar mitzvah." Honors were bestowed upon the taker of the biggest haul, the boy who executed the most daring escape, the boy who made off with the ripest bounty or a bounty from a new tree, a rare variety. They all knew which trees ripened first, Tzimmie's mango, Mordechai's clementine, Smilansky's apricot, Goldschmidt's blood orange. They could tell you exactly where the trees were, in what grove, in what quadrant, and what row; they could tell you which side of the tree tasted better, the north or the south; they could probably tell you the owner's habits—who slept soundly, who was given to the occasional midnight ramble, who had a vicious dog, who didn't, who would notice if a single fruit were missing, who wouldn't notice if his own nose were missing. Older boys passed on the information to their younger brothers, and younger brothers hero-worshiped the older boys whose exploits they told and retold. How Micky had outrun the German shepherd, one ripe grapefruit in each hand, how Yoni had run right into Goldschmidt in the middle of a particularly ripe summer night, how Yoni had thrown the fruits high up into the air and then made a dash for it, knowing full well that Goldschmidt, who loved his fruit like babies, would have to catch the grapefruits rather than chase him, and that by the time they landed either on the earth with a thud or in his grasping, old-man palms, Yoni would be far away, racing across other orchards, so many denials and alibis already sprouting on his tongue. They told these stories to each other as they bit into pieces of fresh fruit that no one had tasted in an entire year, the juice running down their faces, their fingers so sticky. There was magic in these first stolen bites. It was as if the fruit were created anew each year, each season, especially created anew for them by a God who loved boys and mischief.

Smilansky was a particularly favorite target, even though the boys were terrified of him. He was big Lithuanian with huge hands and a fat, bulbous nose and eyes that were as gray as the winter ocean. His nose, which was as long as it was fat, looked remarkably like a cucumber for which reason they sometimes referred to him in code as "Mr. Salad." Smilansky was a favorite target because of his prized apricot trees. There weren't many other apricots in the village, and certainly none like Smilansky's, which were as perfect as they were unusual. An apricot is a fruit whose appeal lies in the way it has both a sour taste and a sweet taste. In regular apricots, the sweet taste wraps around the sour—the tongue delights in the fleshy sugar and then, lulled into a false sense of security, the sour infiltrates the mouth, biting back for having been bitten. But Smilansky's apricots were different. In his fruit, the sour wrapped around the sweet, giving the tongue first a tarty challenge and then an ethereal mellow reward for having made it past the outer orbit. Smilansky's apricots were famous as far away as Haifa, where his sister lived and where a sister grove to his own bore perfect fruit on exactly the same day and minute. Smilansky knew that his apricots were a target, and so he usually checked on them once or twice a night from the time they were almost ripe until they had made it safely through the harvest.

On this particular night, in this particular month, in this particular year, when the apricots had just turned from too-hard into perfectly delicious, the boys had elected Moti Peleg to steal the apricots from Mr. Salad's tree. They had drawn lots, and Moti had drawn the short stick. When he drew the losing lot, he rose stoically from his seat and bit his protruding lower lip, and looked at each one of them as if they were personally responsible for his imminent execution. But he was a good sport, and he left the group silently, determined to perform his duties honestly, even if they were to be his last.

Eliezer, Yoni, Micky, and Amos left just after him. They ran the other way, along the shore path, around the periphery of the village, and in the back way, up the hill, past the chicken coops, and straight to the prize tree in Smilansky's orchard. They knew that Smilansky wasn't there that night. This was their secret information. He was in Haifa, visiting his sick sister whom he loved even more than he loved his apricots. Eliezer pumped his arms up and down as he ran. They ran in a tiny clump, almost attached to each other, bumping into each other, their arms on each other's elbows, shoulders, so that the speed of one carried the other and their heaving but muffled breaths, though seemingly taken from separate lungs, were all invigorated with the same air of excitement. Eliezer looked at Micky and smiled. Yoni let out a loud guffaw. And they all almost started laughing, but they swallowed their laughter and just kept running. "Happy times," someone said. "Happy times," they all echoed. It was true, they had rigged the lots. Moti had been doomed from the very moment they had congregated. Micky had actually done it. Though blessed with an honest smile, he was a natural-born master of deceit, a font of tricks, jokes, and schemes. The rest of them weren't quite sure how he had done it. He told them that he had gotten his "technique for making the straw seem different" out of a book of magic tricks he had received for his last birthday. But they weren't so interested in his "technique" as in his skill. Could he actually do it? He could, and he did, and Moti picked the short straw and now the rest of the boys flew through the village over the beach. Ordinarily, they could easily outrun Moti, but since they had to go the back way, which was significantly longer, they had to run as fast as they could. When they got to the beautiful apricots they just stood there for a few seconds. The fruit was perfectly ripe and it dotted the dark green leaves like precious diamonds placed there just for them. Yoni reached up a hand to touch one, and he would have picked it, but they heard Moti clumsily coming through the grove, sticks snapping, his footsteps heavy, even though he was so light. Moti had taken extra long, not because he was afraid (even though he was) but because he had chosen to execute his mission scientifically, sneaking from tree to tree, and peeking out and then running to another clump and peeking out again, thus advancing on the target with supreme stealth. He had also taken a moment to camouflage himself. He had smeared his face and arms with mud, and had tied a rather large branch of a clementine tree to his back so its foliage stuck up over his head and made him look both suspicious and ridiculous. The other boys saw him coming and had to stifle their laughter in their hands. They were hiding in the surrounding trees and they were waiting for the perfect second. They meant to scare Moti before he had taken any fruit. But they weren't quick enough—or Moti, whom they had always thought slow, was fast in this one stealthy moment. His white hand shot out through the dark night, and he quickly picked three perfect apricots from the perfect tree. And at that moment they jumped out at him, barking and howling and yelling like an entire zoo full of animals vicious and untamable.

Moti shrieked, dropped the fruit, and started running. He ran in a zigzag fashion, in and out of the rows, down to the shore path, his white skin shining in the moonlight, his heavy steps echoing all over the valley, disturbing light sleepers, waking up curious and angry dogs. They stopped following him when he reached the sand. The clementine branch tied around his waist had come loose and was bobbing up and down with his strides, eventually falling in between his legs, but he didn't even stop to free it. He ran over it, almost tripping on the branch until it just fell off.

Moti never once turned back to see just who was behind him, he just kept running, zigzagging even on the shore. When he finally made it back to the hideout, he had peed his own pants, was drenched with sweat so the dirt on his face was melting in brown smeary rivulets over his eyes, and his chest was heaving. "Smilansky . . . with a gun . . . he had a gun . . . he was there waiting for me . . . and he chased me all the way to the ocean!" When they asked him how he had escaped, how he had avoided not only the big man's huge hands, but also the gun, the gun, Moti told them about his strategy, about running in serpentine fashion. "That way, when he shot at me," he explained, "and he did shoot at me, several times at least, the bullets didn't know where I was. I was quick, he couldn't find me, and then, when he got close, I threw myself into a *duna,* a dune, and I burrowed on the other side of the sand, where he couldn't see me." Moti stood up straight and smiled now as he was particularly proud of this accomplishment. All the boys listened with solemn faces while holding their noses because Moti smelled. And then they burst into laughter, and jumped up and ran in serpentine fashion around each other, and then they flung themselves into each other, calling each other a *duna,* their bodies crashing into each other like waves. Nobody had the heart to tell Moti Peleg that Smilansky wasn't even in the village that night. But they couldn't stop laughing. They laughed so hard that their eyes hurt and their lungs began to tingle. Moti laughed, too, even though he thought he would be out of breath forever.

Eventually the boys dispersed. Each made his way to his parents' house. Eliezer walked with Yoni to the corner of their road. And then Yoni turned left and Eliezer walked the rest of the way alone. When he got there, he didn't go up the front walk, but scooted around the back, through the orchard, around the little room where the new tenant was sleeping. He meant to go up the back porch stairs and in through the kitchen but before he climbed the stairs he heard a noise. Eliezer heard something inside the house, footsteps maybe, or a particularly loud creaking of furniture—perhaps his parents rolling over in their bed? The noise scared him. He felt a familiar pang of terror. What if his father had woken up? Eliezer shut his eyes and saw the three perfect apricots orangy pink on the ground, their perfect flesh bruised. In the afternoon of the next day, Smilansky would return from visiting his sick sister in Haifa, he would find the apricots on the ground, and see their footprints in the earth, who knows, maybe he would even follow their prints to the ocean, and find the very dune behind which the scared ghost of Moti Peleg was probably still hiding. Yes, they would be caught, or at least suspected. Even though nothing had actually been taken, and even though he himself had not shaken the apricots down, Eliezer knew that he was in trouble. He sighed out loud. And he cracked his knuckles, folding his fingers backward against his own face.

Eliezer looked toward his parents' dark window. He knew that if he could just sit down with his father, not as a son but as a friend, that if he could sit down with him and tell him the story, tell him how Moti Peleg had thrown himself into a *duna*, how they had raced back in front of him, and how Moti had peed himself and how he had lied, telling them that Eitan Smilansky had pounced out of the trees with a gun, Zohar's eyes would disappear and his cheeks would grow red and he would laugh so hard, because the story really was so very funny. Skinny Moti Peleg throwing himself into a dune. But Eliezer couldn't just sit down with his father. There would be no laughter over this. Because Zohar's anger didn't make allowances for ordinary bouts of boyhood mischief. Because Zohar's anger was an extreme anger, occupying not the visible or audible range of perception but the too-visible, the ultra-audible, the regions of sound and sight that burned the eyes' lenses and popped the ears' drums. Zohar had an anger that was terrifying because it was extreme. And perhaps it was terrifying also because on the other side of his soul lay a peace and a calm, a joy of life, an almost kingly kindness and grandeur that made everyone love this man, and made his son love him too, love him so much that Eliezer saw the anger not as an organic part of his father's personality, but as a kind of invader or a thief who stole the best moments of their lives.

Now, Eliezer felt that he had to hide from his father. Zohar would immediately suspect that Eliezer had been out with the boys and that they had stolen something. Eliezer never stole anything. He was too scared. He didn't even bother to draw lots with the other boys—and they didn't make him because they were even more afraid of Zohar than he was. All of the boys liked Eliezer and none of them wanted to incur the wrath of this particular father. No, Eliezer couldn't go back into the house. Even though he hadn't really done anything. All he had done was to run wild and happy through a quiet night that had seemed to need some noise, some good waking up. Eliezer held his breath. Once again, a creaking noise came out of somewhere inside the house. He shut his eyes and saw the three apricots again, not on the ground, but in his own hands. Sour wrapped around sweet. Eliezer took one last look at his parents' window before he turned around, and ran far into the fields to spend the night.

# Chapter 16

# IN THE GOLEM'S GARDEN

My FATHER WRITES:

When I was eighteen, I began my service in the Israeli army. After my basic training I was assigned to Intelligence and served mostly in the north, near the Sea of Galilee. In the army, I worked primarily as a statistician. It was my job to help make tactical field operations safer and more efficient by providing a statistical analysis of battlefield strategies.

I WRITE:

It was strange to be home, not as the boy he had been just a few months ago, but as a soldier with sore muscles and an appetite he couldn't sate. It was his first leave after being drafted into the army. He had been helping his mother in the kitchen when she had shooed him out of the house. She said, "You must rest. Go, go find your friends, or take a walk." They both knew that all of his friends were away in the army. But still Eliezer appreciated his mother's pampering. He gave her a kiss on her damp face, and walked out the back porch door. He walked down the steps and sat on a big rock at the edge of the sticker field and begin to throw little pebbles into the sand. In the army, for the past six weeks, he had felt different. During basic training, he would be doing push-ups, his face would be so close to the ground, and the dusty earth would seem to be just that—dusty earth under his sweaty face and palms. He would watch his own sweat drip down to the earth and he would think how strange it was that not long ago he had had thoughts about the golem conjuring him, conjuring his family—as if dusty earth could have such power. And he would work his muscles hard, harder, strangely enjoying the new pains in his body and the exhaustion he always felt at night that made sleep come easily and blotted out thoughts of anything else but the army and its demands on him.

But now that he was back home, it was all there again. The feeling that they were indeed creatures conjured by someone or something else. He started to pitch the pebbles farther, toward the wall of the house. Some fell on a pipe and made pinging sounds. There were ants around the base of the rock. He put his finger down and let one climb over it. Then he shifted on the rock and stretched out his legs and he wondered, If your family is just a phantom that some other phantom conjured, what does that make you? The figment of a figment? Am I real? He won-

LAKE OF TIBERIAS, OR SEA OF GALILEE

dered, Am I a ghost? Am I really here at all? He held up his
hands, and squinted. For a second, when the setting sun
wrapped its rays around his fingers, he thought he could see
right through his skin and his bones, see right through to the
branches and leaves and to the silvery-gray trunks of the trees at
the edge of the orchard. This convinced him of something that
he had long suspected—that he was as insubstantial as smoke, as
empty as air. They all were. Now that he was back in Shachar he
had no trouble believing that even as his family went about their
regular business, some cosmic force was straying through the
soil of their lives and calling out to them, in a name familiar but
unpronounceable.

Miriam had finished in the kitchen and had gone into the
salon to do some sewing. Eliezer knew this because she had
called out to him from the kitchen window, asking him where he
had put the pair of pants that needed darning. Zohar was in the
front yard, talking local politics with a neighbor. Tomer was next
door—he had fallen in love with the neighbor's niece, a freckled
clarinet-playing brunette recently emigrated from South Africa.
Tomer had taken up the trumpet and the two of them would play
duets. Their music floated all over the village, and everyone in
Shachar was glad that Tomer Sepher was playing music and
making love to a girl, instead of playing tricks and making mischief—for his antics had only grown more mischievous as he had
grown up.

Eliezer listened to the music coming from next door. He envisioned his brother whose eyes were dim and who no longer lived
in their house. And he could feel the mystic form being drawn
around them all—as they were sitting in the salon, as they were
standing in the front yard, as they were next door, playing duets
with a freckled girl, as they were lying, staring at absolutely
nothing, as they were sitting on a big rock in the backyard,
throwing pebbles in the sand. It was the figure not of a single
human being, but of a family. This scared him very much. He

had not meant for this to happen. He tried to wish it all away. But no matter how hard he tried, he could not erase the image of all of them from the ground, nor could he pry his own figure away from their collective shadows. They were indelible, stuck permanently on the citrus soil. Even though they were all walking around, flesh and blood, even though they had been obviously conjured, the outline still remained in the earth, their figures huddled close together—all one, two, three, four, five of them. Later, when he was back at his base, he would often think back to this. And no matter how far Eliezer was from the orchard, from Shachar, from Israel, he would know in the silent part of his soul that they were all still there, etched into the orchard earth that had known them when their family was young and their family's tragedies were even younger. They were a tattoo the soil wore not for decoration but for memory, and no matter how hard they themselves would try to forget what they wanted to forget, the trees would remind them that this was who they had once been, who they still were.

An ant was climbing on his sandal. Now on his toes. It tickled, and he flicked it off with a finger. Eliezer shivered. He looked around—into the trees, and then above the trees, and then to the left by the wash basin, to the right by the shed, and behind him, he stared into the windows of the house. He knew that if he weren't careful, that is, if he didn't follow the rules, he would be quickly turned back into a clump of earth and be cast back down onto the dark floor of the world. The rules, or rather, the rule was simple. "Yes," he said out loud. "A golem is a mute creature. Gavriel," he said out loud. The rules, or rather, the rule was simple. Eliezer arched his back and repositioned himself on the rock. He stretched his arms up into the air and twisted them so that his elbows cracked. He heard his parents yelling in the house. He envisioned his father with his right eye open so wide, and the other one half-squinting, his brow fiercely wrinkled and lopsided. Zohar's angry face was always so uneven and strange.

Eliezer knew his mother would be standing with her feet planted a good distance apart, her hands on her hips, her face looking away from her husband, toward a vacant spot on the floor or wall. The rules. Never to utter and never to know, never to draw the fifth figure in the earth, never to acknowledge that Gabi had ever existed.

Eliezer did not believe in a distant God. God was near, in his own hands even, and in his brother's hands, which though mostly missing, were still hands enough to hold God close. Eliezer listened to his parents. They had come into the kitchen and now he could hear they were fighting about nothing in particular. Something about a woman whose name she had forgotten and a man who fixed cars and shouldn't have been invited to a party they shouldn't have thrown. Eliezer listened as everything they said and didn't say infiltrated not only his soul, but the entire valley with a tale not meant for a God of Here but for a God of There. A distant deity for whom the prayers of mothers and fathers, brothers and sisters are as arrows that regularly miss the mark.

They came outside and walked down the back porch stairs and into the sticker field, by the wash basin. Miriam's mouth was open; she was holding a blanket that she obviously wanted to shake out. Zohar was not helping her. Zohar had a *turia* in his hand; he was gripping it tightly and he was wearing a gray work shirt and pants. They fought on. Eliezer watched until the trees behind them seemed to reach out and pull the couple closer into the grove. He watched how as they continued to argue, their voices took on the quality of breaking branches, and their faces began to blend fiercely with the blooms. And still, Eliezer watched his parents fighting in the trees. "No," he said to himself, "it doesn't add up." For even though he knew the reasons, the why's and how's and horrible when's that had made them into parents who fight instead of parents who love, the equation was still impossible. It belonged to a world where numbers stood not

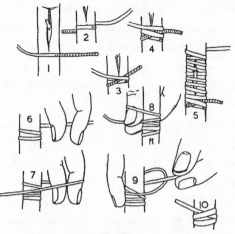

**Fig. 40**

A METHOD OF TYING INSERTED BUDS

*The tie is laid across below the vertical incision (1) and passed behind the stock (2). The short end is held by the next turn in front (3) and a further turn catches the short end down against the previous turn (4). Binding upwards, carefully but closely passing the bud (5), the tie is finished off well above the incisions. In this the tie is held by the right hand, the finger and thumb of the left are placed within the encircling tie, against the stock (6), and draw the tie back behind the stock (7) where they take it from the right hand (8). The first finger of the right hand is now pressed against binding, to prevent loosening, and the tie is drawn through (9) and pulled around the stock to form a half-hitch (10). A second similar half-hitch is added to make a sound job.*

FROM THE GRAFTER'S HANDBOOK BY R.J. GARNER

for set values, but for myriad tragedies, and the lives of men and women were the tortured figures in a queer math, a currency of devils, an algebra of angry ghosts.

Eventually, Zohar did help Miriam shake out the blanket. It billowed between them, up and down, making a sharp, flapping noise. When they walked back into the house, passing by their firstborn son, their new soldier, this time they acknowledged his presence, smiling at him, Miriam's hand straying to his shoulder, tousling his hair. Eliezer watched his parents go up the porch steps and disappear into the house they pretended was their own. He knew that he belonged in there with them, that they were all guests or ghosts in the golem's house, in the golem's history, in the golem's garden. And though a part of him wished for a different address, a different answer, another part of him was relieved to know that he would always belong to the place where their images were etched into the fragrant earth and the oranges, whose rinds were bitter, defiantly tasted so sweet. One last time he pictured his family, all five of them, their outlines stamped into the soil—mother and father in the middle, sons on either sides.

Eliezer reached toward the forms and tried to hold the phantom's hand. But the phantom's hand was limp and the father's faceless face was distorted and the mother's nervous eyes were looking at a vacant spot on a vacant wall. The images receded. He took a deep breath. He told himself that he didn't really mind that he couldn't erase his own figure, that he couldn't pry himself up from the queer tableaux of outsides without insides. Because otherwise, he would be alone, with neither family nor figments to love and hate and forget and remember. Miriam was calling for him to come in to dinner. The last of the pebbles fell out of Eliezer's palm, down to the sand. When his hand was empty he walked forward, across the sticker field. Following the setting sun, he lost himself in the orchard.

*My* FATHER WRITES:

> After my three years of army service were up, I did seriously consider staying in the military. But after much thought, I decided that I would prefer a civilian occupation. Upon discharge, I studied at the Hebrew University of Jerusalem where I received a degree in mathematics. I paid for my studies by grafting piecemeal in the summers. I paid my way through Hebrew University by grafting three-fourths of all the orchards in Shachar in the late fifties. When I was finished with university, in 1961, I traveled to America. It was actually my father's idea. He sent me to the United States in order to study for an

advanced degree in agriculture. First I was to go to Boston, where we had cousins, and then I was supposed to travel to Kansas, in order to go to agricultural school. But quickly, once I got to Boston, I decided to stay there. Eventually I enrolled in Harvard University, where I received a degree in business.

# Part Five

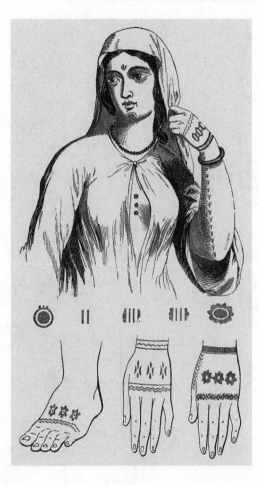

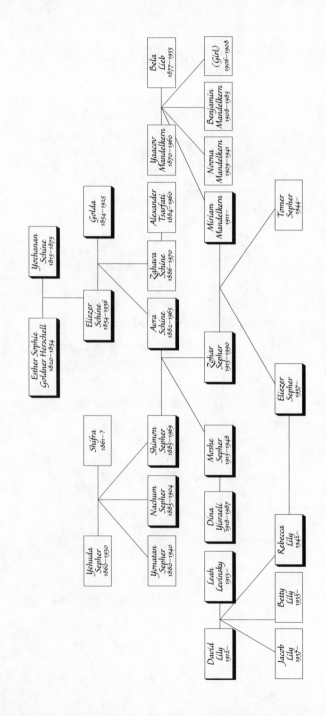

Esther Sophie Goldner Herschell 1820–1854

Yochanan Schine 1815–1875

Golda 1854–1925

Eliezer Schine 1854–1936

Zahava Schine 1886–1970

Alexander Tsarfati 1884–1960

Avra Schine 1882–1965

Yaacov Mandelkern 1870–1960

Bela Lieb 1877–1955

(Girl) 1906–1908

Benjamin Mandelkern 1908–1985

Norma Mandelkern 1909–1941

Miriam Mandelkern 1911–

Tomer Sepher 1944–

Shifra 1861–?

Shimon Sepher 1885–1969

Zohar Sepher 1915–1990

Eliezer Sepher 1937–

Yehuda Sepher 1860–1950

Nachum Sepher 1885–1904

Yonatan Sepher 1880–1940

Moshe Sepher 1915–1948

Dina Yisraeli 1918–1987

Rebecca Lily 1942–

Leah Levinsky 1915–

Betty Lily 1935–

David Lily 1912–

Jacob Lily 1937–

# Chapter 17

## REBECCA

**I WRITE:**

Rebecca was brought up blessed with the knowledge that her great-grandmother, her father's mother's mother, Chana Frieda, had been the "bakery woman to the czar." David Lily would lift his youngest daughter up onto the edge of the baking table. "Yes, honey bun," he would say while pounding a new dough with the heel of his hand. "My own Bubbie baked for the czar, the czarina." Rebecca would nod her head and repeat after him, "Sar, sarina." David kept working while he talked, pounding with the heel of his hand.

**MY FATHER WRITES:**

I met Rebecca Lily in Boston in 1962. I had just come to the United States and was staying with distant cousins of my mother's in the Brookline section of Boston. I met Rebecca at a party that my cousins threw for me to meet their friends. Rebecca was born in 1942. She is an artist. Rebecca's parents had a very well-known Jewish bakery, called Lily's Famous, in Brookline. Her parents, David and Leah, were both immigrants from Russia. The family lived in an apartment above the bakery. David ran the shop in back, and Leah ran the store, up front. It was a wonderful bakery, with all kinds of cakes and breads.

R ebecca dangled her little legs off the side of the table and looked expectantly at her father. David winked at her, and continued: "An illustrious family history ours is, and don't let anyone ever tell you different. My grandmother had a tiny bakery. Very tiny, and yet with a big reputation. Known all the way from Chelminski to the river Volga." And now David always stopped working, and drew a line in flour on the wooden table that grew from a river signified by wavy lines to another hieroglyphic that was supposed to be a crown but looked more to Rebecca like a tall fluffy hat that a chef would wear in the kitchen. Rebecca knew she could draw a better river and a better crown than her father, but because she knew his attempts were noble, she never wiped his drawings out. Instead she just took her own tiny index finger and happily traced the dusty white line in between the two illustrations.

David kept speaking. "One spring day after a particularly heavy winter, a royal messenger appeared at my grandmother's cottage and summoned her to St. Petersburg. Chana Frieda's reputation for 'daring dough—particularly pumpernickel' had reached the royal family. And the rest, as they say, is history—our history, the history of our family, our fortunes, and of course our pumpernickel bread. Chana Frieda, the redheaded Jewess, as she was known, became a court favorite. She was whisked out of her dirt floor cottage and given a staff of seventy-five clean-necked Russians and a fully appointed bakery in the palace with a huge cast-iron oven and an actual stone floor." Over the din of the bakery (or perhaps just under it, under the clattering of metal pans, the voices of the workmen, the slapping and pounding of dough, the creak and belly rumble of the huge walk-in oven), Rebecca could hear the hooves of the royal messenger's horse going clop, clop, clop. David took a deep breath and looked over to his own oven. He couldn't tell this story without feeling somehow as if he and his long dead grandmother, whom he had never known, were

connected. David's oven was a magnificent walk-in machine ten feet long, recessed in the wall with shelves that revolved in a backward pattern and had what David liked to call "the warm glow of a good Hades" in its metal belly. And while Rebecca drew soft concentric swirls with her pinky in the flour, David watched with wonder as the plucky ghost of his grandmother Chana Frieda tended his newfangled oven.

Rebecca said, "Dad?" David reached out a floury hand and with his wrist—the only clean part of him—softly rubbed her freckled cheek, and then gazed proudly at her hair. She, the daughter of his head and heart, was a redhead just like him. Devoutly orange were her locks, and baking was in her blood, too. Rebecca would sit for hours "on the bench" watching her father's hands orchestrate the day's symphony of bread, cakes, and assorted cookies. Rebecca had an older sister and a big brother too, and she always felt like she had a whole shop full of additional siblings. The cakes and bread were beloved company. She grew up surrounded by crackly-thin onion boards and long, hard salt sticks that she loved to suck on when she was very little. There were *mun* cookies, which she hated, and chocolate *babkes* that she loved too much, there were white sugary bow-ties and black, black breads she pretended were made out of wheat from the planet Mars. There were cherry rolls, kaiser rolls, warm, plain white buns sprinkled with sesame, round challahs and honey cake for Rosh Hashanah, *hamantaschen* for Purim (her favorite were the prune), and of course their special "pump," which, through the generations, hadn't lost a pinch of its daring and which Rebecca loved hot out of the oven spread heavily with butter.

※

The bakery hummed and whirred and never slept. David presided over the shop, and Leah minded the store. Leah was a tiny dark-haired woman with a big chest and warm exuberant manners. She greeted customers not only by name but by knowing who they were and where they came from and where they might be going—to synagogue for a *kiddush* with that bag of *rugulach,* to a *shiva* house to pay a call with that chocolate chip loaf, to a grandchild's *bris* with three boxes of assorted danish and a bottle of *schnapps* in the pocket, or just home to dinner with two warm little loaves. Leah was knowledgeable about her customers' lives but never nosy, and her smiles as she handed out change or asked after a son or a daughter were always sincere.

There was a little room between the bakery in back and the store up front. In this room were the stairs that led upstairs to the family apartment. Here they kept paper goods such as unconstructed cookie boxes, rolls of string for tying the boxes, wax paper, and other such essentials. Also in this little room was a little table, and a phone for taking orders. David and Leah often met in the little room. They didn't need to call to each other, they didn't need to arrange a time for meeting. They were spiritually synchronized. When one came back, the other just knew to come front and vice versa. They met in the middle of their little world, like two explorers of an internal equator mutually charting the distance between their bodies, and needing every so often to calibrate equipment or check the weather conditions in a place that was both near and far.

David wiped his floury hands on his pants, and then held them out to Leah. And they stood there, giving each other what everyone called their "honeymoon" eyes. They were so completely in love.

Nine years after they married, David and Leah learned that they had both come to the United States of America on the same ship when they were children. A nephew of David's had been doing research on the family history and had unearthed the coincidence. Ever since the nephew had told them about the boat, David and Leah had held each other closer, and there was an even stronger urgency to their love, as if they were terrified that they would once again find themselves in the middle of a crowd and be completely unaware of the nearness of their own beloved. They were in the little room in between the bakery and the store. David bent down and kissed Leah on the lips; she nodded up at him, and then put one hand on her hip before kissing him back and then breaking out into a big smile. It is true that their terror was made much less terrifying by the knowledge that they had indeed found each other after all, and that perhaps their coming over on the same boat when they were children was not so much a metaphor for potential loss as it was an affirmation that they had been traveling together all along.

❦

On Sunday mornings there was always a long line of customers snaking out of the shop door. The family did not put on airs, but were privately proud of their imperial past. And while most in the neighborhood knew the Lilys as descendants of barrel-makers, gravediggers, even the occasional thief, they ran their business as if the court were still their best customer. And while walking out of Lily's Famous with a cookie in one hand and a warm bag of bread in the other, one felt touched by something edibly majestic. So what if the czar was not a friend to the Jews? "A king is a king," David would tell his three children, "no matter how you slice it."

By the time she was thirteen, Rebecca had taken fast to the family mantel. She continued her father's story in her head, telling herself as she stood by the bench, "I have been placed under house arrest with the czar and the czarina." She looked around and instead of seeing the bakery workmen dressed in white, their faces always kindly, Rebecca saw the doomed Romanoffs. Their faces were kindly, too, but their kindness was sticky, not insincere, but structurally damaged, as if having been exposed to too much heat or sun. The royal family was dressed in rich brocades, fancy purple, red, green, glittery fabrics. They thanked Rebecca profusely for having accompanied them into their desperate exile. When they said this, Rebecca modestly looked down at her hands, which were covered in a thin layer of cake flour, and then she went to work. She tried to brighten the imperial family's gloomy days by designing for them fanciful cakes in the shapes of animals. She fashioned her own odd zoo of cake tins out of spent cannon-shell casings, which were in unfortunate abundance from the recent revolution. Out of chocolate and vanilla batter she made lions and tigers and giraffes and bears with polka-dot coats and happy grinning faces. The young prince loved these creatures the most. He would prance around the bakery while Rebecca was working, telling everyone, as he stuck his fingers in the batter, that he was "going on safari." And when, toward the end of the whole disaster, the princesses sewed their diamonds and rubies and aquamarines into their clothes for safe-keeping, Rebecca braided thin delicate breads into the shapes of precious jewels for them—so they could still feel "princessy." She made cinnamon-twist bracelets for their china-white arms, and crispy sourdough brooches for their chests, even pumpernickel tiaras for their foreheads, which may have lacked glitter but at least gave off a rich glow from being coated with a layer of honey mixed with sugar. The princesses were so grateful, and didn't mind at all when their foreheads were sticky, or the "jewels" left crumbs all over their fancy gowns.

But Rebecca was not always lost in imperial reveries. As she grew up, she worked hard in the bakery, after school or late into the night. She learned from her father how to braid challah into hearts for Valentine's Day, Stars of David for Israeli Independence Day, crescent moons for the eccentric man down the street who liked his loaves celestially inspired. She was her father's "right-hand girl" even though she was left-handed. She could do a six-braid, a nine-braid, an eleven-braid, and eventually the masterful five-foot-long "golden fifteen special." She braided quickly, and with what her father called "a healthy dose of the old family spirit." From the moment Rebecca came home from school, she, her older brother, and her father would work side by side, filling orders, telling jokes. But mostly they would work quietly, their ears soothed and their fingers made more nimble by the slapping sound of dough hitting the wooden table.

Rebecca realized early on that the bakery was not just about baking bread. There was art in her father's hands, which were thick, huge, muscular, callused, and yet sensitive enough to detect the granular differences between kinds of flour.

But it wasn't really the size of her father's hands that made Rebecca think about art. It just seemed to her that her father could make anything out of flour, sugar, yeast, eggs, and water. And the anything usually appealed to much more than just the sense of taste. When she was a little girl sitting up on the bench as her father worked, and later, when she stood at the bench next to him braiding her own challah, Rebecca would forget that she was in her parents' bakery on Harvard Street in Brookline and drift off into imaginings. She would daydream about the czar and czarina, or she would imagine that she had baked giant-sized chocolate-chip cookies for Paul Revere on the night of his famous ride. Or Rebecca would think about how she had been a slave in Egypt and how when Moses gave them instructions, she had bent down to the hearth and pounded dough into flat sheets and baked them unrisen. As Rebecca's fingers worked the dough, and as her father's huge hands pinched the ends of the challah next to her, they told each other stories, or imagined various sweet or crusty worlds in a yeasty silence. As she worked, Rebecca found herself not in a bakery but in a studio where the elegant strands of history and imagination were mixed into one fancy bread and then served not only for dinner but also for decoration. And that to Rebecca was what her father always held in his huge hands—a kind of kneaded art. The bakery was a tasty braided universe where the dough pressed and the spirit relaxed and the princesses wore bread for jewels and Paul Revere took a big bite out of a giant chocolate-chip cookie before mounting his horse, and the Israelites made their matzah out of Lily's famous pump.

Yes, it seemed to Rebecca that her father could make anything out of bread. His breads were beautiful, idiosyncratic. It could even be said that they were amazing. Of course David was usually baking regular orders, but then there were the other times. Like when he was commissioned to make a wedding cake out of challah. It was a perfect wedding cake three tiers high, each tier made of delicate concentric braids. Rebecca had helped with the tiny roses for the sides and top. They made them by pinching the dough with the tips of their fingers. "This," David told Rebecca, pointing to the bread-cake in progress, "is what my grandmother once made for a close friend of the czarina." David baked the wedding cake tier by tier, and when the last layer came out of the oven, everyone in the shop stopped their work, whistled, and applauded. The next day at the wedding, the rabbi who performed the ceremony, upon first seeing the creation at the start of the festive meal, had stood up on a chair and insisted that an eighth blessing be added to the traditional litany. And so, in addition to mirth and exultation, joy and gladness, the glowing bride and groom were blessed with "a local miracle concerning braids, David Lily, and challah bread."

David always drew a new design before trying it. And Rebecca would watch her father sketch out a particularly hard or interesting creation. Her own first "serious" sketches were of the sacks of flour in the back of the bakery. The sacks were stacked near the oven, piled up halfway to the ceiling. She sat down on a huge tin of cocoa, put her sketchbook on her knees, and set about drawing while the men worked all around her, filling jelly donuts, rolling *kmish* bread, sprinkling seeds on the back of the pump. Later Rebecca would think of that first sketch and know that she had loved the flour sacks, how as a little girl she and her siblings had climbed all over them, pretending they were a fort, or the ramparts to an enchanted castle.

Sometimes, before joining her father in the back of the shop, Rebecca would begin to draw. She clutched the pencil down low and began to draw the czarina. She gave her big catlike eyes and a small but elegant mouth and cheekbones that stretched all the way across Mother Russia. Rebecca loved to draw members of the royal family; she consulted her memories of a murky parallel past and tried her best to re-create the faces of her family's patrons so as to do her great-grandmother Chana Frieda appropriate honor.

Rebecca drew in the little room in between the shop and the bakery. She sketched on the flat, unconstructed white cardboard boxes they used to pack cookies in. The unmade boxes were stacked up high on a long shelf to the right of the table in the little room. Once a week a huge pile of them would be taken up front where the shop girls turned them into boxes to fill orders. Of course, Rebecca wasn't supposed to be drawing the feline eyes, the imperious cheekbones of any czarina on the boxes, and when her parents first caught her "doodling on the bakery equipment" they told her to stop it. But she couldn't help herself. When she wasn't working in back with her father, or helping up front with her mother, Rebecca's fingers would inevitably make their way to the boxes, which beckoned, milky white, to be decorated with pretty pictures. And then, whether on purpose or by accident, her drawings would get mixed in with the "clean" boxes, and that is how her art first made its way out into the world. The first customers to receive those boxes were confused. No one was sure if it was a joke, a gimmick, a prize, or some kind of mistake.

Rebecca drew unconsciously. She drew compulsively. She

drew with her stomach muscles taut and her lips half-puckered. Rebecca clutched the pencil down low and began to draw her parents. She drew her mother's sensually swollen lips and her father's strong jaw, angular features, curly hair. She drew the "honeymoon look" they always had in their eyes when glancing at each other. Rebecca paused, sharpened her pencil, and continued to work. She drew and she drew, until finally one day Leah, with her hands on her hips and her full lips pulled tight in anger, sent Rebecca out of the bakery and up into the house. "You are banished from the boxes!" she yelled after her daughter as Rebecca ran up the steps. "Banished! No one on Harvard Street expects portraits on their pastries!"

Leah walked away from the steps and back to the little table. Now, Leah knew her youngest daughter had talent for drawing. But until this point she didn't know the extent to which Rebecca was gifted. It must be said without hyperbole that the drawings Leah saw on those boxes knocked her socks off or, more precisely, grabbed hold of her girdle. Until now, overly busy with the round-the-clock demands of the bakery and shop, Leah really hadn't paid attention to what Rebecca was always drawing. She was drawing faces, and they were extraordinary. Leah flipped through portraits of Gladys the senior salesgirl who always batted her eyelashes at the gentlemen customers; there was Stevie, Leah's own little brother, bald as he could be at thirty-four; there was big-nosed Doris from down the street; handsome Milty the butcher; there was the czar, unmistakable in his old-fashioned mustache and military collar; there was the czarina, of course; and Demchick the corset-maker who made all the ladies look shapely but told stupid jokes. Leah kept flipping through the pictures until she came to one of her husband, David, and then she saw her own face. It peered out at her from off one of the boxes, like a sudden twin from one of life's many mirrors.

Leah thought, My goodness. My goodness. Leah, mistress of this little bakery kingdom, was well aware of the many intrigues,

A COURT RECEPTION IN ST. PETERSBURG

sorrows, and *simchas* that coursed through the lives of her sweet-
toothed congregation. But even she didn't know everything. And
now she was surprised to see Tova Rabinowitz's affair with Morris Goldberg clearly depicted on the cookie boxes. Tova always
came in for jelly donuts, and Morris had a sweet tooth for cherry
danish. Even though they were on different boxes, it was obvious
to Leah that Morris and Tova—Tova with her bouffant blond
hairdo, Morris of the flaring nostrils—were making eyes at each
other. "How did Rebecca do that?" Leah wondered. "What is it
about their eyes that lets me know they are looking at each
other?" The customers spoke to Leah from the sketches, con-
fessing a story of sweet passion sprinkled with a dash of dread
(after all, they were both married, and in-laws to boot). Leah
lifted up another flat box and there was pretty Betty, her own
older daughter, in profile, looking as she did on her last day of

high school, exalted, relieved, and staggeringly grown-up. On another box were Tony the cake-baker's bulging eyes and jowly cheeks, and there on another box was Johnny Johnson the delivery man. Johnny was smiling so widely from off of the box that you could tell from glancing at him that his youngest child had just been born. Leah said out loud, "Thank God! Congratulations!" because she hadn't seen Johnny in days, and so hadn't known that his wife had safely delivered. Leah held the faces and for the first time was aware of the talent in the hands of her youngest daughter. She took a deep breath and lifted up the edge of one of the boxes, only to be again astounded at the portraiture underneath.

That night, she sat on the edge of Rebecca's bed, brushed a lock of red hair out of the way, kissed Rebecca's forehead, and said, "Honey, you can keep it up with the boxes, but please do try your best to draw mostly strangers. We can't afford to scare away the regulars with art."

And that is how Rebecca's drawings ended up on the cookie boxes. At first when the faces began to appear people were surprised by them. But soon there were many in the shop and neighborhood who counted themselves as Rebecca's patrons, her boosters, her collectors. For as their faces began to adorn the sweet packages tied with white string, and were carried out of the bakery and into the streets of Boston, those who carried them felt as if they were purchasing much more than a half-pound of *kmish*, or assorted cookies, much more than a braided or seeded loaf of bread. There was stunning intimacy in Rebecca's fine-lined art. And Lily's Famous became known to its habitués as a place where one knows they will be treated to something delicious and at the same time as a place where being known itself was considered a recipe rare and drawn and delicious.

At first Rebecca tried to draw only strangers—that is, strangers mixed in with the occasional member of the Romanoff clan. But soon familiar faces began once again to come from her pencil. She couldn't help it. It's just what she did. She drew what she knew. It is true that those customers with something to hide (Harry Blackman who hit his wife; Edna Levinsky who stole the occasional pickle from the grocer) stopped coming to Lily's Famous and began to buy their pumpernickel from bakeries less daring or different. But most of the clientele and most of the staff were brought closer by Rebecca's creations. And people didn't even really mind when their secrets made their way onto the boxes. After all, Tova Rabinowitz and Morris Goldberg really were in love. So what if they were in-laws? So what if divorce was out of the question? Love, no matter how illicit, wants to be known, drawn, honestly depicted. Everyone knows that secrets generally come to be known anyway on a city block. And at least this way, in Rebecca's cookie-box drawings, the things they wanted kept quiet were made not into scandals but into art.

# Chapter 18

## REBECCA AND ELIEZER

I WRITE:

Rebecca met Eliezer at a party and immediately knew she was bringing him home. "Eliezer Sepher," he said, "Israel, I just to come." Rebecca was taken by Eliezer's big blue eyes and exotic air. And she was also attracted by the fact that he couldn't put an English sentence together. "School, America States, I to come." She didn't pity him, but she right away trusted Eliezer's choppy irreverent form of communication. She knew that he wasn't doing it on purpose, but still it seemed to her as if this young foreigner was being particularly wise with his words. Rebecca, a visual artist, thought in pictures and resented the fact that people were expected to live their lives under a net of dull, shapeless, colorless, squiggly little words. She held out her hand and smiled, "Rebecca, I to come too," she said, and Eliezer, sensing that he had met a soul mate, smiled back.

After the party, Rebecca took Eliezer home with her. The bakery was just a ten-minute walk away. They walked down Louis Street, right on Chestnut, left on Druett, and then straight until Harvard. The bakery was the third shop from the corner. It was 12:30 a.m. when Rebecca and Eliezer arrived, and Lily's Famous was wide-awake. David, dressed in whites, his red hair very shiny, took one look at Eliezer and immediately decided that it was his

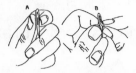

REMOVING THE WOOD FROM THE BUD SHIELD
*A. The sliver of wood has begun to separate from the rind and the rind 'tail' is gripped to the base of the thumb by the second finger. B. The wood is held between finger and thumb, of the other hand, and flicked upwards from the shield.*

FROM THE GRAFTER'S HANDBOOK BY R.J. GARNER

duty to induct this foreign-born boy into the cult of their domestic goddess—bread. It was four days before Rosh Hashanah; David was short-staffed and less interested in Eliezer as his daughter's brand-new suitor as he was in Eliezer as a human being possessed of a pair of workable hands. David sized a man up by his hands and had noticed the second Eliezer had walked into the shop that his were fine-tuned instruments, heroically callused but infused with a balletic grace of palm and knuckle that was instantly recognizable to David as the mark of someone who could do some good with dough. David was not mistaken. Eliezer's hands were hardworking creatures. They had tamed many a recalcitrant graft—not by forcing the tree into place, but by convincing the branches through a mixture of faith and dexterity that the graft was good and the sapling would take. David smiled at the young man. Eliezer tried to introduce himself and to tell David who he was and where he was from, but he just barely managed to pronounce his own name. David mercifully interrupted, saying, "Welcome to our country, young man, now come stand by me and I'll put you to work." Eliezer was given a spot at the bench across from Rebecca and right next to David. There were six other men also working that night, including Rebecca's older brother and three of Leah's younger brothers who looked almost identical, except that two had mustaches and one didn't.

Eliezer, who had never worked with dough before, was a quick study. And as they were just making regular challah, once he learned the pattern—over, under, over, under, over, under, pinch, pinch—he, like the others, fell into a floury silence that was decorated every thirty seconds by the hot percussion of the oven going round. But while quiet ruled the mouths of the small company, a conversation did seem to emanate out from all of their fingers, so that by the end of the night, which was also the beginning of the morning, even though no one had "said" much, Eliezer felt as if he knew this family, and as if they knew him. When they were done, David nodded to the boy, and, after wiping his hands on his pants, motioned warmly for Eliezer to come upstairs for breakfast with him and Rebecca and the rest of the workers, most of whom were family, the rest of whom were friends.

Upstairs, Leah had the table set with coffee, orange juice, hot bagels, a thick white square of cream cheese, and a variety of smoked fish. Leah had been down in the shop during the night and had already met Eliezer. Unlike David, she was interested in him for reasons other than just a pair of hands, though, like David, Leah had also noticed that Eliezer's hands were lovely. Leah knew a suitor when she saw one, and now, at the breakfast table at four a.m., tried her best not to ask too many questions— not only because Eliezer couldn't put two English words together to formulate an answer, but also because she knew that later, after this curly-headed young man left, Rebecca would draw a sketch of his face on which the Israeli's character would be revealed in full detail and the only questions left would be about the colors with which to fill his life in.

As the sun slowly rose over a sleeping Boston, all the workers filled their bellies and talked of the day's coming business. No one seemed particularly tired, but then again everyone looked a little strange. Eliezer could not tell whether their complexions were naturally so white, or if the fine layer of flour that coated his face also coated their own. Eliezer was exhausted but exhilarated, and he smiled at Rebecca as he took a bite of his bagel and fish. Rebecca was sitting next to him at the big round table. At first Eliezer did not try to join in the conversation. But soon Rebecca was saying something to him. He didn't really understand what she was saying, but he tried to answer back, "Cousins know me, now not there, yes, to missing." She took his hand under the table, and Eliezer knew from the way that she squeezed his fingers and gently tickled his palm that his attempt at conversation had not failed completely.

Walking home to his cousins' house, Eliezer thought about the bustle of the bakery and the warmth of Rebecca's family. The happy way that David had looked as he had worked reminded Eliezer of how his father, Zohar, always looked when he was grafting. But later, when Leah and David had looked at each other in the kitchen, it had seemed so strange to Eliezer that parents could be so visibly in love. And then, even though he was so far away from Shachar, the part of Eliezer's soul that had not left the village whispered maliciously that the word for "beloved" had the same *gematria* as the expression for "and primordial emptiness, void and waste"—*Ahooovah* and *Ovoohoo* both added up to nineteen. David had taken Leah's hand and together they had eaten, their heads inclined, their bodies connected. Eliezer walked on, past stores still shuttered, and houses still sleeping. The sky was gray and steadily lightening. It was now almost five a.m. And as he walked on, he willed the part of himself that had left the green village and come here to the city of Boston, to whisper back that math sometimes works magic with opposites and that equivalencies are just one way the world has of righting its own mistakes. He thought about the soft way Rebecca had held his hand under the table. As he turned the final corner, and walked up the steps to his cousins' door, Eliezer willed himself to think about how the machinery in the bakery had been so shiny and modern and huge and then he told himself that if the bakery were a song it would have lots of percussion, and that humming it would make your throat tickle and leave you almost laughing. And Eliezer was almost laughing as he slipped inside his cousins' house, hoping to wake no one up.

※

On their subsequent dates, Eliezer told Rebecca that he had never fasted on Yom Kippur. Rebecca looked at him incredulously and said, "But I thought that Israel was the land of pious Jews." Eliezer had laughed and said, "No, praying here people with you, in Boston." The next day she had drawn him with a full belly. She drew the insides of his stomach stacked high with a whole meal of food—there was a lambchop and a baked potato and a whole piece of fresh fruit. On another date, he described the orchard, telling her how it smelled—not like you would expect, like citrus, but like "orange naked, fruit with no clothes, not embarrassed smell, but new like baby." And the next day Rebecca drew oranges and lemons naked like people. She gave them interesting pulpy-looking privates—dividing them up into boys and girls, and then she drew the trees the oranges hung on, and then she drew the insides of the trees, their rings dating back not thirty, forty, or fifty years as Eliezer had described them, but dating all the way back to King David whose reign she inscribed in velvet circular strokes. And when Eliezer got tired of telling Rebecca the truth, and Rebecca got tired of drawing it, he made things up. He told her that the women in Israel always wore ball gowns to do their housework, and the men wore top hats and canes in the fields, white gloves and tails to graft and plant and harvest. That night Rebecca drew Eliezer all fancy-dressed and proper, more Fred Astaire than Middle Eastern farmer.

But mostly, Eliezer told Rebecca about himself, and she asked questions or just listened. They didn't speak much about Rebecca, not because Eliezer wasn't interested, but because her life surrounded them. She was a child both of the bakery and of

Boston, and the smells and sounds and tastes of her environment did not need to be explained. Sometimes, Rebecca would take Eliezer to the back of the shop, and he would stand next to her at the bench as she worked on a regular order, or on a fancy loaf of holiday bread. Occasionally, Eliezer would work with her, other times he would sit on the hard bulging sacks of flour and work on his English studies, asking Rebecca for help on conjugations.

Once, when he was tired of English, he had stood next to her and she had put a piece of dough in Eliezer's hands. He had fashioned it into something complicated that was also simple. When he was done, Eliezer just stood there looking at it. He sighed, and then scratched an itch on his cheek with a floury hand that left a little mark of white on his skin. Rebecca was watching him. Eliezer had no words to call this dough creature forth, and he did not walk around the bench in any magic circle, but he felt threatened by its presence and at the same time felt as if it had fashioned him, and that even now in this bakery it was calling on a part of him that was both ancestral and frightening. Rebecca watched as Eliezer grew agitated by the little decorative lump of dough, and even though it looked benign and ordinary, it seemed to represent something intrusive and malignant. Eliezer reached out and, in one squeeze of his hand, destroyed his creation. Then he banged his fist on the table with great force, and then, as if nothing had happened, he began to talk too loudly about something they had already finished discussing. And because he talked loudly not only with his voice, but also with his body, Rebecca was not surprised when Eliezer knocked his English books off the bench and onto the bakery floor. Eliezer lifted them up and seemed to look both stunned and insulted that his books would obey the forces of the universe and actually fall when pushed. Rebecca continued to work. She did her best to ignore Eliezer's obvious agitation. He was still speaking so loudly.

This wasn't the first time since they had started dating that he had become strange, hostile, angry at little things that made no sense. Once, when they were walking to the movies on Beacon Street, a fat man had bumped into Eliezer, and Eliezer had been pushed into the open door of the butcher's shop. The fat man was immediately apologetic, but even as the man had extended his hand and offered an apology, Eliezer had had a look on his face that expressed both great pain and great fury that life should have so blatantly mistreated him. Eliezer's intense anger had not lasted long, just a few seconds, but Rebecca had seen it and was nonetheless surprised by it.

Now Rebecca concentrated on the bread: over, under, over, under, over, under. The dough on the bench made a thump-thumping sound, and the flour felt all grainy on her fingers. When Eliezer was done speaking, Rebecca told Eliezer that when she was little she would sit on this bench and her father would tell her stories of how her great-grandmother had been the bakery woman to the czar. Rebecca turned her back to the bench and spoke as if to the oven, telling Eliezer how she used to pretend that she herself had baked for the czar and the czarina when they were under house arrest in one of the eastern provinces. Eliezer listened, but he was annoyed by her story. He looked around at the flour sacks, and at the oven, and at the metal stacked rolling trays filled with fresh and sweet-smelling cookies. He was angry at Rebecca for ever having imagined such things. For ever having wanted to escape a landscape that seemed to him threatless and comforting. He wished she would be quiet, and before she could finish he interrupted her and began to tell her something about his first day of class, which would be the next day. Rebecca let him interrupt, and told herself that Eliezer was just nervous about starting school and that his temper was really not too bad, and that she too would be agitated if she had to start her life anew in a foreign country.

That night, Rebecca drew Eliezer sitting on top of the sacks of flour. She drew his curls, and she drew his big brown English book on his lap, she drew his pretty eyes, and then she finished the true drawing abruptly, leaving the essence of the likeness out when she got to his hands and the fingers under her pencil threatened to curl into a fist and to smash something underneath the paper or on top of it. Instead, Rebecca drew Eliezer's hands flaccid and gave his face a disinterested air as if he were staring at the wall opposite the flour sacks while contemplating a point of grammar. Rebecca drew him this way, even though Eliezer never contemplated grammar, he just suffered through it, and even though his face was never disinterested but, rather, always animated—with its emotional, exaggerated, elastic features. When she had finished, the Eliezer Rebecca had created was not at all familiar, but she pretended not to notice the difference between her paper suitor and the one with whom she had spent the last evening, the one with a spot of flour on his cheek who talked too loudly and obviously was in some sort of pain.

*M*Y FATHER WRITES:

Rebecca and I got engaged in 1964. That summer, before our wedding, she first came with me to Israel. We planned to spend the summer with my parents in Shachar before returning to marry and live in Boston.

I WRITE:

*T*hey were in the city of Netanya; it was only the fourth day of their trip. Rebecca reached for a book with a dark green cover. Later she would tell people, "It all started with the tattooed woman." But Eliezer, smiling, would disagree with her and say, "No, started with man with hair all over face. Tiny, tiny pieces cut hair belong other people. All over face." The man was a barber, an old Syrian Jew with cataracts. He was half blind but he wielded a straight razor like a sword and told stories as he worked of his days cutting hair for British soldiers in Damascus. His face and smock and whole shop were covered with "other people hair, thousands of pieces, tiny, tiny." There must have been a generation's worth of hair in the shop. But to Eliezer, he seemed like an excellent barber. While Eliezer was getting his hair cut, Rebecca went to the antiquarian book shop next door.

Rebecca was wearing a short yellow dress that hugged her buxom figure and matched, in a fun and fruity way, her long red hair. She reached for the book. Her hand closed on the dusty dark-green spine and she pulled it down from the shelf. When twenty minutes later Eliezer came into the bookstore, clean-shaven, his hair enthusiastically short, Rebecca held open the book to him and pointed to a picture labeled "Tattooed woman." The woman in the portrait was exotically beautiful. She had long dark hair that was covered by a traditional kerchief and she was looking up from the page, her head pointed slightly to her right, with an expression of seductive restlessness. She had geometric markings on her face and hands and her loose, peasant-style blouse was opened in between the breasts to reveal three vertical dots holding court in the valley of her womanliness, like special sentries. And the way she was depicted, using an advanced etching technique, gave her the realism of a photograph combined with the exquisite artfulness of an original drawing.

Rebecca and Eliezer stood silently for a little while, both of them half holding their breath. Eventually Rebecca began flipping through other pages, stopping at other faces just as real and just as beautiful as the first. After a few minutes she flipped back to the "Tattooed woman" and pointed to her face, saying, "I love the way the illustrations are all made up of little lines. We walk the world feeling so solid," she said, looking not at Eliezer but down at the book. "So solid, but really, we are all just a pile of little lines, thread-thin sticks. Just like her." As she spoke, her finger was pointing to the tattooed woman, who was looking up at both of them, her dark eyes so curious and piercing. Rebecca turned her head. Then she rubbed her own right hand up and down the skin of her arm slowly, as if to confirm that she were made up of "lines" too and that somewhere, in some artist's studio, was the

TATTOOED WOMAN

original plate on which her own image had been carved out, inked, and then printed. Eliezer looked down at his own hands. He wanted to tell Rebecca that she was wrong. "We are solid, can't you see? Not lines, but living creatures." But he didn't say this. He didn't say anything. And he wondered if solidity, actual physical presence, was just a whim his soul longed to believe in, because the notion of "little lines" scared him and made him feel flimsy, found out, understood.

Eliezer ran his fingers through his new-cut hair and thought of the Syrian barber— of the way he had flicked the straight razor expertly against a white towel on his own forearm to clean it in between strokes. And he thought about the sound that the razor had made, a *ffft, ffft, ffft* sound it was. "Little lines," said Rebecca, and then had she reached out a hand to feel the smoothness of Eliezer's cheek. Later she would tell people, "We bought that book. *The Land and the Book* by Reverend W. M. Thomson, written in 1881. And that was the start of my collection."

The images in that first book were vivid, elegant, delicate, and concrete all at once. Rebecca flipped through the pages. She said the names of entries out loud, hoping to get the models' attention. "Water jugs and bottles," "Dancing girls," "Musical instruments," "Syrian gentleman in full dress," "Amulets," "Artisans," "Cluster of dates." She would sit in her favorite spot in

Shachar—on the wooden swing in back of Miriam and Zohar's house, paging through the book while sipping iced coffee. The swing was old, and it creaked as she swung. It was a hot humid day in the middle of the summer. Eliezer was in the orchard with Zohar, Miriam was lying down for a nap, and Rebecca

PUBLIC GARDEN, DAMASCUS

was grateful to the people in the book for keeping her company.

Perhaps because she was an artist herself, or maybe it was the heat that made her mind fuzzy, but soon Rebecca was half dreaming, half knowing who these people were. The "Tattooed woman" was a second cousin of the artist whose skin smelled like peppermint, with whom the artist was obviously in love. The "Water bearers" were a family from whom the artist rented a room. The little boy in the background of the "Dancer" picture had just recovered from a horrible illness, maybe typhoid. The principal woman dancer had a beautiful voice but she rarely sang. And the "Syrian gentleman" on page 67 never went to bed before two a.m. and was crazy for green bananas. The swing kept creaking, and Rebecca rolled her neck around, stretching it out. Somewhere behind her, a solitary cricket began to sing, even though it wasn't evening. She ran her hands over her sweaty forehead before continuing to turn the pages. Rebecca rarely read the text, but concentrated wholly on the pictures.

That first summer, Zohar and Miriam had thrown a party for "the happy young couple." Rebecca had worn a white dress with black polka dots. Miriam had given her a turquoise pendant, which she wore, even though she didn't think it was pretty. Miriam had suggested that the turquoise looked good with her red coloring, and Rebecca had pretended to believe her. There was a band, and much food, and many people, most of whom Rebecca was meeting for the first time. Tomer was there, dancing with his South African girlfriend, Sheila.

SYRIAN GENTLEMAN IN FULL DRESS

In the middle of the evening, Zohar had walked over to Rebecca and asked her with a wide smile and outstretched arms if she would like to dance with him. Rebecca was not a dancer. She hated to dance, and preferred to sit by the side, or to stand and talk. It's not that Rebecca wasn't social, it's just that she didn't have any sense of rhythm, and always felt that when she danced her body was out of control and her balance so bad that she might fall down. She had been sitting by the side of the dance floor, and when Zohar approached her she smiled, and in elementary Hebrew with crossed gender and a noun that should have been a verb, she said, "*Lo todah.*" No, thank you. "*Ani lo ohev rikud.*" I (masc.) don't like dance. She could never have expected her future father-in-law to take such offense as he did. Zohar became almost instantly angry. His face, so handsome, grew distorted, so that his beauty became almost grotesque—one blue eye opened so wide, the other half closed and his hands were gesticulating, even though he wasn't speaking. When he spoke, his hands grew still. He leaned closer and asked her again in broken English, "Will you with me to dance?" And when she again declined, she saw in his open eye sarcasm, in his half-closed eye scorn, and in the wrinkles on his forehead a regiment of prideful disappointment. Rebecca tried to explain but couldn't. In Hebrew she said again, "*Lo todah.*" And then she said in English, "I just don't like to dance." She looked up at him and held up her empty hands. Eliezer, who had been on the other side of the yard, came to Rebecca's side and said, "*Nu,* just a dance little," but the more they asked, the more they insisted, the less control Rebecca felt, not only of her legs and sense of balance but also of the "little lines" that made up her body—so that when she finally did stand up, it was not to dance but to disappear into the house in tearful shame.

For several minutes she sat alone in the salon wondering why she had ever come here so far from the bakery, from Brookline, from her own parents. But then Eliezer came to her, and she buried her face in his chest and he soothed her with his kisses and wrapped his arms around her. She looked up at him. He was not out of place here, and yet she wished that he were. Like she was. And as they stood there in silence she tried to pretend that he was a foreigner here, too, and that when they left this house, this village, this country, Eliezer's accent would fade away and they would speak the same language, and the colorful idioms of their lives would never tell stories such as this. Eliezer kissed Rebecca's lips and told her how much he loved her and how sorry he was that his father was so angry over nothing at all.

Rebecca kissed him back. She was growing used to Eliezer's

own occasional outbursts of sharp anger, but nothing could have prepared her for the way Zohar's voice had risen in public, the way his eyes had bulged, the way he sneered at her, the way he seemed to be saying, even though she couldn't fully understand, that she was a snob, and that his opinion of Americans was ruined by her singular refusal to come out on the dance floor and waltz with him right now. This was craziness, she knew, and yet Eliezer, Miriam, the other guests had not seemed disturbed by Zohar's behavior. Rather, they seemed either used to it, or used to ignoring it. Inside the salon, the "happy couple" sat and watched the party through a window.

Yes, this was strange territory. Eliezer kissed her again. And he tried to get her to look at him, but she looked away, down at her own lap. The music was loud and joyous. Eventually Rebecca and Eliezer went back outside. They held hands tightly, and everyone, including Zohar, pretended that nothing had happened.

Often, when Zohar and Miriam were fighting, Rebecca and Eliezer would escape to the little room downstairs. They would lie there on one of the beds, on the old gray cotton bedspread, so threadbare and musty they joked, "It must be from the time of *Hamandat Habriti*," the British Mandate. They would lie there talking or cuddling, or turning the old pages of *The Land and the Book*, and they would make up stories to go with the people in the pictures. But sometimes when they looked at the book Eliezer ended up feeling nervous. The longer they stayed in Shachar, and the closer the time came for their marriage, the more nervous he got. It was July. They were to be married in Boston in February. Eliezer tried to love the illustrations as much as Rebecca did. Rebecca's red hair fell on the pages; Eliezer reached out a hand and tenderly pulled it back. But he could not love the pictures, and instead found himself adding up the images like numbers, erasing all of the art into dry equations, which then lay on his soul like yesterday's dust.

❧

It was a hot sunny afternoon when Eliezer and Rebecca walked out to see the mosaics in the lower orchard. He had told her about them in America, and before they got to Shachar she had specifically told Eliezer that she wanted to "hold those old stones" in her hands. As they walked, Eliezer told Rebecca about the different trees, "on our left shamouti," he said, pointing, "also called Jaffa orange, and on our right fruit pummelo." But she looked at him strangely at the mention of this name because she had never heard of this fruit before. "No," she said, "I don't think they sell it in America." Eliezer explained that a pummelo was a "fruit enormous" with a "skin thick" and a "flavor sour sweet." He pulled a branch down and was pointing at something invisible because it was summer and there was no fruit on the trees. But he pointed so emphatically that Rebecca thought that she could see it, her first pummelo. Eliezer let the branch snap back and continued to walk toward the lower orchard.

They walked farther down the sloping orchard away from the house. And Eliezer kept talking, and talking, and talking. But although his mouth was filled with words, histories of each tree, interesting anecdotes about different varieties, and the challenges one faces with their plantings, he was panicked by the only thing he really needed to tell Rebecca about this place. He turned around and glanced at her following after him, and then he turned back, and kept walking toward a decoy destination. The mosaic stones had floated to the surface long long ago, but the ones in his mind had only just risen. He clenched his fists. The panic in Eliezer's face and belly was becoming unbearable.

Eliezer and Rebecca had been dating for almost a year, and in all that time he had never thought about Gabi. He really hadn't. But now, as he was preparing to marry, suddenly the memory had revealed itself. That morning, walking with Rebecca through the village, Eliezer had suddenly seen Gabi. He had reached up a hand and rubbed his eyes, but this didn't help. Gabi was there, a kind of appliqué on his own eyes, marring the peace of regular vision. Gabi was on the sandy road and Gabi was under the ficus tree and Gabi was by the post office, and Gabi was next to the bomb shelter and Gabi was in his own arms, as he, Eliezer, walked next to his future wife through his family's village. And although he had no idea how his brother had suddenly appeared, or if Rebecca could see him too, he did know that Gabi was tiny, light as a feather, still five years old as when Eliezer had last seen him, and that his hair was matted against his forehead, and that he smelled slightly of urine, and that most of his fingers were missing and that his toes were too, and that he, Eliezer, was carefully cradling him, oh so careful not to let this child drop.

Eliezer turned toward Rebecca, and then he looked away. He bent down to lift up a broken branch from the ground and then he broke it in half, and then in half again, snapping the dry wood easily and almost angrily. Now, he wanted to tell her not everything, but the crucial essence of things. Rebecca knew part of the family history—she knew that Zohar's identical twin, Moshe, had been killed in the War for Independence, but she didn't know that Gabi had even existed, or existed still. How to tell Rebecca the thing Eliezer had taught himself never to tell anybody? He hadn't told anybody in years and years. How to tell his future wife that Gabi and Moshe, the two tragedies, had collided in their house, and that the explosive nature of this collision had singed and burned his soul for inner expanses unaccountable in meters or miles. How to tell her that were he to shut his eyes, everywhere he looked would be char and ashes? Eliezer was not a rabbi like his great-grandfathers were. He did not think much about the mystical nature of his soul, but some ancestral voice whispered out from inside of him, telling him that he would never be whole until he could somehow make visible the char, the ashes. Yet he had not the words to do so.

Eliezer opened his mouth but still did not speak. Rebecca, sensing that he had something to tell her, said, "Honey, it's okay." And when he did speak, all he could tell her was that those things had happened here, happened to his family, happened in their house. He told her the bare minimum. As he spoke Eliezer looked away from Rebecca, and he talked about the events with a remote air, as if he was describing the plot to a play someone else had written—a play that they had decided that they might see, but probably wouldn't. He was detached, and though obviously nervous, he seemed to convey a sense that these horrible things did not affect him, were simply a part of his past.

But of course, his remoteness did not work to conceal his true pain. As Eliezer spoke, Rebecca saw the twin tragedies in his eyes. Rebecca could not see Gabi in her fiancé's arms, and she could not sense Moshe's blasted spirit wrapping his strong arms around the family's every moment, but she took Eliezer's arms and put them around her own body and hugged him so close that the brother he thought he was holding turned right back into a figment, a forgotten, and the uncle who was holding the whole family in his grip turned, if only for a moment, into a benign and genial regular ghost. Eliezer could feel Rebecca's warm breath on his neck. He kissed her nose and then her lips and then pressed his fingers into her back, holding on to each of her bones, her ribs, her spine, her shoulder blades, separately, tracing them, pressing down on her inside edges. He was so glad he had finally told her. He breathed quickly and deeply, relieved. He hadn't told her everything. He hadn't told her about the butterflies, and he hadn't told her about the photographs disappearing from the pages of the family albums, and he hadn't told her what it feels like to have to pretend away an entire brother, even if the brother isn't entire himself. Eliezer hadn't told her about the golem. He had only told Rebecca the essence of things. But that was enough. Or at least it seemed to be.

⚜

At the end of that summer, the day before they left for America, Eliezer got out of bed in the middle of the night and wandered to the mango tree, as he had done over and over again when he was just a boy. The night was cool but not too cool, the sky was light with an almost full moon, but not too light. As he made his way through the orchard he felt himself both followed and led, watched and remembered. Cold dewy leaves brushed against his face as he made his way forward.

Eliezer thought back to when he had first come to the mango tree when he was ten, eleven, twelve years old. He had been so determined. Determined to perform an alchemy. Not to turn stones into gold but to turn earth into living flesh.

On the eve of their leaving he was tempted to draw the figure again. Leaving on his own to sail to America two years ago had been temporary, a youthful adventure. But now, leaving with Rebecca was a different and much deeper kind of leaving. He bent down to his knees and reached for a stick that he knew would engrave a fine sharp image. But he stopped short of doing it. Instead he just twirled the stick in his hand and wondered. He asked himself, "When it came time, if it ever came time, what would I actually do?" He wondered if, in his studies or casual observing of the world, he did one day come across the right way to rearrange the letters of the divine name, would he actually come back to this place and conjure a golem? Or would the figure he traced in the ground be a familiar one? Would he draw an uncle's face? Would he dare inscribe in the earth an uncle's body? And would he dare recite the Name while walking seven times around the uncle's familiar figure, caressing the magic on his tongue, loving the emerging Moshe with his breath? Would he?

Or would he write a different story in the soil? Would he take the stick and draw Gabi there, but not the Gabi he had known as a boy, rather, the Gabi who might have been. Would Eliezer grip the stick like an artist's pencil and fill in the eyes, replacing the emptiness with a soul deep and bright? Would he walk around the form saying the proper words as his brother passed through the proscribed stages from glowing coals to soothing waters, passed from the earthy realm to the realm of the actual, passed through until his naked form rose up from the earth and separated from it in a ceremony so sweet that the birds and the flowers and the clouds and the night itself burst into song, so joyful to be bearing witness to this reunion of brothers, this banishment of ghosts.

Eliezer imagined that this actually happened and that he and Gabi left the orchard together. They walked up the back porch steps and into the house, into the happy open arms of their mother. And life was good then. But then he imagined that things went horribly wrong in the orchard, and that the creature who rose from the ground looked like Gabi but was really an evil golem in disguise—a mute soulless monster of tremendous strength who wandered the village wreaking havoc ever after. And then he imagined that the creature he had conjured was Moshe indeed, but not a living Moshe, not a Moshe before the catastrophe, but a dead one with bullet holes blasted all through him. And he too, having been awakened, would walk the world, bearing little resemblance to the uncle he had been, or to the twin he had left behind—and Zohar would stagger backward in horror.

Eliezer leaned against the mango tree, his forehead pressing against the wood, his right arm hugging the trunk, his left arm hanging by his side. The house behind him in the distance was dark and quiet. Rebecca was sleeping there. Eliezer remembered how when he was little, he had pulled his pants down and pressed his naked backside into the earth. He remembered how he and Yoni and the other boys had fooled Moti Peleg, scaring him almost to death. He told himself, and he told the mango tree, and he told Moti Peleg, who was now studying to be an electrical engineer at the Technion in Haifa, and he told golems near and far that he would return. Eliezer imagined that every one had a special place like this. A place that seemed like an anthem your whole world was always singing. He left the mango tree behind. And as he walked farther away, over an ocean and into a life so far off and different from the one he left behind, he would sometimes unconsciously find himself back in the orchard. He would find himself crouching down to the sandy earth listening to the noises of the golems.

So he left the land of his stories. He would return, yes. They would return, with devotion and regularity for two months each summer. But always to leave again, and to fly to a place he couldn't really read at all. Its pages were blank to him. But Eliezer loved the blankness and he loved the bakery, and he even began to love Boston. He loved his new country. He built a life there. And he was so grateful to have found a far-off place whose lack of legible letters saved him from having to live again and live forever the end of his tale.

*M*Y FATHER WRITES:

We decided that we would live in Boston, but that we would spend our summers in Israel with my parents. We were married in Boston on February 19, 1965. My brother, Tomer, was married three years later, on August 21, 1968, to Sheila Barowski, our neighbor's South African niece.

I TELL:

*N*o, Jeremy, there is no way to match my consciousness to the history I am trying to tell you. But perhaps that is the history itself, a patchwork of seeing and not seeing, a collage of knowing and not knowing, a full cloth made up of many intricate, differently colored tatters. Family chronology defies consciousness. Things happen that we don't *know about, and by happening affect the very molecules of our own perception. And so we come to know our own lives as if through a prism: all is distortion. But we do not see the prism, all we see are the bends in light that make the faces of our loved ones seem at times much too beautiful, and at other times, much, much less than pretty.*

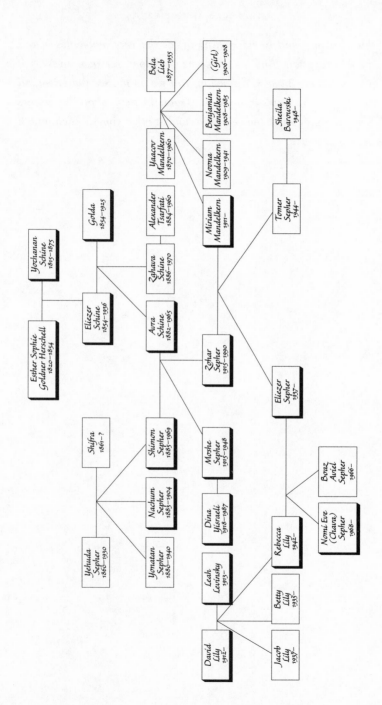

# Chapter 19

## ROUGH ENCLOSURE

*M*Y FATHER WRITES:

Our son, Boaz, was born on January 16, 1966. Our daughter, Nomi, was born on March 13, 1968. We named our children after the biblical story of Ruth. In the Bible, Nomi was Ruth's mother-in-law, and Boaz was Ruth's husband. Their second names are Aviel and Chava—after my late grandmother Avra, and my late cousin Chaim. They are Boaz Aviel and Nomi Chava.

I must explain who Chaim was. In order to do so, I must digress and return to an earlier point in our family history. It is important for me to do so, not only to explain the origins of Nomi's second name, but also because Chaim was a beloved member of our extended family.

Although my father's family came from Russia, we also had many relatives in what is today Eastern Poland. Most of this family died in the Holocaust. But, after the war, my father and uncle learned that two children of their younger Polish cousins had survived and were living in a displaced persons camp in the British zone of western Germany. Their parents had died in the early days of the war. And they had made their way alone across Europe, often hiding from the Nazis. They wandered for three years. Nobody knows how they stayed alive. In 1947 they were found by the Chabad Social Service Committee in a displaced persons camp. Chabad contacted my father and uncle, who, from Palestine, had been actively seeking information about their family in Europe. The children, an eleven-year-old boy and thirteen-year-old girl, were named Chaim and Sima.

In March 1945 my father and his twin decided that one of them would sail to Europe, find the children, and bring them back to Palestine. This was a very dangerous proposition. Because even though tens of thousands of survivors were struggling to leave Europe, the British had placed strict quotas on the immigration of Jews into Palestine. Consequently, the children would have to enter illegally. Anyone trying to enter illegally would be immediately deported, and anyone caught aiding them would be sent to prison for lengthy terms.

The Haganah was very active in illegal Jewish immigration. They advised that either Zohar or Moshe travel to Europe with my passport and Tomer's passport. The plan was for them to bring the children into Palestine on our documents. I was eight years old, Tomer was just one. This was a good plan, but there was an obvious and significant problem. The Polish cousins didn't match our passports. Sima was thirteen years old and female, Chaim was eleven—and though he looked much younger than that, he was certainly not an infant. So there was a tremendous and terrifying probability that the immigration officer at the port in Haifa would notice that the passports didn't belong to them. But since there was no other choice, this was the plan that my father and uncle eventually adopted. And though I don't know exactly why, in the end Moshe was the twin who sailed to Europe. My father stayed in Palestine anxiously awaiting news. Moshe returned safely with the children in three months. He never told us how he made it into the country with the children, but I always assumed that there was someone from the Haganah waiting for them at the dock in Haifa. Somehow, this person must have helped them through customs. All I really know is that it was a very dangerous undertaking and Moshe was very brave to attempt it.

The boy, Chaim, grew up as a member of our extended family in Shachar. I was very close to him. Chaim was killed in 1967. He was a paratrooper—a member of the elite advance guard of the Israeli army. When the country went to war, Chaim's unit was the first unit sent into Jerusalem. He was killed almost immediately. He rushed onto a bus in which he thought there were wounded Jewish soldiers. But there were no wounded; instead, the bus was booby-trapped. It exploded as Chaim entered it. When he died, Chaim's wife was pregnant with their first child. We named our daughter after Chaim. Her name is Nomi Eve. Eve in Hebrew is Chava, the feminine of Chaim. And our son is Boaz Aviel, after my grandmother Avra.

I TELL:

*In the Garden the first couple was Adam, whose name means "Earth," because he came forth from the ground, and Chava, whose name means "Life," because she came from Life and would bring forth life from her body. We walk into my grandfather's groves. Citrus graft. We walk to the place where the double tree stands. Bending down, I hold back the branches on the blood side and then I walk, crouching, underneath the boughs, toward the twinned trunk. Once inside, I wrap my hands around the silver-gray bark. I say out loud, "Pardess." The air all around us smells like the skin of an orange. I breathe in deeply, and I tell you that the word for orchard in Hebrew is* pardess. *It comes from the ancient Persian root, "Pairi daeza," which means "enclosure," and from which we derive, in English, the word* paradise. *I tell you that when I learned this I smiled and thought, No, this does not surprise me. In the Garden the first couple was Adam, whose name means "Earth," and Chava, whose name means "Life." Chava, Chaim, Eve I am, my beloved Adam you are, in this paradise of family stories: rough enclosure of heat and words.*

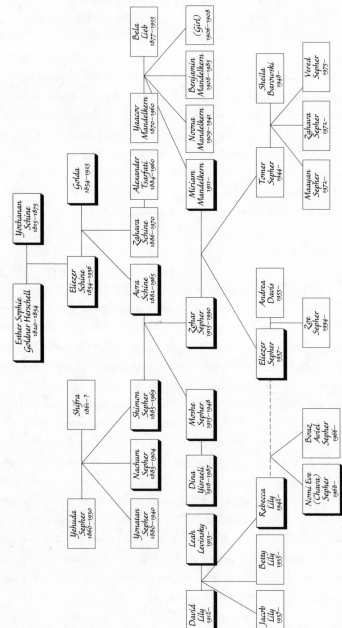

# Chapter 20

## THE PHOTOGRAPH

*M*Y FATHER WRITES:

Rebecca and I lived with the children in Boston. I am a professor of mathematics at Boston College, and Rebecca is curator of the Museum of Judaica at Hebrew College.

We took Boaz to Israel for the first time when he was five months old. We took Nomi for the first time at three months. We returned every summer for two months and lived with my parents in Shachar. Boaz and Nomi attended summer camp in the village for many years. They learned to speak Hebrew and became very close to their Israeli grandparents and our large extended family.

I WRITE:

In the photograph, Zohar is on the right, Moshe on the left, but there is no way to tell this unless someone has told you who was who. Both brothers are smiling; their faces are suffused with confidence and affection. They are approximately twenty-five years old and are facing each other, their foreheads inclined. Zohar is lighting Moshe's cigarette. The picture, in an old wooden frame, is hung halfway up the right-hand wall of the salon.

Boaz and Nomi were mesmerized by this photograph of their grandfather and his identical twin, and from the time they were little, one of the first things they would do when they got to Shachar every summer was to go into the salon and just stand in front of it quietly. Their ritual went mostly unnoticed by the grown-ups in the house. They didn't stand in front of the picture for very long, just long enough. Nor did they speak, not to each other or to the image itself. They just stood there, and then walked away.

Throughout the summer they would return to this spot, just to the left of the television, just to the right of the window. They would never plan on meeting there, but every so often in the middle of a Sabbath afternoon, or early in the morning before they left for camp, they would find themselves drawn to it. Looking back they would see themselves as pilgrims paying homage at a strange shrine and they would see the brothers in the photograph as a pair of wounded sages who had much to tell them. For as long as they could remember they had known the story of how, when Moshe was killed, their grandfather had felt the bullet entering his own back. They never remembered who told them the story, and in fact, they would never remember actually hearing another human being talk about it, but the story seemed always to be told constantly in Shachar. The very walls of their grandparents' house seemed to whisper about the whizzing sound the bullet made as it passed through the *pardess,* the orchard trees seemed to fill in details such as how Zohar had looked up stunned to the heavens when the phantom bullet hit him, and then how he had fallen face down under the double tree with a horrible thud that made the roots deep underground twist more tightly around each other. The photograph of those twins told Boaz and Nomi this one tragic story, but it also told them many others. Mostly it described happy plots, small tales of the mischief the brothers made when they were children. They would listen earnestly. And no matter how many times they returned to it and stood there together, Nomi and Boaz never felt as if they had learned enough.

❧

While Miriam and Eliezer and Rebecca didn't pay attention to the children's affinity for that picture, Zohar noticed it early on, when they were still toddlers. He would often see them standing there while they were growing up, and from the doorway or from across the room he would quietly watch his grandchildren—the little boy, the little girl, staring up at the old faded image of himself and his long-dead brother. Zohar knew that he was speaking to the children from the photograph, but he did not know exactly what he was telling them. He wondered if he was telling them about running on the walls of the Old City with his brother when they were children. How much fun it was! Grandfather Eliezer running with them, his baggy pants flopping in the wind, the neighbors waving to them, shouting "Hello!" Zohar wondered if he was telling Nomi and Boaz about how he and Moshe used to play soccer together in Petach Tikvah. How they would run down the field so fast side by side, kicking the ball back and forth, and how if they ran fast enough sometimes he himself would grow confused by who was who and which was which and unsure of whether the breath pounding in his lungs and even his lungs themselves belonged to himself or to his twin brother. When he would have these thoughts, these memories, he would smile and the nectar of a past life would fill him up with a warm radiant feeling.

But more often, Zohar did not feel the least bit radiant while he watched the children watching him and Moshe on the wall. More often, he would grow angry seeing Boaz and Nomi standing close together, and would feel a sharp distaste, a palpable hostility, even a little bit of hate for them well up inside of him. The feeling he had was like a barricade in his soul. A barricade blocking out the deep love he felt for these children.

While the children were still entranced, Zohar would slip

away. Usually he went out into the orchard where he would bend down low to the earth more urgently than usual, digging holes that didn't need to be dug or pruning trees that did not need pruning. He would work for hours, trying to forget about photographs and grandchildren and barricades and brothers. But the effort was always too much, and by the time he would come back into the house for dinner he would be too exhausted to smile. The grimace on his face would make it hard for Nomi and Boaz to understand how the smiling young man on the left of the photograph and this very angry old man sitting across from them eating tomato salad could both actually be the same person. Sometimes, after dinner, they would steal back into the salon to take another look at the picture on the wall, in order to check that they had not been mistaken.

MY FATHER WRITES:

Tomer and Sheila have three daughters—a pair of twin girls named Maayan and Zahava, who were born in 1972, and Vered, who was born in 1975. They built a house on my parents' property and live in Shachar.

After twenty years of marriage, Rebecca and I were divorced in 1985. Three years later, I married my wife, Andrea Davis. Andrea works as a decorator for an interior design company. We have a daughter whom we named Zoe, after my father, Zohar. My father died on August 7, 1990. Zoe was born on November 5, 1994.

I TELL:

When I was a little girl going to day camp in Israel, once a summer our counselors would take us down into the village bomb shelter to watch Charlie Chaplin movies. There was no war on. It was always the hottest part of the summer and the bomb shelter was simply the coolest place with a movie screen. I made up a name for what took place *underground. I called it "silence speaking." The characters on the screen talked and talked, but they never really said anything. All their talking was just a ruse, a way of communicating nothing while everyone was busy trying to decipher something from faces and gestures of hands. The actors all "silence spoke," saying much while telling nothing. For a long time I thought that my first experience with silence-speaking was down in that bomb shelter. But as time passed and the silences in my family's house became more definite and deafening, I realized that it wasn't.*

*Real silence-speaking is the kind that comes out of people's mouths when they've got a secret stuck on the back of their tongues. I'm not sure if people silence-speak in order to drown the secret by covering it under so many other words, or if they silence-speak in order to dislodge the secret from the back of the tongue—using all the other words as elaborate levers and pulleys and in this way bring it to the front of the mouth, and then out into the open. Probably for both reasons. At least in our family it seems to me that this was true.*

# Part Six

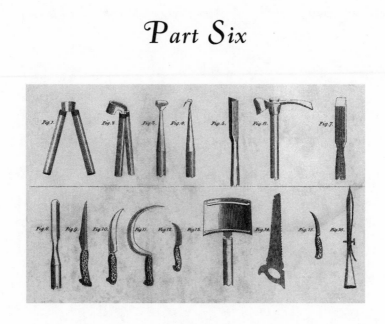

# Chapter 21

## NOMI AND JEREMY

I TELL:

*N*ow, my love, in order to graft our story onto the stories that came before, I choose the ayin *method. The root-stock has already been planted. So I cut the eye in the sapling, careful not to damage the hump of precious embryonic cells. Next, I cut the T in the rootstock, open its lips, and slide our story into the mouth of the old story that grows from this soil and is hardy, and will bear fruit for many generations. Then I bind the wound with bandages and blessings. Finally, I shut my eyes, and imagine that before me is a full-grown tree.*

I WRITE:

*T*he night that Nomi saw Jeremy for the first time in four years was the night before Purim, two weeks after she had gone to see Gabi for the first time. Already the streets of Jerusalem were beginning to fill with people in costumes—downtown the *midrachov* was made merry by giant rabbits, astronauts, belly dancers, caricatures of political figures wearing brightly colored three-cornered hats. Nomi and Amanda hurried through the crowd, toward the dance hall, which was just behind the old cinema. They were late.

When they walked into the hall, she saw Jeremy immediately. He was turned sideways, his hair falling down into his eyes. He was talking to a man in a blue shirt. When she saw him, Nomi was shocked. He was across the room, in the middle of all the dancers. He didn't see her. The hall was very crowded, But since Jeremy was so tall—the tallest man in the crowd—he stood out. The music was starting. The entire room was joining hands.

Nomi didn't know a thing about Israeli dancing. She had never been able to get the hang of it. Her lack of any spatial sense whatsoever made all of the dances seem impossible to her. Any time she had tried to learn, growing up, she had found herself lost on the dance floor, as estranged from her own legs and feet as from the other dancers, whose grace and syncopation seemed to Nomi like some foreign language that her own body had no idea how to speak. But this night, Nomi had agreed to come. "Just watch," Amanda had said. "Just watch, and maybe if you want, join in the beginners' circle. People are nice, and patient. You'll see."

When they had walked in, Amanda had smiled at Nomi and then gone immediately to one of the inner circles. Nomi didn't even take off her coat. She kept pressing herself back into the hallway wall, and then peeking around the doorway to catch glimpses of the man who had been her lover in college. She watched him dance, and even though she was filled with a sharp and panicked uncertainty—What would he say when he saw her? Was he seeing anyone now? What was he doing here? What would happen this time? Would they start again? Would they be able to get over their old end?—Nomi found herself smiling.

Jeremy danced with the same elegant physicality that had always marked all of his movements. He danced as if he had both the strength to lift the dance when it was heavy and the grace to hold it carefully with his whole body when it was light. Nomi pressed herself further back into the wall. She looked for Amanda and tried to catch her friend's eyes, but Amanda was immersed in the dancing and didn't see her. So Nomi, with a questioning kind of confidence, and a panicky kind of passion that was second cousin to the strongest kind of hope, shut her eyes and swayed to the lusty drumming music that was filling the whole room. When she opened her eyes again, the dancers were stamping their feet and raising their arms and arranging their bodies, it seemed to Nomi, into the geometric and yet organic forms of fields, birds, and flowers. Nomi kept her eyes open and tapped her own fingers in rhythm against the wall while holding on tight to the vision of the man in the middle of the room. She wondered what it would be like to dance with him, Jeremy Starr, this time around. She put her hands on her hips and then she arched her back and cracked it. The tiny cracks around her spine felt so good. The music was softer now, the circles moving slower. Nomi tried to catch Jeremy's eyes and then the same instant, just before he could see her, she ducked behind the wall and felt her face fill with blood, her body tingle with an electricity that almost hurt. Then she peeked out again. Jeremy was sweating, smiling, twirling, hopping, moving. He didn't see her. Nomi kept watching him dance. And she knew then that even though she didn't know the steps, and even though she doubted she could ever learn them, her body was aching to join the kinetic fray his body was a part of. She bit her lower lip.

※

Nomi watched the dances all night. It seemed to her as if the dancers were acting out part of the country's history. They joined hands and plowed the fields with their footsteps and then their footsteps grew stronger, louder, harder, and they were shocking the land with their own rhythmic and absolute attempts to make the weapons with which to protect the same earth they danced on. Quiet. Breathing. Sweat wiped from the brow. Another dance. They gathered in two lines and hiked through the desert on gentle music as delicate as flowing sand and then the music became rowdier and less refined, but their hands were still

clasped while their bodies seemed possessed of alternate ener-
gies. Then the dancers were no longer holding hands but were
dancing alone, their arms up, their legs kicking, their faces glowing, as if they were an entire room full of King Davids, dancing
before the ark of the covenant asking God with their bodies to
bless the people and rain down centuries of glory on the earth.

Jeremy was dancing a couples' dance with the pretty blond
woman. Nomi had heard someone announce the dance, calling it
*Etz Harimon,* the pomegranate tree, and she thought that it
looked incredibly romantic. The couples were all turning and
facing each other and then turning around and doing these little
hops, but as their bodies were turning, they kept gazing back at
each other and then hopping and turning to a complicated
intense rhythm, all along keeping eye contact as they moved.
Nomi couldn't bear to watch. Jeremy's partner was wearing a
tight red shirt and jeans. When she danced she tilted her head to
the right, and the other dancers seemed to look at her and
Jeremy and take their lead.

Pressing her body back against the wall, Nomi was filled with
memories of her time with Jeremy. She turned away, looked
toward the door. They had been together for two years—the last
two years of college. They had broken up for reasons that had little to do with who they were, and a lot to do with who they had
both needed to become. Nomi knew that she in particular had
had a lot of becoming to do. Four years' worth, at least. She
peeked her head around the corner and watched Jeremy finish
*Etz Harimon* and then start another couples' dance, with the
same woman.

Nomi was filled with specific memories of their romance. She
saw his hands buttering toast and placing it on the plate of the
first breakfast they ever shared. She saw his curly hair sub-
merged in water and then breaking the surface in the pool after
they graduated from college. She saw the earring in his right ear,
a little silver hoop. She saw, or rather, she felt him reaching for

her in the middle of the night when they were both asleep and they had made love in darkness, the peace of their dreams borne aloft by passion. And they had reached for each other and then they reached for each other again and again and again. Nomi was breathing deeply. She felt as if the whole hall were filled with visions and potent icons of the time she and Jeremy had spent together. She wondered if these visions were their rootstock, and if they were, if perhaps in their own particular orchard, their roots had needed more than just a single year before they were ready for grafting. One year, two, three, four. You cut the top so that it will branch out. It will branch out.

❧

Nomi breathed in deeply and even though the music in the room was playing loudly she couldn't really hear it. She was floating in a bubble, the world sounded to her like it does underwater, her head was filled with an echoing cottony gurgle, and as she stared at the whirr of moving dancers she marveled that they could breathe in such an atmosphere, let alone dance in it. The dancers moved constantly and never seemed to tire. The various circles never seemed to stay the same and so there was a fluidity coursing through the room, dappling the dance floor with movement in every direction. Sometimes Jeremy, moving between circles, came dangerously close to Nomi's hallway. When this happened, she walked to the other end of the hall, near the door, and stayed there until the dance was over. Jeremy continued to dance all of the couples' dances with the tall blond woman. Nomi thought of the tools her father had shown her that were used in grafting: the grafting knife for cutting, the *turia* for digging, *rafia* for binding, and a good strong sealant to cover the scar. Nomi wondered if the tools her grandfather had used to make his garden grow were manifestations of the tools she had, over the past four years, painfully collected, or if perhaps the relationship between things went the other way. Were the tools that people needed just to be people modeled after the tools that gardeners regularly hold in their hands? A tool with which to dig, a saw with which to cut, a tool with which to perform elegant surgery revealing all that is embryonic underneath the surface, a bandage for the wound, a balm for the scar. Nomi watched Jeremy kick up his legs, he was in a line with other men, their arms were linked, and they were kicking up fast, faster. They kicked and then tapped, and then kicked and then turned, and then kicked again while moving their hips side to side, now looking straight ahead, now looking to the right, and then left. The music sounded eastern, Yemenite, the beat had a peppery intensity, and Nomi thought that Jeremy and the other men were so beautiful and sexy. They danced as if on top of the music, high up on the hard shiny shell of something simultaneously familiar and exotic. Nomi had suspected back then, and told herself now, that Jeremy had had the tools to love her properly when they were in college. And she suspected that even if he hadn't had them, he would have persevered with whatever blunt or ill-suited instruments he did have in his possession. And with perseverance, he would have loved her long and well, perhaps forever. But she had turned away from him. And driven away from him with a fist in her belly not because she didn't love him, but because of the bruising emptiness in her own soul and arms.

※

When they finally spoke it was for only a few minutes. They made plans to have coffee the next day at a cafe on the *midrachov,* in the center of town. When they greeted each other in the cafe it was awkward. They kissed, but it was a clumsy kiss, and when they sat down both of them were blushing.

That day, they began to get reacquainted. And they continued to get reacquainted for the better part of that year. They spent

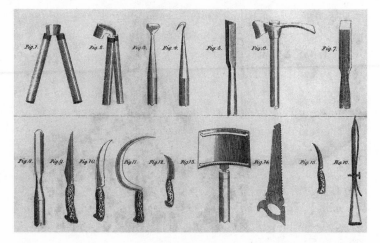

TOOLS

time together. Sitting in cafes, walking around the Old City, wandering through the streets and alleys of golden stone. They told each other everything. They talked for hours and hours, thirsty to know, hungry to confess all of the crowbar words and worries that had formerly, in their first incarnation, kept them apart. Looking back, Nomi knew that if she could have held those months in her hand they would weigh more than most of the other months of her life, not because of what they held, but because of the promise of all that they would deliver. They were patient and yet impatient. They were chaste. He was faithful to his girlfriend, even as his relationship with her was ending. What Nomi and Jeremy mostly did was talk, and talk, and talk. Now they found that they could say everything that they hadn't been able to say before. And even though they were chaste, and even though they were only friends, each word they traded on those Jerusalem streets seemed to bind them more tightly together.

❧

As the days went by the evenings began to grow cool and Nomi began more and more to ache to feel Jeremy's arms around her. She would sit late at night at her desk writing, wearing thick wool socks and extra sweaters. It was so cold in her apartment, she dreaded getting into bed, the cold sheets never comforting. But as she looked up from her work and glanced across the room at her bed she had a sudden image of herself and Jeremy lying there, embracing. She knew that she would be warm with him there, beside her in bed. And she smiled, thinking of how she would kiss his neck, his ears, his cheeks and how in the middle of the night she would wake up and watch him sleeping, his sweet reassuring presence soothing the room so that by the time they both woke up the atmosphere in her apartment would be as soft as petals or cotton. But then the vision disappeared and she was left alone.

Jeremy was not with her, but with his girlfriend, on the other side of town, perhaps curled up in bed or sharing a late dinner. Nomi was alone, sitting at her desk with her pages, in which the characters she regularly created were also just incarnations. Visions of sorts. But she believed in them. Esther looking lopsidedly at the world out from under the brim of her big floppy hat; Golda and Eliezer illicitly embracing; Avra stealing precious pieces from an ancient mosaic; Nachum Sepher approaching the Russian draft board with an invisible pin stuck between his toes; Zohar and Moshe "attending" to the redheaded queen; Miriam, a beautiful little girl, sewing mischievous incantations into cloth; and, last of all, Nomi's own father, Eliezer, in the orchard, trying with all of his might to conjure a golem from out of the ground by the mango tree. They were all real to her. Nomi rubbed her eyes and stretched her arms out and then pressed down hard on the keyboard, which made the table legs squeak. She bit her lips and told herself as she worked, that just as she believed in the existence of the people in her pages, so she also believed in the existence of the two lovers whom she had just seen lying happily entangled under crumpled covers on the bed. So she wrote herself toward them.

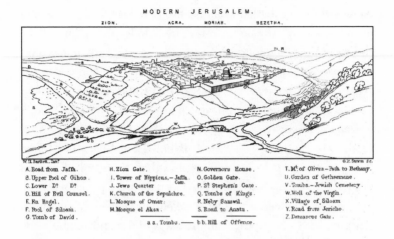

MODERN JERUSALEM.

ZION.　　　　ACRA.　　MORIAH.　　　BEZETHA.

A. Road from Jaffa.
B. Upper Pool of Gihon.
C. Lower D?　D?
D. Hill of Evil Counsel.
E. En Rogel.
F. Pool of Siloam.
G. Tomb of David.

H. Zion Gate.
I. Tower of Hippicus. — Jaffa Gate.
J. Jews Quarter
K. Church of the Sepulchre.
L. Mosque of Omar.
M. Mosque el Aksa.

N. Governors House.
O. Golden Gate.
P. St Stephen's Gate.
Q. Tombs of Kings.
R. Neby Samwil.
S. Road to Anata.

T. Mt of Olives — Path to Bethany.
U. Garden of Gethsemane.
V. Tombs. — Jewish Cemetery.
W. Well of the Virgin.
X. Village of Siloam.
Y. Road from Jericho.
Z. Damascus Gate.

a a. Tombs. —— b b. Hill of Offence.

In the beginning of November Jeremy went back to the States for a month. He returned alone. His girlfriend was no longer his girlfriend. The day after he came back, Nomi and Jeremy went together to an observation tower in Jerusalem. Jeremy had never been there before. On the way, Nomi told him that the first time she had ever gone up into the tower she had realized that she had come upon a very important part of her own private theology—a *midrash* in stone, or maybe even a whole Torah jutting up out of the earth. The building was so beautiful, and the tower, with its bells and reliefs and golden stones, seemed to her like a kind of prayer.

They took the little elevator to the top and walked up a small stone flight of stairs and into the observation tower. The tower had four glass walls with four glass doors leading out to four stone ledges. On each ledge was an old bronze relief map nailed to the stone. The maps were of the city view seen from each of the four vantages. In between the ledges were statues of the Christian apostles carved in Jerusalem stone. They walked out onto the eastern ledge, the one facing the Old City. It came up to

Nomi's chest. At first, she leaned into the ledge, and Jeremy put his arms around her body, resting his hands on her hips. Then she raised her hands to the map and he lifted his hands over hers. Together, they traced the raised buildings. The metal was cool, and they pressed hard on it so that the lines linking names to places indented themselves into Nomi's fingers. David's Tower, the Monastery of the Cross, the Post Office, Hebrew University, the Russian Compound. Reading out loud, they found the places signified on the map, and then they looked up and located the real places signified in the real city; a place that some people, over the centuries, have called only half-real but wholly representative of a mystical municipality of fire and air and heavenly water. The King David Hotel, the Valley of Jehoshaphat, Sultan's Pool, the Valley of Gehinom, and in the distance, on top of everything else, they read the Dead Sea, a thin blue paragraph stretched atop the hazy tan pages of the Judean desert. They said the names out loud, and with outstretched arms and pointing fingers, they finally located themselves on top of the tower.

When they finished reading they stayed out on the ledge. They stood quietly, listening to the silent but somehow murmurous conversation being held by the statue apostles and the stones, and the metal maps and the height and the view and the white feathery wind that brushed their faces so softly.

Then they ascended up into the meditation room. It was a tiny, improbable, and charmed room with gold stars on the ceiling, kneelers against the wall, and a prayer encircling the dome ceiling in gilt calligraphy. Jeremy looked up at the dome and began to laugh. Then he took Nomi in his arms and they danced together for the first time. He held Nomi in a traditional dance position and then moved forward two steps and over another step. Then again, two steps and over another step quickly. At first Nomi was unsure of her feet. But Jeremy was a strong leader and slowly she realized that if she didn't concentrate on her feet so much they seemed to know exactly where to go without her. Two back, one over, two back, one over, and then again and again. When they reached the end of the tiny room Jeremy turned both of their arms facing forward, like a joint arrow, and they went back the same way, two front, one to the side, two front, one to the side. While they were moving under the gaze of the gilt prayer, he whispered. He said, "This is the tango," and he told her that when they danced like this she shouldn't look at him, but she should look over his shoulder, "as if there were someone else, another man, catching your attention on the other side of the room." He said, "The tango is a story. The story is that I, the man, am trying to get your attention, while you, the woman, are coyly playing very, very hard to get. Every time I turn you like this, or move you like that, in or out or over, I do it dramatically, because I am desperately trying to get you to look at me, to look at me no matter what. But you always look away, and so I try again." His hand was pressing into her back, and when he moved, his hips, sexy and strong, carried them forward. Nomi felt his body close to hers, and his smell filled her consciousness like a more-than-memory, a time capsule of consciousness. He smelled spicy and manly and kind. Nomi hadn't even known that they were tangoing, and as they continued to dance she couldn't believe that her legs were cooperating. She couldn't believe that she was dancing. She could feel where she was in space, and did not feel lost, not for a single second. She felt the precision of his steps inlay themselves in her soul like a precious gem. She couldn't take her eyes off him even though she was supposed to be distracted by some other man making eyes at her over his shoulder. She told herself, "That is for some other time, when we care more about style and less about the old-new shock of this love." She stared into Jeremy's eyes, and he stared into hers, and even though there was no music but the soft tangoey melody he hummed for them, all the drama was there, in their locked gaze—a good story if she had ever heard one.

There, high above Jerusalem, they inscribed their story in Time. They wrapped their arms around each other. And as they stood

MY FATHER WRITES:
Boaz married Diana
Berkowitz on December
17, 1990. They live in
Brooklyn, where they own
a kosher falafel restaurant.

Nomi married Jeremy
Starr on May 24, 1995. I
have recently learned that
part of Jeremy's family is
from the same small
village in the Ukraine as
my mother—Noviye
Mlini. I am currently
researching his family
lineage in an attempt to
see if our families are
distant cousins or other-
wise related.

hugging they felt themselves oddly excavated—as if the tower were magically concentric with some distant tomorrow, and as if at that very moment an archaeologist of the future were digging into the ruins of their today and finding them standing there embracing, or at least finding the precious shards of their love, like pieces of a clay pot that he would then devote his life to putting back together.

Nomi kissed Jeremy's chest, he kissed her forehead, her face. They were high above the city together. Nomi looked up at the blue dome with its gold stars. "Yes," she thought, "this is an ancient place that we have settled, but there is a modern quirkiness to our every move and measure." And they stood there embracing until she became the dome and he became the stars, or perhaps it was the opposite: he dome, she stars. But regardless of the configuration of their own private sky and shared constellation, she was sure there was fixity to their claim on this high-up bit of heaven.

They left the meditation room and went back down to the obser-vation tower. They walked out onto the ledge overlooking the Old City. No other visitors came up the whole time. And they just stood there alone together, embracing, all the while writing a code on some crucial bit of consciousness that was inside of them, but was at the same time outside and far away on the circumspect horizon.

And they stayed out on the ledge, high above Jerusalem, kissing, while far away, in the orchard of another existence, two tired ghosts were happily relieved of the good burden of haunting this pair.

# EPILOGUE

**I TELL:**

*J*eremy, whenever I am in the orchard I see on the leaves infi-
nite images. First comes a breeze, and then the branches
shake but not for long. When the air becomes still again, the
leaves are different. Painted with the people I have known. I
stand in the middle of the trees surrounded by these little ghosts
whose haunting seems part of the yearly growth. The cycle that
turns sapling to strength, bud into bloom. I often wonder if I am
the only one who sees these images. But since no one ever says anything about them, I have come to believe that while everyone sees
them, the orchard is an arena for a story that has to be deciphered
not through words but through expressions, not through sound but
through a silence intricately scripted. I try to read the words out
loud. But they read me instead, and I find myself mutely mouthing
syllables of a story that will not let me drape its skeleton in ordinary
sound. When this happens, I turn around. Around and around and
around with my hands held out and my eyes closed and the sun is
so high overhead and the heat grows overwhelming.

You look away from me, and toward a nearby Jaffa tree. You seem
to be examining the tree from a distance. Soon you say, "I think I
know what you are talking about." And you point to the tree and
read our names off the boughs. You squint because it is very sunny
and you say, "Nomi was a writer and Jeremy was a scientist." I can

*hear the rest of the story in my head. I can feel our own chapter sliding into the eye. We work together, pressing the embryonic cells in place, and then I hold a higher branch back as you bind the wound and say the blessing. You say, "Nomi was pious in a peripheral way." I say, "Jeremy was a lover in every way." And the trees put in the punctuation. So many exclamation points, so many sentences that run into each other because our bodies are entwined, our souls constantly touching. And yet, we can read us. We continue to walk through the groves, all the way to the lower orchards. The sky is blue and the air is cool but not cold. I follow you, our feet making static rhythmic stomping sounds, and every so often one of us stops to pick a sticker off of our pants. Finally, you stop at a random lemon. And we stand by the tree listening to ourselves telling and being told to the landscape. You have the end of a branch in your hand and you are ever so gently tugging, so that the branch sways a tiny bit.*

*The tree is craggy, its trunk is elephant-skin-old, and its boughs are fragrantly bountiful. I tell you that lemons are the only trees that give fruit and flower and buds simultaneously. And then I point out that buds and flowers and fruit are all on the tree together. All three life-processes at once, an overlapping cycle. Around the base of the trunk are chazirim, pigs, thorns from the old root graft. We have to watch out for them. I can see you. You are walking around the tree. Scientist that you are, you are examining it. Your hands are reaching through the small dark-green leaves. You let an early dark-green lemon rest on your palm and you move your hand up and down a bit, as if you are weighing it. The sun is picking up the highlights in your beard and hair. I can see you, your blue eyes smiling. Here is our fruit, this very moment, here are our flowers, our love, here is our future, little green embryo lemons promising future harvest, and here are our thorns, our separate seconds, our years apart, wild and sticking up at all angles from the ground. And here is our fruit again, this telling moment. You round the tree completely and we clasp hands.*

❧

*M*y love, I have been in the orchard alone for a very long time. I watch you making your way toward me. I can hear your footsteps. I can see you ducking to avoid the scratch of branches. You are wearing a blue-and-white shirt and jeans. I am wearing a black shirt, also jeans. You stand in front of me. I reach for you. I lean my forehead against your chest. You breathe into my hair.

It is a story, like the others. A story told with buried stones. We dig into the family orchard and find the stones, the very ones. I hold them in my hands, flat on my palm, and I use the words she never taught me. "Here lived an ancient Babylonian clown, here lived a Phoenician princess, here lived a wheat thresher, and a soapmaker, a dye master whose fingers were all a different color." I know these words not because my grandmother told them to me, because she didn't. I know them because I, too, lived in that house. I was there long after the stones had risen up to the surface hiding their charms and horrors in plain sight. We dig. We go together out to the orchard and we dig down deep.

We are on our knees. I turn to you and take your hands in my own and I say, "Here lived one thousand generations of fruit and love and family dust." I hold up the stone and I say nothing. When I speak again I know that I have left the realm of the stones and have fallen or perhaps risen into the realm where stories are not made of rock but of air, and to tell is to breathe. I gasp. I say, "This stone once offered itself into the hands of the man who worked in this garden." I say, "It came up out of the ground and offered itself to him like a present." You take my hands. The stone falls thumping to the ground. We look all around us sensing that we are far from alone; the orchard, though empty of other people, seems crowded.

We both know why we are here. Why I have returned and will keep returning to this little spot of land—this orchard, our library.

We know that my speaking is really a reading and that we two together will press our bodies backward into the pages of the book that grows here, from the soil of this orchard.

We walk to the double tree. When we get close, we have to duck down low in order to avoid being scratched by its branches. You are so tall, you have to duck much more than I do. We smile at this. When we reached the twin trunks you put your hands in between them—in the thick V where they melt together. You are still crouching. I can stand up almost upright. The fruit isn't ripe yet, and we are surrounded on all sides by so many small dark-green early oranges of the two varieties. It is fragrant, lushly dim, and so beautiful in here.

The quiet of the orchard is a quiet of rustling, a quiet of branches touching other branches, a quiet punctuated by the occasional piece of early fruit falling with a tiny crash to the ground. I tell you that the word history comes from the Greek root "istor," which means "knowledge" or "knowing." Then I tell you that my history isn't true to its root because I know nothing. You hold out your arms and I come to you. I follow you, again crouching low in order to emerge from the boughs. I walk into your arms and we stand together in the middle of the orchard. You whisper, "So don't tell me your history, but tell me what has taken its place. Tell me the story's story. Tell me the lying root."

I ask, "How do you tell a lying root when you are one of the living branches?"

We are quiet for what seems a very long time. Then I tell you that I do know something. I say, "I know many stories." You smile. I keep talking, I say, "I know so many stories about them. I know the twin stories, the double tree, Avra the thief, my grandmother and the grenade, my grandfather on the motorcycle riding across the sands of Lebanon. I know about Esther and Yochanan and about the rabbi who was murdered in his parlor when he sat down for lunch." I am flushed now and am talking loudly, waving my hands

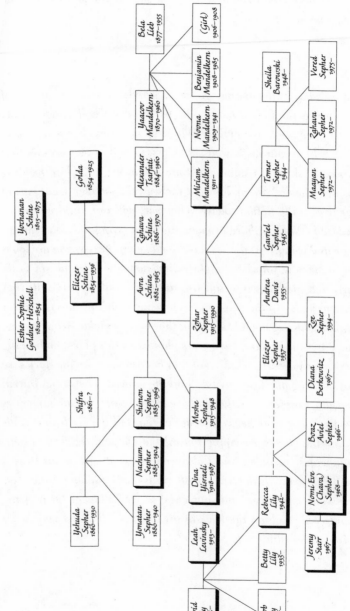

# MANUAL OF ORCHARD TERMS

## Pardesanim, *the Orchard Workers*

The city where my father grew up, Petach Tikvah, was the citrus-growing center of Palestine. Almost all the men in the town and many of the women worked in the orchards. My grandfather, Shimon, was a real *pardesan*, a real "orchard man." Shimon was a citrus grower and a manager of citrus groves. He took my father and uncle out into the orchards with him the day they started to walk. For many years the financial situation of the family was desperate. When the twins finished six years of school, their father gave them shovels and hoes (*turia*) and sent them to work full-time in the groves. But long before that they were helping in the orchard. The *turia*, the grafting knife, and the saw were an integral part of my father's life. He called the *turia* a "fiddle" and taught me, my brother, and many others to "play."

My mother also worked in the orchards. She was an expert packer. When she and my father were first married, the settlement depended very heavily on citrus exports for revenue. Each orange was precious, like gold. In those days it was a real skill to pack the fruit in the wooden crates. They were packed fresh from the tree in the orchard in such a way that the fruit would not be bruised on the way to market. My mother was quite an expert and my father would brag about how she was always the fastest and most careful packer.

When Shachar was founded in 1932 the villagers planted *limeta* rootstock (sweet lime). A year later, when the roots had matured and were ready for grafting, the villagers sent to Petach Tikvah for expert grafters. So who came to graft in Shachar? My father! Not knowing it, he actually grafted his own future orchard. This was an incredible coincidence. Of course, he and my mother eventually moved to Shachar, and for the rest of his life my father worked those same groves.

## Shorishim, *Roots*

The first thing you do, no matter which graft you are going to use, is to plant the rootstock. Rootstock is a citrus variety whose fruit is not good for eating—too bitter, too many seeds, hard to peel, etc., but whose roots are very hardy. Some rootstocks are more suitable for a specific citrus variety than others—for example, clementine do better, give more fruit, if grafted onto *limeta* rootstock.

Examples of rootstocks are: *Limeta* (a kind of sweet lemon) and *choushchash*. *Limeta* is good for light sandy soil. Typically the annual yield of a variety grafted onto *limeta* is quite stable from year to year, but its life span is relatively short. *Choushchash* is better for heavy soil that does not drain water very well. Its life span is very long, but its yield fluctuates dramatically.

After the rootstock grows about two feet in height, you cut the top so that it will branch out. When it branches out you keep about three or four of these branches—cut the rest. When they are about one inch thick, you can graft on each a different variety. From the day you planted the seedling until you can graft will take about one year.

## Klei Avodah, *Tools*

A grafting knife is really like a pen knife, but the other side is flat so that you can use it to slide open the lips of the bark without damaging it. The flat part, which we called the spoon, used to be made of bone, but now is made of plastic. I have a grafting knife at home—I actually have my father's too, his last one.

A *turia* is handled like a pickaxe. It is swung forward from over the shoulder to dig a hole in the ground. It has a short handle, and a rather large metal shovel/spoon head. Using a *turia* is literally backbreaking work. It requires that the worker bend down constantly. But with the *turia* you can accomplish a great deal. Your work goes faster than if you use the longer-handled *maadar*. The shorter handle on the *turia* gives much more leverage and power than a regular shovel or a *maadar*. You use a *turia* to dig holes around a tree for irrigation purposes or to uproot big weeds. You can also use it for scraping jobs or for digging any hole for any of the various jobs involved in planting. While it is very difficult to get in the United States, a *turia* is one of the most common orchard tools in Israel. A friend suggested to me that Americans don't like *turias* because the bending down is reminiscent of slave work. Perhaps this is so.

A saw is of course essential. On a regular basis an orchard worker will use several different kinds. Most useful is a standard all-purpose sharp-toothed saw. This is definitely needed for cutting through trunks. But for slicing off branches one usually uses a more slender, more knifelike saw that cuts well and can fit more easily into narrow, hard-to-reach spots.

A shovel will be used for digging all holes. But once a grove is planted the shovel becomes less necessary—though, of course, must always be available.

## Harkavot, *Grafts*

There are three kinds of *harkavot,* or grafts:

*Ayin* (eye) graft
*Temech* (support) graft
*Rosh* (head) graft

In Shachar, over the course of fifty years, we used the three different grafts in succession in order to prolong the life of the trees, and to make the groves more marketable, by changing variety without sacrificing the growing strength of the established plantings.

## Harkavat Ayin, *Eye Graft*

In the early 1930s they planted the sweet-lime rootstock in Shachar and
then a year later they grafted onto them Jaffa oranges. They used the
*ayin,* or eye technique. For the *ayin* technique, you take a young sapling
branch from the variety that you want to graft—in this case, Jaffa
oranges. The branches should be about half an inch in diameter; they
look like long whips. The color is usually light-green, as opposed to the
dark green-gray color of older branches. Grafting is cloning, not a sexual
flower multiplication. What you are looking for on the sapling are a
group of embryonic cells. You need very young branches with very young
cells. At the base of each leaf on the young branches is a little hump in
the skin. In Hebrew we call this hump the *ayin,* or eye. It is made of
embryonic cells—cells that do not yet have an assigned function and
under the correct conditions can grow to be almost any portion of the
tree. This little hump is what we want to attach to the rootstock. Cutting
it without damaging it is the most challenging act of the entire grafting
process. With pruning shears you cut a wedge in the skin around the
base of the leaf and the hump. Then with a grafting knife you cut a piece
of the skin in the shape of an arrow and you lift it off the little branch
that you want to clone. The arrow should be about an inch or a bit
longer in length and a quarter of an inch in width. On the rootstock, you
cut an upside down T. What you need to do is very carefully loosen the
skin from the branch with the "spoon" of the grafting knife. It is as if you
are opening up its lips in order to slide the wedge of the graft into it.
Then you cut the bottom of the wedge so that it fits exactly into the T. In
the old days, what used to happen next was that the grafter would go
ahead to another tree while a woman would follow the grafter and tie his
grafts with *rafia. Rafia* is from a plant, maybe a bit like papyrus; it is like
a natural tape (they make baskets out of it). They used to measure the
quality of the grafter in two ways. First, clearly by the outcome, that is,
how many of the grafts actually took. And second, by how many women
had to go after the grafter to do the binding. My father was a pro, he had
four women going after him, they never caught up with him. Nowadays,
they don't use *rafia* anymore, but plastic tape. And the grafter does it

himself—he wraps tape around the cut so that it is bound airtight, leaving only the hump exposed.

Within several weeks the young branches and leaves begin to grow from the hump. After about six months you can cut the branch of the rootstock above this new growth. Over time, the rootstock stump will melt into the graft—it will not grow behind it. That is how you create a mature, good-bearing tree using the *ayin* technique.

## Harkavat Temech, *Support Grafts*

The next technique is the *temech,* or support graft. It is the most interesting, and really craziest of all the grafts, but also very common. You use it to actually change the rootstock. In the midfifties, in Shachar, my father and the other *pardesanim* predicted that the *limeta* roots on their Jaffa oranges had only about another twenty years to go. So what they did, in order to increase the life span of the trees, was to literally replace the roots. A citrus tree generally has a tiny trunk—no more than a foot or so high and several very thick branches that come out of the trunk like fingers. What you are doing with a *temech* graft is turning those five branches into the trunks of new subsidiary trees.

First, you take year-old *choushchash* rootstock seedlings. The *choushchash* should be about a half inch in diameter. Then you run under the tree with a hose of water—this is to determine the best places to plant. What you are looking for are spots in between the original roots of the tree. Using the water, dig holes and plant seedlings. For each of the branches you should plant one seedling. Slice open the tops of the seedlings. Next, open little rectangular windows in the skins of each of the Jaffa orange branches. Match the seedling wounds with the rectangular windows in the branches. Secure the grafts with very thin nails and a sealer. Be careful—you don't want to crack the seedlings when you put the nail through. The seedlings should grow diagonally from the main tree to the ground, like the slope of a triangle. You want to make sure that you don't bend the seedling—you must have a natural flow. If you plant it too low the rootstock will bend and not take.

If a tree has five main branches then you plant five *temech* grafts.

Eventually, the branches will get wider and wider and the grafts will heal. You can sever the attachments between the five new "trunks" and the original trunk directly below the grafts. In time, the original trunk will shrink and die, while the new trunks, anchored and nourished by the young roots, will quickly grow thicker than the original. If the root grafts are successfully planted they will take over the main roots, anchoring the new sister trees in place for another fifty years. The upper branches of these sisters are entwined and generally inseparable, as they were once part of the same tree.

I discovered the trick with water on my own. There are so many roots next to the established tree that you won't easily find a place to plant the *temech*. With the water, I would find room between the roots. Otherwise, you will kill your fingers digging to find the right spot.

## Harkavot Rosh, *Head Graft*

Using this graft, you do the opposite of *temech*. Instead of replacing the roots, you are replacing the trunk. This would be useful on an old grove of large trees whose trunks are quite thick and whose roots are still good. You cut down the tree—say, one or two feet above the ground—by making a horizontal (very flat) cut. Carefully separate the bark from the tree and stick in very young branches of the varieties that you want to grow. These branches should be very thin. Before you insert them, you cut the bottoms of the branches as if you are sharpening a pencil into pointy tips.

My father used this technique to rejuvenate his orchard in the last decade of his own life. The Jaffa oranges went out of favor in the 1980s. The international market practically stopped. So my father cut down the Jaffa oranges. He left only the rootstock—the *choushchash* that I planted in the fifties. On top of it he grafted mineola mandarins. This created a grove of trees that grew very fast because of the mature second-generation roots. In only three years they became full trees. Oh, they were something else! Because of the previous graft—the *temech*— they were like four or five trees in a cluster, and because of the new graft—the *rosh*—their branches were beautifully new but also very strong and fruitful. Agriculturalists, farmers, professors, even government officials came from all over Israel to see this beautiful young/old grove. The very last work I did with my father in the orchard was caring for these mineola trees.

## Chazirim, *Pigs or Thorns*

The rootstock occasionally sends up wild branches. They project from the earth at the base of the tree. In Hebrew they are called *chazirim*, pigs. The reason this happens is that they always have some young embryonic cells—even though they are roots—and these cells try to grow into regular trees.

Typically, the branches that come up from the roots are much more thorny than the regular branches. And if they would be permitted to bear they would bear wild oranges. The thorns are really huge and quite dangerous. Sometimes they come up from the ground at some distance from the trunk of the tree.

## Etz Kaphool, *a Double Tree*

In order to make a double tree, you really have two options:

*Harkavat ayin* (eye graft) or
*Harkavat rosh* (head graft)

If you choose to make your double tree with the *ayin* graft then what you do is graft different varieties of citrus branches onto the one-year-old rootstock. If you choose to use the *rosh* graft, you insert different varieties of citrus branches in between the bark and wood of the trunk that you have cut down to one or two feet in height. With either technique you can easily make double or triple or even quadruple trees. Also, it is important to remember that a double tree is not kosher. According to Jewish law, you aren't supposed to mix varieties. So while the rest of our orchard's fruit is harvested for sale, we always save the fruit of the double tree for ourselves and our friends.

# Hadarim, *Citrus: Origin*

Citrus fruit is native to the southern regions of China, where the tree has been nurtured for thousands of years. In German the fruit is called *Apfelsine* ("apple of China"). Citrus is a subtropical tree that cannot survive below freezing temperatures. It seems that the fruit was carried out of ancient China as seeds, mostly by sailors. And so it spread to Southeast Asia, the Arabian Peninsula, and the Middle East. The etrog (citron), *choushchash* (sour orange), and the lemon existed in Israel during the Second Temple period. The Arabs, conquering the Mediterranean basin in the 600s, brought citrus trees to all of the basin countries, especially Israel, Lebanon, Egypt, and the rest of North Africa and Spain. The Spaniards brought citrus into the New World.

Citrus fruit became popular because of its numerous attributes. The trees are very decorative and green year-round and while the tree blossoms, it is always very beautiful. The flowers give wonderful perfume (the fruit and leaves too), and its nutritional value is well recognized. Sailors used citrus against scurvy (they especially used lemons). This probably explains the success of the citrus in South Africa, because the Cape of Good Hope was an important stopover for expeditions in those days.

## Citrus Varieties

All the citrus varieties are part of the very same species. This is the reason that you can graft them onto each other without rejections. The varieties can be divided in two large groups: those that are commercially grown for consumption, and those that are rootstocks. Rootstocks have all kinds of advantages under varied soil, weather, disease conditions. But the fruit of rootstock is never tasty enough.

The commercial category can be divided into four main fruit groups: oranges, mandarins, lemons, grapefruit.

## Oranges

Among the most famous orange varieties are: navel, Jaffa, Valencia, shamouti, blood (Sanguinelli).

## *Mandarins (or Tangerines in the United States)*

Among the most famous mandarin varieties are: satsuma, clementine, michal, tangelo, nova, Murcott, Dancy, mineola, and *Yosefefendi* (Lord Joseph in Arabic).

## *Grapefruit*

Here is an interesting fact about grapefruit. On the tree, the fruit grows in clusters, like grapes. That is why it is called grapefruit (*eshkolit* in Hebrew; *eshkol* is a cluster of grapes). Among the most interesting grapefruit varieties are the pummelo and the pummelite. The pummelo is extremely large and heavy with a very thick skin. It is often used to make jelly. The fruit itself is very meaty. The pummelite is a recent development. It is a mix of grapefruit and a pummelo that was developed in Israel. It is smaller than the pummelo and has a much thinner skin, like the grapefruit.

## *Lemons*

The lemon is a unique variety since it can be made to bear fruit year round. In this case, you have the flowers, very small lemons, and large ripe lemons on the tree at the same time. The lemon varieties usually have thorns that can be very painful.

## *The Ripening Season*

The citrus season in the Northern Hemisphere starts in September and continues to the early summer. Each variety has a season of about two to three months. The satsuma ripens in late September. Clementines are also in late September. Michal ripens in October. Nova and Murcott are a bit later—November. The navel orange ripens from October to November. Jaffa ripens from late November to January. Valencia (also called late oranges) ripen in April. The lemon season is also at the beginning of the fall, but it is a longer season, and as I said some lemons can give fruit all year long (the summer crop is smaller). The grapefruit has the longest season—from November until the late spring.

## Marketing

Originally, the mandarins were not exported since they are smaller with a thin skin and very short shelf life. Today, with much faster shipping facilities (faster vessels, even air-conditioned, and even via air), more and more of the mandarin varieties have become popular for export. This has been especially true since new seedless varieties were developed (like michal or the Spanish seedless clementines). Oranges, lemons, and grapefruit have always been exported as well as sold on the domestic market.

Many (or most of) the citrus varieties are ripe and very tasty while their skin is still very green. Shipping, and exporting the fruit while it is still green, will give it a longer shelf life, but the consumer does not tend to buy it if it is green. People assume that green oranges cannot be ripe. This is why artificial methods have been developed in order to turn green ripe fruit orange.

## One More Interesting Fact

The word for citrus, *hadar,* in Hebrew means splendor or glory. The biblical *"Pri Etz Hadar"* (fruit of the goodly tree) is the etrog or citron in English. Citrus is mentioned (I believe) once in the Bible, in Leviticus 23:40, "And you shall take you on the first day the fruit of the goodly trees. . . ."

# ACKNOWLEDGMENTS

I would not have been able to write this book had my father not devoted himself to exploring our family history. My writing grows from the soil of his passionate research. For every word, and for every page, I am so grateful to my father, and appreciative of *his work*. Also, in every stage of this writing, both my mother and my father helped me with my research. They constantly answered questions on big, small, and rather esoteric points, and they also hunted down resources for me. I am so thankful.

For many years, I lived in this book. Of course, while this arrangement worked very well for my prose, it was often hard on my wallet. I have many people to thank for supporting me in various ways while I devoted myself solely to my writing. I am indebted to my parents: my mother, Rita Rosen Poley; my late stepfather, Arthur Poley; my father, Dr. Yehoshua Buch; and my stepmother, Debbie Fay Buch.

A laptop doesn't do a very good job of keeping out the elements. Many people opened their doors to me, and let me set up my life in their houses and hearts, as well as my computer on their kitchen tables. In the United States, I am forever indebted to Burt, Joan, Abby, Max, and Zach Horn; Nancy and Greg Vorbach; Sue Sherr; Sue Standing; Sandy Bodzin and Shoshana Gross; Ora Pearlstein; Mindy Gellman; Margo Borden; Lisa Padalino (dance teacher extraordinaire); Monica Wood; Peri Buch; Ida and Sam Rosen; Bernice and Harold Horn; Marty and Shelly Rosen; Bruce Rosen; Lauren Rosen; Nelson and Jeanne Rosen; Ivan, Lynn, Jennifer, Danielle, and Adam Horn; Phyllis, Earl, and Charles Epstein; and the Poley, Hyman, Hagman, and Saunders fam-

ilies. I also want to thank Andy and Karen Schloss—Karen designed the original version of the family tree that runs throughout the book.

In Israel, I am so grateful to Rivka Buch; Merav, Michal, and Orna Buch;
Udi Buch; Noadia Heldig; Aviva Pele and Jochanan Mintzker; Ahoova Shnek;
Eti Peleg; Lon Pele; Menacham, Dalia, Alex, and Eli Kaplan; Nadav, Orli, Noa,
Dana and Micha Kaplan; Eli Buch, and the entire extended Buch family; Dr.
Avraham Shaked; Jessica Steinberg; Alan, Eli, and Missy Stein Goldman;
Harold Messinger; Yoni Gordis; Arie, Maya, Daniele, and Roee Ofir; Yael and
Nissim Dahan, Arik and Michal Kaplan, Tami and David Politi, and all of their
wonderful children.

I must thank my dear Aleister, whom I visited for a weekend and never left.

I am forever grateful to my teachers, Paul West and John Moore.

I would also like to thank the MacDowell Colony and my dear fellow
colonists. During my residencies at MacDowell I wrote crucial parts of this
novel. Also, I am grateful to the following people for publishing pieces of this
book along the way: M. Mark, Van Brock, Susan Burmeister-Brown, and Linda
Burmeister-Davies.

And I would like to thank the people who helped my book find *its* home. I
am so grateful for Danzy Senna, Amanda Urban, Jordan Pavlin, Sonny Mehta,
and Marty Asher. Thanks also go to Vrinda Condillac, who so kindly and
patiently took care of business.

The following books greatly aided me in my work: *A View from Jerusalem
1849–1858: The Consular Diary of James and Elizabeth Anne Finn*, edited by
Arnold Blumberg; *Israel Guide*, by Zev Vilnay; *The NILI Spies*, by Anita Engle;
*A History of Israel*, by Howard M. Sachar; and *The Timetables of Jewish History*,
by Judah Gribetz, Edward L. Greenstein, and Regina S. Stein. I am also grateful to the many kind gentlemen who e-mailed me from around the world (Scot-
land, England, Israel, Japan!) in order to help me identify my grandfather's
motorcycle. I applaud the "Rudge Enthusiasts."

I am grateful to the memory of my late great-aunt, Sarah Kaplan, and to the
memory of my late grandfather, Peretz Buch. He was called *Mar HaPardess*, Mr.
Orchard. Surely all the trees on my pages were also tended by his deft hands.

My book is for, about, and written because of family. Lastly, I thank all of my
family near and far, named and unnamed. I will be forever picking up branches
and using them to write beloved names on the orchard floor.

# ILLUSTRATION CREDITS

'Enchanting, highly readable. . . . *The Family Orchard* captures two centuries of Israel's modern history through the dreams, the sacrifices, the bravery of one remarkable Jewish family. It's a marvelous debut."
—San Francisco Sunday Examiner & Chronicle

'Wonderfully crafted, beautifully illustrated. . . . Eve is terrific at evoking a sense of place." —*The Miami Herald*

'Rich and lively. . . . Eve's tight, poetic language allows her to revel in the extraordinary gift of being able to trace her own family back so far." —*The Oregonian*

'Blends traditional Jewish storytelling with the ingredients of postmodernism: magical realism, multiple authorial voices, [and] a playful conflation of fiction and nonfiction." —*The Boston Globe*

'Wonderfully accomplished . . . in a league with other multigenerational epics like *One Hundred Years of Solitude*." —*Talk*

'Ripe with vivid images. . . . An earthy, unorthodox view of family history, one imbued with love and warmth and humor."
—Detroit Free Press

*at you and at the trees. You say, "Tell me all the stories. Tell me them one by one."*

❧

*We embrace by the old mango tree. I wonder, Jeremy, what part of our lives is the fiction today—the part that we will either simply forget or refuse to remember? Will it be my arms that reach up to clasp behind your neck, your shoulders? Or will it be your eyes that survey the sky now catching a glimpse of a very large bird heading out over the orchard and toward the water? I wonder, what part of our lives is the fiction today? What part will our children or our children's children have to make up when trying to know who we were and weren't? Will they have to make up the way you are look-ing at me now, your head slightly tilted down to the right, your eyes flirty and piercing, your soft lips upturned and parted? Will they have to make up the way you are pressing your lips into the top of my head, kissing me in code? Will they have to make up our stance, our story, our passion, our bodies planted in this place, embracing in the early evening wind? Will they have to make up the stories we are standing on? I dig my toes into the ground. The stories buried beneath our feet? Or will they have to weave nets to catch the ones floating above our heads, the stories that tell our souls, our souls riding the clouds, swooping toward the horizon like doves unen-cumbered? I wonder. And I also wonder, what part of our lives is the truth today? Is the truth these words that I put down now? Is it the words I whisper into your chest as we embrace? Or is it the words still stuck on the back of my tongue—all that I may never write, never whisper, never utter?*

*at you and at the trees. You say, "Tell me all the stories. Tell me them one by one."*

⚜

*We embrace by the old mango tree. I wonder, Jeremy, what part of our lives is the fiction today—the part that we will either simply forget or refuse to remember? Will it be my arms that reach up to clasp behind your neck, your shoulders? Or will it be your eyes that survey the sky now catching a glimpse of a very large bird heading out over the orchard and toward the water? I wonder, what part of our lives is the fiction today? What part will our children or our children's children have to make up when trying to know who we were and weren't? Will they have to make up the way you are looking at me now, your head slightly tilted down to the right, your eyes flirty and piercing, your soft lips upturned and parted? Will they have to make up the way you are pressing your lips into the top of my head, kissing me in code? Will they have to make up our stance, our story, our passion, our bodies planted in this place, embracing in the early evening wind? Will they have to make up the stories we are standing on? I dig my toes into the ground. The stories buried beneath our feet? Or will they have to weave nets to catch the ones floating above our heads, the stories that tell our souls, our souls riding the clouds, swooping toward the horizon like doves unencumbered? I wonder. And I also wonder, what part of our lives is the truth today? Is the truth these words that I put down now? Is it the words I whisper into your chest as we embrace? Or is it the words still stuck on the back of my tongue—all that I may never write, never whisper, never utter?*

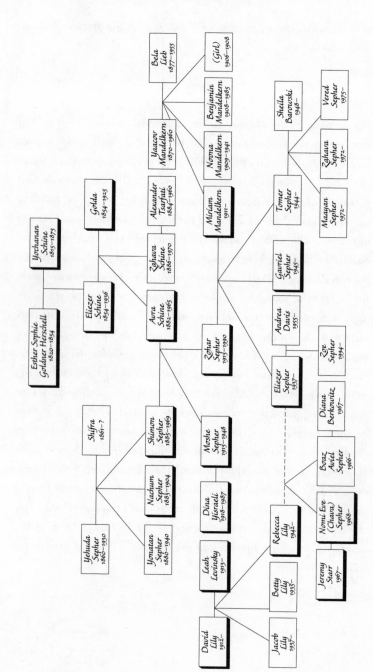

at you and at the trees. You say, "Tell me all the stories. Tell me them one by one."

❧

We embrace by the old mango tree. I wonder, Jeremy, what part of our lives is the fiction today—the part that we will either simply forget or refuse to remember? Will it be my arms that reach up to clasp behind your neck, your shoulders? Or will it be your eyes that survey the sky now catching a glimpse of a very large bird heading out over the orchard and toward the water? I wonder, what part of our lives is the fiction today? What part will our children or our children's children have to make up when trying to know who we were and weren't? Will they have to make up the way you are look-ing at me now, your head slightly tilted down to the right, your eyes flirty and piercing, your soft lips upturned and parted? Will they have to make up the way you are pressing your lips into the top of my head, kissing me in code? Will they have to make up our stance, our story, our passion, our bodies planted in this place, embracing in the early evening wind? Will they have to make up the stories we are standing on? I dig my toes into the ground. The stories buried beneath our feet? Or will they have to weave nets to catch the ones floating above our heads, the stories that tell our souls, our souls riding the clouds, swooping toward the horizon like doves unen-cumbered? I wonder. And I also wonder, what part of our lives is the truth today? Is the truth these words that I put down now? Is it the words I whisper into your chest as we embrace? Or is it the words still stuck on the back of my tongue—all that I may never write, never whisper, never utter?